ONLY LOVE

Elizabeth Lowell

ONLY LOVE

Published in Large Print by arrangement with
Avon Books, a division of The Hearst Corporation
in the United States and Canada.

Wheeler Large Print Book Series.

Set in 16 pt. Plantin.

Library of Congress Cataloging-in-Publication Data

Lowell, Elizabeth, 1944–
Only love / Elizabeth Lowell.
p. cm.—(Wheeler large print book series)
ISBN 1-56895-260-0
1. Man-woman relationships—Rocky Mountains Region—Fiction.
2. Large type books. I. Title. II. Series.
[PS3562.O8847O55 1995]
813'.54—dc20 95-34679
CIP

THE "ONLY" FAMILY

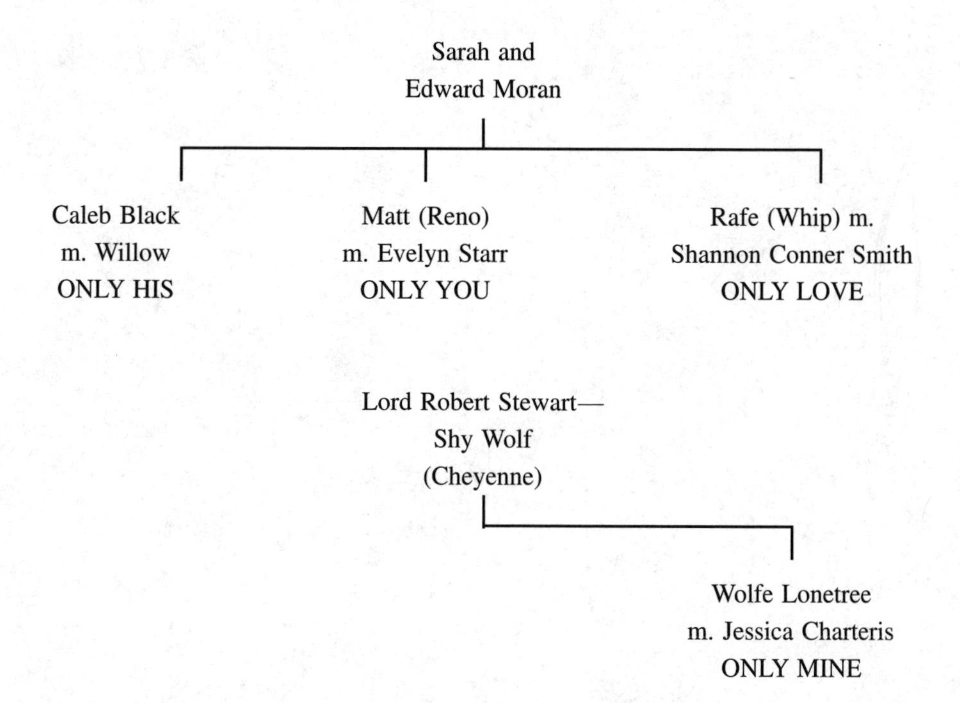

1

Summer 1968
Echo Basin, Colorado Territory

She's frightened.

She has a walk like honey.

The two impressions came simultaneously to the man called Rafael "Whip" Moran. Whip didn't know which drew him to the girl more immediately, the fear or the honey.

He hoped it was the fear.

The heat in Whip's blood told him otherwise. Underneath the girl's threadbare man's wool jacket and trousers there was a very female body. And beneath her straight spine, high chin, and determination, there was very real fear.

Whip didn't know what caused the girl's fear or why it should matter so urgently to him. He did know that he was going to find out.

For a moment longer Whip stood in the cold mud in front of Holler Creek's only general store. The chill of the high-country wind cut through his thick wool jacket. The girl must have felt the chill too. She shivered as she hurried through the grubby door of the mercantile.

With the easy motions of a man who was both fit and thoroughly at home in his own body, Whip followed the girl inside. The wind blew the door shut behind him with a loud bang. He barely noticed. He had attention only for the girl with the sweet, softly swinging walk.

She stopped in a shaft of light from the one window that hadn't been broken and boarded over. For a few moments her eyes ran hungrily over the scattered piles of dry goods, tools, and clothing. The fingers of one slender hand were clenched around something she held in her palm.

As though sensing Whip's intense interest, the girl turned toward him suddenly. He had a vivid impression of eyes the color of a wild autumn sky, a blue so clear and so deep that a man could look forever and never find an end to the beauty. What he could see of her hair beneath the hat was the color of autumn itself—glossy chestnut with red and gold running through it like leashed fire.

I've seen her before, he realized. *But where*?

With the next breath, realization went through Whip like lightning through a storm.

My dream. She's the girl in the cabin door, waiting, always waiting . . .

For me.

Motionless, Whip stared at the girl. A lock of hair had just escaped from beneath the girl's battered Stetson. The hair gleamed like silk against her pale cheek.

Without thinking, Whip walked closer and lifted his hand to tuck the strand back into place above her ear. When he realized what he was doing, he stopped, stepped back and touched his hat instead.

"Morning, ma'am," Whip said, nodding to her.

The girl blinked and looked at his big hand. Whip knew why. He had moved so quickly that she couldn't be certain he had ever intended to touch her instead of tipping his hat politely.

Her glance went from his long fingers to the bullwhip coiled over his right shoulder. Her eyes widened.

Teamsters with bullwhips weren't particularly unusual in Colorado Territory, certainly not enough so that the presence of a bullwhip should startle anyone. The girl's involuntary response told Whip that she probably knew him.

Or, to be precise, knew *of* him.

With a tight motion of her head, the girl acknowledged Whip's polite greeting. Then she turned away from him with cool finality.

"Mr. Murphy?" she called huskily.

Whip felt his body tighten as though the girl had stroked him from forehead to heels. Her voice, like her walk, was pure summer honey.

I've been too long without a woman.

No sooner had the thought come to Whip than he knew it wasn't true. He had never been a man to be controlled by his sexuality. He had spent too many years in too many cultures where women were prohibited to foreigners; even to a polite, soft-spoken foreigner with strong shoulders and smoke-gray eyes and hair the color of the sun.

"Mr. Murphy?"

There was a rattle and muttering, followed by the sound of reluctant footsteps from the back room. The storekeeper left his cozy seat by the stove for the barnlike, unheated room where supplies were heaped about in untidy piles. Owning the only store in Echo Basin's remote gold country had spoiled Murphy. He made his customers feel that he was doing them a favor by selling them his overpriced goods.

Behind Whip the mercantile's door opened. Reflexively he spun around and stepped out of the way. As he moved, his left hand went to the butt of the bullwhip that was riding his right shoulder. Though quick, the motion wasn't threatening. It was simply the action of someone who was accustomed to living alone in dangerous places among the most dangerous of all animals—man.

The four men who crowded through the door were examples of why Whip was careful not to turn his back on anyone in Echo Basin. The Culpepper boys were worse than the usual run of gold hunters. Loud, lewd, unwashed and lazy, they weren't especially beloved by anyone. Including, if rumor could be trusted, their Arkansas mother.

Few people were really sure which Culpepper was Beau, or which was Clim, or Darcy, or Floyd. No one cared. There wasn't a finger's worth of difference in the lot of them. Brown hair, pale blue eyes, rawboned, quick to anger; the Culpeppers were all the same. They were pack animals. They prospected, hunted, fought, and whored together.

It was whispered that the Culpepper boys also worked together to rob miners who were taking their gold from Echo Basin to Canyon City, but no one had ever caught them at it. Nor had anyone pushed the matter, publicly or privately. Men who crossed the Culpeppers had a nasty habit of waking up bruised, bloodied, and of a mind to pull up stakes and try their luck in some other part of the Rocky Mountains.

The Culpeppers might have been lazy when it came to hammering gold out of hard rock, but they fought savagely with fists, knives, guns, and boots.

Casually Whip eased farther back toward the wall, giving himself plenty of room. He didn't expect anything violent to happen, but a careful man was always ready.

Whip was a careful man. From where he now stood, he could see the girl on his right and the Culpeppers on his left.

If the men noticed Whip's movements, they didn't show it. Their pale blue eyes tracked each breath the girl took as though she was a lamb born only for their fangs.

"What'll it be, Shannon?" Murphy demanded. "Talk fast. My chilblains is aggravating me something fierce."

"Flour. Salt." Shannon took a quick breath." And a handful of lard and a pinch or two of baking soda."

Murphy grunted. "How you payin'."

It was a demand, not a question.

Shannon's clenched hand opened. A circle of gold gleamed on her palm.

"My wedding ring."

Disappointment swept coldly through Whip when he realized that the girl was married.

Of course she is, he told himself acidly. *A girl with a walk like that wouldn't live alone in a place like Echo Basin.*

Her husband must be a damned fool to let her come to Holler Creek by herself.

"Gold?" Murphy asked, looking at the ring.

"Yes."

The stark word said a great deal about

Shannon's emotions, as did the fine tremor in the hand she held out to Murphy.

Whip's eyelids flinched in sympathy for the girl. The past winter must have been very hard for Shannon and her husband if she was forced to sell her wedding ring for the most basic supplies. And not much of them, either.

Slowly Murphy took the ring. At least he was slow while his dirty fingers touched Shannon's palm. When he finally dragged his hand away from the girl's clean skin, he moved quickly enough to test the quality of the gold ring.

While Murphy bit down on the wedding band, Shannon's right hand dropped to her side. Her clothes, like her hands, were almost painfully clean. She rubbed her palm against her ill-fitting pants as though removing the feel of Murphy's touch.

The Culpeppers saw, and laughed.

"Hey, old man. She don't want your dirty paws on her," one of them said. "How about mine, darlin'? I washed 'em just last week."

"Your hands ain't no cleaner than mine, Beau," said another Culpepper.

"Shut up, Clim," Beau said. "Go find your own rag doll to fondle. I done found mine. Ain't I, darlin'?"

Shannon acted as though the Culpeppers didn't exist.

But Whip could tell that she heard each word clearly. She was standing straighter than ever, and the generous lines of her mouth were drawn flat in fear or distaste.

I hope those boys have better manners than I think they do, Whip told himself grimly. *I'd hate like hell to take on the four of them with only a bullwhip and a prayer.*

Murphy bit the ring again, grunted, and tucked it into the pocket of his greasy flannel shirt.

"Your husband must've cleaned out his claims if this is all the gold you got left," Murphy said.

"Ask him," said Shannon. "If you can find him before he finds you."

Murphy grunted and the Culpeppers hooted.

"The bit of supplies your ring fetches won't see you through a fortnight, much less a whole summer," Murphy said.

"My husband is a fine shot, no matter what the game."

Shannon said nothing more.

Nor did she have to. The Culpeppers looked among themselves uneasily. Then Beau smiled like a Comanchero.

"Yeah, I keep hearing about what a fine shot your husband is," Beau said. "But I ain't never *seen* him shoot. Come to think on it, I ain't never seen Silent John a'tall, and we been comin' and goin' from here nigh onto two years."

As Whip made the connection between "fine shot" and Silent John, he understood why Shannon felt brave enough to come into town alone. Silent John's reputation as a bounty hunter was of the kind to make a man whisper Silent John's name—and leave his wife alone, no matter how beguiling her walk.

"Silent John's not sociable," Shannon said. "Most men never see him and go on to talk of it."

Her voice was thin, almost brittle. Not once had she turned to face the Culpeppers. It was as though she already knew who they were.

And what.

"Flour and salt," she repeated to Murphy. "I would appreciate your getting them now that I've paid. It's a long ride back to the cabin."

"Sure enough is, especially on that old mule your husband fancies," Murphy said indifferently. "Soon as I take care of that big stranger and the Culpeppers, I'll see to your order."

"I'm in no hurry," Whip said. "See to the lady. She was here first."

Murphy grunted, unimpressed by the stranger's logic. The storekeeper looked at Shannon's right hand, the one she had rubbed along her pant leg to remove the feel of his fingers. He smiled, revealing teeth stained by chewing tobacco.

"You want to throw in a little something to sweeten the pot," Murphy said to Shannon, "and maybe I'll get around to your supplies before dusk."

"My husband would be very disappointed in you."

"So would I," Whip said.

Murphy didn't miss the warning. He bent beneath the counter, pulled out a shotgun, and slapped it on the scarred wooden countertop. The muzzle was pointed away from everyone, but Murphy's hand wasn't far from the trigger guard.

Whip smiled grimly. Murphy wasn't the first man to mistake Whip for a wandering teamster and think a shotgun was faster than a bullwhip. That kind of misunderstanding was fine with Whip. Surprise would help to even the odds a bit.

But Whip still hoped it wouldn't come to a

fight. Four to one was about three too many as far as any careful man was concerned.

"Just fill the lady's order," Whip said calmly. "If those boys are in such an almighty rush, I'll go to the back of the line."

A quick flash of sapphire came as Shannon glanced toward Whip again.

"Thank you," she said.

"My pleasure, ma'am," Whip said, touching the brim of his hat with a graceful motion.

Despite Whip's politeness, Shannon turned away before he could prolong the conversation.

Whip was startled by the disappointment he felt. Listening to Shannon's voice had been as pure a pleasure as watching her walk or trying to see to the bottom of her matchless blue eyes.

"Hey, darlin'," Beau said.

Shannon kept her back turned to the Culpeppers.

"Nice of her to show me the shape of her butt," Beau said to no one in particular. "A mite narrow, but still enough to grab hold of so as not to get bucked off when the going gets rough."

The Culpepper boys laughed as though Beau had said something funny.

Shannon didn't move.

"Does Silent John do it to you that way, darlin'?" Beau asked. "Or does he bend you over the back of a chair and have at you like the randy old goat he is?"

Shannon's face became as pale as salt, but she neither moved nor spoke.

Neither did Whip. He simply watched Beau, measuring the distance between Shannon and the four Culpeppers. Two of the men seemed to be leaning on one another, swaying very slightly.

The smell of sweat and stale whiskey rolled off them.

Maybe the two of them will only add up to one man in a fight, Whip thought hopefully. *In any case, I'll start on the others first and leave those boys for last.*

Murphy moved through the room as though wading in chest-deep mud, slowly putting together Shannon's small order.

"Now, was it me," Beau said, "I'd pull down those ragged trousers and grab a handful of—"

"Murphy!" Whip said clearly, cutting across Beau's words. "No need to measure the salt a grain at a time. I want to be out of here before sundown."

Beau gave Whip a hard look.

Whip smiled. Beneath his golden mustache the curve of his mouth was cold rather than reassuring, but Murphy was too far away to notice and the Culpeppers were looking only at Shannon.

"Don't git yer water hot," Murphy said from the other end of the room. "I'm movin' fast as I can."

"Move faster. The lady is in a hurry."

Something in Whip's voice made the Culpeppers turn and look at the fair-haired stranger.

Nothing had changed. He was still a big, easy-moving man with a bullwhip riding his right shoulder, a tolerant smile, and neither rifle nor revolver in sight. The Culpeppers each had belt guns, and no reluctance to use them.

"You better take Murphy's advice, boy," Beau drawled to Whip, "and don't get your water hot for nothin'."

As Beau spoke, his hand settled on his belt, just above the scarred wooden handle of his revolver.

"You're big enough for two," Clim said, "but we're four to your one, we ain't exactly tiny, and we're packing guns."

"I can see that," Whip said.

It was all he said.

The Culpeppers muttered among themselves. They must have decided that the stranger was suitably cowed, because they began baiting Shannon again.

"Why don't you turn yourself around, darlin'?" Beau said. "As pretty as your butt is, I'd a damn sight rather look at your teats."

"Yeah," Clim said. "We been wonderin' all winter what you'd look like without them men's rags you always wear. Are your teats dark like old Betsy's, or are they red like Clementine's?"

"Clementine rouges hers," muttered one of the Culpeppers. "And they ain't the only place she greases."

"Hell you say, Darcy," Clim retorted. "I done left enough tooth marks on them teats to know what's real and what's rouge."

A small shudder went through Shannon.

Only Whip noticed, for only he was looking for a reaction from the silent girl.

Beau gets it first. Definitely. That boy's manners need some real polishing.

Whip took a step forward.

"No," Shannon said quietly, turning her head, looking right at Whip. "Ignore them. Their words mean no more than a dog breaking wind."

The Culpeppers didn't hear Shannon. They were too busy arguing among themselves about what else Clementine rouged.

Whip gave the Culpeppers a narrow, icy look and wondered how often Shannon had been forced to endure their lewd talk. Probably every time she came into town for supplies.

Damn her husband for letting it happen, Whip raged silently. *If he's half as mean as his reputation, he should cut out their filthy tongues and use them for cleaning the barrel of his buffalo gun.*

But he hasn't, and now it's left for me to do.

A movement at the back of the store caught Whip's attention. Murphy was slowly lifting the lid off a barrel of flour. He handled the wooden lid as though it weighed more than a side of beef. His head was turned toward Shannon rather than toward the contents of the barrel.

"What do you think, Floyd?" asked Beau over the sound of the other Culpeppers' arguments. "Is that little girl's teats big enough to squeeze until they turn red and white and blue like a Yankee flag?"

Whip tried to control the anger tightening his gut. It was a losing battle. He couldn't stop thinking how he would feel if it were his woman shopping alone while men talked loudly about how she would look naked and what size her breasts were.

If Shannon were my wife, when I came back from yondering I would hunt the Culpeppers down like the coyotes they are.

The thought didn't satisfy Whip. Sometimes a yondering man didn't come back. And even when he did, nothing could erase the sickening memory of humiliation in his woman's eyes.

Damn Silent John anyway! *If he can't take care of a girl like Shannon, he never should have married her and brought her to such a rough place.*

"Well, Floyd," Beau persisted. "What do you think about them teats?"

Floyd belched, scratched his crotch thoughtfully, and said, "I think Silent John is a damned good shot."

"So what?" Beau retorted. "We ain't touchin' her. Thet was all we was warned about. Touchin'."

"And followin'," Clim added.

"We ain't done thet, neither," Beau said.

"Not after the first time," Floyd agreed.

He pulled off his hat and stuck two fingers through two bullet holes in the brim.

"Damn fine shootin'," Floyd said. "Must have been near a thousand yards. Sure never saw hide nor hair of him, neither."

"All we done is try to be friendly-like to his wife," Clim said. "Follow her an' see she got home safe."

"Yeah. We was bein' neighborly." Beau smiled, showing a line of sharp, uneven teeth. "Like now. Right neighborly. Thinkin' warm thoughts about birds and tight little nests."

"Downright hot nest, I'll bet," Darcy mumbled.

"Stuck-up bitch," Clim muttered.

"Murphy," Whip said sharply. "Start measuring that flour instead of staring at it. I'm getting tired of hearing dogs break wind."

"Huh?" Clim said.

For a few moments there was silence while the Culpeppers tried to figure out if they had been insulted, and if so, how.

Murphy slammed the lid back on the flour barrel and walked slowly to the front of the store. He was carrying a small sack of flour over one shoulder and a much smaller bag of salt in his left hand.

"Do you think she yells?" Darcy asked no one in particular.

"What you yammerin' about now?" Beau demanded.

"Her, what else?" Darcy said impatiently. "When the old fart bends her over a chair and goes to rutting on her, does she fight and yelp and beg for mercy, or does she just let him do it any way he wants and whimper for more like a bitch in heat?"

Darcy will be the second one, Whip decided.

A subtle movement of Whip's right shoulder dislodged the bullwhip's coils, sending them sliding down his right arm. His left hand closed around the butt of the long lash as the coils fell toward the floor.

The bullwhip came alive.

With each small motion of Whip's left hand, waves of energy rippled through the bullwhip, making the long, slender length of the lash seethe and whisper delicately like a snake gliding through dead grass.

Whip began whistling softly through his teeth, looking at nothing, yet seeing every move the four Culpeppers made. None of them noticed. They had already decided Whip was no threat.

Last chance, boys. Clean up your talk or have it cleaned up for you.

Murphy walked past Shannon, leered at her, and plunked the flour and salt down on the counter.

"Be back with the lard in a minute," Murphy said. "Take good care of her, boys."

The Culpeppers laughed. Then they stopped

laughing and eased closer to Shannon. Beau looked Shannon over with speculative, watery eyes, eyes that stripped her as she stood there, eyes that probed every curve and shadow for the vulnerable female body beneath the cloth.

Shannon stood like a wild animal frozen in the moment of discovery by a hunter, poised on the edge of panicked flight. She was white and flushed by turns, obviously fighting for control.

"Dunno how she likes it, Darcy, or if she likes it a'tall," Beau drawled.

Shannon flinched despite her desperate attempt not to show that she heard Beau's words.

"Know how I'd like it, though," Beau continued. "I'd cut her pants open with a knife, put those little feet behind her ears, and—*Ow*!"

Beau's screech covered the pop of the bullwhip, but nothing could hide the bright gush of blood from his mouth.

Like lightning, Whip's hand flicked again.

The long lash writhed and snapped, striking too quickly for the eye to follow. Darcy bent over, grabbing his crotch and trying to yell through a throat closed by pain.

Whip didn't even hesitate. Surprise was on his side, but only for a few more seconds.

Snap.

Clim grabbed his shirt, which was suddenly split from collar to waist.

Snap.

Floyd's hat was sliced in two.

Snap. Snap. Snap.

Beau grabbed for his trousers. The steel buttons that had once held up his pants were bouncing and rolling across the mercantile's uneven wood floor.

The rest of the Culpeppers were still dancing in place and looking around for the hornet nest they must have kicked over.

"Wonder how you boys would look without your clothes?" Whip asked sardonically.

Snap. Snap.

"Rawboned and filthy, I'll wager," Whip continued, "with privates smaller than a rat's."

The lash hissed and snapped in savage counterpoint to Whip's words, flaying buttons from cloth and cloth from flesh.

While the Culpeppers hopped and yelped and their clothes were shredded too quickly for the eye to follow, Whip kept on giving the Culpeppers back the words they had used to bait Shannon.

"Are you going to scream and beg for mercy?" Whip asked. "Or do you like being whipped so much you'll whine and ask for more? Which will it be, boys? Speak up. Usually I'm a patient man, but you've plumb rode my temper raw."

By now, three of the Culpeppers were bent over, covering their crotches with whatever remained of their pants.

The fourth Culpepper went for his gun.

The bullwhip uncoiled in a blur of speed. Leather shot hungrily around Floyd's wrist. After a quick, hard jerk, Whip flicked the lash free, retrieved it, and struck again. Floyd yelped and flailed and fell to his knees. Blood streamed from a long cut just beneath both eyebrows.

"I'll kill the next one who goes for his gun," Whip said. "That includes you, Murphy."

"I ain't reachin' for nothin'," Murphy said calmly.

"Keep it that way."

Then the lash was still.

Silence gathered like a storm while Whip looked over the Culpepper boys. Other than Beau and Floyd, there was no blood, simply stinging welts. Yet everyone in the room knew that Whip could have reduced the Culpeppers to scarlet shreds as easily as he had disarmed Floyd. The attack had been so unexpected and so swift that they had never had a chance to gather their wits, much less fight back effectively.

"Boys, I've known outhouses with cleaner mouths than yours," Whip said. "I'm purely sick of your filth. If you all want to keep a tongue in your head, put a bridle on it when you're around a woman. Hear me?"

Slowly the Culpeppers nodded.

"Good," Whip said. "Shuck your irons."

Four revolvers hit the floor.

"Leave that girl alone from now on," Whip said. "Hear me?"

One by one the Culpeppers nodded sullenly.

"I've given all my warnings," Whip continued, "and it's more than the likes of you deserve. Now get out of my sight."

Dazed, uncertain, Beau allowed himself to be pulled upright by Darcy. Clim helped Floyd to his feet.

The front door slammed open. The four Culpeppers staggered out into the cold wind. None of them looked back. They had seen as much of the big stranger as they wanted.

The door banged shut. The room was empty but for Whip and the storekeeper. Whip looked at the countertop. The flour and salt were gone. He turned to Murphy. The storekeeper's hands were in full sight and empty of all but grime.

"You be the one they call Whip," Murphy said.

Whip said nothing. He was looking through the mercantile's dirty window. The Culpepper boys were mounting up and riding out on their lean racing mules.

Shannon was nowhere in sight.

"Leastwise," Murphy said, "folks done called you Whip ever since you skun out them Canyon City boys for talking dirt to that half-breed Wolfe Lonetree's white wife."

Whip turned and looked at Murphy with eyes the color of winter.

"Where is Shannon?" Whip asked.

"She lit out when you cut Beau's tongue."

The bullwhip seethed restlessly. Murphy eyed it as warily as he would have a rattlesnake.

"Where?" Whip repeated.

"Yonder," Murphy said, jerking a dirty thumb toward the north. "Silent John works some claims up a fork of Avalanche Creek."

"Does she come into Holler Creek often?"

Murphy shook his head.

The bullwhip shivered and leaped softly, whispering to itself.

Murphy swallowed. At the moment, Whip bore an uncomfortable resemblance to an avenging angel.

Or Lucifer himself.

"How often does she come in?" Whip asked.

The gentle tone didn't fool Murphy. He had gotten a good look at Whip's eyes. They were a preview of hell.

"Once a year," Murphy said quickly.

"In the summer?"

"Nope. Just the fall. For the last four or five years she fetched the winter supplies for Silent John."

Whip's eyes narrowed.

"Now her tail is in a right narrow crack," Murphy added. "That snake-mean old man is all what keeps the Culpepper boys away from her. Talk now is he's dead."

Hope leaped in Whip.

Maybe Shannon is free.

A young widow.

Damn, a yondering man like me couldn't ask for more than a widow like Shannon between now and whichever tomorrow the sunrise calls my name again.

When Whip had first come to the Rocky Mountains, he had seen their emerald and granite heights and felt that somewhere ahead of him there was a cabin he had never seen and a woman he had never known, and both of them were waiting for him, filled with warmth. The certainty was so deep in him that he even saw it in his dreams, the open door of golden light and snow all around and peaks reaching up into the dawn. . . .

But in the past few years Whip had been from east to west and north to south in the beautiful, deadly mountains, and he had found only his own shadow riding ahead of him, pushed by the rising sun.

"Do you think Silent John is dead?" Whip asked.

Murphy shrugged, looked sideways at Whip, and decided to keep talking.

"He ain't been seen since the pass opened," the storekeeper said. "A few days later it snowed somethin' fierce. Pass didn't open again for weeks."

"Where was Silent John last seen?"

"Heading out to his claims on Avalanche Creek on that old mule he favors."

"Who saw him?"

"One of them Culpepper boys."

"How long ago?" Whip asked.

"Five, six weeks. We don't keep track of time much here. It's either snowing or it ain't. That's the only clock what matters."

"No one has seen Silent John for six weeks?"

"That's about it, mister."

"Is that unusual?"

Murphy grunted. "Ain't nothin' usual about that old snake. He's chancy as a hog on ice. Come when you least expect and leave the same way. A hard man, Silent John. Real hard."

"Most bounty hunters are," Whip said dryly. "Has he ever been gone longer than six weeks before?"

Squinting, Murphy scratched the tangled hair that covered his chin.

"Can't rightly say. Once, maybe, back in sixty-six," Murphy said slowly. "And in sixty-one, when he fetched the gal from back east."

"Seven years ago," Whip said. "The War Between the States . . ."

"That be the one. Lot of folks come westering during them years."

The thought of Shannon married to a "snake-mean old man" for seven years dug at Whip. He had been in Australia during much of the War Between the States, but he knew how brutal it had been for the people caught between North and South. His sister Willow had barely survived.

It could have been Willy forced to sell herself to an old man in order to survive, Whip told himself silently. *But Willy was lucky. She managed to stay alive and single until she met a man she could love. Caleb Black is a hard man, and a damned good one.*

"Yup," Murphy said. "I figure the gal is a widow by now. There was a mess of avalanches this spring. Silent John's probably froze solid as stone somewhere way up a fork of Avalanche Creek. Culpeppers must think so, else they wouldn't be so free with their talk."

Whip said nothing. He simply stood, listening. The bullwhip writhed and hissed at his feet like a long, restless snake.

"The gal will be froze solid, too, come fall," Murphy said with faint satisfaction. "Them supplies she bought wouldn't keep a bird alive. Now, if'n she been more neighborly and less uppity . . ."

The storekeeper's voice died as Whip looked at him.

"I saw a crowbait black picketed just outside of town," Whip said. "Would he be for sale as a packhorse?"

"You got gold, ain't nothin' you can't buy in Holler Creek."

Whip dug coins out of his pants pocket. Gold coins. They rang as they hit the counter.

"Start rounding up supplies," Whip said.

Murphy's hand flashed out and scooped up the coins with surprising speed.

"And when you weigh the dry goods," Whip added gently, "keep your dirty thumb off the scales."

Surprisingly, Murphy grinned. "Not many folks are quick enough to catch me."

"I am."

Murphy laughed and started gathering Whip's supplies.

By the time Whip returned to the mercantile leading the thin black packhorse, his supplies were waiting. Within an hour everything was loaded and ready to go.

Whip swung into the saddle of his big, smoke-colored trail horse and grabbed the packhorse's lead rope. He rode out with a storm building around him, tracking the girl with frightened eyes and a walk like honey.

It was sunset when Whip rode down a wooded draw into a clearing. At the far edge of the clearing a cabin was waiting, the cabin he had seen in his dreams.

And the girl he had dreamed was waiting, too.

But Shannon had a dog the size of Texas by her side, a shotgun in her hands, and an expression on her face that said she didn't want a damn thing to do with the man called Whip Moran.

2

Shannon stood in the doorway of the cabin and looked into the eerie radiance that came to the high country during a stormy sunset. All around her thunder rumbled and echoed like distant avalanches. She could smell the storm coming down the mountainside. She could taste it. She could feel it in the freshening wind.

But the fierce thunderstorm didn't worry her

nearly as much the lone man riding out of the sunset.

Lord, that's one big man the storm is pushing toward me.

The rider was mounted on a silver-gray horse that was the exact color of the stranger's eyes back in Holler Creek. When the rider turned to check on the progress of his packhorse, the long leather lash coiled over his right shoulder gleamed in the twilight.

Whip.

Is it really him? Cherokee said nobody alive could handle a long lash like the man called Whip.

But what brings him here?

The answer was a memory of Whip's clear, quicksilver glances following her, touching her like ghostly caresses.

Other men had stared at Shannon, followed her, wanted her . . . but none of them had looked at her like Whip. In his eyes there had been a combination of elemental male hunger and profound human yearning, as though he had spent a lifetime in darkness and she was sunrise shimmering just beyond his reach.

Shannon's heartbeat hammered wildly inside her chest while Whip rode slowly closer. The double-barreled shotgun lay cold and heavy in her hands. The gun was loaded, the hammers were back, and her finger rested across both triggers.

Beside Shannon a huge brindle dog snarled softly, sensing his mistress's unease. Bigger than a mastiff, leggy as a timber wolf, as thick through the chest as a pony, the dog clearly outweighed Shannon. Just as clearly, the dog was protective of her. Fangs as long as Shannon's thumb gleamed whitely below the beast's curled upper lip.

"Easy, Prettyface," Shannon said softly to the dog.

Prettyface subsided, but the ruff still stood out on his powerful neck. His ears remained flat against his massive skull in blunt warning of his temperament.

Whip kept riding closer, until Shannon could see the clear silver of his eyes. His hunger was equally clear, a yearning both direct and complex. That yearning had haunted Shannon all the way back to the cabin.

It haunted her still.

"That's far enough, mister," Shannon said steadily. "What do you want?"

To her relief, Whip reined in his horse and tipped his hat politely to her.

"Evening, ma'am," he said. "You left Murphy's store so quickly that you forgot most of your supplies."

Shannon's eyes searched the quicksilver and shadows of Whip's eyes.

She hadn't made a mistake. She wasn't dreaming. The stranger called Whip was here, in her clearing.

And he wanted her.

"It *is* you," she said huskily. "Whip. That's what they call you, isn't it?"

"Out here, yes."

Shannon knew better than to ask if Whip had any other name, a given name, a Christian name, a home and a family. West of the Mississippi you called a man sir, mister, or whatever nickname he accepted. If he wanted to be called something else, he would tell you quickly enough.

Shannon's glance went over Whip with a curious longing. The rhythm of his words and his muted drawl were those of a man who hadn't been raised in eastern slums or crude western gold camps. He was southern, but not from the Deep South. Perhaps not even Confederate.

"Are you . . . Did you . . .?" Shannon took a quick breath. "Did those Culpeppers hurt you?"

Whip smiled slowly.

Shannon's breath lodged in her throat, making her ache. Whip had the smile of a recently fallen angel, gentle and rueful and so darkly beautiful it almost brought her to her knees.

"No, Shannon," Whip said. "They didn't hurt me."

"You're sure?"

"Yes."

The breath Shannon had been holding came out in a ragged sigh.

Lightning raked the mountain peaks that rose around the clearing. Wind surged, bending delicate aspens whose branches were still bare of leaves. With the wind came a prolonged rumble of thunder and a quicksilver taste of rain.

"You shouldn't have interfered," Shannon said earnestly. "The last man who stood up for me against the Culpeppers got stomped so bad that he died."

Gray eyes narrowed.

"Those boys have the manners of a wolverine," Whip said.

"I tried to warn you."

"And I tried to warn them. They didn't listen. So as Caleb would say, I read to them from the Book. Maybe they'll listen better in the future."

Shannon's dark eyes jerked toward the braided

leather coils riding so comfortably on Whip's powerful shoulder. She hadn't seen the lash strike Beau, but she knew it had. At the first sight of blood on a Culpepper mouth, she had grabbed her supplies and run for old Razorback.

"Caleb?" Shannon asked.

It was the only thing she could think of to say, for the smile was gone from Whip's face. Now he was looking at her like she was food and he was a man who had gone hungry far too long.

What frightened Shannon was how much a part of her wanted to ease this one man's hunger.

I'm still scared after what happened in town, Shannon told herself stoutly. *Tomorrow I'll go see Cherokee. Then I won't feel so alone that a stranger's smile turns my heart upside down and makes my knees shaky.*

"Caleb Black," Whip explained gently, "is my sister Willow's husband. They have a ranch west of here. So does my brother Reno, and his wife, Eve."

"Oh."

Shannon forced herself to breathe normally. Her hands ached from being clenched around the heavy shotgun, but she wasn't about to put the weapon down. She had seen how terrifyingly fast that bullwhip could move.

"I'm Shannon Conner, uh, Smith," she said. Then added hastily, "Smith is my married name."

Whip frowned as though he didn't like the reminder that she was married.

"Is it all right if I get down and give you the supplies you left behind?"

"All right?" she asked, perplexed.

"The shotgun," Whip said gently.

"Oh. That."

Whip made no attempt to hide his amusement at his effect on Shannon Conner Smith.

"Yes," he said in a deep voice. "That."

Shannon flushed.

And she kept the shotgun's muzzle where it was, pointing just in front of Whip's horse.

"Go ahead," Shannon said. "Get whatever Murphy figured he couldn't cheat me out of."

Whip dismounted with a muscular grace that did nothing to set Shannon's mind at ease.

Lord above, this is one dangerous man.

Beautiful, too.

The second thought was so startling to Shannon that she almost laughed out loud.

I must be going cabin happy. Flowers are beautiful, and butterflies, and a baby's smile.

Whip isn't like those things.

Lightning burned whitely across the indigo base of clouds whose towering heads were still washed in crimson light. The mountain wore the storm with the muscular ease of a man carrying a bull-whip coiled on his shoulder.

But mountains are beautiful, too. And thunderheads. And lightning burning through the storm.

Whip is like that. Lightning and storm and a mountain's strength.

Prettyface's rippling snarl brought Shannon's wandering attention back to the clearing.

Whip was walking toward her.

But instead of the small parcels of baking soda and lard she had expected, his big arms were filled to overflowing with supplies.

"Hold it, Mr. Whip."

The shotgun was no longer pointing at Whip's horse.

Whip stopped where he was.

"My name is Rafael Moran," he said calmly, "but call me Whip if you'd rather."

"It's how I've been thinking of you," she said.

"Have you?"

"What?"

"Been thinking of me?"

Shannon blushed, realizing what she had admitted.

Whip smiled and started toward her again.

"I said hold it!" she ordered.

"I'm already holding as much as I can," Whip said reasonably, "but I'll try."

Shannon bit her lips against an urge to smile, to laugh, to put away the shotgun and trust the big stranger who seemed as familiar to her as her own breath.

Why didn't Cherokee ever tell me I would react like this to a man? Lord above, no wonder women do fool things for men.

At least, for men like Whip.

"Don't come any closer," she said grimly. "Prettyface doesn't like strangers."

Whip blinked. "Prettyface?"

"My hound."

Whip looked at the huge, snarling animal whose head came up to Shannon's breasts.

"That's Prettyface?" he asked.

"Of course. Or maybe you'd like to be the one to tell him he's ugly?"

There was an instant of silence. Then Whip threw back his head and laughed with surprise and delight.

A ripple of pleasure went through Shannon at the sound. Whip's laughter was even more beautiful than his smile.

"Prettyface it is," Whip agreed. "You'd have to be dumb as a roomful of Culpeppers to call that brute anything else."

This time Shannon couldn't help smiling.

"Where do you want your supplies?" Whip asked.

Her smile vanished.

"They aren't mine," Shannon said flatly.

"That isn't what Murphy said."

"Murphy wouldn't know the truth if it wore a sign."

Whip smiled again. "Can't argue that. So think of this as Murphy's apology for all the times he kept his dirty thumb on the scales when he was weighing your supplies."

With a hunger Shannon couldn't entirely conceal, she looked at the sacks of beans and flour, bacon and dried apples, salt and spices, and other things she had gone so long without she could hardly remember their names.

Abruptly Shannon looked away from the bounty that was being offered to her. Her throat worked as she swallowed, for just the thought of food was enough to make her mouth water.

"I'll take the baking soda and lard I paid for, and thank you for your trouble," she said tightly. "You can take the rest back."

Just as Whip started to speak, lightning slashed through the condensing night. Thunder rumbled, closer now. The air itself tasted of sleet. The storm was closing in on Shannon's clearing, bringing the icy rains of high-country summer.

"If you think I'm going to ride all the way back to Holler Creek in this weather," Whip said, "you're crazy."

"Where you go is your business. What you take with you is mine."

For a long time there was no sound but that of the twilight storm, of wind rushing and trees bending, thunder growling, the muted drumroll of rain beating against the mountain with tiny silver hammers.

"You need the food," Whip said bluntly. "You're too thin."

Shannon didn't bother to deny it. She had lost so much weight during the past winter she could barely get Silent John's cast-off clothes to stay on her. If it hadn't been for the pronounced flare of her hips, Shannon would have found the pants around her knees every time she moved.

But Whip doesn't have the right to notice something that personal, much less to take it upon himself to feed me.

Both Cherokee and Silent John had repeatedly warned Shannon about the problems that would come if she allowed herself to get beholden to a man during Silent John's frequent absences. Shannon couldn't allow herself to owe a man anything. Even a man with a smile like a fallen angel.

Perhaps *especially* not that man.

When Whip saw the determined line of Shannon's mouth, he knew before she spoke that she was going to refuse the supplies. That made him angry, but what really triggered his temper was the fact that he couldn't force Shannon to take so much as a single bite of the food he had brought for her.

He had no right to take care of Shannon. Only her husband had that privilege, and obviously the man was no damned good at it.

"Think of it as a loan," Whip said through clenched teeth.

"No."

"Hell's fire," Whip snarled, "you're so weak you can hardly hold that shotgun up!"

"I'm not too weak to pull the trigger."

The sound Prettyface made then echoed Whip's anger, a low rumbling like a storm coming.

Whip got a grip on his temper. The last thing he wanted to do was fight Shannon's dog. As a way to get into a girl's good graces, thumping on her dog was a losing strategy.

Besides, the damned beast was as big as a barn.

Yet, even knowing that, Whip had to struggle with his desire to yank the shotgun out of Shannon's hands, clout the dog a good one, and then sit Shannon down to a real meal.

Realizing that his temper was at flash point shocked Whip. Normally he was the easygoing Moran and his brother Reno was the hardheaded one. But there was something about Shannon's sheer stubbornness that put the spurs to Whip's temper.

"There's no harm in accepting a hand now and again," Whip said, forcing himself to speak gently.

"Cherokee, the shaman, told me that men tame mustangs by offering them food when they're hungry and water when they're thirsty. Of course, the men run the mustangs nearly to death first, so they get plenty hungry and thirsty. Then the men offer the mustangs a hand—with a rope in it."

Humor briefly softened the planes of Whip's face.

"That's one way to do it," he agreed.

But Wolfe Lonetree taught me a better way, Whip remembered. *You stay on the edges of the mustang's senses, not crowding, not rushing, until the wild thing gets used to having you around. Then you get closer and the mustang gets nervous and you stop until you teach it to accept you at that distance.*

And then you go closer and wait and go closer and wait and go closer until finally the sweet little beauty is eating right out of your hand.

Of course, damned few mustangs are worth that much trouble.

The wind swept down, billowing Shannon's loose clothes one moment and molding them to her body the next.

Whip's breath stopped. Shannon might have looked skinny, but underneath that frayed cloth were the kind of curves that would keep a man awake at night, thinking of new ways to get close to her.

Really close.

Damnation. If she were mine, I sure as hell wouldn't be off chasing gold or hunting men. I'd be right next to her, seeing how many ways we could pleasure each other.

And I'd keep at it until we both were too tired to lick our lips.

"Shannon . . ."

As Whip spoke, lightning arced in white violence across half the sky. Thunder battered the mountains until the ground trembled. In the calm that followed, a rushing sound swept across the clearing toward the cabin, rain streaming down in wild silver veils.

Whip was fascinated by the beauty of the storm racing down toward him, but he wasn't deceived.

He knew all about the seductive, deadly beauty of the Rocky Mountain high country. Though it was early summer, at this altitude sunset brought a sharp chill to the air. By moonrise it would be freezing. By morning there might be snow chest-high on a Montana horse. The snow could be gone by the next day.

Or it could stay for a month, as it had late this spring.

The little bit of supplies Shannon had would barely keep her alive for two weeks.

"Where the hell is your husband?" Whip asked in exasperation. "You need him!"

Shannon hoped it was too dark for Whip to see the alarm in her eyes. Cherokee was right. Whatever had happened to make Silent John disappear, men had to believe that Silent John was still alive, still likely to appear without warning, still able to bring down a buck or a man at three thousand yards.

"Silent John is wherever he is," Shannon said flatly.

"Word in Holler Creek is that you're a widow," Whip retorted. "Word is that Silent John is dead and you're starving all alone in this miserable, godforsaken clearing!"

Prettyface snarled.

Whip felt like snarling right back.

Shannon said not one word. She simply stood with her feet braced and the shotgun steady in her aching arms.

Sudden, heavy rain drenched the clearing, dousing all the colors of sunset. Within moments cold water was dripping from Whip's dark Stetson and beading up on the heavy wool of his jacket.

Shannon had the shelter of the cabin's eaves, but it wasn't enough to turn the cutting wind. She shivered as the first raw blast of rain pelted her.

"Be sensible," Whip said, forcing his voice to be even.

"I am. You're the one who's been puffing on the dream-pipe."

"Murphy has been cheating you for years," Whip said, ignoring Shannon's retort. "When I pointed that out, he decided he could fatten up your supplies some. That's all there was to it. No obligation on your part at all."

Shannon opened her mouth.

Whip just kept talking. "You don't need to worry about being obligated to me for bringing the supplies, either. I was going to check out the Avalanche Creek gold fields and your cabin was on the way."

"That's a nice story," Shannon said, wishing she could believe it. "But I've heard it before. I'm not looking for help from women-hungry men."

Whip's hold on his temper slipped as the cold rain lashed one side of his face and the truth lashed the other.

"I'm not like the others," Whip said through his teeth.

"Do tell," Shannon said coolly. "Does that mean you don't want me?"

Whip opened his mouth, then closed it. Lying simply wasn't his style.

"I want you," he said flatly.

Shannon couldn't control the shiver that went through her at Whip's blunt words.

"But I'd never force you, Shannon," he said gently. "That's a promise."

"I'll make that promise easy for you to keep. Mount up and ride."

"Listen," Whip began.

"No, you listen," Shannon said tightly. "You're just like all the others. You want my body and not one other damned thing. No offers of marriage and kids and sharing good times and bad for the rest of our lives. All you want is a few minutes in the dark with the 'poor little dear' who might or might not be a widow."

"It's not just that," Whip said angrily.

"Oh? Does that mean you're offering marriage along with the rutting?"

The look on Whip's face told Shannon more than she wanted to know. Her short laugh was as bitterly cold as the rain.

"That's what I thought," she said. "Thank you, but no thank you. I've got everything I need until Silent John gets back."

"What if he never gets back? Damn it, what if he's dead? What then?"

Shannon's finger tightened on the shotgun's double trigger. Hearing her own fears spoken by Whip's deep, angry voice reinforced them.

And undermined her.

Don't argue with him, Shannon warned herself. *You'll lose. Then you'll be like those two sad whores in Whiskey Flat, with every man in Colorado Territory knowing the color of your nipples.*

"You earned the name Whip," Shannon said harshly, "but even you aren't faster than a shotgun shell. So take your supplies and your hungry silver eyes and ride out."

To Shannon it seemed like a week before Whip finally turned around and began loading supplies back onto his skinny black packhorse.

Lightning split the rainy twilight, turning the world to burning silver. Thunder followed instantly, loud enough to drown out all other sounds. Rain came down harder and then harder still, a torrent fit to put out the fires of hell.

Though Whip was only twelve feet away, Shannon had to strain to see him. She blinked her eyes fiercely, knowing she must see through tears and rain alike.

When lightning came again, the clearing was empty.

Whip was gone.

Shannon bit her lip against the urge to scream Whip's name into the teeth of the storm, calling him back, offering him whatever he wanted in return for food and safety.

And she knew exactly what he wanted.

The Culpeppers had made what men wanted savagely clear to Shannon on more than one occasion. What men wanted was to bend her over a chair and rut on her until she begged and bled and begged some more.

The thought of it made her stomach clench, sending bile into her throat.

Maybe Whip wouldn't ask that of me. Maybe he did just want to help and wouldn't have asked for anything more than thanks and a home-cooked meal.

Then Shannon remembered Whip's words and the heat in his silver glance. She gave up trying to fool herself.

Whip wants me, all right. Just like the Culpeppers want me.

Shannon shuddered and felt cold all the way to her soul. Nothing in her experience had led her to believe that women did more than endure men's brutal rutting in exchange for shelter and food and safety.

And children. Sweet-faced little bits of humanity to sing to and cuddle and love.

Prettyface whined and set his teeth gently around Shannon's hand, reminding her of his presence. It also reminded Shannon that she was standing in the icy evening rain, feeling as empty as the clearing had become when Whip rode out.

Stop dreaming, Shannon told herself savagely. *Mother dreamed, and what did she get? A no-account traveling man who left her flat.*

And she got me. I loved her, but all she loved was laudanum.

Cherokee is right. Love is a fairy tale spun to keep women from setting off on their own and leaving men to take care of themselves.

Slowly Shannon turned and went into the cabin that was little warmer than the rain itself.

3

When Shannon awoke before dawn, the storm had spent itself. Night was slowly draining from the sky, leaving it a transparent silver that reminded her all too much of Whip's hungry eyes.

Prettyface made a low sound in his throat and nudged Shannon's cheek again.

"Brrrrrr," she muttered. "Your nose is as cold as the floor will be."

But Shannon ruffled Prettyface's fur anyway. He was the only living thing that had ever returned her love. If it hadn't been for Prettyface, she didn't know what she would have done when Silent John disappeared in the winter of '65.

Not that her great-uncle had ever been much company. He had fully earned the nickname "Silent John." But Shannon was grateful to him just the same. No matter how remote, no matter how lonely, no matter how hard life was in Echo Basin, she much preferred it to the life she had left behind in Virginia.

In the Colorado Territory, Shannon was free.

In Virginia, she had been little more than a slave.

"Good morning, my beautiful monster," Shannon said to the dog, stretching. "Do you think summer will ever truly come? Sometimes I feel so cold even the hot spring can't warm me."

At the words "hot spring," Prettyface's ears came up. He cocked his head, whined, and looked toward the back of the cabin, where a cupboard door opened onto a narrow tunnel. At the end of the tunnel was a cave with a hot spring that was sweet rather than sulfurous.

Silent John had used the healing waters when his arthritis bothered him too much. Shannon simply liked the steamy warmth of the hidden cave. It saved having to chop wood to heat water in order to wash clothes—and herself. The hot spring meant that the secondhand clothes she wore were clean, as was the skin beneath them. In such a remote place, where the soft comforts of civilization were almost entirely lacking, the hot spring was a delicious luxury.

And during Shannon's first winters alone, when she had neither the strength nor the skill to bring down trees big enough to heat the cabin, the hot spring had saved her life. She was better with ax and maul and saw, now, yet far from good. There was barely a few days' worth of stove wood stacked outside the cabin right now.

Thank the Lord for the hot spring. Otherwise I might get as dirty as Murphy or those Culpeppers.

Seeing the direction of his mistress's glance, Prettyface whined hopefully. For all his rough appearance, the dog enjoyed chasing shadows in the warm creek that flowed out from the hot spring's pool before disappearing into a crack in the bedrock.

"Not this morning," Shannon said to Prettyface. "We have to return the salt we borrowed from Cherokee. She—blast it, *he*—will need it."

Shannon frowned at Prettyface, who waved his tail gently.

"It's a good thing no one else is ever around," Shannon said unhappily. "I got used to being called Silent John's wife, but I have an awful time speaking of Cherokee as a he when I know full well now that she isn't."

Memories of the Culpeppers' coarse comments tightened Shannon's mouth for a moment.

"Not that I blame Cherokee for the charade. The longer Silent John is gone, the more I know why she decided to dress like a man, let herself be called a shaman, and live way up on the north fork of Avalanche Creek."

With a determined sweep of her arm, Shannon pushed off the bearskin cover that kept the worst of the chill at bay during the night. There was no dressing to do, for she had quickly learned the habit of bathing before bed and sleeping in clean clothes for their warmth.

There weren't many chores to do around the cabin in the morning. Since Shannon wasn't going to stay inside, there was no point in building a fire. Just as there was no point in lighting a lantern and wasting precious oil when the sun would be up pretty soon.

Shannon poured a cup of water from the small silver pitcher that had been her mother's. The water was so cold it made her teeth ache, but even so, the water made scraps of venison jerky easier to chew.

She was still chewing when she pulled on Silent John's second-best jacket and went to the front door. As she walked, she stuffed a few more strips of dried venison into her pocket.

That's the last of the jerky, she thought unhappily. *Thank God the deer are coming back to the high country.*

Before Shannon unbarred the cabin door, she lifted the shotgun from its pegs over the doorway. As she had done the previous night, she broke open the weapon, pulled out the two precious shells, picked up a soft buckskin cloth, and went to work on the gun.

Even when Shannon had been barely fifteen, Silent John had been merciless in his demands that Shannon learn to use and care for his weapons. She had never been much good with the heavy .50-caliber buffalo gun that he preferred, but she could shoot the lighter guns well enough to defend herself.

Putting food on the table was another matter entirely. There was no money to spare on extra ammunition to hone her shooting skills, so she had to get very close to the quarry before she could risk a shot. As a result, she nearly always gave away her presence before she felt confident enough to shoot.

"But I'm getting better," Shannon assured herself. "By this winter, Cherokee won't have to hunt for two."

With quick, efficient motions Shannon wiped down the shotgun, making certain that no moisture had condensed overnight inside the firing chambers. When she was satisfied that everything was clean and dry, she put a shell in each chamber and closed the gun firmly. She put four more shells in her pocket, leaving only three shells in the box.

Like the venison jerky, Shannon's supply of ammunition was nearly gone.

"When I go into Holler Creek again, I'll have to buy ammunition. And next time I go, you're coming with me, Prettyface. I know you don't like settlements and strangers, but that's too bad. I need you to guard my back."

Prettyface stood with barely restrained eagerness, watching the door and his mistress by turns.

"But before I can buy anything in Holler Creek, I'll have to wring a bit of gold from one of Silent John's claims," Shannon continued, thinking aloud as had become her habit. "Mother's wedding band was the last thing of any value I owned, except the small poke of gold I'm saving for winter supplies in case the hunting is real bad."

Silently Shannon hoped that she wouldn't have to use that tiny anthill of Silent John's gold. It was all that stood between her and the kind of destitution that forced women to sell their bodies to strangers.

"If only you could teach me how to track and

stalk better," Shannon said to Prettyface. "Then I could get close enough to the blasted deer to turn them into venison."

Prettyface watched Shannon with dark, adoring eyes, but was of no other help. When he hunted with his mistress, the dog chased whatever he scented at a pace that left Shannon far behind. Sometimes Prettyface ran a deer down and shared with his mistress. Often he settled for less tasty game.

Silent John had taught Shannon the basics of shooting and dressing out the kill, but there never had been enough time for her to learn the kind of skill that would allow her to stockpile game for winter. When the hunting had been good, Silent John hunted, and he hunted alone.

The rest of the time he grubbed gold from the hard rock of the mountains. That, too, was a survival skill he hadn't taught the young grand-niece he had brought back from Virginia to live in his home.

"But I'm learning," Shannon said firmly. "I brought down one deer and some foolish grouse last fall. If the weather holds now, I'll hunt some more, until I have enough food to go up the east fork of Avalanche Creek and dig for gold, and then I'll hunt for more food and jerk the meat and take the gold and buy supplies for winter and . . ."

Shannon's voice died. Summer wasn't very long for all that had to be done. At nearly eight thousand feet, summer came and went as quick as a mayfly.

"The wood!" Shannon said, remembering. "Oh, lord. How could I forget sawing and chopping and splitting and stacking and curing the wood? I'll need a lot of fuel, even with the hot spring for washing clothes and such, and I'll need to get it all before the first heavy snows close the passes and cover the downed trees and send the game to lower elevations."

Shannon drew in a deep breath, trying to calm the fear that sometimes took her unawares since Silent John had ridden away from the cabin and never come back.

I'm scared, Prettyface. I'm really scared.

But those were words Shannon would never speak aloud. She had learned when she was thirteen that giving way to fear only made things worse. It told people you were ripe for the taking.

"Sufficient unto the day are the troubles thereof," Shannon said grimly. "I'll have plenty of time to do everything if I stop standing around wringing my hands!"

With quick, light steps, Shannon went to the leather-hinged box that held dry goods. Except for the salt and flour she had bought yesterday, the cupboard was empty. Last night she had divided the salt into two portions. The smaller one was hers. The larger one was destined to repay Cherokee for her loan at Christmas.

"I should have told Whip to leave the supplies that I paid for," Shannon muttered.

The memory of the Culpeppers made Shannon's mouth tighten in fear and distaste.

But the memory of a big man riding toward her out of the storm made her breath unravel with an excitement she had never known.

"Come on, Prettyface. It's time to see Cherokee. She'll talk some sense into me."

Prettyface bounded out the door ahead of Shannon. She watched him carefully, knowing that the dog's senses were much more acute than hers. If anyone was prowling around, Prettyface would discover the intruder long before she did.

The dog lifted his muzzle into the cold, clear wind and sampled the air with all of his senses. Then he bounded forward, telling Shannon that there was no danger on the wind.

Even so, Shannon was cautious. She stepped outside and looked around carefully. There were no tracks in the frost-stiffened grass around the cabin. She sighed with relief even as she took another look just to be certain.

The shotgun was in the crook of her arm and her hand was never far from the trigger. The wind tugged at her hat, but she had tied it on securely with a faded silk scarf, one of the few luxuries that had survived from her Virginia childhood.

Pulling the door shut firmly behind her, Shannon set out toward Cherokee's cabin. She could have ridden Razorback, but he was still tired from the trip into Holler Creek. She left the old mule on a picket rope, cropping tender young grass.

It was less than two miles to Cherokee's cabin. As Shannon set out, dawn was coming up all around in glorious shades of rose and gold and deepest pink. The beauty of the day lifted her spirits. Humming very softly under her breath, she pulled the colors of dawn around her like a glorious cloak and hurried along the trail.

When Shannon reached the cleared area around Cherokee's cabin, she stood at the edge and called out. Since the Culpeppers' arrival at Echo Basin, folks had been less welcoming to visitors. People who walked up on someone unannounced stood a good chance of getting shot. Even Cherokee's reputation as a shaman wouldn't keep the likes of the Culpeppers at bay.

Shannon didn't step forward until a friendly invitation came from the cabin.

"Come on in, gal," Cherokee yelled. "Too durn cold out there for standing around."

"Okay, Prettyface," Shannon said.

The dog bounded forward. Just as he reached the cabin, the door opened completely. A tall, lean figure stood in the doorway.

A single glance at the way Cherokee was standing told Shannon that something was wrong with the old woman's right foot.

"Howdy, gal," Cherokee said. "Fine day, ain't it?"

"Indeed it is," Shannon said. "Prettyface, get out of the way. If you're hungry, go rustle your own breakfast."

The cabin door closed, leaving Prettyface on the outside. In truth, there was barely room for two people in Cherokee's tiny cabin, much less two people and a big dog.

"Hear you went into Holler Creek for supplies," Cherokee said.

"How did you hear that?"

"Injuns, how else? Wounded Bear's nephew was trading gold for whiskey in Holler Creek. He heard tell how them Culpeppers finally got their comeuppance."

"Did they?"

"Bet your sweet smile they did. Where was you when the dust settled? They was fighting over you, after all."

"When that bullwhip cracked, I grabbed the flour and the salt and took out of there like my heels were on fire," Shannon said dryly.

Cherokee's husky, chuckling laughter filled the tiny cabin. She wore her salt-and-pepper hair in two thick braids, Indian style. Her seamed, dark face, combined with shapeless trousers, wool shirt, and worn moccasins, created the appearance of an old half-breed who had chosen to live alone rather than endure the insults of being not white and not Indian. Only the amulet bag hanging around her neck hinted at the wisdom lying behind her calm, dark eyes.

If anyone other than Shannon knew that Cherokee was an old woman rather than an old man, no one had spoken publicly about it. Her gifts with herbs and healing had earned her the title of shaman among Indians and whites alike.

"Light and set," Cherokee invited.

Shannon settled onto the stool that was pulled close to the ancient wood stove. Cherokee limped slowly over to sit on her bunk. The cabin was so small that their knees nearly knocked together as they sat.

"What did you do to your foot?" Shannon asked.

Cherokee turned and began stuffing something noxious into a stone pipe. She struck a match and puffed the mixture of tobacco and herbs into life.

"It was a hard winter," Cherokee said, "but Wounded Bear's band only lost one old squaw and a stillborn baby. The rest of them are as frisky as your durn dog."

Shannon wanted to pursue the subject of the other woman's injury, but didn't. Cherokee talked about what interested her and ignored the rest.

"If they weren't frisky, one of your spring

tonics would put them right," Shannon said, grimacing.

Cherokee's tonics tasted awful, though she swore that was part of their virtue.

"That's the God's truth," Cherokee said.

Discreetly Shannon looked around the cabin. Normally there was a full bucket of water beside the stove, wood stacked nearby, and something edible simmering. Sometimes there were even fresh biscuits.

But today there was only a nearly empty bucket, the scraped remains of stew in the bottom of a pot, and nothing edible in sight. Nor was there any wood bigger than kindling.

"Walking here made me thirsty," Shannon said, reaching for the empty bucket. "Mind if I fetch some water?"

Cherokee hesitated, then shrugged.

"The creek is cold enough to freeze hell itself," the old woman muttered. "Makes my teeth ache all the way to my elbows to drink the durned water."

"Then I'll just fetch some wood and warm the water a bit."

Again Cherokee hesitated. Then she sighed.

"I thank you kindly, Shannon. I'm feeling a mite puny today."

Quickly Shannon performed the necessary chores of drawing water and bringing wood in from the woodpile. When she was finished stacking the wood between the bunk and the stove, Shannon stole a sideways look at the other woman. Cherokee looked pale and worn.

"While I'm at it," Shannon said cheerfully, "I'll just scrub out this old pot and make a little soup. There's nothing like soup to take the gloom out of a day."

This time Cherokee didn't even hesitate. She simply lay back on her bunk with a muffled curse.

"I slipped whilst I was bringing in water about six days ago," Cherokee said. "Bunged up my ankle. The poultice helped, but the durned thing still bothers me."

"Then stay off it," Shannon said, scrubbing the pot. "Give it time to heal."

Cherokee smiled slightly. "That's the same advice I gave to Silent John when old Razorback stepped on his foot."

"I hope you take it better than he did."

"Still no sign of him."

It wasn't a question. Cherokee sounded quite certain. But Shannon acted as though it was a question.

"No," she said. "No a trace."

"You got to face it, gal. You're a widow."

Shannon said nothing.

"Even those no-account Culpeppers have figured it out," Cherokee said," and nobody would accuse them of being overly bright."

"Then I'll just have to put on Silent John's riding coat and take Razorback over the pass again."

Cherokee grunted. "Don't think that will fool them again."

Shannon shrugged. "No help for it."

"What about that man called Whip?" Cherokee asked. "Small Bear said he followed your tracks out of Holler Creek."

"Small Bear is as big as gossip as his uncle Wounded Bear."

Cherokee waited for Shannon to tell her about Whip.

Instead, Shannon made soup as though her life depended on it.

"Well?" prodded Cherokee finally.

"Well, what?"

"Whip, that's what. Did he find you?"

"Yes."

"Blast it, gal. You done hung around Silent John too long! What happened 'tween you and Whip?"

"I sent him packing."

"How?"

"Prettyface and a loaded shotgun."

"Huh," Cherokee grunted, unimpressed. "If that Whip fellow left, it's because he decided to, not because you had him buffaloed. What did he want?"

"Same thing the Culpeppers wanted," Shannon retorted.

"Doubt it. He don't have no reputation for beating gals bloody to get his satisfaction."

Shannon looked up from her work, surprised that Cherokee had a good word to say about any male of the species.

"Do you know Whip?" Shannon asked.

"Not directly, but Wounded Bear and Wolfe Lonetree are thick, and Lonetree is real thick with Reno and Reno is Whip's brother."

"Reno? The gunfighter?" Shannon asked, for she hadn't wanted to ask Whip.

"Yep, but only when he's pushed to it. What Reno is really good at is hunting gold. Durn near makes you believe in spirits talking to men when you watch Reno and his wife Eve quarter the land for gold. Leastwise, that's what Lonetree told

Wounded Bear, and Wounded Bear told Small Bear, and—"

"—Small Bear told you," Shannon finished. "I swear, you beat that fancy Denver telegraph when it comes to passing on news."

Cherokee chuckled.

"Not much else to do but talk, when you get to my age," Cherokee said. "Besides, men is the worst gossips there is, and that's God's own truth. Except for Silent John, of course. Talking to him was like talking to a tombstone. Don't know how you ever stood it. The man durn near drove me to drink."

"I didn't know you ever were around Silent John long enough to be bothered."

Cherokee bent down and fussed over her ankle before she spoke again.

"Don't take long for that kind of silence to wear on me," she muttered.

"I don't mind silence. John loved to read, and he taught me to love it, too. Though I admit I prefer poetry to Plato."

Cherokee snorted. "I seen that trunk o' yours stuffed with books. Waste of time, all of them, 'less they talk about herbs and such."

"In winter there's lots of time to spare."

"It ain't natural not to talk to folks."

"Oh, I talk all the time to myself and Prettyface," Shannon said.

"Sensible. Leastwise you get a smart answer from one of you. Ain't saying which one, though."

Smiling, Shannon checked the water she had put on the stove. It was heating nicely.

"How about some willow-bark tea?" Shannon asked.

Cherokee grimaced. "Blasted stuff. Tastes like the bottom of hell's own slops bucket."

"It would make your ankle feel better."

"Slops."

Ignoring Cherokee's muttering, Shannon went to a battered wooden chest and lifted the lid. A complex, herbal aroma drifted up to her nose. The willow bark was easy to identify and not hard to administer. Other herbs were more chancy to use.

A few were frankly deadly. Shannon knew which they were. She avoided even touching them.

While Shannon made the tea, Cherokee reached under the bed and dragged out a battered canvas bag. She reached inside and pulled out a small, tissue-wrapped parcel. Saying nothing, she sat back on the bed. Her gnarled, scarred hand rested lightly on the parcel, as though it was a beloved pet.

When Shannon brought the medicinal tea to Cherokee, the old woman ignored the battered metal mug and looked Shannon straight in the eye.

"We got to talk," Cherokee said bluntly. "No two ways about it. You're a widow."

"You can't be certain of that."

"The hell I can't. I prayed over his grave."

Shannon's eyes widened. "What?"

"Autumn, it were. Night sky like God watching me, and that poor old mule all bloodied and worn from running down the creek."

Shannon's breath froze in her lungs. Cherokee had never talked about how she found Razorback. She had just brought the mule to Silent John's cabin, told Shannon that like as not Silent John would be late coming off his claims that year, and she better start rustling grub for herself.

Then Cherokee had said that her true name was Teresa, so Shannon didn't need to fear asking her for help if she needed it.

"You never told me," Shannon whispered.

Cherokee didn't even pause. "I patched up the mule and set out at dawn to backtrack. Trail ended in hell's own landslide. I assumed it was Silent John's grave."

"Why didn't you tell me?"

"No point," she said tersely. "If I'm wrong, Silent John turns up in the fall. If I'm right, and word gets out, every man in Echo Basin goes to howling around your cabin. No good to come of that. A man with a stiff pecker ain't no more trustworthy than a rabid skunk."

Shannon tried to speak. No words came.

"An' what good would telling you do?" Cherokee asked. "The passes was already closed, so you couldn't leave nohow. Your cupboards was full. You was safer up here than anywheres, long as no one knew Silent John was dead. So I just shut my mouth and kept it shut."

When Shannon tried to speak, only an odd sound came out.

Red appeared on Cherokee's weathered cheekbones.

"I shoulda told you 'fore now," the old woman muttered, "but I get . . . lonesome. It ain't like you had a family all pining and sighing for your company. Towns and such just ride roughshod over pretty young things like you. You was better off here, but if you knew Silent John was dead, I feared you'd up and leave."

"This is my home. I won't leave it."

"But I was wrong to keep you here," Cherokee said, ignoring Shannon's words. "Purely selfish. My conscience stings me real good when I think on it. I was going to tell you real soon and give you money to—"

"No," Shannon cut in.

Cherokee muttered under her breath. Then she straightened her shoulders.

"Things is changed, now," the old woman said flatly. "You got to leave."

"Why? Just because I know what I've suspected for the last two years, that Silent John is dead?"

"You got to git out of Echo Basin, and Whip is—"

"Why should I leave the basin?" Shannon interrupted. "It's the only home I have."

"You can't survive alone in that cabin, that's why."

"I've done it so far."

Cherokee grunted. "Silent John had enough food to feed three with some left over. You ate the leftovers the second winter and bought more. But not enough more. Look at you. Skin and bones and hair, that's all."

"I'm winter lean. I'll fatten come summer, just like all the other creatures."

"And if you don't?"

"I will."

"Blast it, gal. You're too bullheaded by half."

"That's why I'll survive," Shannon said. "Sheer stubbornness. Here. Drink your tea."

Cherokee waved off the cup. "I helped you the last two winters, but—"

"I know," Shannon interrupted. "I'm grateful. I brought your salt and as soon as the deer come back, I'll repay the—"

"Damnation, that ain't what I meant!" Cherokee blazed. "Now you listen to me, gal!"

Cherokee's anger was unexpected. Shannon closed her mouth and listened.

"Some men is better than others," Cherokee conceded reluctantly. "Lots better. Leastwise, that's what Betsy and Clementine say when they come to get their childbane potion from me."

Shannon closed her eyes. She knew the prostitutes sometimes came to "the half-breed shaman" for medicines; Shannon just hadn't known what kind of medicines, until now.

"I see," Shannon said weakly.

"Doubt it," Cherokee retorted, "but we're sneaking right up on it. Now, what we got to do is find you a man what wouldn't shame a rabid skunk. This here Whip feller fills the bill."

Shannon started to object.

"Shut your mouth, gal," Cherokee interrupted, holding out the parcel. "This here piece of frippery was given to my mother by some fool man. She gave it to me. I'm giving it to you."

Before Shannon could say anything, Cherokee was unwrapping the tissue with reverent hands. The paper was worn nearly to transparency with age and gentle handling.

But even the tissue wasn't as delicate as the creamy silk and lace inside. Shannon's breath came in with a rushing sound of surprise and pleasure as she saw the subtle sheen of satin.

Cherokee smiled gently.

"Pretty, ain't it?" Cherokee said. "First time I saw you, I thought of this here chemise."

"I can't take it."

"You ain't taking it. I'm giving it to you."

"But—"

"Hell, it don't fit me," Cherokee interrupted impatiently. "Never has. I'm too big. Never fit Ma, neither. Never been worn by no one."

Hesitantly Shannon touched the chemise. The cloth was as soft as a cloud. Even the deep lace that edged the garment was silky and supple.

"Go on, take it," Cherokee said.

"I can't."

"Sure you can."

Cherokee wrapped the chemise once more and held it out to Shannon.

"You just put it in that deep front pocket of Silent John's old jacket," Cherokee said. "It will ride safe till you get home."

"But—"

"Gal, I ain't drinking so much as a drop of that there tea unless you take this."

Slowly Shannon took the package in her free hand.

"Go on, now," Cherokee said, taking the cup of medicinal tea. "Put it away."

Not until Shannon had eased the package into the pocket of her jacket did Cherokee drink the tea.

"I don't know how to thank you," Shannon said hesitantly.

"No need. I'll feel better knowing you have it. High time it was put to its real use."

Shannon flushed.

"No, not as a whore's decoration," Cherokee said, laughing. "As a satin snare for a man. Whip, for instance. There's a man worth—"

"No."

"Yes," Cherokee retorted. "He gets one look at you in that little bit of satin and lace and he'll forget all about hitting the trail alone. You'll be married before you can say aye, yes, or maybe—"

"No," Shannon interrupted.

Cherokee sighed. "Gal, you don't—"

"No," Shannon said again, cutting across the old woman's words. "It's your turn to listen. My mother and I lived on the kindness of my uncle until I was thirteen and Mama died of lung fever. My uncle died shortly after. Then his wife worked me like a slave."

Cherokee nodded without surprise.

"I was indentured to a tailor," Shannon said. "I couldn't leave the shop, ever. I worked there, ate there, and slept there. When the tailor got drunk, which was about twice a month, I fought him off with the shears I kept beneath my pillow."

Again Cherokee nodded, unsurprised.

"One day my mother's uncle came to town," Shannon continued in a flat voice. "A letter I wrote to him when Mama was dying had finally reached him and he came to fetch me. He got Mama's silk scarf and gold wedding ring back from my aunt. He put the ring on my finger. After that, I was Mrs. Smith."

"That's about how I had it figured," Cherokee said matter-of-factly. "No gal like you takes up with a man like Silent John unless she's desperate."

Shannon's smile was bittersweet. "Compared to what I came from, Silent John and Echo Basin looked like paradise."

"I always felt that way, myself. Except I come here older than you, and alone, and I come as a man. My pa was a Mexican and my ma was a raw-boned Tennessee whore, strong as a mule and durn near as stupid. I been hired out to do men's work since I was ten, been paid like a gal, and treated like trash. After Ma died, I just took out and never looked back."

"Nor did you look for a man to marry," Shannon pointed out.

Cherokee shrugged. "Like I said, I was full tired of being some man's slave."

"Yet you want *me* to go looking for a man."

"That's different."

"Yes," Shannon said dryly. "It's my slavery, not yours."

Cherokee swore and smiled at the same time. "You're always too quick for me. But then, anybody is, these days. I'm getting old. This blasted ankle ain't healing worth a handful of spit. I'll be lucky to hunt for myself this summer, much less for you."

"Then I'll hunt for both of us."

"Gal, you've got sand enough for three men, but you're mighty thin beer when it comes to hunting."

"I'll get a lot better before the end of summer."

For a long moment Cherokee's dark eyes searched Shannon's face. Then Cherokee sighed and said no more on the subject of men and marriage and survival. She simply shook her head. There wasn't enough time between now and winter's famine for Shannon to learn how to hunt well enough to feed two people.

But Shannon would have to discover that for herself, because she wasn't listening to the older woman's advice.

Cherokee could only pray that Shannon wouldn't learn too late, after the high pass over Whiskey Creek was closed by snow. Then every living thing left in Echo Basin would be locked in until the pass opened, or they died of starvation.

Whichever came first.

4

It was sunset by the time Shannon wearily dragged herself to the top of the steep, rocky rise that overlooked her cabin. From where she stood the cabin was nearly invisible, shielded from the clearing by tall firs and half buried in the mountainside itself.

Rarely had the clearing looked so good to Shannon. The hours since she had left Cherokee's cabin had been spent hunting food. All Shannon had to show for her work was a tired body and a stomach that was growling loudly enough to draw curious looks from Prettyface.

"Take it easy," Shannon muttered. "I'm not going to catch you and skin you out for supper."

Prettyface waved his tail and licked his chops.

"Don't look at me," she said tiredly, rubbing the dog's head. "If you're hungry, go catch something. And this time, make it big enough for both of us to eat, okay?"

Because Shannon was alone, she made no attempt to hide her hunger and fatigue. Her posture and her tone of voice showed just how worn out she felt.

Other than a few scraps of jerky just after she had gotten up, there had been nothing to put in her stomach all day long. The jerky she had stuffed in her pocket that morning had ended up in Cherokee's soup, along with whatever tender greens Shannon had found growing near the old woman's cabin.

It was a better dinner than Shannon would have for herself. She had been hunting ever since she left Cherokee's cabin. But no matter how hard Shannon had tried, no matter how stealthily she had followed tracks, the deer always fled before she was close enough to risk shooting one of her few precious shells.

Glumly Shannon started picking her way down the rise where the back wall of the cabin was the mountainside itself. Somewhere beneath her feet was the cave where a hot spring breathed warmth and moisture into the darkness, but no sign of that showed on the surface. Off to the left was a pile of jumbled rocks where Silent John had dug out a second, hidden exit to the cabin. Nothing of that showed on the surface, either.

Prettyface trotted ahead of Shannon, sniffing the wind that swirled through the clearing. Suddenly the hound froze. His ears flattened to his skull and his lips lifted in a soundless snarl.

Instantly Shannon put her back to a tree, raised the shotgun, and began searching the area ahead, her weariness forgotten.

Prettyface reacted like that only in the presence of men.

Someone was near her cabin. Perhaps even inside it, hiding, waiting for her to walk in unawares.

Trying to make no noise, Shannon angled down the rocky, wooded rise. When the ground flattened, she began circling the cabin without ever leaving the forest.

Prettyface showed no interest in any of the

scents he found along the way. Only the cabin held his attention.

When Shannon finally circled to the far side of the clearing, she found out the reason for the dog's reaction. A freshly killed, fully dressed-out buck was hanging from the crossed logs at one corner of the cabin.

Silent John had used the same logs to hang game on while he sliced it up to be dried.

"Silent John?" Shannon whispered.

Suddenly Prettyface whipped around and looked back up the steep rise that they had just descended. His ruff stood on end.

Shannon turned and looked, too. There, silhouetted against the crimson and orange of sunset, was a man on horseback. The breadth of his shoulders was unmistakable to Shannon, as was the shape coiled around his right shoulder.

Whip.

He tipped his hat to her, then reined his big gray horse around. Moments later he vanished down the far side of the rise.

Though Shannon waited for a long time, breath held, Whip didn't reappear.

Finally Prettyface yawned, prodded Shannon with his nose and looked longingly toward the cabin.

"All right, boy. Guess Whip knows better than to come back now that we're onto him."

As she spoke the words, Shannon told herself that she wasn't disappointed that Whip had gone.

But she knew that she was lying.

Shannon also told herself that she would leave Whip's gift to rot where it hung.

But she knew that was also a lie. She was too hungry, and the little bit of flour she had brought back from Holler Creek would be gone all too soon.

Half grateful, half angry, thoroughly unsettled, Shannon went to the cabin. She pulled Cherokee's gift from her jacket pocket. The chemise gleamed through an opening in the tissue.

He gets one look at you in that little bit of satin and lace and he'll forget all about hitting the trail alone. You'll be married before you can say aye, yes, or maybe.

A curious, tingling sensation went through Shannon at the thought of wearing the chemise, feeling its cool softness against her breasts.

"Would I look pretty enough to hold him?" Shannon whispered. "And would he be gentle with me?"

There was no answer but the echoing silence of the cabin. Quickly Shannon put away the gift and went about dealing with another gift—Whip's buck.

Soon the first real meal Shannon had sat down to in months was steaming in front of her. Despite her hunger, she ate carefully, savoring every delicious bite.

The deer was only the beginning of Whip's gifts.

When Shannon woke up the next morning, she found two burlap bags hanging from a tree limb near the creek. The first bag was full of dried apples, sugar, cinnamon, and lard. The second bag held the supplies she had left behind in Holler Creek, and more besides.

Shannon resisted the temptation for several hours. Then she decided that she could make better use of the supplies than whatever varmint managed to climb the tree and get the bags for itself.

Decision made, Shannon wasted no time in getting an apple pie baking. And biscuits. And bread.

When Shannon went to Cherokee's cabin to share Whip's bounty, she sensed that she was being followed. It was like a prickling just under the nape of her neck, a shivery animal awareness that she wasn't alone.

Yet every time Shannon whirled around, hoping to catch a glimpse of Whip, there was nothing behind her but rocks and trees and a wild high-mountain sky.

Nor did Prettyface ever scent Whip the entire way to Cherokee's cabin.

"Come in, gal," Cherokee said, opening the door.

"Thank you."

Shannon wriggled out of the awkward back-pack she had made from strips of leather and an ancient saddlebag.

"How is your ankle?"

"Fine as frog's hair."

Shannon looked at Cherokee and knew her ankle wasn't fine.

"That's good," Shannon said. "Here, I brought you some food to pay back what you gave me this winter."

"Now lookee here. It weren't no loan, so it don't need no repaying."

"I'll hang the venison back in the corner," Shannon said, ignoring the old woman's protests. "The rest I'll put where it belongs in your dry goods cupboard."

Dumbfounded, Cherokee watched while Shannon suited actions to words.

"That's fresh venison," Cherokee said finally.

"Yes."

"Well I'll be go-to-hell. You got yourself a deer!"

Shannon said nothing.

"Now, you just take back them bags of flour and sugar," Cherokee said quickly. "I got plenty to last me till I scratch out more gold or trade some herbs down to Holler Creek."

Shannon ignored her.

"Apples!" Cherokee said reverently. "Do I smell apples?"

"You sure do. I put half of an apple pie on the back of your stove to warm."

"Bread. Pie. I *will* be go-to-hell! You done went back and claimed all your supplies!"

Shannon made a sound that could have meant anything.

"That was a damn fool thing to do," Cherokee said. "Two of them Culpeppers didn't have no more than their pride hurt in the fight with Whip. They could have caught you."

"They didn't."

"Still, they—"

"I didn't go back to Holler Creek," Shannon interrupted.

Cherokee was silent. Abruptly her seamed face split into a wide, gap-toothed grin.

"It was Whip, by God," she crowed. "He's courting you!"

Shannon started to deny it, then decided not to. Cherokee wouldn't refuse to share in the unexpected bounty of courting gifts from Whip.

But Cherokee might refuse to share in the spoils of attempted seduction.

"Maybe," Shannon said. "Maybe not."

"'Course he is. Where's your mind, gal? He's got an eye for you. Or did you wear that frippery for him already?"

"I'm married, remember? That's what everyone is supposed to think, and don't you forget it."

"Huh. Wearing a ring didn't make no marriage. Anyways, you're widowed."

"Get off your ankle," was all Shannon said. "I'll bring in enough water and wood for several days, because I might not be able to get back before then."

"Going somewheres?"

"Hunting," Shannon said succinctly.

Cherokee looked puzzled. Then she laughed her husky, chuckling laugh.

"You gonna run him a right smart chase, ain't you, gal?"

Shannon's smile was as hard as the blade of the hunting knife she had sheathed at her waist.

"I'm going to run that old boy's tail right into the ground," she drawled, imitating Cherokee's accent.

Cherokee's laughter redoubled until she was breathless.

"You just keep on thinking that," Cherokee said finally. "You just go ahead, right up to the moment Whip grabs you and drags you in front of a preacher."

Shannon's smile slipped. Whip didn't have marriage in mind, and she knew it very well.

But Cherokee didn't need to know. She looked so delighted that Shannon's future was solved.

"You stay off that ankle, now," Shannon cautioned. "If I catch you up and around, I'll make you do your own chores."

Still chuckling, Cherokee limped to the rumpled bed and stretched out.

As soon as Shannon stepped out of the cabin, she knew that Whip was somewhere close by, watching her. Yet Prettyface gave no sign. He lay at ease in the sun in front of the cabin, letting the wind ruffle his thick salt-and-pepper fur.

While Shannon drew water and carried wood, she kept glancing downwind, the one place where Whip could hide from Prettyface's keen senses.

She never spotted Whip.

But she heard something that could have been the wind keening through distant rocks . . . or the sound of a man making the mountain silence tremble with the soft wailing of panpipes.

After she left Cherokee, through the long, futile hours of hunting, Shannon looked for Whip. She knew he was there, for the prickling at her nape told her that she was being watched. If that weren't enough, the cry of the primitive flute came to her at odd times, a mere echo of sound that made Prettyface cock his head and listen, but not snarl. The disembodied music carried no threat for the dog.

Yet for all Shannon's watchfulness and Prettyface's acute senses, she never caught a glimpse of the man whose presence haunted her as surely as his music haunted the mountain silence.

The next day she followed a game trail, walked between two boulders—and found three grouse neatly dressed out and tied by their feet, dangling from a tree branch.

Frantically Shannon spun around, looking everywhere at once. There was nothing to see but trees and rock, sunshine and pure white clouds. She looked at the ground, but saw no tracks, no disturbance of twigs or leaves or dirt.

Nor had she heard any shots. Yet there the birds were, obviously freshly killed.

He got them with that bullwhip. Lord, that man is fast!

Prettyface circled the ground beneath the grouse, growling almost silently.

"Well, I'm glad you can smell Whip," Shannon whispered. "I was beginning to think he was a ghost."

She hesitated, then took down the grouse and stuffed them into her makeshift backpack.

"No point leaving good food for varmints," she mumbled.

Prettyface sniffed the wind several times before he lost interest. His ruff settled and he looked at Shannon, waiting for a signal.

Shannon looked at her hands and realized they were trembling. The knowledge that Whip might be out there just beyond the reach of Prettyface's senses was unnerving.

At least he's keeping his distance. He won't come closer so long as I have Prettyface and a loaded shotgun.

Squaring her shoulders, Shannon set off across the mountainside once more. As she looked for game, she gathered fresh greens and stuffed them into the backpack with the grouse.

When Shannon returned to her cabin, she found a side of bacon hanging from the crossed logs where the buck had been until she had taken it down, sliced off strips and set them to drying.

She looked around quickly.

No one was there. Nor did the nape of her neck prickle with primal awareness of another's presence.

Yet hours later, as the moon rose to send a rush of silver glory over the land, the husky music of panpipes was breathed through the night.

Shannon sat up with her heart pounding and Prettyface's throaty growl vibrating just beyond the bed. Then the growling subsided.

Slowly Shannon realized that the keening sound was Whip's flute talking to the night. She went to the window, opened the shutters and crack, and looked out. She saw nothing but moon shadows and silver light and the massive ebony shawl of the forest flung over the sleeping mountainside.

Prettyface grumbled quietly and flopped down in the corner again. His actions told Shannon what she already knew. She was in no danger from the husky, keening notes.

She went back to bed and listened to the sound of loneliness distilled by a man's breath blowing through a primitive flute.

The next day was much the same for Shannon, the prickling of her nape and the sweet haunting of the flute while she hunted game that eluded her. The only difference was in the gift Whip left waiting for her—three fine trout, still cold from the stream.

That night the flute woke Shannon again, but her heart raced less this time. Prettyface growled, prowled the cabin several times, then curled up and went back to sleep.

Shannon lay awake, listening to the husky lamentations of the flute, yearning toward the unspeakable beauty of something she couldn't name.

The third day Whip's gift was onions and potatoes, luxuries Shannon hadn't tasted in six months.

That night she lay half asleep, waiting for the sound of the flute. When it came she shivered and listened intently. Prettyface awakened, prowled the cabin briefly, and settled back into sleep once more. Finally Shannon slept, too.

The fourth day, Whip's gift was a pot of jam that was like tasting a sweet summer morning, holding it on her tongue, and licking it from her fingertips.

The sound of the flute came early that night, whistling up the stars, giving them to Shannon like another gift. Prettyface cocked his head and listened, but didn't bother to get up. The big mongrel no longer associated the sound of the flute with something unknown and, therefore, dangerous.

The fifth day, Shannon returned from hunting to find logs dragged up to the dwindling woodpile. The maul Silent John had used to split wood—and Shannon had broken—was repaired. The ax was sharpened. So was the crosscut saw.

Prettyface sniffed every object suspiciously, his ruff raised and his chest vibrating with a low growl. But nothing came forth to challenge him. Nor did he catch any sense of unease from his mistress.

The big dog's ruff settled. Slowly he was coming to accept Whip's scent as something normal.

That night Prettyface barely cocked his ears when the flute's husky cries wove through the twilight. Shannon paused in the act of draping clothes across the line to dry over the stove. She tilted her head back and closed her eyes, letting the beauty of the music caress her tired spirit.

On the sixth day that Shannon came back empty-handed from hunting, Whip's gift was freshly chopped wood of the exact length to burn in her stove. The wood was neatly piled by the cabin door, close at hand whenever she needed it.

While she looked at the wood, Whip's flute whispered to Shannon from the surrounding forest, a haunting three-note cry. When she turned, she saw nothing.

Nor did the flute sing again.

On the seventh day, a bouquet of wildflowers waited for her.

Shannon looked at the flowers and bit her lip against an unexpected desire to cry. Letting out a shaky breath, she searched the forest at the edge of the clearing, hungry to see more of Whip than a shadow slipping away at the edge of her vision. Sometime in the past six days, she had stopped worrying about Whip circling around behind her and catching her unawares. She no longer believed he would jump on her like an animal and rut on her whether she wanted it or not.

If that was what Whip wanted from Shannon, he could have taken her more easily than he had taken the grouse or the trout. She knew her vulnerability when she left the cabin as surely as he must have known it.

And the Culpeppers. She feared they knew it as well.

Shannon wondered if Whip, too, had come across the tracks of four saddle mules just two miles below the cabin. Seeing the tracks, Shannon had been relieved to know that Whip was just beyond reach in the forest somewhere, watching out for her.

Protecting her.

The thought made Shannon smile, though the smile quickly turned upside down. She knew Whip's protection wouldn't last very long. As soon as he realized that she wasn't his for the asking, he would ride on until he found a more willing woman.

But until then, Shannon welcomed the knowledge that she wasn't wholly alone.

Slowly Shannon bent down and picked up the flowers Whip had left for her. It was like holding a handful of butterflies. She looked at the glorious colors, brushed her lips against the smooth petals, and tried to remember when someone had given her anything that wasn't needed for sheer survival.

She couldn't think of one time. Even Cherokee's unexpected gift had been meant to further Shannon's survival, like a box of shotgun shells or a haunch of venison.

With a ragged sound, Shannon put her face into the soft, fragrant flowers and wept.

When she looked up, she saw Whip silhouetted against the burning blue of the sky. She blinked away tears, trying to see him better.

She saw only empty sky.

Whip walked down the far side of the rise to the place where his horse was tied. The sight of Shannon crying disturbed him in ways he couldn't name.

Why would she cry over a handful of flowers?

There was no answer.

Whip muttered a curse and swung into the saddle. Then he cursed again and shifted his weight in the stirrups. Seeing Shannon walk through the clearing to the cabin had drawn a pronounced response from his body. She had a way of moving that could set fire to stone, and Whip was a long way from stone.

He was both annoyed and amused by his own arousal. He hadn't been this hot and bothered over a woman since West Virginia, when Savannah Marie had set out to tease one of the Moran brothers into marrying her. Whip had known precisely what she was doing, but the scented sighs and rustling silk petticoats and peekaboo glimpses of her nipples still had made his body as hard as an ax handle.

But Shannon wasn't wearing silk petticoats, and her breasts were hidden unless the wind blew hard enough to press cloth against the surprisingly lush curves of her body. Whip hadn't gotten close enough to discover whether Shannon's breath was scented, but he had discovered the spearmint someone had planted by the creek, and he had seen her pick sprigs and take them to the cabin.

Whip wondered if Shannon would taste of cream and mint when he dipped his tongue into her.

Then he wondered again why she had cried over the flowers.

Maybe she's just lonely.

He considered that possibility as he began casting for sign on the trail that led away from Shannon's cabin to Holler Creek. He knew that widows were often lonely, especially if they had no children or nearby family or friends.

Hell, any woman would be lonely in those circumstances.

Of course, there's that old shaman in the cabin on the north fork of Avalanche Creek. Shannon visits him often enough. That's company, of a sort.

Whip had been surprised the first time he had tracked Shannon to the tiny, remote shack where the shaman lived. Then Whip had seen the old man's crooked stance and realized that Shannon was helping him out.

She must be used to taking care of old men. If gossip can be trusted, Silent John is no spring chicken.

Or was.

Is he dead like the Culpeppers think, or did he take a bead on the wrong man and find himself ambushed in turn and is lying low until the other man gives up?

The only answer Whip could think of was another question.

Maybe Silent John is like that half-breed shaman, bunged up and waiting to heal before he comes back. After all, he was seen riding out over Avalanche Creek Pass at the first thaw.

The thought made Whip's mouth thin. Much as he wanted the pleasure he would find within Shannon's body, he no more wanted to seduce a married woman than he did a virgin. It wasn't something a decent man did.

That was why Whip had spent much of the past week quartering the land and scrambling up the various forks of Avalanche Creek, looking for any sign that Silent John was working on his claims or had gone to ground to wait out an injury.

Whip had found nothing for his trouble but a

few ragged holes far up the mountainside, signs that someone had taken a pickax to hard rock and gone looking for gold. But there was nothing to tell Whip how long ago the holes had been worked. All he could be certain of was that the ashes of the various campfires he discovered hadn't been disturbed since the last rain, three days before.

Three days.

Three weeks.

Three years. No *way to tell.*

Hell, Caleb told me of coming across charcoal from fires built against cliffs high in these mountains. Nothing had changed since his daddy surveyed those same charcoal remains thirty years ago for the army.

And the fires had been built by Indians three hundred years ago, before they had stolen horses from the Spaniards and learned how to ride.

I don't have three hundred years to find Silent John.

Whip didn't know how much more time he would spend in the Rocky Mountains. Already he had stayed here longer than he had in any place since he had left West Virginia all those years ago, when he was man-sized and boy-stupid.

Part of what still held Whip in the Rockies was the presence of his brother Reno and his sister Willow, and friends like Caleb and Wolfe. But the land itself was also an extraordinary lure. The taste of the wind and the colors of the land were like nowhere else on earth. Something about the clusters of high, icy peaks and the long, green divides between the groups of mountains fascinated Whip.

Yet as much as he loved the landscape, he

didn't expect to settle down and live in the midst of the wild Rockies. Sooner or later wanderlust would reclaim his soul and he would go wherever the mood took him, searching the earth for something he was able to describe only as the sunrise he had never seen.

But until the yondering urge comes, there's nothing to keep me from enjoying the sunrise I have right here.

Accompanied only by his thoughts and a restless wind, Whip cast for sign in the long, raking light of late afternoon. He saw tracks of elk and deer and mountain lion. He heard the high, fluting cry of an eagle calling to its mate. But he neither heard men nor saw signs of anyone moving over the land.

There were no new mule tracks where Holler Creek's racing white water joined with Avalanche Creek's eastern fork. The tracks of four mules were still there, blurred somewhat by a light rain but unmistakable.

The Culpeppers had ridden to the fork in the trail that led to Shannon's cabin. Three of them had stayed there for a time, sitting on their mules and drinking while the fourth Culpepper scouted the east fork of Avalanche Creek.

Whip had been on the rise behind Shannon's cabin when he saw Darcy sneaking through the woods. Whip had pulled his carbine out of the saddle scabbard, sighted, and sent rock splinters peppering over Darcy's chest. Darcy had run back to his mule and set off at a hard pace.

Whip had backtracked him to where the others sat their mules and awaited their brother's return. The Culpeppers didn't hang around for whoever had taken a shot at Darcy. They threw two empty whiskey bottles onto the rocks and put spurs to their racing mules.

When Whip got there, all that was left were telltale tracks and shards of glass glittering in the sun.

Days ago, Whip thought, looking around the valley where the two creeks joined. *The Culpeppers haven't been back since.*

But they'll get around to it, soon as they work up the nerve.

For a long time Whip sat on his horse, thinking about the Culpeppers and Silent John and the frightened girl with a walk like honey. Nothing Whip had found as he searched the Avalanche Creek watershed made him believe that Silent John was still alive, much less working any of his claims.

I suppose he could be out man-hunting on the other side of the Great Divide.

The thought made Whip frown.

But if I had to lay money on it, I'd say Silent John was dead. No man as canny as he's supposed to be would leave Shannon alone for six weeks when coyotes like the Culpeppers are sniffing around.

But if Silent John were dead, Shannon was left to fend for herself without a husband's help. She was a young girl in a woman-hungry land, a silky lamb among snarling coyotes. No matter how big and savage Prettyface was, no matter how careful Shannon was, sooner or later the Culpeppers would catch her off guard.

Sooner, probably.

Whip didn't like to think about what would happen when the Culpeppers got their hands on Shannon.

Silent John or no Silent John, it's time for me to close in on my beautiful, almost-tamed mustang.

5

The next day Shannon awoke not to the sound of Whip's flute calling up the sun, but to the rhythmic sounds of a man splitting wood.

It was a sound she hadn't heard for years.

Instantly Shannon looked toward Prettyface. The dog was lying with his head on his massive paws and his ears cocked in the direction of the noise. He was growling slightly, but with no real menace.

Shannon left the bed in a rush and ran to one of the cabin's two windows. Neither window had glass. Instead, they were covered with shutters that were solid but for a gun slit plugged by a rag. Despite the plug, cold air came through the slit in a ceaseless, invisible flow.

Removing the rag, Shannon eased the shutters apart just a bit and peeked out.

Whip was standing just fifteen feet away. Despite the cold, sleet-streaked dawn, he had taken off his thick jacket. The red of his wool shirt burned like wildfire in the gray light and heat lifted from his big body in tongues of mist.

Legs braced slightly apart, sleet lashing across his body, Whip lifted the heavy maul and brought it swiftly down on a round of fir. The wood split cleanly into half circles. He bent, set one of the halves on end, and brought the maul down again, splitting the wood once more.

The grace and power of Whip's movements sent an odd, glittering sensation from Shannon's breastbone to her thighs. For a long time she stood motionless, watching the measured, masculine dance of maul and wood, strength and balance.

Finally a stray piece of sleet stung Shannon's nose, breaking her trance. Shivering, stiff from not moving, she stepped back and eased the shutter closed, sealing out the icy dawn.

But there was no way Shannon could seal out the memory of Whip's male beauty, the elegance and easy power of his body, and the heat rising like smoke from him as he warmed to the work.

Feeling almost light-headed, Shannon went about her morning tasks. Because she wouldn't have to spend hours gathering downed wood in the forest to replace whatever she burned, she decided to make a hot of breakfast.

Humming softly, not realizing that she was singing one of the tunes Whip played on his haunting flute, Shannon raked the coals in the wood stove to new life. She added wood and dipped up a bucket of steaming hot spring water, smiling in anticipation of breakfast.

One of Whip's gifts to Shannon had been coffee beans. It had been two years since she had ground beans and made coffee, but she hadn't forgotten how.

It wasn't long before the smell of biscuits, bacon, coffee and a wood fire filled the cabin. When the coffee had brewed, Shannon carefully poured some from the battered kettle into an equally battered tin mug. Then she let herself out of the cabin and walked toward the man whose presence no longer alarmed her.

When Whip bent down to stand another log on end, he saw Shannon standing quietly a few feet from him. Sleet was tangled in her shiny chestnut hair. In her hands was a steaming cup of coffee.

She was holding the cup out to him.

Whip took it, careful not to touch Shannon as he did, even though he was wearing leather work gloves. He didn't want to do anything to spook his shy mustang.

Not now.

Not when she was so close to eating from his hand.

"Thank you," Whip said, his voice deep.

Shannon's breath caught.

"You're welcome, Whip."

Her voice was as sweet and husky as Whip had remembered. Smoke and honey combined. Hearing his name on her lips was like being licked by a tender flame.

And looking at Shannon was like breathing pure fire.

Her eyes were sapphire gems gleaming in the midst of the colorless dawn. Her silky chestnut hair had refused to be completely confined by braids. Soft tendrils escaped to brush against her cheeks and curl against her vulnerable neck.

When the breath Shannon exhaled touched Whip in a silver rush, he breathed in deeply, hungry to touch her in even so small a way.

A color that had nothing to do with the cold dawn appeared on Shannon's cheeks. Belatedly Whip realized he was staring at her. He lifted the tin cup to his mouth, silently cursing himself for acting like a boy who had never seen a pretty girl before.

"Careful!" Shannon said quickly, reaching out to prevent Whip from lifting the cup any farther.

Whip froze, but not because of the warning. Shannon's fingers had slipped from his glove to rest on bare skin just above his wrist. Her fingers were warm, amazingly delicate, and smelled of spearmint. Her breath was the same.

The realization that Shannon had eaten mint so that she would smell sweet to him made Whip want to pull her into his arms and show her just how much he liked the taste of spearmint.

But he didn't do it. He had come too far to lose his sweet, silky mustang by startling her into flight.

"The coffee is devilish hot," Shannon explained.

Whip smiled, revealing teeth as clean and white as her own.

"It's best that way," he said slowly. "Hot. Steaming hot. And sweet."

Shannon's smile was a little shaky, but then, so was her heartbeat. Whip radiated heat like a big stove, only nicer, because she didn't have to worry about burning herself.

"I'm sorry," Shannon said. "I didn't think to put sugar in your coffee."

"No need. I like it black."

"But you just said it was best when it was steaming hot and sweet."

"Did I?"

Shannon nodded.

Whip smiled slightly. "I must have been thinking of something else."

He took a sip from the battered metal cup, closed his eyes, and savored the heat and taste of the fragrant brew.

"Now that's fine. Really fine," Whip said. "And no sugar on earth could be sweeter than having you bring me coffee."

Color burned on Shannon's cheeks, but she almost smiled before she looked shyly away.

"Breakfast will be ready soon," she said, turning back toward the cabin. "I'll leave warm water by the door so you can wash up."

"I'll eat out here."

Shannon turned around, surprise clear in her extraordinary eyes. She pushed a flyaway strand of hair behind her ear and frowned at Whip.

"There's no need to eat in the cold," she said. "I may be poor as a church mouse, but I have two chairs for the table."

"It's not that. I just don't want to make you nervous by coming inside."

Shannon's glance went to the bullwhip that lay neatly coiled on a log, easily within reach of Whip's long arm.

"My cabin isn't as big as Murphy's mercantile. Once you're inside, that bullwhip of yours won't be much use," she said dryly. "Prettyface is quicker, anyway."

Whip looked back down at his coffee, not wanting Shannon to see the light of amusement in his eyes. There were more ways to fight than with a bullwhip, as his travels in the Far East had taught him. As for Prettyface, the dog was quick enough—and big enough—to kill a careless man.

Whip wasn't a careless man.

But it would be stupid to point that out to Shannon. Whip didn't want to disturb her peace of mind. It was pure pleasure to see a smile on her mouth rather than the grim lines of a girl trying to do work that would have taxed many a man.

"Then I'll be honored to share breakfast with you," Whip said. "Call me when you're ready."

He took another deep drink of coffee, set the tin cup aside, and picked up the maul once more.

"I'll do that," Shannon said.

She lingered for a moment longer, hoping to catch another glimpse of Whip's unusual, quicksilver eyes, but he didn't look in her direction again. He simply braced his legs slightly apart, lifted the heavy maul, and brought it down with an easy motion.

The fir split cleanly, but Shannon hardly noticed. She had eyes only for the casual, purely male grace of the man called Whip. She wondered what it would be like to be that skilled, that sure, to feel power flowing through her with every motion of her body.

Then Shannon realized she was staring at Whip as though she had never seen a man before. Cheeks bright, she turned and hurried back into the cabin as though pursued.

Whip split four more round logs into eighths before he trusted himself to look over his shoulder.

Shannon was gone.

He let out a long, whistling breath. He was aching from his forehead to his heels, and the knowledge that she liked watching him move hadn't helped to cool him off one bit.

But he had to cool off.

The closer Whip got to Shannon, the more he realized that she wasn't like the widows he had met from time to time and shared a few days or weeks with. She blushed when she looked at him.

She glanced away an instant after she met his eyes. Yet it wasn't flirting. She no more knew how to flirt than she knew how to stalk deer.

Silent John mustn't have been any great shakes when it came to making a girl feel like a woman, Whip thought as he slammed the maul into a big log. *Shannon acts more like a nervous bride fresh from the church than a widow who's done it all a thousand times before.*

Damnation. I wonder just how green she is when it comes to being a woman with her man?

The thought was unnerving.

Whip shifted his grip and brought the maul down so hard it whistled through the air. The wood broke apart violently and leaped beyond his reach.

With a muttered curse at his own clumsiness, Whip grabbed one of the chunks and set it on the chopping block once more.

"It's hot and waiting for you," Shannon called from the window.

The maul missed its target completely.

"Well, son of a bitch," Whip muttered softly. "Looks like I'm no more use than a broken handle."

He lifted the maul over his head again and swung down, using less force. The log obediently fell into two pieces and lay within easy reach.

Let that be a lesson, Whip told himself sardonically. *Whether it's logs or women, finesse beats raw strength any day of the week.*

Whip split the log again for good measure before he set aside the maul, removed his leather work gloves, and stuffed the gloves into the back pocket of his pants. From long habit he picked up and settled the bullwhip on his shoulder.

As he went to the cabin, sleet fell against his face and lodged in his clothes. When he removed his hat to wash up, sleet mixed into his hair. He bent down over the washbasin, then stopped, sniffing the steam that rose from the water. Though it was mint rather than Willow's favorite lavender scent rising from the basin, the smell of the water kindled a memory in him.

Willow's bathhouse. All full of warmth from the hot spring water Wolfe and Reno piped in for them. No real sulfur to it, just a richness of minerals.

Whip scooped up steaming water and lowered his face into his palms. He made a sound of pleasure as the water spilled over him, washing away sweat and sleet alike.

Wish I'd had this when I shaved this morning. Cold water is pure hell, no matter how sharp the razor is.

Whip paused as a thought struck him. He looked at the surrounding forest and the clearing itself. No telltale plumes of white rose into the cold, clear air.

I haven't seen sign of a hot spring around here for miles in any direction, either. It must be in a cave somewhere.

"Come and get it before I feed it to Prettyface," Shannon said from the window.

"Don't you dare, woman!"

Quickly Whip splashed hot water over his face and hands. He followed it up with the morsel of soap that was balanced on the basin's wide rim. Then he rinsed again, making certain he was clean. When he lifted his head, dripping, the cabin door was closed and Shannon was standing very close.

"Here," she said softly.

Whip looked at the piece of cloth Shannon was holding out to him. It was faded and threadbare, but enough remained for him to see that the fabric once had held a vivid pattern of flowers and birds. It was a very feminine design, as clean and graceful as the hand that held it.

Looking at the rag, Whip guessed that it was the remainder of a favorite dress. Or perhaps Shannon's *only* dress. Certainly he had seen her in nothing but secondhand men's clothing that had been cut down to fit her slender frame.

"Thank you," he said huskily.

When Whip took the towel, he thought he felt the silky brush of Shannon's fingers against his own, but he couldn't be certain.

Yet Shannon was certain she had touched him. Whip could see it in the sudden expansion of her pupils, the rush of color to her cheeks, the breath that hesitated and then came out in a ragged sigh.

"I'll—I'll wait by the door," she said breathlessly.

"You don't have to," Whip said. He lowered his face into the fabric Shannon had once worn against her skin. "I won't bite."

"Prettyface might. That's why I'm keeping him inside for now. He's not used to being around men."

"How old is he?"

The question was muffled, but Shannon understood.

"Oh, a little more than two years, I guess," she said.

Whip's head came up quickly.

"What about Silent John?" Whip asked. "He's a man, isn't he?"

Shannon blinked, bit her lip, and flushed.

"Silent John is the exception, of course," she said, looking at her hands.

Whip had a strong suspicion that Shannon was lying. He just didn't know why.

Maybe she doesn't want anyone to know how often Silent John is gone. And for how long.

Then Whip understood more than he wanted to: Shannon's husband had been absent so much that her dog never had a chance to get used to men.

Judas Priest!

Shannon has had God's own luck keeping out of reach of gold miners and renegades. But she can't count on luck to keep the Culpeppers at bay forever.

Before I go yondering, I'll have to have another talk with those boys. Make them understand all the way to their black souls just how lacking in Christian charity their manners have been.

Absently Whip wiped off his hands and started toward the cabin door.

"Wait," Shannon said, stepping closer.

Whip looked down at her through half-lowered lids.

"Change your mind?" he asked.

"About what?"

As Shannon spoke, she took the damp rag from Whip's hands and blotted his mustache right above the peak of his lip.

"There," she said, examining the cleanly drawn curves of Whip's mouth. "Now the biscuits won't taste like soap to you."

Then Shannon looked up into Whip's eyes and forgot to breathe. Close up, his eyes were a clear, luminous gray surrounded by a glittering circle of black. Intriguing splinters of blue and green radiated from the pupils, which were expanding as she watched them. Soon there was only a smoky crystal band of color left in his eyes.

Whip was looking at Shannon's mouth with a smoldering intensity that made her feel weak.

"You missed a bit of lather," she explained, her voice shaky.

"Just one?"

She nodded.

"Sure there aren't any more?" he coaxed.

His dark, husky voice made shimmering sensations chase down from Shannon's breastbone to her thighs, as though she were watching him in secret from the cabin window again.

"More?" she whispered.

"Bits of lather. To wipe off."

With shuttered eagerness, Shannon's glance went over the pronounced planes and masculine angles of Whip's face.

"No," she said, unable to conceal her disappointment. "Not a speck."

"Maybe next time."

The smile Whip gave Shannon was like his voice, dark and very male. It sent another odd cascade of sensation through her, making her breath break.

"I'd better go inside first," Shannon said. "Prettyface might get the wrong idea otherwise."

Her voice was faintly husky, reflecting the quickening of her pulse.

Well, Whip thought in relief, *whatever Silent John did to Shannon as a husband, he didn't ruin her. There's real passion in that sweet body.*

And real hunger.

Whip watched with a barely veiled hunger of his own while Shannon opened the cabin door.

Instantly, gleaming fangs appeared in the

narrow opening. Shannon stepped between the dog's muzzle and Whip. Snarling, growling, the big hound stood squarely in the opening.

"No," Shannon said firmly. "Prettyface, stop that! Whip is a friend. Friend, Prettyface. *Friend.*"

Slowly the dog's lips came down over his fangs, but the rumbling sounds of menace didn't stop.

"It's all right, Prettyface," Shannon said. *"Friend."*

Whip looked into the dog's feral eyes, saw the wolf blood staring back at him, and knew that Prettyface wasn't convinced he was any man's friend.

"No wonder you didn't bring Prettyface into town," Whip said. "That's one hardheaded son of a bitch. What is he?"

"Mastiff, mostly. And some wolf, I think. I'm sorry he's so edgy."

"Don't apologize. I know the hardheaded breed well," Whip said dryly. "Got a brother just like him. And a brother-in-law."

Shannon looked at Whip, startled.

"Come to think of it," he added with a slight smile, "I've been accused of being too slow to back down, myself."

Shannon tried to look as though the thought of Whip's being hardheaded had never occurred to her. The effort dissolved into something that sounded suspiciously like a giggle.

Prettyface looked at his mistress as though she had lost her mind.

Whip smiled. He was discovering what a keen pleasure it was to bring the light of laughter to Shannon's beautiful eyes.

"Go lie down, Prettyface," Shannon said, pointing toward the dog's favorite corner. *"Go."*

Prettyface went. Slowly. With every step he looked over his shoulder at Whip. A low, almost inaudible growl seethed inside the dog's big body.

Despite Whip's easy smile, he never looked away from the beast who combined the savage traits of mastiff and wolf alike. Prettyface was both powerful and fierce.

Whip would have called the dog vicious, but in the past week he had seen Prettyface lying tamely on his side while Shannon pulled burrs from between the dog's tender pads and from inside his big, sensitive ears.

The dog was possessive, not vicious.

"Does Prettyface act this way when you're around the shaman?" Whip asked.

"Cherokee?"

"Yeah."

"Of course not," Shannon said absently as she lifted biscuits from the pan onto a platter. "He only hates men."

"What does that make the shaman—a eunuch?"

Shannon realized her mistake and mumbled, "Guess Cherokee must smell different, being so old and all. Whatever, *he* doesn't set off Prettyface."

"Maybe I should borrow some of his herbs and change my smell."

"His herbs?"

"Cherokee's."

"Oh, of course. Cherokee's. *His*. Well, it's a thought."

Quickly Shannon turned back to the stove, hiding her amusement at the idea that a handful of herbs would diminish Whip's manhood enough to put Prettyface at ease.

She set the platter of biscuits and bacon on the scarred, handmade table and pointed to a chair.

"Have a seat," Shannon said.

Instead of sitting, Whip pulled out Shannon's chair and waited to seat her. She looked at him, confused. Then she remembered courtesies from a time so long ago she sometimes thought it must have been a dream.

"Why, thank you," Shannon murmured.

But as she sat in the chair that Whip held out for her, Prettyface came to his feet in snarling rage.

"No!" Shannon said sharply. "Lie down!"

Prettyface started forward with menace in every gliding stride.

Whip reached for the bullwhip's coils.

"Step away from my chair," Shannon said urgently. "Quickly! Prettyface doesn't like it when you get between him and me."

For a moment Whip considered having it out with the dog then and there, but decided against it. Maybe if Prettyface had a little time, he would settle down. That way Whip wouldn't be forced to frighten Shannon by jerking the dog off his big feet and teaching him who gave orders and who obeyed.

Maybe it will work out peacefully, Whip thought. *Sure as hell hope so. I'd have to take a lot of chewing to put that dog in his place without killing him.*

But Whip wouldn't have bet a Confederate dollar that Prettyface would accept Whip as his superior without a fight. The wolf in him would demand it.

Calmly, without any hurry at all, Whip moved away from Shannon's chair. He held Prettyface's eyes every inch of the way.

"Now lie down!" Shannon said sharply.

"Me or the dog?"

Shannon winced at the tone of Whip's voice and remembered what he had said a moment earlier.

I've been accused of being too slow to back down, myself.

Yet Whip had meekly given way to the dog when she had ordered him to do so.

"I'm sorry," Shannon said unhappily. "Prettyface is just . . ."

"Jealous?"

"Protective."

"I don't think so."

Whip held Shannon's eyes with the same unflinching stare he had used on the snarling dog.

"A protective dog takes his cue from his master," Whip said. "A jealous dog acts like Prettyface, purely pissed off when anyone gets close to you, no matter how you might feel about it."

"He hasn't had much time to get used to strangers."

"You might think on ways to get Prettyface to accept your friends," Whip said mildly. "Or else your friends will have to do it for you. May I pour you some coffee?"

The change of subject distracted Shannon. By the time she realized what had happened, it was too late. Whip was pouring her coffee and holding out the platter of biscuits and bacon to her.

Prettyface snarled when Shannon's hand touched the platter. She turned and gave the dog a level stare.

"No, Prettyface," Shannon said, her voice firm. "Nothing is wrong. Now behave yourself!"

The dog whined uneasily and settled back to watch the stranger in his cabin with the unblinking, feral eyes of a wolf.

At first Shannon and Whip ate without talking. It wasn't an uncomfortable silence, for they were hungry. When Shannon had eaten her fill, she poured another cup of coffee for Whip and herself and settled back in her chair to savor the unexpected luxury of the coffee.

Whip reached for another round of bacon and biscuits. As he did, he found himself wondering how chickens would survive in Echo Basin. A few eggs would have gone very well with the meal.

You're dreaming, Whip told himself sardonically. *Eggs are for people who are settled enough to raise chickens, like Willow, or those folks who are rich enough to buy eggs that are damn near worth their weight in gold.*

Whip bit into a tender biscuit and sighed with pleasure. The biscuit was steamy, fragrant, and light as smoke.

"I always thought no one could match my sister Willow's biscuits," Whip said, reaching for more. "Looks like I was wrong. These biscuits are pure heaven."

Shannon watched Whip's big hands move from biscuit to bacon and back again. He handled the food deftly, which didn't surprise her. He was a man of rare coordination. What did surprise her was the care he took with the food itself. His manners told her more than words just how much Whip appreciated the meal.

Seeing Whip enjoy the food she had prepared was an unexpected pleasure. It was as though a little bit of her was in each bite . . . part of her becoming part of him. Quietly Shannon watched

Whip eat, her mouth slightly curved, her eyes gentle, liking the thought of it.

"You keep looking at me like that," Whip said finally, "and I'm going to do something that will put Prettyface on the warpath."

Belatedly, Shannon realized she was watching Whip far too warmly.

"I'm sorry," she muttered. "I'm not used to company."

Whip's smile was as gentle as his eyes.

"Honey girl, I'm just teasing you. You can look at me all you like. My head might get too big for my hat, but I'll just go without one. It would be worth it to see your beautiful eyes watching me and liking what they see."

Shannon's color heightened, but she didn't look away for more than an instant before her glance was drawn back to Whip. His sun-colored hair caught light with each motion he made. Thick, fair, shiny, his hair made Shannon itch to sink her fingers into it. Only then would she find out if it felt as warm and silky as it looked.

Whip glanced up, wondering what had caught Shannon's attention so much that she sat without moving. When he realized that he was the source of her fascination, his eyes narrowed and his pulse kicked hard. There was approval in Shannon's eyes, and a sensual curiosity that aroused Whip as much as a hungry kiss would have.

Damnation. Maybe I shouldn't have told her she could look at me all she likes.

Something is growing fast, and it's not my hat size.

With an effort Whip forced himself to look anywhere but at the sapphire eyes that were watching him with luminous pleasure.

"How did you come to Echo Basin?" Whip asked.

For a moment the question didn't register on Shannon. Then she blinked and looked down at her coffee cup.

"Silent John brought me here seven years ago."

"You must have been a child."

"I was husband-high and had no relatives who wanted me. Even before the war . . ." Shannon shrugged. "A lot of children were orphaned."

"Eve, my brother's wife, was like that. She came west on an orphan train and was bought by two old gamblers to make their lives easier." Whip looked at Shannon. "Echo Basin must have been a harsh place for you."

Surprise showed on Shannon's face. She shook her head, making the mahogany lights in her hair gleam.

"It's better than where I came from," she said. "Here I'm beholden to no one for my bread and salt."

Whip waited, but Shannon said nothing more on the subject of her past or Echo Basin.

"What about you, Whip? How did you end up here?"

He smiled slightly. That was a question few westerners dared to ask a man.

On the other hand, he had just asked her precisely that question.

"Turnabout is fair play, is that it?" Whip asked.

"Unless you mind?"

"Not as long as you're the one doing the asking. I came to Echo Basin because I'd never been here before."

Shannon frowned slightly. "You sound like there aren't many places you haven't been."

"There aren't. I'm a yondering man. I've been all over the world."

"Truly?"

Whip smiled. "Truly."

"Have you seen the pyramids of Egypt?"

"I saw them," Whip said.

"What are they like?"

"Big. They rise out of the desert all pitted and racked by time. There's a city nearby, a place where women go veiled from head to heels so that only their eyes show."

Shannon made a surprised sound. "Just their eyes?"

Whip nodded. "You would be a sultan's prize, honey girl. Eyes as blue as heaven itself."

And a walk that's hotter than hell, he added to himself.

But Whip wasn't about to say it aloud. If Shannon knew just how much he wanted her, Whip doubted that she would be sitting so at ease across the small table from him.

"Paris," Shannon said. "Have you seen it?"

"Paris, London, Madrid, Rome, Shanghai . . . I've seen them, and more besides. Do you like cities?"

"I don't know. I haven't been in one for years and years."

Shannon looked past Whip to the strips of light coming between the ill-fitting shutters.

"But I think," she said slowly, "having that many people pressing close would wear on me."

"Are you eager to find out?"

"No. I only asked about cities because the history books are always going on about Paris and London and Rome. They're the only places I could think of. And China, of course."

Whip's eyes took on a faraway look.

"China is a special place," he said quietly. "It had empires and art and philosophy long before Christ was born. The Chinese have a real different way of looking at life, from music to food to fighting."

"Did you like it?"

"Like, love, hate . . ." He shrugged. "Those words have no real meaning when it comes to China."

"I don't understand."

Whip lifted his cup of coffee, sipped, and tried to find words to explain to Shannon what he had never explained to himself.

"Once," he said slowly, "I stood on the banks of a river at midnight and watched men fish with lanterns and black birds instead of hooks and nets."

Shannon made a startled sound.

"Did it work?" she asked.

"Oh, yes. It had been working like that for thousands of years, golden lantern light swirling with each dive the birds made, the fluting whistles of the fishermen as they called to their birds, midnight and the ebony river flowing by. . . . It was like breathing time itself to be there. China is old, older than I had ever imagined anything could be."

A shiver coursed through Shannon as she watched Whip's eyes. They were hazed with memory and distance and a black river flowing.

It was like breathing time itself.

"Are there other places like this?" Shannon asked when she no longer could bear Whip's silence and distance.

"Echo Basin?" he asked.

"The Colorado Territory."

Frowning, Whip ran his hand through his hair.

"I haven't seen one to beat it," he admitted finally.

"In all the world?"

"Oh, Ireland is green enough, but it lacks towering mountains like these. Burma and Switzerland have huge mountain ranges, but they're stone and ice with little place in them for man."

Shannon leaned forward, her eyes brilliant, fascinated.

"South America has a long, muscular chain of mountains with green lands in between clusters of high peaks," Whip said, "but the high plains are so high that it makes a man weary just to walk a mile. Australia has green mountains with some snowy peaks. They're pretty enough, but they aren't real high. And the smell of the gum forest never appealed to me as much as the evergreen scent of the Rockies does."

"Then it sounds like the best place on earth for you is right here," Shannon said.

Whip laughed and shook his head, but when he looked at Shannon, his expression became very serious. He sensed the question buried within her words: *Are you going to stay in the mountains that are like nowhere else on earth*?

"The Rockies have held me longer than any other place," Whip said softly, "but someday a distant sunrise will call to me, promising me everything I've ever wanted and have never been able to name. Then I'll set out again, because there's nothing as grand as the sunrise I haven't seen. Nothing."

Shannon fought against a sorrow so sharp it

made her breath break. There was no reason for her to feel such grief. Whip was barely more than a stranger to her. She shouldn't care if he stayed forever or left in the next hour.

But she cared so much it was a knife turning deep inside her. She closed her eyes and fought the unexpected pain.

"Like I said, honey girl," Whip said gently, "I'm a yondering man."

Shannon's eyes opened. She looked at the man she knew only as Whip. Then she looked at his savagely clear eyes, eyes that had seen so much and yet moved on to another view, a different place, one more distant sunrise, for there was always more to see.

Always.

I hear your warning, yondering man. Don't try to hold you. Don't dream on you.

Don't love you.

Yet Shannon had the uneasy feeling Whip's warning had come too late. Somewhere deep inside her, something she had never felt before had awakened.

She prayed that it was only desire.

6

A week later Shannon awoke just after dawn to the sound of an ax taking big bites from a tree. Relief washed through her.

Nothing changed while I slept. He's still here.

If the Culpeppers came skulking around, they would find Shannon with a shotgun in her hands, a snarling dog at her heels . . . and a man called Whip by her side.

"See?" Shannon whispered to herself. "I told you he would still be here in the morning."

This time.

When Shannon hadn't heard Whip's panpipes last night, she wondered if he had saddled up and left Echo Basin, never to return again. But he hadn't. He was still here, still doing all the chores that had been difficult for Shannon to do alone.

Whip had repaired the lean-to where the old mule spent the worst of the winter, then he had trimmed and shod the beast's hooves with horseshoes Silent John never had gotten around to using. Whip had rehung the cabin door so that it closed evenly without being shoved or leaned on or kicked. Then Whip had rammed caulking so tightly between the cabin's logs that the wind couldn't get past to steal the fire's warmth. He had chopped down eight trees and was working on a ninth.

Not only would Shannon have firewood curing for winter, with those trees gone there would be enough sun on the south side of the cabin for her to have a small kitchen garden. It was something she had always wanted, but she had given up on the idea four years ago. It had taken six days for her to gnaw through a tree with an ax, and then the tree had knocked her silly by falling the wrong way.

Silent John had laughed when she told him the story about the tree falling on her. But when she told Whip about it a few days ago, he hadn't laughed at all. He had said something under his breath and then told her in very plain English that if he ever caught her trying to chop down a tree, they would both regret it—but she would regret it more.

Then, yesterday morning, the trees on the south side of the cabin had started to come down one by one, felled by a man who attacked each tree as though it was an enemy.

Humming quietly to herself, Shannon got out of bed and started the breakfast fire. As she worked, anticipation swirled through her like heat through flame. Soon Whip would call out and she would bring a pan of warm water to the bench at the side of the cabin. Then she would watch while he washed and shaved.

If she was lucky, he would overlook a bit of lather on his mustache or in the dimple on his chin. She would stand close to dab at the soap . . . and then she would look up and see the quicksilver of his eyes burning down at her, and the flare of his nostrils as he caught the scent of spearmint on her hands and breath.

"You're a fool, Shannon Conner Smith," she told herself firmly. "You're letting that yondering man get too close."

Yet all Shannon truly cared about was getting Whip closer still. She hungered for him in ways that were as old as desire and as new as sunrise.

She struck a match and bent over the open door of the wood stove. The flames caught and entwined with an ease that reminded her of Whip's masculine grace. Heat filled the stove and radiated out into the room as wood and fire consumed one another.

Is that what it would be like with Whip? Would we feed one another until everything was gone but the memory of heat?

A shiver coursed through Shannon, touching her secret flesh like a match touched tinder; and like tinder, she burned.

Is this what the wood feels like? Does it ache and tremble and cry to be burned to an ash so fine it can fly right up to the sun?

"Lust, that's all," Shannon said beneath her breath. "Pure lust."

Prettyface scratched at the cabin door, distracting Shannon from her study of the fire.

"Oh, all right. But if you snap and snarl at Whip when he comes up to wash, I swear I'm going to get a stick and beat you."

The dog grinned and waved its long brindle tail. Rows of white, sharp teeth gleamed at her.

"Yeah, I don't believe me either," she admitted. "But I have to do something, Prettyface. You watch Whip like you can't wait for an excuse to jump him. He'll go soon enough. Much too soon. You don't have to drive him away."

Shannon opened the cabin door. Prettyface bounded out and began casting around for scent. Though Whip had shot more deer, the dog still hunted for himself. Whatever venison wasn't eaten fresh was cured into jerky. It was the same for the trout. Whip was determined that Shannon have plenty of food for the coming winter.

As Shannon shut the door and headed for the dry goods cupboard, she noticed the fresh bouquet of wildflowers set on the small, scarred table. Very gently she ran her fingertips over the tender, scented petals. She was smiling when she reached into the cupboard and began to measure out flour into a battered tin bowl.

Whip was always bringing something to her,

little things to brighten up the cabin's dark interior. Usually it was flowers. Sometimes it was a pebble that was all smooth and rounded from the creek. Once it was a butterfly freshly come from its cocoon. Watching the wings slowly unfurl and become rich with color had been like having a rainbow gather and dance softly in the palm of her hand.

Shannon would never forget the look on Whip's face as he watched the butterfly lift from her palm and spiral upward into the aching blue of the sky—pleasure, envy, understanding, satisfaction, yearning, all had been part of Whip's smile.

I know he's going to leave someday. But please, God, not today.

Not today.

Shannon's hands jerked. Flour spilled. Carefully she gathered it with the edge of her hand and coaxed the white powder back into the cup.

Don't think about Whip leaving, she told herself firmly. *He will leave today or he won't, and all I can do is watch him eat and blot lather from his chin and feel his smile like sunlight on my soul.*

Instead of worrying about tomorrow, I should thank God for sending me a gentle, generous, decent man to help me. There's fresh meat in the larder and jerky curing and fish being smoked outside and firewood piled high along the east side of the cabin.

Those are blessings enough for anyone, and a lot more than I had when I sold Mama's wedding ring to keep from starving while I got better at stalking deer.

Bending down, Shannon felt the air inside the oven. It wasn't hot enough to make the skin around her nails draw up. She added more wood to the fire, cut several slabs of meat from the ham that hung in the corner, and put the meat in a pan to fry while the biscuits were cooking.

The next time she tested the oven, it was ready. She went to the window and opened the shutters wide. Sunlight spilled in, bringing with it the scent and excitement of an untouched day.

"Biscuits are going in," Shannon called to Whip. "I'll bring the water out in a moment."

The rhythmic chopping sounds ended. Whip stepped back from the tree. A single look told him that it would take him longer to fell the tree than it would take Shannon to cook the biscuits. With an easy, one-handed stroke, he sank the blade of the ax deeply into wood. There the cutting edge would stay safe and dry until he needed it again.

Whip looked over his shoulder and saw Shannon hanging partway out the window, a smile on her face and a comb in her hand. She drew the comb through her hair with swift strokes, as though impatient to be through with the small chore.

Sunlight made her hair an autumn glory, like dark fire shot through with streaks of gold and red.

Someday soon you're going to let me comb all that beautiful hair for you, Whip promised silently. *Soon. Real soon.*

Your hair will be as soft and hot as fire running through my fingers, but nothing will be as soft or as hot as the dark woman-flower concealed between your thighs.

You'll bloom for me, honey girl. I'm as sure of it as I've ever been of anything.

But first I've got to get past that hellhound of yours without scaring you to death.

"I'm on my way," Whip called.

His voice was curt. Prettyface was a whole row of thorns in Whip's side. Though only partly wolf in his body, the dog was mostly wolf in his temperament. Despite Whip's best efforts, the animal refused to treat Whip as anything but a dangerous intruder. Several times Whip had found himself on the edge of reaching for the snarling dog to teach it the only kind of lesson it seemed capable of learning from a man.

Fear, pure and simple.

Whip knew it was the wolf's nature to give way only to superior strength. After Whip's strength was established, respect would come, and then, finally, he could begin teaching Prettyface that not all men took pleasure in abusing a mongrel with the eyes of a wild wolf.

Given time, Prettyface would not only accept Whip, the dog would give Whip the same trust and loyalty he gave to the girl who had found him beaten nearly to death on the trail from Holler Creek.

All Whip needed was time.

How much time do I have before that sunrise calls my name?

There was no answer to Whip's silent question. There never had been. When the wanderlust took him, he packed up and left. Nor did he ever come back to the same place again.

Sunrise called to him only once from each new land.

Before he left Echo Basin, Whip planned to see that Shannon's cabin was in good repair, the larder was overflowing, and the firewood was stacked to the eaves on three sides of the cabin. It was what he had always done for the openhearted widows whose paths he crossed, even if the women did no more than cook his meals and mend his shirts and share the warmth of their kitchens with a yondering man.

The world was a difficult place for a woman alone, a fact that Whip understood better than most men. That was why he was haunted by the vision of Shannon lying beneath a fallen tree . . . Shannon injured and alone, no one to help her, no one even to know that she needed help.

She's a widow whether she admits it or not. She's got to be. Hell, she doesn't even act married. She keeps watching me like she's never seen a man before.

And I watch her like she's the first woman I've ever seen.

Frowning, Whip pulled off his leather work gloves, stuffed them into his back pocket, and picked up the bullwhip that always lay within easy reach. As he walked toward the house, Prettyface appeared from the surrounding forest and snarled viciously at him.

"Good morning to you, too, you evil-tempered son of a bitch," Whip said pleasantly.

"Prettyface, stop that!" Shannon called from inside.

The dog's snarling increased.

Shannon rushed to the cabin door. Half-braided hair spilled out of her hands and fanned over the faded blue flannel of her shirt. The contrast between the worn fabric and the lustrous silk of her hair tempted Whip almost beyond endurance.

"Stop that!" Shannon commanded, staring right at the dog's yellow eyes.

Prettyface gave Whip a predatory look. Then, reluctantly, the dog obeyed his mistress.

Whip gave the look back with interest before he turned to the basin of steaming water Shannon had put out for him. His folding razor lay by the basin, along with soap and the faded, flower-printed rag. As he bent over the water, the familiar scent of mint floated up to him.

Without warning, desire raked Whip, tightening every muscle in his body. He drew a deep, careful breath, then another, until his body slowly began to relax. The ease and intensity of his arousal around Shannon was a warning to him.

And an incredible lure. Whip had never wanted a woman the way he wanted Shannon Conner Smith.

The sensible part of Whip's mind told him that his growing obsession with Shannon was the best reason in the world for him to pack up and ride on. Only heartbreak could come of an affair between a yondering man and a young widow who watched him with dreams in her eyes.

But Whip wasn't listening to caution or conscience anymore. He sensed too clearly the unspeakable ecstasy that awaited him within Shannon's body. Until he drank the dark wine of her sensuality to the last, lush drop, he wouldn't leave.

He couldn't.

I need her.

Come heaven, come hell, I have to have her.

The intensity of his own thoughts shocked Whip. Some time in the past ten days he had gone from straightforward masculine desire to a more complex passion—darker, more intense, a fierce hunger that had no beginning and no possible end other than shimmering oblivion deep inside Shannon's body.

Whip's thoughts had an inevitable reaction on his body, increasing the ache of flesh that was already pulsing with need. Cursing silently, he rubbed soap into lather between his big palms and applied it to his face. He began shaving, using an exquisite sense of touch as well as his small shaving mirror.

Shannon watched, fascinated.

"You act like you've never seen a man shave," Whip said, flattered and irritated at the same time. The feminine approval in her dark blue glance aroused him all over again.

"Silent John just wore a beard," Shannon said.

Whip grunted, stroked, and flicked lather off the blade.

"You always speak of him in the past tense," Whip said after a few more strokes.

"Who?"

"Your husband."

Shannon opened her mouth, closed it, and hugged herself as though suddenly cold.

"I'll be more careful," she promised. "Those Culpeppers are brazen enough as it is."

"You think Silent John is dead."

Although it wasn't quite a question, Shannon sensed Whip's intense interest in her answer.

"I don't think I'll see Silent John again," she admitted in a low voice. Then, anxiously, "But please don't say anything about it in Holler Creek. Murphy isn't much more polite to me than the Culpeppers. If they thought Silent John wasn't ever coming back . . ."

Shannon's voice died.

But she didn't have to finish the sentence. Whip knew exactly what she meant.

"Maybe you better plan on leaving Echo Basin," he said flatly.

For an instant hope flared in Shannon that Whip was asking her to go with him when he left.

"Where would I go?" she asked softly.

"I don't know, but I do know that at least one of those Culpeppers is always camped about two miles down the road."

"Why?"

"Waiting for me to leave. When—"

"But—" she interrupted.

Whip talked over Shannon. "When I leave, they'll start bothering you again."

Quickly Shannon looked away, not wanting Whip to see the hurt in her eyes.

When I leave.

Not if.

When.

Until that moment Shannon hadn't known how much part of her had counted on having Whip stay. Each day he watched her more intently, wanted her more obviously. Yet despite his urgent male hunger, he cared enough for her not to speak crudely to her of his need or to back her up against a wall and buck against her the way she once had seen a man do with Clementine.

"I'll manage," Shannon said in a low voice. "I always have."

"Not without Silent John."

"Prettyface protects me now."

"That's not good enough and you know it."

"It isn't your concern," she said tightly. "It's mine. Breakfast is ready."

With a muttered word, Whip bent and splashed

more water on his face, rinsing it. Then he held his hand out for the rag.

His hand remained empty.

Whip looked up, ignoring the water running down his face. Through narrowed eyes he saw that Shannon had gone back into the cabin.

There would be no mint-scented cloth given to him by her hands. There would be no careful dabbing at his face by minty fingers. Worst of all, there would be no sapphire eyes going over his face like loving hands, transparently admiring him, blushing when he caught her watching him.

Whip said something harsh beneath his breath, groped for the rag, and wiped himself with more irritation than care. He hadn't realized how much the morning shaving ritual pleased him until the moment when he found himself with empty hands and water running down his neck.

You're a damn fool to be arguing with that girl instead of petting her like a Christmas puppy, Whip told himself sardonically.

So I'm a damn fool. But not a total damn fool. It isn't safe for Shannon here. Not when I'm gone.

When you're gone, it will be just like she said—not your concern.

That answer didn't appeal to Whip, but he didn't have any other one to put in its place.

Maybe I'll just have to sidle up to those Culpepper boys and read to them from the Good Book—chapter, verse, and line—until they see the error of their ways.

That thought appealed to Whip. A lot.

Smiling like a wolf, Whip resettled his bullwhip over his shoulder and went into the cabin. He was looking forward to a hot breakfast and Shannon sitting catty-corner from him at the small table, close enough to rub against his leg with every small shift of her body.

Prettyface growled at Whip from his preferred place in the coldest corner of the cabin. The dog's thick fur kept him warmer than any stove. His teeth gleamed like ice beneath his raised upper lip.

"Whatever made you decide to save that misbegotten cur?" Whip asked, irritated all over again.

"Could you have ridden past him and done nothing about his pain?" Shannon asked.

Whip looked at Prettyface through narrowed eyes. The scars the dog bore showed as pale patches against the brindle of his fur. There were a lot of marks.

"No," Whip admitted. "At the very least I'd have put him out of his misery."

"You're a yondering man," Shannon said. "I'm the settled type. There was room in my life for something else."

"Most women would have wanted a baby instead of a savage mongrel with the eyes of a wolf."

The oven door closed with a metallic clang.

"Be careful, the pan is hot," Shannon said as she put it down near Whip.

"Didn't you?"

"Didn't I what?"

"Want a baby."

"Silent John was hard put just keeping two souls alive," Shannon said evasively, sitting down again. "There was nothing left over for a baby."

Whip took several biscuits from the pan.

"Babies have a way of coming whether you want them or not," he said.

"Do tell. How many do you have?"

Whip choked on the biscuit he was trying to swallow. He took a gulp of searing coffee, swallowed hard, and looked at Shannon with disbelieving eyes.

"What a question," he said.

"You brought it up."

"Did I?"

"You did. How many, Whip?"

"Not a damned one."

"That you know of," Shannon added mildly, but her eyes were dark.

"What is that supposed to mean?"

"It takes an instant to make a baby and about four months for it to show. Did you ever hang around that long?"

"No."

"Then you don't know, do you?"

"I know," Whip said flatly.

"How?"

"Same way Silent John knew how not to get you pregnant. Are you going to share that jam or just sit on it like a mother hen with only one egg?"

The change of subject caught Shannon with her mouth still open, staring at Whip in disbelief. She was staggered that a man like Whip was celibate. But he had just said as much.

Same way Silent John knew how not to get you pregnant.

No wonder Whip had changed the subject. It couldn't have been a comfortable topic for him, for Shannon knew that Whip certainly was capable of coupling with a woman. As often as not, when he was around her, she saw the unmistakable sign of his ability pressing hard against his trousers.

Silent John had been too old for such discomfort. The marriage had been a way to keep men like the Culpeppers at bay; a wife was more respected than a grandniece.

"Uh . . . jam," Shannon said, trying to gather her scattered wits. "Yes. Of course. Here."

"Thank you," Whip said, the courtesy automatic.

He took the jam and began spreading it over biscuits. Though Whip never appeared to move quickly, food disappeared into his mouth with astonishing speed.

Shannon had learned after the first breakfast that Whip could eat a lot of food and still look around for more. Now she routinely made a double batch of biscuits for breakfast and didn't expect to have any left over for lunch.

"I'd better see to that second batch of biscuits," Shannon muttered. "Should be about done baking."

"I'll get it," Whip said.

"Thank you, but it's no trouble."

"Don't bang the stove door, then. The hinge is nearly broken off. I'll try my hand at hammering out a new one as soon as I finish with the firewood."

Shannon felt the last of her hurt slide away, leaving her vulnerable once more to her longings. She no longer doubted that Whip would move on, leaving her behind. But while he was with her, he watched out for her more tenderly than anyone ever had.

If she was greedy for more, it was her own

fault, not his. He had told her plainly that he was a wanderer with no intention of settling down.

"Thank you," Shannon said. "I tried to make a new hinge from an old horseshoe, but no matter how hard I hammered . . ."

She shrugged and didn't finish the sentence.

"Have you ever seen a blacksmith's arms?" Whip asked dryly.

"No."

"They're bigger than mine."

Shannon's eyes widened.

Whip smiled at the look on her face. He was used to his unusual height and physical power. Shannon wasn't. At first the contrast between his strength and her own had made Shannon uneasy. Lately, though, Whip had seen appreciation rather than fear of his strength when she watched him working.

When Shannon pushed back from the table to get the biscuits, Prettyface's eyes followed his mistress the short distance to the stove. She pulled out the pan and turned toward the table. As she turned, the sole of her boot caught on an uneven floorboard.

Shannon made a startled sound and tried to regain her balance, but it was too late. Whip's big hands grabbed her and set her upright before she could fall.

"Are you—" began Whip.

The rest of his words were lost in a savage snarl as Prettyface came out of the corner in a lunge and went for Whip's throat.

7

Whip pushed Shannon out of danger even as he spun to face the attacking dog. Horrified, Shannon watched Whip yank the coiled lash off his shoulder. His left arm collided with Prettyface in mid-leap.

Man and dog went down in a snarling, cursing tangle. Prettyface ended up on top. His teeth were sunk into Whip's left hand and the coils of leather it held.

"No, Prettyface! *No*!"

Shouting and yanking frantically, Shannon tried to drag Prettyface off Whip. The dog ignored her.

Whip didn't.

"Get the hell out of the way!" he ordered.

"But—"

Shannon never finished her objection. With a powerful movement of his body, Whip turned over, dragging Prettyface beneath him and sending Shannon staggering away from the fight.

She caught her balance on the old trunk full of books and looked around wildly for something to use that would subdue Prettyface. But there was nothing at hand that would free Whip before Prettyface got his feet under him again and sank his teeth into Whip's throat.

"Prettyface! No!"

Her shouts had no effect.

Struggling, flailing, man and beast slammed into the legs of the old table. It skidded and crashed against the bed, sending blankets flying. An instant later the table careened into the front door, propelled by the thrashing bodies.

Now all Shannon could see was the corded muscles of Whip's back and Prettyface's hind feet raking Whip's legs.

"Stop it!"

Even as she screamed, Shannon knew it wouldn't do any good. Prettyface had no intention of surrendering.

Shannon's wild glance fell on the bucket of steaming water on the stove. She reached for the bucket, but a single touch told her that the water was much too hot. It would scald Whip and yet barely penetrate Prettyface's thick coat.

Abruptly the sounds of the struggle diminished. Shannon looked around.

Prettyface was on top. Whip wasn't moving very much at all.

"Oh, God," Shannon cried. *"Whip!"*

There was no answer.

Shannon lunged across the room and yanked away the table that was blocking the door. She dragged the shotgun from its pegs over the top of the door frame. Tears running down her face, she cocked the shotgun and turned back to shoot the dog that believed he was defending her.

But he wasn't. He was killing Whip.

"Put that damned gun down," Whip said grimly. "I'm not going to kill your mongrel wolf. But by God I'm going to teach him some manners."

Shannon was too shocked at hearing Whip's voice to tell him that Prettyface had been her target. Impatiently she wiped her eyes on her sleeve and looked again, thinking tears must have blurred her view of what was happening.

She saw the same thing she had seen before. Whip was mostly on the bottom of the pile, and he wasn't moving very much at all. Prettyface's muzzle was still pressed against Whip's neck.

Abruptly Shannon realized that the dog's teeth were set in the bullwhip rather than in Whip's throat.

Relief swept through Shannon, only to give way to dismay. Whip's left hand was jammed into the dog's mouth along with the bullwhip. Dismay became fear when she realized that Whip's other hand was clamped around Prettyface's windpipe.

Whip was slowly choking air and life out of her dog.

"You're killing him!" Shannon cried.

"The hell I am. The son of a bitch is still kicking like a steer."

"Let go! He's barely moving!"

"Barely is too damn much with a beast this size."

Whip bore down harder with his right hand. His mouth was set in a harsh, determined line.

"Whip!"

He ignored Shannon, even when she grabbed his hand and tried to drag it away from Prettyface's throat. When she set her feet and started to pry at his thumb with both hands, he gave her a glittering, narrow-eyed look.

"Get out of the way before you get hurt," Whip said through his teeth.

Shannon kept clawing at his hand.

Prettyface kicked feebly and went limp.

Abruptly Whip released the pressure on the dog's windpipe. Slowly the animal slid off Whip's chest onto the floor and lay without moving, as slack as a pile of wet laundry.

"You killed him!" Shannon cried. "Damn you, Whip! You killed him!"

"Hell," Whip said in disgust. "If I'd wanted to kill him, I would have broken his neck when he jumped me."

Wordlessly Shannon shook her head, denying Whip's words. Sobbing quietly, she tried to go to Prettyface, only to find her way barred by Whip's hard arm.

"He's not dead," Whip said roughly. "Look at his flank. He's breathing just fine now that my fingers are off his windpipe."

Hurriedly Shannon wiped her eyes on her sleeve and looked at Prettyface. The dog's flank was indeed rising and falling slowly, dragging air back into his lungs.

"Thank God," she whispered.

Shannon tried to go forward again, and again found her way barred by Whip.

"Go stand by the stove," he said.

"But I want to—"

"Right now what you want doesn't matter a whole lot," Whip interrupted, his voice harsh. "You had your turn at controlling this beast and you couldn't do it. It's my turn now."

"But—"

Whip looked up at Shannon.

"Move," he said softly.

Too softly.

"Don't hurt him any more," Shannon pleaded. But she was backing toward the stove while she spoke. Like Whip's voice, his eyes were calm, clear, and cold as a dagger made of ice.

Prettyface whimpered and tried to raise his

head. Instantly Whip was there, holding the dog's head against the floor, making it impossible for Prettyface to regain his feet.

"Easy," Whip said in a gently tone. "Before you get up and start feeling feisty again, focus those damned throwback eyes on me and know who's head wolf around here."

Prettyface whined softly. He blinked his yellow wolf's eyes and looked around to see what was holding him down.

The dog met Whip's eyes, recognized him, held the man's glance for the space of a breath . . . and then Prettyface looked away, silently acknowledging that Whip was the master.

Nor did the dog attempt to get up again.

"That's it, Prettyface," Whip said, stroking the dog's head gently. "I knew you were a damn sight smarter than you looked. All you needed was proof that you weren't the master."

Prettyface whined and tentatively nudged Whip's hand.

"Hello, boy," Whip murmured, rubbing the dog's head, reassuring him. "We're going to get along a lot better from now on, aren't we?"

A long, rough tongue swept over Whip's bloody hand.

"Like that, do you?" Whip laughed. "You're a hell of a fighter, Prettyface. Now you need to learn how to be a partner, too."

When Whip's fingers ran over every inch of Prettyface's body, the dog stiffened, but he didn't object in any other way to the man's touch. Even when Whip probed between the sensitive pads on the dog's feet, Prettyface didn't so much as growl.

Shannon was shocked.

"All right, Prettyface," Whip said, rubbing the dog's ears affectionately. "I think you got the point. You take orders around here. You don't give them."

Whip came off the floor with a catlike grace that was startling in such a big man. The bullwhip was still in his left hand, still coiled.

"Up you go, boy," Whip said.

Prettyface came to his feet, shook himself thoroughly, and looked at Whip.

Whip opened the cabin door.

"Go out and rustle your breakfast instead of trying to eat me," Whip suggested dryly.

Prettyface looked once at Shannon, then trotted outside. Whip shut the door.

"You broke his spirit," she said hoarsely.

"No, I just—"

"You're like the Culpeppers," Shannon interrupted wildly.

Her voice was cold. Her body shook with rage and fear and the aftermath of too much adrenaline.

"The hell I—" began Whip.

"You're cruel and you're brutal. You force anything weaker than you to grovel at your feet!"

Whip took one gliding step toward Shannon, then another. His eyes were like hammered silver. Blood dripped from cuts on his left hand.

He looked as dangerous as he was.

Shannon's heartbeat doubled, but she didn't back up one step. She couldn't. She didn't trust her legs to hold her.

"Prettyface," Whip said softly, coldly, "is a spoiled, savage mongrel that weighs more than most men. He has too much wolf in him to understand anything from a man but force. So I beat him at his own game. Force. Now he'll accept me."

Shannon's chin came up defiantly, but she was smart enough not to say a word. Whip was right and both of them knew it. She just didn't like hearing it put so bluntly.

"As for the rest of your tirade," Whip said, "when you give yourself to me—*and you will*—it won't be because I choked you into submission. If that was all I wanted, I would have killed Prettyface the first time I walked into the cabin. Then I would have thrown you down on the floor and raped you."

A small sound came from the back of Shannon's throat as she understood the raw truth of Whip's statement. Deep inside, she had always assumed it was Prettyface's snarling presence that had kept Whip from touching her in any way at all.

Now Shannon knew how badly she had misread the situation. Whip was as smart and quick as he was strong.

And he was frighteningly strong.

"But that isn't what I want from you," Whip said, his voice lethally calm.

"Wh—" Shannon's voice broke.

She licked her dry lips, took a quick breath, and tried again.

"What d-do you want from me?" she asked.

At first Shannon didn't think Whip would answer. Then he took one last, gliding stride toward her. When he stopped, he was so close to Shannon that she couldn't take a breath without her breasts touching his hard chest.

Slowly, giving Shannon every chance to flinch away, Whip lifted his hands to her face.

She didn't move. She simply watched him with eyes that were both wary and defiant.

The bullwhip he still carried in his left hand caressed Shannon's cheek so lightly it felt more like a breath than a touch. The supple leather coils traced her eyebrows, the straight line of her nose, her high cheekbones.

It was the last thing Shannon had expected from Whip. The touches were so gentle she barely felt them. They shouted of Whip's restraint.

And they teased her even as they reassured her.

She closed her eyes, wanting to concentrate on the elusive, shimmering sensations that shivered through her body. She took in a quick breath and smelled the wood smoke and evergreen on Whip, as well as the primal, disturbing scent of blood.

"Whip?" Shannon whispered through trembling lips.

His wrist flicked and the leather coils vanished. A vague thump told Shannon that the bullwhip had landed on the floor.

Whip took the shotgun from her hands and uncocked it with a few swift, easy motions. When he replaced the weapon on its pegs over the door, Shannon numbly noted that there was blood on both of his hands.

Whip saw the look on her face when he turned back to her.

"It's all right, honey girl," he said. "You don't need the shotgun. I won't hurt you. I'm just trying to answer your question about what I want from you. But I don't have any words to tell you. . . ."

Callused fingertips lightly traced Shannon's hairline, the rims of her ears, the dense mahogany eyelashes quivering against her cheek, the trembling line of her lips, the pulse beating frantically in her throat.

"Are you truly afraid of me?" Whip asked huskily.

Shannon shook her head. "N-no."

"You ought to be."

"Why?"

"I want what I first saw in your walk," he said simply.

"I—I don't understand."

"Neither do I. I've never wanted a woman the way I want you, all at once, no thought, no caution, no right or wrong, nothing but a hard need riding me all day, every day. And the nights . . . Jesus. The nights are pure, undiluted hell."

Shannon tried to speak. No words came out of her dry throat.

Whip's thumbs traced her mouth, caressing it as intimately as a kiss. Her softness lured him, and her heat, and the ragged sigh she finally gave, a sigh that was also his name.

"You have a walk like honey," Whip said huskily, bending down to her. "Kiss me, Shannon. I want to find out if your mouth is half as arousing as your walk."

Shannon made a soft, startled sound when Whip's teeth nibbled at her lips and his tongue probed the corners of her mouth. Tingling sensations rippled through her, shortening her breath until she felt dizzy. Her hands went up to his arms, anchoring her in a world that was dissolving beneath her feet one frantic heartbeat at a time.

"Whip?" she whispered raggedly.

"That's it," he said against her mouth. "Open those soft lips a little more. I have to taste you."

"Taste me?"

"Yes. Now."

Whip's tongue slid into Shannon's mouth, caressing her, tasting her with a hushed intensity that made her tremble. An answering tremor went through Whip.

Curious, Shannon looked at him. His forehead was creased and his eyes were closed. His cut, bleeding hands held her face as though she were more fragile than a butterfly's wings. Despite the potent hunger that tightened every muscle in his body, Whip's mouth only sipped lightly at hers.

Beneath her hands, Whip's arms felt like steel bands. His muscles were corded and his breath was ragged. He could have taken whatever he wanted from her much more easily than he had subdued Prettyface. Shannon knew it.

And so did Whip.

Yet still he demanded nothing of her. He simply asked, coaxed, mutely pleaded to be allowed into the lush darkness behind her lips.

Shannon sighed and gave Whip what he desired. His tongue glided over hers, coaxing her to touch him in turn. The caress was tantalizing, irresistible, as warm and gentle as sunrise itself.

A small sound came from the back of Shannon's throat as she understood Whip's silent message. He was telling her without words how much he wanted her and how careful he would be if she gave herself to him.

The thought of such a tender sharing took the world from beneath Shannon's feet. Her fingers dug into Whip's arms as her knees loosened.

"Whip?"

Shannon's muffled whisper was barely understandable. Whip was tempted to ignore the question in her tone, but didn't. Despite her previous assurances, he was afraid that fear rather than passion had caused her fingers to clench around his arms.

Reluctantly Whip lifted his head and looked down into Shannon's dazed blue eyes. When she still didn't speak, he nuzzled the corner of her mouth with his mustache.

She smiled slightly and kissed the rough silk mustache that was caressing her. Whip eased the tip of his tongue into the corner of her smile. Then he probed between her lips several times, slowly, easing in and out of her warmth, teasing and tasting her lightly, hotly.

Shannon made another throttled sound and shivered.

"What is it?" Whip asked in a low voice. "Are you afraid of me after all?"

She shook her head. While she did, she watched Whip's mouth, wondering how anything that looked so hard and sharply controlled could feel so soft and wild against her lips.

"I—" Shannon blinked, touched her tongue to the corner of her mouth, and whispered, "I feel dizzy."

Whip's smile was dark, swift, very male. Shannon's eyes were a smoky sapphire that sent tongues of desire stabbing through him. His own eyes became a smoldering quicksilver as he watched Shannon lick her lips again.

"Dizzy," Whip repeated huskily.

She nodded and touched the tip of her tongue uncertainly to her lips.

"Put your arms around my neck and hold on," Whip said. "I'll make sure you don't fall."

As Whip spoke, he drew Shannon's arms around his neck. The movement brought her up on tiptoe and pulled her against his body. Her breath came in with a soft, ripping sound that acted on Whip like a shot of whiskey.

"Now we can do this properly," Whip said.

"What?"

"Lick your lips again, honey girl. I'll show you."

Shannon hesitated, then did as Whip asked.

No sooner had Shannon's tongue touched her lips than Whip bent down and caught her mouth beneath his. His tongue pressed into the moist darkness behind her teeth, caressing her even as he filled her. He felt the hesitation of her body, the quick intake of her breath, and then the trembling pressure of her tongue against his in secret caress.

Whip made a low sound and gathered Shannon even more closely along his body. His tongue began a sultry rhythm of penetration and retreat, return and withdrawal. After a few moments her arms tightened around his neck, lifting her into the kiss.

Without realizing it, Shannon opened her mouth more. She wanted to know every bit of Whip's mouth, from the satin just behind his lips to the velvet of his tongue. Hungrily she probed the heated darkness that lured her unbearably.

The world spun swiftly around Whip as Shannon give back the deep kiss. His hands went from her shoulders to her thighs in long, slow sweeps. Fingers widespread, he measured the feminine elegance of her back, the lush flare of her hips, the siren call of her breasts pressed more closely against his chest with each stroke of his hands.

When Whip could deny himself no longer, he allowed his hands to slide along Shannon's ribs until his thumbs met at the bottom of her breastbone. Without warning his hands shifted, cupping soft, taut flesh.

A threadlike groan was dragged from Whip when he discovered that Shannon was even more womanly beneath her men's clothes than he had guessed. Her softness filled his hands.

Probing, caressing, his thumbs circled Shannon's sensitive nipples. They blossomed in a rush that sent a fierce answering fire through Whip. Delicately he caught the tips of her breasts between his fingers and squeezed.

Shannon made a high sound of surprise as desire splintered through her, tightening her body, arching it against him in a wild caress. Her nipples had been transformed by Whip's touch. Now they were hard peaks that stood out proudly against her old flannel shirt, begging for Whip's hands, his mouth, his passion.

"Honey girl," he groaned. "You could set fire to stone, and I'm one hell of a long way from stone."

Before Shannon could answer, Whip took her mouth again. His tongue shot between her teeth as his hands slid down to her hips, lifting her, fitting the soft nest above her thighs to the rigid male flesh she had called from his body. He rocked her sensuously against his arousal while his tongue mated with hers in a fierce, elemental rhythm.

Wild pleasure streaked through Shannon, shaking her. She couldn't get her breath because she was holding on to Whip too hard. He was holding her even harder in turn, but she still couldn't get close enough to him. She was dizzy for lack of air, yet she pressed even more violently against Whip's mouth, needing the deep kiss in a way she didn't understand.

And then he dragged her hips against his rigid flesh.

A ragged moan was torn from Shannon's throat. The sound could have been pain or fear or passion, or all three together.

Abruptly Whip realized that he was devouring Shannon's mouth, crushing her to his body with both arms and grinding his hips against her as though he would have her here, now, standing up like a whore in an alley.

Shuddering, Whip tore his mouth from Shannon's and loosened his arms. He let her slide down his body until her feet touched the floor.

She made a questioning sound and touched her lips with fingers that jerked slightly with each quick breath she took.

Unhappily Whip looked at Shannon's face. Against the bloody marks left by his savaged hands, her skin looked pale. Her eyes were dilated and her lips were soft, trembling, parted as she dragged raggedly at air. She swayed until she reached out blindly and steadied herself against the wall.

"Are you all right?" Whip asked.

He wanted to be gentle, but the question came out rough. His voice was harsh with the blood that was still pumping fiercely through his body.

"I feel—" Shannon's breath broke. "Dizzy. Crazy. I can't breathe and I'm shaking like I'm cold but parts of me are on fire and I'm burning and I want—I want—oh, God, I don't know what I want! What did you do to me, Whip?"

For a long moment Whip looked at Shannon, hardly able to believe what he was hearing.

"How long have you been married?" he asked finally.

"What does that—have to do with—how I feel?"

The breaking of Shannon's breath acted on Whip like tongues of fire licking over his aroused flesh, making him ache until he had to clench his teeth against a groan.

"It has everything to do with it," Whip said thickly. "What you're feeling is passion, honey girl. Pure and wild and hotter than hell."

"I don't—understand."

Whip made a sound that could have been a curse or a prayer or both at once.

"Your husband wasn't much of a man to cozy up with on a cold night, was he?" Whip said between his teeth.

"Silent John wasn't—that is, he *isn't*—a warm man."

"Are you telling me that you haven't ever felt sexual desire like this before?"

"This?" Shannon drew a ragged breath and looked at Whip with burning blue eyes. "This is desire?"

"Son of a bitch," Whip whispered, shocked. "You mean it, don't you?"

She nodded.

"As naive as an egg," Whip muttered. "*God.* Silent John must have been about as much fun in bed as a rattlesnake. No wonder you don't mind being his widow—he's been as good as dead to you for years!"

Shannon's breath caught at the contempt in Whip's voice. She shivered and wrapped her arms protectively around herself.

As naive as an egg.

Abruptly, Shannon's desire was transformed into anger.

Whip has no right to act so superior just because I'm not as knowing about men as Clementine or Betsy.

But Shannon wasn't going to open the subject again by pointing that out.

"Don't call me a widow," Shannon said through her teeth.

"Why? It's likely the truth and you know it."

"But if the truth goes beyond this cabin, who will protect me from the Culpeppers after you leave? And you will leave, won't you? *Yondering man.*"

"Yes," Whip said harshly, stung by the anger and distance in Shannon's voice. "I'll leave one day. But not until I find a safe place for you to stay."

"As long as I'm Silent John's wife, I'm safe enough here."

"That's crap, Shannon. You're his widow, not his wife, and this place isn't safe for a girl alone. Especially one as naive as you!"

"It has been for seven years."

"Only because Silent John was here with you," Whip retorted. "Without him you wouldn't last two months."

Shannon barely bit back the hot retort that was crowding her tongue. Telling Whip the truth would do no good, and could do a great deal of harm.

"I'll live where I please," she said tightly.

"Alone?"

"Yes."

"You can't."

"I can!" she said savagely. "And what business

is it of yours how I live, yondering man? You have no right to order me about like I was bound by law to you."

Whip was appalled by the idea of Shannon's living alone through the winter in Echo Basin's high, icy wilderness, having no one to depend upon but herself. He shook his head, said something profane beneath his breath, and raked his hand through his hair in frustration.

His fingers were bright with his own blood, blood drawn by Prettyface in defense of his naive, stubborn mistress.

When Shannon saw Whip's fingers, she felt her hot, inexplicable rage at him drain away, leaving only an edgy kind of concern for his wounds.

"Come on," Shannon said, turning away. "One secret spilled between us won't matter."

"What?"

Without a word Shannon walked to the dry goods cupboard. She opened the door, pushed on the center of a shelf, and stepped forward into the darkness.

An instant later she vanished.

The warm, humid smell of a hot spring floated back out to Whip, along with Shannon's voice.

"Silent John told me never to tell anyone about the hot spring, but . . ."

Shannon's voice died. Light flared as she struck a match and set it to a lantern's wick. Glass clinked quietly as she replaced the chimney. A warm yellow glow spread out to Whip.

"Well, come on," Shannon said impatiently. "Silent John swore by—*swears* by—the healing power of the spring, and your hands are pretty well chewed."

"I'll be damned," Whip said, stepping toward

the cupboard. "So this is why he built the cabin right into the mountainside."

Shannon shrugged. "All I know is the hot spring boils meat and washes clothes and dishes real clean at the far end, and is just right for bathing at this end. Everywhere else, the hot spring keeps the worst of the cold at bay when I can't get out to gather wood in the winter."

Shannon set the lantern on a wooden crate that had once held ammunition. Light transformed twists of steam into ghostly golden wraiths.

Whip ducked low as he went through the cupboard. Once inside the cave, he saw that the ceiling was high enough for him to stand upright. Lantern light glanced off the rocky walls and uneven floor, and made the many deep cracks in the rock look like ragged slices of midnight. But for the tiny hissing of the lamp and the seething, whispering swirls of water, the cave was utterly still.

A metal pan scraped over rock as Shannon dipped up hot water for Whip. She put the steaming pan on the crate next to the lantern, fished a lump of soap from a smaller wooden box and stepped aside to make room for Whip.

When Whip looked from the water to Shannon, but didn't move farther into the cave, she made an exasperated sound.

"Surely you aren't afraid of caves?" Shannon asked curtly.

"No. But you ought to be."

"Why? I've been here a thousand times."

"Not with me. Not when lantern light outlines your breasts and shows me that your nipples are still hard, still hungry. Do they ache, honey girl?"

Shannon flushed to the roots of her hair. She

did ache, and not only in her breasts. But she wasn't about to mention that to Whip. He had had enough fun at her expense already.

"Go to hell, yondering man. What I feel is none of your business."

Frustration fairly vibrated through Shannon's body and voice. Whip knew what its source was, knew its cure, and worst of all he knew the naive little widow would be the hottest woman he had ever shared a bed with.

Abruptly Whip closed his eyes, unable to look at Shannon any longer without touching her.

And if he touched her, he would take her.

He didn't want that to happen. Not yet. Not after he had just discovered how naive she was. Seducing her now would be like shooting fish in a barrel.

Whip wanted Shannon to give herself to him knowing full well what she was doing, not because her judgment had been clouded by her first taste of real pleasure.

"I'm counting to three," Whip said, his voice rough. "When I open my eyes, you better be—"

"But—"

"—in the cabin or I'll strip those ragged clothes off you and teach you everything your damned husband should have about men, women, and sex."

Shannon drew a swift, audible breath at Whip's bluntness. If it hadn't been for his bleeding hands, she would have grabbed the lantern and left him standing alone in the dark.

"Your hands need tending," she said through her teeth.

"They don't ache nearly so much as my crotch does. Do you want to tend to that, too?"

"You are a crude, miserable, surly—"

"Get your sweet little rump out of here," Whip interrupted savagely, "or I'll do something we'll both regret. *One.*"

The temptation to throw the pan of water at Whip was so great that Shannon had her hands wrapped around the warm metal rim before she realized what she was doing.

For an instant her fingers tightened, getting ready to lift the pan.

Then common sense returned in a cold rush. No matter how angry and unsettled she was, it would be plain foolish to bait a man as dangerous as Whip, especially after she had received the clearest kind of warning about the state of his temper.

With a stifled curse Shannon let go of the pan and stepped back.

"Two," Whip said.

He hesitated for a time before he spoke the next number. Motionless, he listened. He heard no sounds of Shannon's retreat. He heard nothing at all but the muted noises of lantern and hot spring.

"Three."

Whip opened his eyes and discovered that Shannon had gone as silently as steam rising from the hot spring's gently seething surface.

Damn.

I was hoping she'd lose her temper and sling that pan of water at me. It would have been fun using every stitch of her clothing to dry myself off.

It would have been even more fun getting her wet in return.

Whip took a deep breath and let it out slowly,

trying to release the aggressive, coiled hunger of his body.

It's better this way. She's too naive.

Whip kept repeating that bit of wisdom all the way to the pan of water, but it didn't convince him worth a damn. He still wanted Shannon like hell burning.

He plunged his hands into the hot water, hoping pain would take his mind off the hunger that was knotting his guts.

It didn't.

Swearing, Whip began to work soap into the ragged cuts on his hands. As he did, he remembered what Jessi, Wolfe's wife, had told him about keeping wounds clean so that they would heal quickly.

Silently he wondered if soap would wash away desire as well as blood and dirt.

Somehow, I doubt it, Whip thought sourly.

He was right.

8

For the rest of the day, Whip and Shannon were as polite to one another as well-bred strangers. She cooked for him; he split wood and replaced a rotten log in the cabin wall. She washed his clothes; he picketed the old mule in a fresh section of meadow and caught a half dozen trout for dinner. She mended his clothes; he began tanning buckskin for moccasins for her.

The subject of passion and naive little eggs

never came up. Nor was there any discussion of death and Silent John or of widows and safety.

The weather was a favorite topic for what little conversation Whip and Shannon had.

Prettyface was the only creature in the cabin that was fully at ease. He begged scraps from Whip and Shannon equally, offered his head to both people to be petted, and looked to man and woman alike as a source of open doors and romps in the meadow.

Shannon should have been pleased by Prettyface's acceptance of Whip. Most of her was, but a part of her wondered acidly if the dog would leave her when Whip did.

The following morning Shannon slept later than usual. She had spent a restless night filled with dreams and yearnings she couldn't express in words. She woke up to a familiar sound. Whip was splitting wood.

"Good," Shannon said beneath her breath. "Maybe he can work out his bad temper on the woodpile instead of on me. Besides, what did I ever do to him except . . ."

Sensual memories licked through Shannon with tiny tongues of fire. Her nipples tightened to aching peaks.

Oh, no. Why won't it go away?

Shannon threw back the blankets and shot out of bed as though it were on fire.

But it wasn't the bed. It was her body.

No wonder Whip is giving the wood such a going over. He must feel as edgy-achey-strange as I do.

Hurriedly Shannon went about the familiar chores of making breakfast and putting the cabin back in order. When she was finished, she went to the cabin window, unlatched the shutters, and let the crisp air wash over her.

A glance told her that Whip had split an impressive amount of stove wood since she had first heard him at work shortly after dawn. She had meant to get up then, but instead had rolled over and slid back into the subtly fevered dreams that had claimed her for most of the night.

With a hunger Shannon didn't understand, she watched the taut strength of Whip's body while he transformed lengths of fir logs into clean pieces of stove wood. Never once did he look up to see if she was standing in the window. He simply kept working as though his strength was truly limitless.

"At this rate, I'm going to be buried alive in wood," Shannon muttered to herself.

When she realized that watching Whip was only increasing the restless fever of her body, she turned her back on the open window.

"His hands will never heal if he keeps that up."

Shannon frowned. That was another topic Whip had refused to discuss. The one time she had asked Whip how his hands felt, he shot her a narrow-eyed look and changed the subject.

To the weather, of course.

Both of them agreed it was just lovely, from sleet to sunshine and back again.

Shannon sighed. She hadn't felt quite so alone since her mother died and left her to the mercy of a step-aunt who had no mercy in her. The odd thing was that Shannon had never felt particularly lonesome in Echo Basin before now, but remembering how much fun it had been to share the days with Whip made her feel the present distance from him all the more keenly.

Without warning, Shannon had a vivid, tactile memory of what it had been like to be kissed and petted by Whip. In the wake of memory, a primitive kind of heat blossomed in her. She couldn't help hoping that once his anger was past, he would kiss her again, and touch her, and . . .

"What do you think, Prettyface? Is Whip's temper going to give out before the logs do?"

Prettyface yawned.

"You're right. His surly mood will outlast the whole blasted forest."

"Count on it."

Shannon jumped at the sound of Whip's voice just behind her at the open window. She spun around, blushing at having been caught thinking aloud.

Whip was standing with his forearms crossed on the windowsill, smiling at her. Then he laughed.

Shannon's answering smile was as beautiful as an unexpected sunrise.

Honey girl, don't smile at me like that. All my good intentions will burn to ash.

"Does this mean you've forgiven me?" Whip asked softly, knowing he shouldn't, unable to stop himself.

"Forgiven you? For what?"

"Teaching Prettyface a few manners, and then forgetting my own."

"I wasn't angry about Prettyface."

"Could have fooled me. I saw you holding a fully loaded, fully cocked shotgun on me."

At first Shannon believed Whip was teasing her. But there was no deviltry in his quicksilver eyes. Abruptly her good humor turned to anger.

"I was going to shoot Prettyface," she said starkly.

Whip looked shocked. "What?"

"I thought he was killing you. You weren't moving and there was blood and it looked like his jaws were locked on your throat."

The horror of that moment came back all too forcefully. Shannon turned her back on Whip again.

"So I got down the shotgun," she said distinctly.

"To save my life?"

"You needn't sound so shocked," Shannon said through her teeth.

But Whip was shocked. He knew how much Shannon loved her dangerous mongrel. He also know how much she depended on Prettyface for companionship and safety.

Yet she had been ready to kill Prettyface in order to save a man who had made no promises to her.

Not one.

"I see," Whip said.

"Do you? That would be a first."

The irritability in her own voice surprised Shannon.

"Sorry," she muttered. "I don't know why I'm so touchy lately."

"I do. It comes from wanting someone and going to bed aching and alone."

"Then it's a pure blue wonder that couples survive courtship," Shannon retorted.

Whip tried not to laugh. He didn't succeed.

He tried not to touch the buried fire in Shannon's hair. He didn't succeed in that, either. Slowly he reached through the open window and stroked down between her braids to the graceful nape of her neck.

Shannon shivered.

"We'll survive, honey girl."

"That's because yondering men don't court ignorant little widowed eggs," Shannon said crisply, stepping beyond Whip's reach. "Come in when you're ready. The biscuits are almost done."

While Whip washed his hands, Shannon took a quick look at the larder. Supplies that would have lasted months for her were vanishing at a startling rate.

Dear Lord, that man eats enough for three. Of course, he works enough for six.

She bit her lip. Whip kept them in meat and fish, and she gathered fresh greens, but flour couldn't be stalked and shot in the forest. Nor could it be gathered in the meadow. Neither could beans, apples, rice, salt, and other necessities. Not to mention luxuries like coffee and cinnamon.

"I'll have to go into Holler Creek and buy more," Shannon muttered, closing the cupboard.

Sure. And just how will I pay for them?

Shannon thought of the miserable amount of wealth she had concealed in an old poke back in the cave. It was the last of Silent John's gold. When it was spent, Shannon would be exactly what she had been at thirteen—dead broke, alone, and no one giving a damn whether she lived or died.

No. I won't touch that gold.

I'm not that desperate.

But Shannon was afraid she would be. Soon. After she spent the last of Silent John's legacy, she would have to depend entirely on her own ability to wrest gold from the stubborn rocks. So far, she had enjoyed even less luck hunting gold that she had hunting meat.

Shutting the cupboard door firmly, Shannon turned her back on its empty shelves.

Whip was standing only a few feet away, watching her with quicksilver eyes.

"I'll go into Holler Creek for more supplies tomorrow," Whip said.

"Thank you, but no. You've given me too much already."

"I've eaten nearly all of it myself."

"Whose stove wood are you chopping?" Shannon asked mildly. "Whose cabin are you fixing up for winter winds? Whose mule got shod? I should be paying you wages."

"I'm barely earning my keep."

"You're earning food, wages, and then some. You never stop working."

"I like working," Whip said.

"I'll find a way to pay you."

"I won't take money from you."

"But you've *earned* it," she insisted.

"No."

The single word made Shannon feel as though she had run into a granite wall.

"You're as stubborn as that mule you shod," she said.

"Thank you. I've often thought the same about you. But I'll outstubborn you, widow lady. You can count on it."

Irritation surged through Shannon.

"No, yondering man. All I can *count* on from you is that someday I'll wake up and you'll be gone. Maybe you'll outstubborn me before then, but I doubt it."

Without another word Shannon stepped around Whip and began serving breakfast. He watched her movements with eyes as gray and hard as gunmetal.

Not until both of them had eaten some food and drunk a cup of coffee did Shannon feel civil enough to break the silence.

"What kind of jobs have you worked at since you became a yondering man?" she asked.

Whip's mouth thinned at the words "yondering man." He didn't know why Shannon's use of the term rankled him so much.

But it did.

"Teamster, sailor, surveyor, jackaroo, teacher, shotgun rider," Whip said in a clipped voice. "You name it and I've probably done it, one time or another."

"What's a jackaroo?"

"An Australian cowpuncher."

"Oh." Shannon frowned and asked, "Did you ever prospect for gold?"

"Here and there."

"Find any?"

Whip shrugged. "Here and there."

"But not enough to stake a claim?"

"Claims are like wives. They tie you down."

"You mean you've walked away from gold just because it would tie you down?"

"Yes," he said succinctly.

She swallowed. "I see."

"Do you?" Whip asked, echoing her earlier words.

"Indeed I do. You'll walk away from home, family, friends, gold, land, any or all of them.

And for what, yondering man? What's worth more than all that put together?"

"The sunrise I've never seen," Whip said flatly. "For me, there's nothing more beautiful or compelling than that."

Shannon wanted to shake Whip, but knew it would do no good. He believed what he believed.

And she had just realized a truth that would break her heart.

"Love is more compelling," she whispered. "Love is like the sun, burning through darkness . . . always burning, always beautiful."

Whip started to argue, but Shannon's smile stopped him. Her smile was one of the saddest things he had ever seen, as haunting as the sorrow in her eyes, her voice, her very breath.

"And like the sun," Shannon said softly, "love is always beyond reach. It can no more be caught and held than sunlight itself. Love touches you. You don't touch it."

Whip shifted uncomfortably and reached for the biscuits again.

"For you, maybe," he said in a clipped voice, rankled again. And again not knowing why. "For me, love is a cage."

"No one can build a cage of light."

Whip bit back a savage word and drank scalding coffee.

"What about you?" he asked after a moment. "What do you want? Love?"

"I don't know."

"You mean you don't have any dreams?" he asked curtly.

"Dreams?"

Shannon's soft laughter taught Whip what sorrow really was. He fought against the sensation of living in her skin, breathing her breath, feeling her pain as though it was his own.

"Once I dreamed of a home," Shannon said, "a garden, children, and most of all a man who loved me like the sun burning . . ."

Shannon's voice died.

Whip paused in the act of reaching for a biscuit. He didn't want to pursue the subject, but found it impossible not to do just that.

"Once you dreamed of those things, but not now?" he asked.

"No, not now."

"Why not? You can still have your dreams, Shannon. Plenty of fine, upstanding men would be glad to marry a pretty young widow like you."

"Marry me?"

Shannon laughed, but there was no humor in the sound. Nor was there any sadness. There was simply a bleak acceptance of what was and what was not.

"All those *fine, upstanding men,*" Shannon said sardonically, "want the same thing from me a certain yondering man does, and—"

"Just because I won't be tied to—"

"—a home, a garden, and love don't have a damn thing to do with what those men want," Shannon continued, talking over Whip. "As for children, the men don't want them either, but they sure as sin don't mind leaving their seed behind for the pretty widow lady to raise."

Whip's cheekbones became ruddy against the tan of his face.

"I told you, I never left any kids behind," he said flatly.

"What does that have to do with anything?" Shannon asked, arching her dark eyebrows.

"We're talking about *fine, upstanding men* who would be glad to marry a pretty young widow like me. We already know you're not one of them, yondering man."

"I would make a piss-poor husband!"

"Am I arguing with you?" she asked gently.

Whip opened his mouth, then closed it with a distinct clicking of his teeth.

"No," he said curtly.

"Then why are you yelling at me?"

"I'm not yelling."

"I'm so relieved. I fall apart when I'm yelled at."

Whip shot Shannon a searing gray glance, but she seemed to be too busy eating bacon to notice.

"Now," she said, chewing thoughtfully, "where were we? Ah, yes. We're not yelling about the fact that neither one of us is in a rush to get married."

"It's fine for me to be on my own," Whip said grimly. "It's different for you."

"Really? Why?"

"Because you can't take care of yourself and you damn well know it!"

"Oh, good. Another subject not to yell about. Pass the jam, please, and isn't the weather lovely?"

Whip said something blasphemous under his breath.

Shannon acted as though she hadn't heard. She reached past Whip, took the pot of preserves, and began slathering jam on a biscuit.

"Do you prefer sleet or snow?" she asked.

"Shannon—"

"I know," she interrupted. "Such a difficult

choice. What about hail? Do you think we could not yell about that?"

"Doubt it," he retorted. "I wouldn't yell about another cup of coffee, though."

Hiding a smile, Shannon twisted in her chair and reached back to the stove, grabbing the coffeepot without getting up. She turned back gracefully, surprising an expression of frank hunger on Whip's face as he looked at her breasts. An instant later the expression was gone.

Silently Whip held out his coffee cup. Just as silently Shannon poured coffee and replaced the pot on the stove.

"How about half of whatever you find on Silent John's gold claims?" Shannon asked. "Would you yell about that?"

The tin cup of coffee stopped an inch from Whip's mustache.

"What?" he asked.

"Silent John had—*has*—several claims on Avalanche Creek."

Whip shrugged.

"He worked those claims to pay for food he couldn't hunt," Shannon explained.

"Do tell," Whip said dryly.

"I'm trying, yondering man. I'm trying."

"My name is Whip," he said finally, rankled by the nickname.

"Why do you get upset when I call you yondering man? It's what you are, isn't it?" Shannon asked reasonably. "I don't get upset when you call me a widow, and you're not even sure I *am* one."

Whip started to argue but knew it was futile before he said a word. He let out a long breath and concentrated on his coffee and bacon for a few minutes.

Shannon was tempted to push Whip to agree that there was no reason for him to be irritated. Then, reluctantly, she decided that she should quit while she was ahead.

It was difficult, however. The temptation to bait Whip was nearly irresistible. Frowning slightly, she concentrated on her coffee.

"My little sister Willow used to do the same thing," Whip said finally. "My brothers and I decided mothers must teach it to girls along with how to make good biscuits."

"What's that?"

"Tying men up with words."

Shannon didn't hide her smile before Whip saw it.

"But we do get even," Whip drawled.

"Do tell. How?"

Whip simply smiled.

"Tell me about those gold claims, honey girl."

"There's not much to tell."

"Start with where they are," he suggested dryly.

"Up Avalanche Creek."

"Which fork?"

"East. Way, way up, where it comes out of a shattered rock wall."

Whip grunted. "Rugged country. Some of the roughest I've seen."

"Amen," she said. "Each time I climb up there, I get dizzy and breathless and I just know I'm going to fall."

"You have no business going up to such a dangerous place!"

Shannon ignored Whip.

"A grizzly got one of the mules there," she said, "the second summer I was in Echo Basin. After that, Silent John packed in supplies, brought Razorback home, and walked back to the claims."

"Did you go with him?"

"Sometimes. Sometimes I stayed at the cabin. I didn't know from day to day what I would be doing. That's the way he wanted it. He said a hunter can't kill game that doesn't have a pattern to its movements."

"Cautious man."

Shannon shrugged. "It was just Silent John's way."

"Did he have any other work besides prospecting?" Whip asked, curious if Shannon knew about her husband's other life as a bounty hunter.

"No."

"Didn't find much gold for all the time he was gone, did he?"

"We never went hungry."

"Didn't he work for other people if the prospecting was slow?" Whip probed.

"Silent John? Hardly. He hated people. Anyway, who would hire him? He was wiry but he wasn't what you would call a strong man. And he was old. He would be more likely to hire something done than to hire out himself to do another man's labor."

"There are some jobs that don't need a lot of strength," Whip said dryly.

Shannon frowned. "Silent John never would have tended bar or been a storekeeper or whatever. He was no good with people."

Whip looked at Shannon's clear, innocent eyes and realized that she hadn't the faintest idea that she was the widow of one of the most feared man-hunters in the Colorado Territory.

"You mentioned that Silent John had several claims," Whip said, changing the subject. "Which was the best one?"

"Rifle Sight."

"Which one is that?"

"The highest one," Shannon said. "Way up against the rock wall, a ravine not much bigger than the notch on a rifle sight, and a steep drop-off at the mouth of the ravine."

"Hard rock mining?"

Shannon nodded.

"Damn," Whip said. "Tunnels?"

"Just one."

"One is too many." He grimaced. "After digging Reno out of a cave-in last year, I don't hold much love for tunnels and mines."

"We could try the Chute first."

"What's that?"

"Another gold claim. It's in the belly of an avalanche chute."

Whip looked out the window. Last winter's plentiful snows still gleamed on the peaks.

"I'll pass on that one, thanks," he said. "There's too good a chance of an avalanche."

"Silent John usually worked that one later in the summer," Shannon agreed," after most of the snow was gone."

"What of the other claims?"

"There's just one more that I know of."

"What's it like?"

"Cold. Wet. It's a miserable crack in the rock where rain collects."

"Silent John wasn't a man for comfort, was he?"

"He never said one way or the other."

Whip grunted and gazed past his coffee cup, considering the claims.

"None of the claims sound real appetizing," he said finally. "But then, if I liked digging gold, I'd have stayed in the west with Reno years ago instead of going on to China. Is there any feed for horses up at Rifle Sight?"

"Some. There's a meadow a quarter mile from the mine."

Whip grunted. "Grizzlies?"

"That's where the other mule died."

"I don't think Sugarfoot will have a problem that way."

"Sugarfoot?"

"My gelding," Whip said absently. "They cut him too late, so he still thinks he's king of the mountain."

Shannon waited while Whip held his coffee cup and stared into a distance only he could see. As she waited, she memorized the arching line of his fair eyebrows, the catlike tilt of his gray eyes, and the clean planes of his cheekbones and jaw. His mustache gleamed like captive sunlight above his lip. There was a faint sheen of coffee on his mouth.

"What are you thinking?" Whip asked softly.

"That I'd like to lick the coffee from your lips."

Hearing her own words, Shannon flushed.

Whip's breath came out with a low sound that could have been a curse.

"Dangerous words, honey girl."

"I'm . . . sorry. I didn't realize how it would sound until I said it."

"Give me your hand," Whip said softly.

Hesitantly Shannon held out her hand to him. He turned her palm up and inhaled deeply.

"Spearmint," he said huskily. "God, I'll die remembering the sweet scent of you."

"Whip," she whispered, her throat aching.

Whip held Shannon's palm to his mustache, rubbing softly against her sensitive skin.

"I'd give you the kiss we both want," he said, touching his tongue to her skin, "but if I feel your mouth open beneath mine right now . . ."

Slowly, thoroughly, Whip tasted Shannon's palm.

"If I felt your mouth," he said in a deep, low voice, "I'd start unbuttoning clothes."

He bit her tenderly, felt her tremble, heard her whimper with passion and surprise.

"If I start unbuttoning clothes," Whip said, "I'd have you right here, right now, sitting astride my thighs, and I'd watch you ride me all the way to the sun."

Whip looked up, pinning Shannon with blazing gray eyes.

"Would you like that, honey girl?"

"I . . . I . . ."

"Don't know?"

"I can't think when you touch me," she said, her voice husky. "And when you aren't touching me, all I can think about is the next time you'll touch me."

Whip shuddered and gripped Shannon's hand a little fiercely. He slid his tongue between two of her fingers in a hot, tender rhythm.

"Your honesty makes me burn," Whip said

against Shannon's skin. "When you burn in the same way, come to me. I'll wait as long as I can."

"Then you'll leave?" she whispered unhappily.

"No, honey girl. Then I'll come to you."

9

"I still think we should split any gold we find fifty-fifty," Shannon said stubbornly over her shoulder.

Beneath Shannon, Razorback plodded at a surprisingly good pace up the steep game trail that led to the headwaters of the east fork of Avalanche Creek. On the trail behind Shannon, Whip sat easily astride his big gray gelding, following her to Silent John's solitary claims.

"Whip?"

Ignoring Shannon, Whip looked over his shoulder. The packhorse was following more slowly with each foot of elevation gained. And there had been a lot of elevation. Avalanche Creek's east fork went up the side of the mountain like lightning, zigzagging from ravine to cascade to ravine.

"Cat got your tongue?" Shannon asked acidly.

"I'll take wages, just like any other coolie," Whip said.

"Someone should bridle you, shoe you, and use you as a mule," she said under her breath, believing Whip couldn't hear.

"Anytime you want to ride me, just ask," Whip said in a deep voice.

"You have a mule's long ears, too," she retorted.

Whip saw the flush on Shannon's pale cheeks and laughed aloud.

"You're so sweet to tease," he said. "I swear, I could get drunk on you."

"It's the altitude."

"No, honey girl. It's you."

Shannon shook her head vigorously, but her eyes were sparkling. Whip's tender, sensual teasing was a constant surprise to her.

"I never know when to take you seriously," she said, sighing. "You're the first man I've ever known who wasn't hell-bent on gold or fighting or . . ."

Too late, Shannon realized where her words were leading her.

"Sex?" Whip asked dryly.

She nodded.

"Oh, I'm hell-bent on that," he assured her.

"You have an odd way of showing it," Shannon muttered.

His smile flashed against his tan face.

"You noticed," he said.

"What?"

"That I haven't touched you since breakfast two days ago."

"Now why would I notice a thing like that?" she retorted coolly.

Whip's laugh was as darkly masculine as his smile.

"Are you burning yet, honey girl?"

"I don't know what you're talking about."

"I know. That's why I haven't touched you."

Shannon bit her lip. "How will I get less naive if you don't touch me?"

"Good question. When you think of the answer, let me know. I'll do the same for you."

She made an exasperated sound and turned back to the trail, ignoring Whip's gentle smile.

Prettyface was waiting up ahead where the trail forked. One vague path led to the Chute, which was still buried under summer avalanches. The other path led to the Rifle Sight claim, by way of a place Silent John called Grizzly Meadow.

"Go right, Prettyface," Shannon called, waving her arm to the right.

The big dog promptly trotted off to the right.

Shannon glanced behind to see if Whip was suitably impressed by the dog's obedience. But Whip wasn't watching her. He was looking through a gap in the trees back down the trail. His narrow-eyed intensity was nearly tangible.

"Whip?"

He held up his hand in a sharp signal for silence.

Uneasily Shannon waited, eyes scanning the back trail for anything out of the ordinary. She saw only trees bending slightly beneath the breeze, and cloud shadows dappling the green-and-gray flank of the mountain.

After another minute Whip finally turned in the saddle to face Shannon.

"Nothing," he said. "Just a bird startled by a deer, I guess. Indians have no reason to climb this high and outlaws are too darned lazy."

"Grizzly?"

"Wouldn't surprise me. We're following a game trail. Bears follow it, too. They don't break any trails they don't have to, unless it's berry season. Then they'll plow through hell itself to get to a ripe thicket."

Shannon looked around at the mountainside. Spruce, fir, and aspens grew thickly, shutting out much of the view. Ahead, there was a thinning of the forest that signaled the approach to Grizzly Meadow. The meadow with its rim of bushes and willows was the last good browsing for deer. After the meadow, plants grew more and more scarce until there was nothing left but rocky heights rising naked to the windswept sky.

"Have you seen any sign of grizzlies?" Shannon asked uneasily.

"Look on that tree to your right."

Shannon looked. All she saw was a place well above her head where the evergreen's thick bark had been scraped off, revealing the lighter wood beneath.

"Do you mean this scar?" she asked.

Whip nodded.

"But it's at least eight feet off the ground," she objected.

"Closer to ten."

"What does that have to do with grizzlies?"

"Silent John didn't teach you much, did he?"

"No. My learning comes from books he brought—*brings* me from time to time so I won't bother him with my chatter."

"When a male bear marks out his territory," Whip said, "he rears back on his hind legs and slashes as high up on a tree as he can."

"Why?"

"An old trapper told me it was to warn off other males. If a wandering male couldn't measure up to the resident claw marks, he just put on his best behavior and drifted to new territory."

Shannon looked at the claw marks and tried

not to think about the size and power of the grizzly bear that had left its sign so high in the tree.

"From the looks of those marks," Whip added, "there's a fair-sized grizzly that stakes his claim here in the summer."

Instinctively Shannon's fingers went to the saddle scabbard. The shotgun's cool stock reassured her. The weapon was loaded, needing only to be cocked before it was ready to fire.

"Don't worry," Whip said without looking at Shannon. "It's early for bears at this altitude."

"Maybe. After the mule was killed, Silent John told me bears are notional creatures. Like Indians. They do or don't do according to their own whims. And a female with cubs is pure poison. You see one and you go the other direction. Quick."

Shannon looked away from the forest and smiled oddly at Whip.

"I think that was the most words Silent John ever spoke to me all at once," she said. "It was his way of telling me how important the information was."

The thought that Shannon had been so essentially alone for the past seven years troubled Whip. It made him feel like he was scheming to steal candy from a baby instead of planning to share mutual pleasure with a widow who understood what passed between men and women.

"Don't worry," Whip said tightly. "Those claw marks aren't fresh. Anyway, most of the time bears want nothing to do with men, except to steal food if you're fool enough to leave some lying around where you're sleeping."

Despite his reassuring words, Whip kept

checking the back trail, as well as both sides of the vague track that led to the high claim.

As Silent John had warned, bears were notional creatures.

Whip saw nothing for his efforts but the untamed beauty of the country itself. It was a place of jagged stone crowns thrust up to the clean wind, of high green divides, and of quaking aspens whispering among themselves while thunderstorms stalked the skyline on stilts made of lightning.

"Can't you get more speed out of the mule?" Whip asked after a long time of silence.

"I'll try."

"There will be sleet before long."

"Hail, more than likely," Shannon said. "Those are mean-looking clouds the wind is pushing toward us."

She urged Razorback to a quicker pace. The mule didn't object much. It, too, had smelled the raw edge of ice on the wind.

Once in the meadow, Whip and Shannon went about making camp as quickly as possible. While she picketed her old mule and Whip's horse, he took the packhorse he had named Crowbait to the south edge of the meadow. There among the trees was a burned ring where Silent John had camped from time to time.

But not recently.

"How did you know this was the most sheltered campsite?" Shannon asked, coming up behind Whip.

"I've been here before."

"When?"

"When I was looking for signs that Silent John was still in the area."

"And?" she asked tightly, afraid that Whip might have discovered proof of Silent John's death.

"No new sign. Not then. Not now. Near as I could tell, no one has been here but me, and I left damn few tracks."

"Did you get up to Rifle Sight?"

"Yes."

Shannon's eyes widened. "Was there any sign of Silent John?"

"Nothing fresh. A broken pickax. A tin can filled with paraffin and sporting a tail of rag for a wick. The rag hadn't been burned at all. The charcoal had been scattered by wind. There were signs of avalanche and a rock slide old enough to have wild-flowers growing in the cracks."

Shannon swallowed and tried very hard not to think of Silent John buried beneath the rubble.

"What about the Chute?" Shannon asked.

"If it's over that ridge and off a bit to the north—" Whip began, pointing.

"It is."

"—then it's still buried in snow. Anyone there is buried, too. There are a few other places someone has been digging, but they're up the north fork and don't show any signs of recent—"

"Why didn't you tell me?" Shannon interrupted.

"That I was looking for Silent John?"

Shannon nodded curtly.

"You weren't talking to me then," Whip said, his voice dry.

"Then why were you looking?"

"Because I don't hold with adultery."

The blunt words weren't what Shannon had

expected. She didn't think of herself and Silent John in those terms, because it hadn't been a real marriage.

Whip turned and faced Shannon fully. He looked very large to her with his broad shoulders and heavy wool coat and his collar lifted to turn the wind. But it was his eyes that held her. His eyes were as untamed as the sky.

"More than once in those first few days," Whip said, "I tried to ride off and keep on riding. But I wanted you too much to keep my hands in my pockets."

"You've done a fine job of overcoming that," Shannon said ironically. "I'm proud of you."

"You're proud, period." Whip smiled a slow, off-center smile. "I like that, Shannon. Gives you sass and vinegar to go with all the honey and cream."

Abruptly Shannon turned her back and found something to do. She was no longer able to meet the sensual knowledge in Whip's eyes without putting her arms around his neck and begging for a kiss that would never end.

Not until camp was secure and a cold supper had been eaten did Shannon say anything to Whip again. She hadn't meant to speak at all, but lightning struck and thunder pounded and then hail started hammering down.

Quickly Whip pulled Shannon beneath the tarpaulin he had drawn over himself when he realized how fast and furious the storm would be. With a few deft, powerful motions, he seated Shannon between his drawn-up knees with her back to his chest.

"Pull your knees up or else your feet will get hammered," Whip said.

Shannon was drawing up her knees even before Whip spoke. Beneath the canvas it was like a sheltered golden dusk, except for the times when the wind tugged some of the tarpaulin out of Whip's fingers or lightning burned so brightly that it turned the world white for a few instants.

"Hang on to this," Whip said.

With her right hand, Shannon grabbed the corner of cold, stiff canvas he was holding out to her.

"And this," he said.

The fingers of her left hand closed around the second bunch of tarpaulin Whip gave her.

"Got them?" he asked.

"Yes."

"Good. Whatever you do, don't let go, or we'll get the coldest bath you've ever taken."

Shannon nodded.

The motion knocked her hat askew. Instinctively she reached up to right the hat. A blast of ice-tipped air swept beneath the tarpaulin. Quickly she dragged her hand—and the cloth—back into place on the ground.

"Sorry," she muttered. "My hat."

"Come back more toward me."

Shannon scooted backward until she felt the warm vise of Whip's thighs closing on either side.

"More," he said.

She edged back an inch or two. "How's that?"

"Not enough. I still can't reach your hat without letting in the storm."

Shannon dug in her heels and rocked her bottom slightly, pushing herself against Whip until she felt the heat of his muscular thighs seeping into her.

"Okay?" she asked.

Whip dragged in a slow, hidden breath. The feel of Shannon's hips rocking softly between his thighs had hardened him in a wild torrent that all but stopped his heart.

"Closer," he said thickly.

"I can't. There's no room."

"There's lots more room. You'd be surprised how close two bodies can get if they put their minds to it."

Shannon muttered beneath her breath and dug in her heels once more, rocking backward a fraction of an inch at a time. She felt Whip's breathing break, heard a low sound that could have been a groan, and sensed the vibrant tension in his body.

"Whip?"

He managed a questioning sound.

"Are you all right?" Shannon asked.

"A little cold around the edges," he said, lying through his teeth. "How about you?"

"A lot more comfortable than I was. You're better for warming than a campfire."

She sensed as much as heard Whip's amusement.

"But my hat is still halfway off," Shannon added. "It's tickling my nose."

"Sit tight. I'll move around until I can get a hand free without freezing us."

Before she could answer, Shannon felt Whip's big body shift against her. The sensual, moving prison of his chest and thighs rubbed over her, sending heat like lightning through the center of her body.

"What are you doing?" she asked in a strained voice.

"Trying to sit on a corner of the damned

tarpaulin so I can get a hand free to fix your hat. Why?"

"Nothing."

Shannon's nose twitched as a lock of hair slid free and slithered over her face. Hail drummed down on the tarpaulin, gathering coldly in the creases. Thunder chased lightning through the storm. Whip's movements continued to send a different kind of lightning spearing through Shannon.

"There," Whip said. "That should do it."

Shannon let out a sigh of relief and tried to relax. She didn't know her own body when Whip was this close to her, moving against her, sharing the very air she breathed.

"Lean back against me," he said.

"Why?"

"Do you want that hat fixed or not?"

Grumbling, Shannon leaned back until she felt the hard coils of the bullwhip on Whip's shoulder. Her hat loosened, shifted, and was tugged firmly back into place on top of her head by Whip's hand.

"How's that?" he asked.

"Better. But now my hair is in my face."

"You're more trouble than a sack full of puppies."

Despite his complaint, Whip was smiling as he reached around Shannon, caught the lock of hair, and tucked it behind her ear.

"All set?" Whip asked.

"Yes. Thank you."

"Nothing else bothering you?"

"No."

"Good. I want you to be able to concentrate on what you're feeling."

"Right now I'm feeling—*Whip*!"

"Hang on to that tarpaulin, honey girl. The hail is damned cold."

Shannon barely heard Whip's words. His big hand had slid inside her jacket and cupped her right breast. Slowly, tenderly, he caressed her until her nipple peaked. He caught the hardened tip between his fingers and pinched lightly.

A gasp came from Shannon as fire licked out from her breast, consuming her. The flames leaped higher as Whip kneaded her soft flesh and tugged at the nipple until it stood proudly against her worn shirt.

"There are times when leather gloves are a real nuisance," Whip said. "Help me, honey girl. Set your teeth in the leather and pull."

"But—"

"I'm just giving you the answer to your question about how you can learn without being touched. You can't. So I'm touching you. If you don't like the way I'm doing it, tell me what's wrong and I'll change it."

Shannon bit down on her lip, trying not to cry out as Whip's fingers teased and delighted her at the same time.

"Shannon?"

The low word was her name and a question and a caress spoken against the nape of her neck.

"Do you want me to stop?" he asked.

"Yes. No. I don't know!"

She took a swift, wild breath. The movement pressed her nipple against Whip's hand. Pleasure rippled through her.

"Yes," Shannon whispered. "Touch me. Teach me."

Whip tried to still the elemental response of his body to her husky words.

It was impossible.

Thank God it's the middle of a hailstorm, Whip thought ruefully. *I'm going to have a hell of a time stopping at a little petting.*

"Help me with this glove," he said in a low voice. "It will feel much better. For both of us."

Whip's hand lifted from Shannon's breast and slid up to her chin, then her lips. Blindly she found the tip of one of his fingers, bit down on the leather, and tugged. She did the same with each finger until he was able to free himself of the glove.

Instantly his hand returned to her breast. Beneath her unbuttoned jacket, his fingertips circled the rigid peak without touching it.

"Does this feel better for you?" Whip asked huskily. "It damn well does for me. You make me think of hot satin and sunlight and a slow, aching kind of lovemaking."

Shannon bit back a cry. Her back arched as she tried to bring Whip's hand closer to her hungry nipple.

With a smile that Shannon couldn't see, Whip bent his head and nudged her hat upward until he could set his teeth against the nape of her neck.

The primitive caress dragged a low sound from Shannon's throat. She bent her head to give Whip greater freedom and was rewarded by another hot, tender bite. At the same time, his fingers caught her nipple and plucked.

Fire blossomed in Shannon's belly. She didn't know that her shirt was giving way a button at a time, making room for Whip's big hand. She only knew that her skin was on fire and his fingers were hard, cool, delicious in their blind caresses.

Whip felt the shiver that went through Shannon's soft breast, felt the rigid crown he had drawn from her, and wished that they were naked in a warm bed rather than fully clothed with a hailstorm beating at their frail shelter.

With a throttled groan, Whip eased his hand over to Shannon's left breast. It was already firm, pouting for his touch, and when he plucked the nipple, it became a velvet dagger thrusting against his palm.

"You have the most responsive breasts," Whip said. "A touch, and they harden."

"I don't—they don't usually—I mean—unless it's cold—wet—oh Lord, I can't think."

Whip smiled to know that he had taken the sharp edge off Shannon's wit and replaced it with the scattered words of a woman whose body was focused entirely on pleasure. It was worth the ache in his crotch to hear her ragged breathing, to feel her writhe slowly against his hand, to sense the sweet violence of the heat gathering between her legs.

"Passion," Whip said huskily.

"What?"

It was a sigh as much as a question. His hand slid from satin slope to velvet crown and back.

"You," Whip said. "It's passion that draws your nipples so tight."

"It's—your fingers."

Laughing, Whip bit the nape of Shannon's neck again. Then he licked the indentations where his teeth had tested the sweetness of her skin.

She moaned and pushed back against him, increasing the force of the caress.

A torrent of heat went through Whip, focusing him in the aroused flesh that now was pressed against Shannon's hip. His teeth raked over her nape less gently than he had intended, but she didn't complain. Instead, she moved against him again, and again he let her feel the lover's caress of his teeth against her nape.

"Like that?" he murmured.

Shannon's answer was a sound that had no meaning, but the slow rocking of her hips between Whip's thighs told him all that he needed to know. He bit her with savage restraint as his hand swept down her body and burrowed between her thighs.

Her breath came in with a swift, ripping sound. Her whole body stiffened as though struck by lightning.

"Easy," Whip murmured.

The advice was as much for himself as it was for Shannon. Through the old trousers she wore, Whip could sense the steamy heat between her legs.

A blast of hail hammered over the tarpaulin. Neither Shannon nor Whip noticed. They were both riveted by the sultry flesh that throbbed only inches from his hand.

"I won't hurt you," Whip said in a low voice. "I just want to feel the fire I've started. I want you to feel it, too. Open your legs, honey girl."

With a shudder, Shannon leaned against Whip fully and gave him what he wanted. Long fingers slid over her, pressed teasingly, cupped her, and held her in the palm of his hand. Slowly his hand rocked back and forth, opening her legs wider, pressing suddenly, urgently, sending a shock of pleasure surging up her body.

Shannon whimpered.

Whip's hand gentled, simply holding her.

It wasn't enough. Instinctively Shannon moved her hips, wanting more of the pleasure he had given her.

Whip unfastened her pants, smiling as he realized that he had never undone a fly before and found a woman's very different flesh awaiting him.

"Whip—your hand—"

"Yes. My hand. Your softness. God, you are soft. Creamy soft and so hot it makes me want to—"

With a curse Whip bit back his incautious words. If he thought about how good it would feel to press into Shannon's sultry, clinging heat, he would probably do something stupid like open his pants and slide her soft little rump into his lap and himself into her at the same time.

Not yet. She's still too naive. She's got to know what she's asking me for when she watches me and smiles and crosses the room to stand next to me.

When she knows what she wants, I'll give it to her. Every hot, aching inch of it.

Shannon made a ragged sound as she felt Whip's palm nestling deeper and deeper between her legs, rubbing over her while pleasure coiled and coiled and coiled until it burst and spilled hotly over his caressing hand.

"I didn't mean—I'm sorry—I don't—I can't—help it—" Shannon said jerkily.

"Help what?"

His hand moved and satin fire pooled again in his palm.

Shannon moaned as pleasure coiled even more deeply for having known just a small release.

"That," she said raggedly.

Whip smiled despite the need raking him. He stroked Shannon again, pressing against the satin knot that stood out from her lush flesh. She shivered and heat licked over him in sultry caress.

"That," Whip said huskily, "is the purest kind of honey."

Shannon looked down and saw Whip's hand moving inside her loose trousers, between her legs, touching her as she had never been touched.

"I shouldn't—let you."

"We're just playing, honey girl. Men and women do this all the time. It's a way of finding out if you want to play for real."

Slick fingertips circled the knot Whip had drawn from Shannon's softness. Instantly she stiffened and shuddered and cried out with surprise.

"Am I hurting you?" Whip asked.

"No," she said, her voice ragged. "It feels—strange."

"Strange bad or strange good?"

As Whip asked, he plucked and felt the hot rush of Shannon's response spilling over his hand.

"Your body says that it feels good," he said, biting her neck. "Damned good."

Shannon's only answer was a whimper and a jerk of her hips with each deft motion of his hand. Pressure coiled and coiled and coiled, driving her toward something she had never known.

"Whip! I can't—stop! Stop! I'm scared!"

"It's all right, honey girl. You're nearly there. Lie back against me and let me take you the rest of the way."

Shannon tried to answer, but Whip was caressing the lush, soft flesh between her legs. She whimpered as pleasure clenched tightly, summoned by his fingers and the pressure of his teeth at the nape of her neck. Helplessly her hips rocked and lifted, seeking something she couldn't name.

Whip knew what Shannon sought. He circled the knot of her passion, caressing her with fingers slick from her wild response. He heard her whimpers come more quickly, felt the tension drawing her body until it was rigid, shaking.

Shannon's breath fragmented over Whip's name and she convulsed with a pleasure that was beyond anything she had ever imagined. Helpless in the grip of ecstasy, she called his name again and again.

It took an act of will for Whip to stop caressing the honey and silk between Shannon's legs. He wanted to sheathe himself in the fire of her body, to feel her softness caress him with every sweet surge of her release.

And then he wanted to spend himself in her fire until he couldn't remember what it was like to go hungry, aching with each breath, each heartbeat.

Shannon made a broken sound and moved against his hand. Heat pulsed between their skin. The air beneath the tarpaulin was steamy, mysterious, exciting beyond anything Whip had ever known.

"You're everything your walk hinted you were," he said roughly. "Honey and fire."

Whip set his jaw against the temptation offered by the girl lying so seductively between his legs, her body open to his hand. Slowly, feeling as though he were tearing off his own skin, he forced himself to release the sultry, honeyed flesh.

He wasn't nearly so slow about getting out from under the steamy intimacy of the tarpaulin. A few swift, savage motions of his hands tucked the tarpaulin around Shannon, protecting her from the violent weather.

"Stay here until the storm's over," Whip said.

"What about you?" asked a muffled voice.

"I'm hot enough to burn ice."

Hail beat on Whip's body as he went to check on the horses. Grimly he hoped it would put out the fire.

It didn't.

10

"Any better luck?" Shannon asked, looking up from the campfire.

"Same as yesterday," Whip said, bending to scratch Prettyface's ears.

Afraid that Whip would see her fear, Shannon looked away from him to Grizzly Meadow where the two horses and the mule were grazing, their tails lazily swatting flies. Golden, slanting light spilled over the land, infusing it with the first rush of true summer heat.

Six days.

For six days Whip had gone up to the Rifle Sight claim while she stayed in the camp. For six days he had hammered with pickax and determination on the stone shoulder of the mountain.

For six days all Whip had found was the sweat dripping down his nose.

"Tomorrow," Shannon said. "It will be better tomorrow. Or the day after."

Whip didn't say anything. He simply slid his big hand under Prettyface's chin and rubbed until the dog's eyes glazed over with pleasure.

When Shannon turned back to Whip, she saw the dark smudges beneath his eyes and the trails perspiration had made through the rock dust coating his entire body. Each afternoon she washed in a basin and rinsed in the stream before he came back. Then she heated more water for Whip's bath. Each night she washed his clothes, and the following day they came back to her stiff with sweat and grit.

Whip had protested that he could work in dirty clothes. Shannon had simply shaken her head and scrubbed harder. It was all she could do to make his work easier. She wished she could do more.

"You should take a day off," Shannon said softly. "You look tired. You work too hard. All day. Every day. You hardly even take time to eat."

"It makes me sleep well at night."

That was true, as far as it went. But it said nothing about how often Whip woke up during the night, sweating from forehead to heels, aching, his body rigid with a kind of hunger he had never known.

Whip wondered if Shannon felt the same.

He wondered, but he didn't ask. Six days ago he had shown her what passion was all about. If she didn't want more, he wasn't going to push himself on her.

It was Shannon's turn to do the asking, and to do it plainly. Blushes and longing looks were for virgins who didn't know what they were asking for, much less how to ask for it. Pretty widows who had just had their first taste of pleasure knew enough about men and sex to recognize the signs of male hunger.

"Sit down on that log," Shannon said. "I heated enough water so that you could take a basin bath."

"Are you saying I smell like old Razorback?"

Shannon ducked her head and looked at Whip from beneath her eyelashes, trying to decide if he was teasing her or simply asking a question. Since the hailstorm, her relationship with Whip had changed in ways she didn't understand. He rarely teased her anymore.

And he never kissed her, held her, caressed her until the world came apart around her and she cried out with pleasure.

"You always smell good to me," Shannon said hesitantly. "I just know that rock dust is uncomfortable."

"Another thing Silent John told you?"

She shook her head. "I learned it the same way you did, at the dumb end of a pickax."

Whip's mouth opened but no words came out. He simply stared at Shannon, unable to believe that her slender arms had ever swung a pickax.

"Well, don't look so shocked," Shannon said. "I'm not nearly as helpless as you think."

He grunted. "You're not nearly as skillful as *you* think."

"I can't swing an ax or a pick like you," she said tartly, "but I can get a job done if I stay with it, and getting the job done is what matters."

With that, Shannon turned back to the fire. Irritation prickled through her. It had become a common sensation in the past few days. She was forever balanced on the razor edge of her temper . . . and she didn't know why.

"Did you find any gold while you were swinging that pick?" Whip asked Shannon.

"No, but I was working a landslide that covered most of the Chute. Rifle Sight is richer."

"According to Silent John."

"I've seen some of the ore he brought back," Shannon said. "There was so much gold in the quartz that the chunks came apart in your hands. He called it jewelry rock."

"He must have cleaned out that vein. From what I've seen, you could work all summer in Rifle Sight and not find enough gold to pay for your supplies."

Fear breathed coolly down Shannon's spine. The gold claims were her freedom. Without them, she was at the mercy of strangers.

"The gold is there," she said tightly.

Whip grunted.

From the corner of her eyes, Shannon watched Whip stretch his arms and shoulders, loosening muscles drawn tight from hour after hour of hard labor. The shirt he wore was dark with sweat, and it clung to every powerful line of his body.

Lord, but that is one beautiful man, Shannon thought. *Just looking at him makes me all edgy and short of breath. When I think of him touching me again . . .*

A delicious sensation cascaded through Shannon's body at the memory of what had happened beneath the tarpaulin. She hadn't imagined that pleasure like that existed short of paradise.

At first the experience had left her feeling shy with Whip. The fact that he hadn't spoken about it in any way since then, or even so much as touched her in passing, had only increased her shyness.

And her irritation.

She didn't understand what had happened when Whip touched her so intimately. She only knew that she wanted it to happen again. Soon.

But obviously Whip didn't feel the same way. He hadn't touched her.

Maybe I should try touching him.

"Would you like me to wash your hair?" Shannon asked. "I know how awkward it is to do in a basin."

The thought of how good her fingers would feel rubbing over his scalp made Whip's body tighten despite the punishing hours of labor he had just finished. His own relentless sexual response to Shannon made his mouth flatten into a harsh line. He didn't like wanting a woman to the point that his body wasn't his own anymore, no matter how hard he worked to exhaust himself.

"No," Whip said curtly. "I've managed my whole grown life without a handmaid. No point in taking up such foolishness now."

"Well, do go and eat some wasps," Shannon retorted. "It will make your tongue seem sweet by comparison."

Whip grabbed the basin of hot water and stalked off toward a nearby grove of aspen trees, where there was an icy creek to use for rinsing off soap. Prettyface followed, leaping and prancing like a puppy. He loved playing tag with shots of water from Whip's quick hands.

"That's it, Prettyface," Shannon called after them. "Desert me! Go follow the yondering man who smiles like a fallen angel and has a temper fully suited to hell!"

Both males ignored Shannon.

With a frustrated sound, she turned back to camp, looking for something to vent her irritability on. All that came to hand was the pickax leaning against the log next to her shotgun.

"I'm not mad enough to hammer stone . . . *yet*," she muttered.

She tested the water in the bucket, which was hanging from a cast-iron tripod over the fire. The water was lukewarm. Barely.

"Go ahead, take all day to heat up," Shannon muttered. "I've got nothing better to do than stand around sticking my finger in cold water."

She hovered around the campfire, feeding fuel into it, testing the water, and wondering if fire burned colder in the high mountains. Surely it didn't take this long to heat water at the cabin.

"I've got the hot spring at the cabin," Shannon reminded herself. "It takes no time at all to get a bucket of hot water for washing clothes."

Sighing, Shannon tested the water for the fifteenth time. It was passably warm.

"Finally. Now I can do the wash. Thunder and blazes, I can see why folks run around in dirty clothes a Comanchero would be ashamed to wear. Heating water for baths and such could make a body crazy."

Just as Shannon bent to take the bucket from the tripod, Prettyface broke into a savage kind of barking that was more a snarling howl of rage than anything else.

A shot rang out.

Water sloshed as Shannon slammed the bucket handle back over the tripod and ran for the shotgun. The sound of another shot overwhelmed the dog's furious sounds.

Whip's shout came as Shannon broke into a run, heading for the aspen thicket. As she ran, she understood what her ears had been trying to tell her—the "shots" she was hearing were the sounds of a bullwhip at work, not a rifle.

The bullwhip cracked and then cracked again, splitting the air like lightning. Whip shouted something that Shannon couldn't understand.

Then came a terrifying kind of chomping, snarling cough, as though the mountain was clearing its throat. Shannon had never heard the sound before, but Silent John had described it often enough.

Grizzly.

"Whip!" Shannon screamed, running harder than she ever had before in her life. "Oh, God, you don't even have a gun!"

She leaped a fallen log, staggered for an instant on landing, then gathered herself and raced on, cocking the shotgun even as she ran.

Shannon saw the grizzly before she saw Whip. The bear was reared up on its hind legs, taller than Whip, wider, terrifying in its strength. The enraged bear was snapping its jaws together. Saliva showed stark white against the dark muzzle. The grizzly's massive paws swatted at the bullwhip that cracked again and again around its head.

Naked to the waist, Whip stood with his back

against a thicket of aspen that was too dense for him to penetrate. It wouldn't have done any good even if he could have hidden among the trees—the grizzly would have broken through the aspens at a gallop.

Nor could Whip outrun the bear, even if the terrain had been flat and open. On level land, grizzlies were as fast as horses. On broken land, grizzlies were faster.

Prettyface leaped and snarled behind the bear, fangs slashing, seeking the grizzly's hamstrings beneath the thick coat of fur. With horrifying speed the bear turned and slashed at the dog with claws longer than Shannon's hand.

The bullwhip cracked and the grizzly straightened. It spun away from the dog and raged deep in its chest, jaws working as though crunching through bone. Blood glistened redly above the grizzly's right eye, proof that the bullwhip had reached flesh despite the protective fur.

But rather than driving the bear away, the slashing bullwhip seemed only to enrage the grizzly further.

It was obvious that sooner or later one of the bear's massive paws would tangle with the long whip, ending its usefulness. Or the grizzly could simply charge the man like an enraged bull. Then the uneven fight would end very quickly.

Shannon ran harder, knowing she had to get in close enough to be certain of killing the bear. Silent John had warned her that a wounded grizzly was the most dangerous animal on earth.

As Whip's arm moved, launching the lash like a bullet right at one of the bear's eyes, he caught sight of Shannon running at the grizzly from the side.

"Get back!" he yelled.

If Shannon heard, she ignored him.

Whip worked the lash with startling speed, creating a high, ripping crackle that held the bear's attention while Prettyface snapped at its heels.

Shannon kept running until the shotgun was almost touching the grizzly's side. She triggered both barrels at a spot just under the bear's left arm.

There was no time for Shannon to brace herself before she fired. The shotgun's fierce recoil knocked her flat in an instant. The grizzly gave an outraged roar and swung a massive paw at the place where Shannon's head had been only an instant before.

Deadly leather coils whistled and snapped tightly around the bear's neck. Whip set his feet and jerked hard, making muscles stand rigidly all the way down his back. Grimly he dragged the choking, mortally wounded grizzly off balance, forcing it to fall away from Shannon's motionless body. The bear hit the earth, bucked and roared savagely, and slashed out with claws at an enemy it could no longer see.

Abruptly the grizzly jerked and went still.

The grove became silent but for the ragged sawing of Whip's breath and Prettyface's snarls as he stalked stiff-legged toward the unmoving grizzly.

"Get back!" Whip ordered.

Prettyface froze.

A deceptively lazy movement of Whip's wrist sent the tip of the lash flicking over the bear's open eyes.

The grizzly neither flinched nor blinked. It was truly dead.

Whip ran to Shannon's side and knelt in a rush. He let out a rough sound of relief when he saw that her eyes were open and she was breathing.

"Where do you hurt?" he demanded.

Numbly she shook her head.

"The hell you don't hurt," Whip muttered. "I saw that grizzly hit you."

Whip's hands hadn't shook during the fight, but they were shaking now as he gently touched the back of Shannon's head, searching for the wound he was sure she must have.

"I'm—all right," Shannon said jerkily, trying to catch her breath and speak at the same time.

"Easy, honey girl. Just lie still until I see how bad you're hurt."

"Just—breath. Shotgun—knocked me—"

Whip's hands hesitated. He looked down into the beautiful sapphire depths of Shannon's eyes.

"Recoil?" he asked.

She nodded and concentrated on breathing.

Saying nothing, Whip probed Shannon's hair with long, surprisingly gentle fingers. When he found only the warmth of her scalp, he moved on down her body. His hands ran over every bit of her and found nothing but heat and a silky female softness that made him feel like he was caressing fire.

Abruptly Whip came to his feet. He looked down at the breathless but otherwise uninjured Shannon for a long, tense moment.

Then he held out his hand to her.

"Can you stand?" Whip asked quietly.

Too quietly.

Warily Shannon looked at Whip's eyes. Where

there had been tender concern a moment before, now there was only wintry gray. His eyes were almost opaque.

She had seen Whip look like that only once before, when the Culpeppers were baiting her. Whip had been furious then.

He was furious now.

Shannon scrambled to her feet without touching his outstretched hand.

"I'm fine," she said. "See?"

"I see that you're a fool, Shannon Conner Smith."

She winced. "Why are you yell—"

"You could have been killed!"

"But you were—"

"I told you to get back," Whip continued, talking over Shannon harshly. "Did you listen? Hell no! You came running up and shoved that antique shotgun right up the grizzly's ass!"

"It was his arm, not his—"

"If the recoil hadn't knocked you down, you would be dead right now! Do you hear me, you little idiot? *You would have died and I couldn't have done a damn thing about it*!"

Adrenaline and anger combined to overcome Shannon's good sense. She put her clenched fists on her hips and glared right back up into Whip's face.

"So what was I supposed to do?" she demanded. "Stand by and darn socks while that grizzly clawed you into pieces too small to use in a rag rug?"

"Yes!"

"Ha! And *you* have the gall to call *me* a fool! Well, let me tell you something, yondering man. When it comes to being a fool, you not only win the race, you also take second, third, and fo—"

Shannon's tirade ended in a surprised sound as Whip yanked her off her feet and buried his tongue in her mouth. She fought for an instant, then gave back the kiss every bit as fiercely as he was giving it to her.

Prettyface snarled and circled the grizzly again, then darted in and set his teeth into the furry hide. He shook his head hard, harrying the prey.

Neither Whip nor Shannon noticed.

It was a long time before Whip let Shannon slide down the length of his torso until her feet touched the ground once more. The rigid arousal of his body told Shannon the same thing the kiss had.

Whip wanted her. All of her.

And all of him was doing the wanting.

"Oh, my," Shannon said raggedly, hanging on to Whip as her knees buckled. "I've been hoping you would kiss me like that every day since the hailstorm."

Whip let out a long, long breath. Then he tilted back Shannon's head and looked at her with eyes that were no longer the color of winter.

"Why didn't you say something?" he asked. "I thought you didn't want me to touch you anymore."

"What was I supposed to do? Walk up to you and say I wanted you to—to—"

"Yes," Whip said simply.

Shannon blushed, bit her lip, and looked up at Whip with eyes as wide and deeply blue as the sky.

"Cat got your tongue?" he teased.

She made a fist and hit him lightly on his muscular shoulder.

Laughing softly, Whip gathered Shannon close

and rocked her slowly from side to side, resting his chin on top of her head.

"How anyone can be so fierce and so shy at the same time is a pure wonder," he said after a few moments.

"I'm not fierce. And I'm not shy."

"Of course not," he said gravely. "You're a tender little mouse who cowers at the first hint of danger. And you're a brazen little hussy who throws herself at a man."

"You're teasing me."

"Not just yet. I'm thinking about it, though." Whip smiled like a cat licking cream. "I'm giving it a lot of thought, in fact."

Shannon couldn't see Whip's smile, but she could hear it in his voice. She smiled in turn and nuzzled against his chest.

Hair tickled her nose.

She made a startled sound as she realized anew that Whip wasn't wearing a shirt.

"What is it?" he asked, holding Shannon away so that he could see her face. "Are you hurt after all?"

She shook her head.

"Then what?" Whip asked.

"You."

"What about me?"

"You're not wearing a shirt."

"I was just getting dressed when the bear showed up. But if it will make you feel better, you can take off your shirt, too."

Shannon stared at him, then laughed out loud.

"Now you *are* teasing me," she said.

She smiled, but didn't rest her head on Whip's bare chest again.

"Does it really bother you to see me like this?" he asked.

"No," Shannon admitted softly. "It's just that the sight of all that silky fur makes me want to pet you like Prettyface."

"Head to heels and back again?" Whip suggested in a deep voice.

For a shimmering instant Shannon looked at Whip from head to heels and back again. The thought of touching him in the same way made her almost dizzy.

"The look on your face . . ." Whip said, laughing. "Come on, honey girl. We'll leave Prettyface to worry over the bear in peace."

Whip swung Shannon up in his arms like a child and began walking back toward camp. He didn't stop until he reached the opposite edge of the forest, where he had made a night camp separate from hers.

"I've been meaning to ask you why," Shannon said, looking at his bedroll, "but you were so darned touchy I thought better of it."

Whip made a questioning sound.

"Why did you camp over here instead of by the fire with me?" she asked.

"This is close enough to hear you if you need me, and far enough that I don't lie awake listening to you breathe, listening to you move, listening to the blankets slide over you the way I want to."

Shannon tried to speak but couldn't. The look in Whip's eyes stole her breath and made heat glitter through the center of her body.

"You couldn't sleep either?" she managed to whisper.

"Passion is a two-way street. Didn't you know?"

She shook her head.

Whip opened his mouth to say something about Silent John's limitations as a lover, but thought better of it. Right now Whip didn't want to think about Silent John.

And he sure as hell didn't want Shannon thinking about Silent John, either.

"Tell me again," Whip said almost roughly. "Tell me that you want me."

"Yes," Shannon whispered. "Oh, yes. I didn't know this kind of wanting existed."

Her words aroused Whip fiercely, yet gave him more self-control than he had had since he first saw Shannon's hips swinging gently as she walked past him in Holler Creek.

The waiting was finally over. She was going to be his lover. Nothing could stop it now.

"It's going to be good, honey girl," Whip said, lowering Shannon to his bedroll. "It's going to be so damned good."

"As good as before?"

"Better."

"I think I'll die of it, then."

Whip's smile was as sensuous as his lips brushing over Shannon's mouth.

"Lie still for me," he whispered against her mouth. "I've been dreaming about how it would be to undress you, look at you, touch you. Now I won't have to live on dreams anymore."

A shiver that was part nervousness and part delicious anticipation went through Shannon. With half-closed eyes, she watched Whip kneel at her feet and remove her boots. He peeled away her much-darned socks and wrapped his hands around her slender feet.

"You're always as clean as sunshine," Whip said.

"The hot spring," she said, and could say no more.

"The Culpeppers ride by hot springs every day, and those boys are dirtier than any Comanchero."

Whip looked at Shannon's long, shiny braids and creamy skin.

"At first I thought you bathed so often because you wanted to be pleasing to me. Then I realized it was just your way. Spearmint and fresh water, honey and cream."

Whip's hands shifted, caressing the sensitive soles of Shannon's feet. She made a throttled sound as her feet arched in sensual reflex.

"Ticklish?" he asked.

"Not . . . quite."

"How about this?"

Whip bent his head and smoothed his mouth over the arch of her foot. Just at the point it would have tickled, he sank his teeth delicately into her skin.

Shannon gasped as she discovered how deliciously sensitive the arch of her foot was.

"Am I tickling you?" Whip asked.

"No," she whispered, staring at him with wide, luminous eyes. "I just didn't know that men kissed women there."

"Did you like it?"

"Yes . . ."

She shivered and made a low sound of pleasure as Whip caressed her other foot. Her response sent an answering tremor through his powerful body.

"There's so much of loving you don't know

about," Whip said, looking at Shannon hungrily. "All the sweet tastes and hidden textures of passion. I'm going to know every last one of yours, honey girl. And when we're too tired to breathe, I'm going to fall asleep deep inside you and wake up with the taste of you on my tongue and then we'll begin all over again, touching and tasting and knowing, being alive in each other."

Shannon didn't understand most of what Whip was saying, but she didn't care. The sensual blaze of his eyes and the gentleness of his big hands told her everything that mattered.

No matter how great Whip's strength, no matter how fierce his hunger, she was safe with him.

Watching with curious, hungry eyes, Shannon allowed Whip to unfasten her shirt and ease it down her arms. Her breasts peaked before he touched them, for she had seen the smoky approval in his glance. Then his head bent, his mouth opened, and he shocked her to her toes by taking the tip of one breast into his mouth.

"Whip."

He made a hungry, questioning sound, swirled his tongue around the hardened nipple, and drew her deep into his mouth.

The rhythmic movements of Whip's mouth sent pleasure stabbing through Shannon, arching her back even as her fingers blindly raked through his hair, holding him close. She had no breath, no thought, nothing but the changing pressures and textures of his mouth as he suckled her, shaping and hardening the nipple even more with each stab of his tongue.

By the time Whip lifted his head, Shannon was twisting slowly beneath him and whimpering softly, feverishly. He looked at her breast, taut and glistening from his mouth, and he let out a ragged breath.

"I've been around the world three times," Whip said in a husky voice, "and I've never seen anything more beautiful than you all shiny and proud from my loving."

"I—didn't—know," she said raggedly.

"You've never been kissed like that?"

Shannon shook her head even as she watched Whip's mouth with shocked, curious eyes.

"Does it matter that I'm as naive as an egg?" she whispered.

"No," Whip said. "Teaching you, watching you respond . . . it gives me a kind of pleasure I've never known."

Whip bent down to Shannon again, and again he taught her something about pleasure. She learned that it could build and build until her body was burning with a need so great she pleaded helplessly with him to end the sweet torment.

He laughed softly and refused to be drawn closer.

"Not yet, honey girl. There are a whole lot of ways of touching and kissing left to explore."

Shannon's eyes opened in disbelief.

Smiling, Whip raked his teeth lightly over one proud breast, then the other. Then he sheathed his teeth with his lips and tested the velvet tension of her nipple.

Pleasure lashed Shannon, making her gasp.

"Whip?"

The husky voice licked over him like fire.

"What?" he asked.

"I can't—take it."

"If I can, you can."

"But I'm not kissing you."

"Not this time. I'm way too hungry for that. Next time, though. Next time I'll teach you how to make me sweat and shake with need of you."

Whip's hands moved with the quickness that was as much a part of him as his fallen angel smile. Shannon felt the rest of her clothes sliding down her legs. Unease went through her, but far stronger was the memory of pleasure she had once known at his hands.

"That's what you're going to be doing before I'm through," Whip said in a low voice. "Sweating and shaking with need of me."

Slowly he ran the back of his fingers up between her legs from her ankles to the dark mahogany cloud just above her thighs. His big hands shifted, circling the top of her thighs, flexing deeply, urging her legs farther and farther apart even as he caressed them.

Then Whip became very still but for the quickness of his breathing.

"I thought nothing could be more beautiful than your breasts," Whip said finally. "I was wrong."

Shannon followed his glance down her body and made a startled sound. She was sprawled wantonly, wholly naked to his eyes, his touch. Reflexively she moved to cover herself, but found that impossible. Whip was kneeling between her thighs, bracing them apart with his knees while he caught both of her hands in one of his own. He was holding her in a gentle, immovable vise.

"Too late, honey girl," he said huskily. "You set free something in me that no other woman has. I don't know what it is, but I'm damned sure I'm going to find out."

One of Whip's fingertips circled the lush flower that had opened for him. Shannon trembled and made a broken sound.

"Tell me again that you want me," Whip said thickly.

As he spoke, he parted the flushed petals with two fingertips, seeking the honey within.

"Yes," she said huskily. *"Yes."*

Shannon's hips moved as she cried out, and his fingertips knew the hot, silky kiss of her desire.

"Honey girl," he whispered. "God, I love feeling your pleasure."

She started to speak, but her breath wedged in her throat as she felt Whip's caress slowly deepen. The feeling of having him within her even by so small a measure was as unexpected as it was extraordinary. Heat swept through her, leaving her skin flushed, sultry, exquisitely sensitive.

But nothing was as sensitive as the flesh Whip was softly stretching even as he caressed her. Pleasure coiled relentlessly inside Shannon, twisted, redoubled, and then held her arched and quivering on a rack of need.

Shannon moaned and moved her hips in a reflex as old as desire, seeking to draw Whip more deeply inside her body.

Instead, Whip's touch lessened as he forced himself to withdraw all but his fingertips.

"Not yet," Whip said, his voice hoarse with fierce restraint. "You're not ready. You're so tight, honey girl. And I'm not as small as your husband was. We'll have to take this slow and gentle for a little longer. Like this."

Shannon moaned as pressure and pleasure

built inside her once more, pushing her toward the shivering culmination she had known once before at Whip's hands. Yet before she could touch that sweet ecstasy, he began withdrawing again, leaving her aching, restless. Then he returned, bringing pleasure with him, a hot teasing that promised heaven and delivered only a bittersweet kind of hell.

Sweating, shaking, Shannon begged him to end her torment. Whip closed his eyes as sweat broke over his whole body. He couldn't look at her, touch her, hear her pleas, and not take her.

"Hold on, honey girl," he said hoarsely. "Just a little more. You're so damned tight. And so hot. Just a little deeper and—"

Whip's words stopped as though cut by an ax. He stared at Shannon in fury and disbelief.

"You're a virgin."

Shannon simply looked at him, not understanding what had made him so angry.

Whip shot to his feet and stood over Shannon.

"Naive, huh?" he said savagely. "Ha! You're naive like a fox, pretty little *widow* lady. You figured I would give you a wedding ring if you could tease me into taking your maidenhood."

Dazed, trembling, Shannon understood only that the culmination she desperately needed had been yanked away from her without warning. She wanted to weep and scream and rail at Whip, but she had no breath.

Whip didn't have the same problem with breathing. And talking. He had never been more furious—or more frustrated—in his entire wandering life.

"What kind of twisted marriage did you have with that old man-hunter?" Whip demanded.

"I don't understand," she said shakily.

"The hell you don't. Silent John was a piss-poor gold prospector, but he was first-class when it came to tracking down men and killing them where he found them, then collecting rewards for their sorry hides."

Shock widened Shannon's eyes.

"He never said—" she began.

"Hell," Whip interrupted savagely. "He never said anything, right? Silent John. Silent as a tombstone. And that was what some folks called him. Tombstone John. He earned that moniker, too."

Whip's glance raked Shannon from forehead to heels. Shame flooded her as she looked at her own nakedness. Her groping fingers found her shirt. She pulled it on and fastened it with shaking hands.

"That man must have had ice water in his veins," Whip said through clenched teeth, watching as Shannon's beautiful breasts vanished beneath worn, faded fabric. "He had you for seven years and barely touched you."

"He *never* touched me."

"Never?" Whip laughed harshly, not believing a word of it. "Even an old killer like him must have liked undressing you and—"

"Silent John was my great-uncle!" Shannon cried, cutting across Whip's words. "He never touched me! Not ever! Not a handshake when I brought down my first deer. Not a quick tug on my braids when he passed my chair. Not even a pat on the head when I learned to make biscuits the way he liked. Nobody has touched me in a tender way since Mama died!"

Blindly Shannon pulled one of Whip's blankets over her hips, shielding her nakedness from him.

"And then you came with your hungry eyes and fallen angel smile and gentle hands," she whispered.

Shannon closed her eyes, shutting out the sight of Whip's face hard with anger and contempt.

"Why didn't you tell me you were a virgin?" Whip asked, his voice flat.

"I did."

"Horseshit."

"Go to hell, yondering man. *Go soon.*"

Whip looked at the girl huddled in a crookedly buttoned shirt with part of his bedroll drawn up over her hips. There was nothing of the hot temptress about her now. She wasn't pleading for his mouth, his hands, his body locked with hers in primal ecstasy.

Whip drew a quick, sawing breath and fought for self-control. Shannon didn't know what she was missing.

But, by God, he did.

"When did you tell me you were a virgin?" Whip asked less harshly.

"When we were talking about me not having a baby."

He thought about it, frowned, and shook his head.

"The subject of virginity didn't come up," Whip said.

Shannon threw him a glittering glance. Her eyes were as brilliant as sapphires.

And twice as cold.

"I asked how you could be sure that you didn't leave any bastards behind," Shannon said flatly. "You said the same way Silent John knew how not to get me pregnant. Well, the way Silent John used was—"

"He never touched you," Whip interrupted, finally understanding, believing. "You've really never been touched at all. My God."

"Hallelujah," Shannon said sarcastically. "If I repeat something often enough, even a gray-eyed yondering man finally learns."

Whip opened his mouth, closed it, and stared at the virgin widow who had turned to honey and melted all over him at a touch.

"My God," Whip repeated. "I—" He shook his head as though coming out of deep water. "It never occurred to me that Silent John and you hadn't been truly man and wife."

"No more than it occurred to me that you didn't understand why I didn't get pregnant," she shot back.

"Chastity. The oldest way of all. Judas H. Priest."

Shannon's anger drained away as she saw how shocked Whip was. In the wake of anger came a fatigue so great that she wanted to put her head on her knees and cry. It was all too much to take in—the grizzly and her fear for Whip and his rage that she had come running up, then the heady sensuality of his touch, and then his fury.

"Shannon?"

"What."

"What did you think would happen after I had you?"

"Think? *Think*? Yondering man, when you touch me I can't think worth a handful of cold spit."

"You weren't trying to trap me into marriage?"

Shannon lifted her head. Between the grizzly and the lovemaking, her braids had come mostly undone. Long, dark strands slid over her cheeks and down over her breasts. Her eyes were dark, unreadable.

"Why on earth would I want to do that?" she asked.

For the second time Shannon had managed to shock Whip speechless.

"What possible use is a man who puts a baby in you and then flits off around the earth until it's time to come back and put another baby in?" she asked.

"I'd never get you pregnant and then leave you," Whip said coldly. "You know me well enough to know that."

Reluctantly Shannon nodded. "You're not the kind to run out on your responsibilities."

"Is that what you were counting on? Getting pregnant so I wouldn't leave?"

Anger stirred in Shannon, but she was too tired to sustain it.

"I'm naive about sex, but I'm not stupid about life," she said wearily.

"What does that mean?"

"Pregnant or not, I will never marry a man who wants me less than he wants a sunrise he's never seen."

Whip flinched at the conflicting emotions in Shannon's voice, in her eyes, in her hands clenching the blanket over her nakedness.

"But you would have given yourself to me," Whip said, angry for no reason.

A shiver of memory and desire went through Shannon.

"Yes," she said.

"Why?"

"Why do you care?"

"Because I'm afraid you're naive enough to believe you love me," Whip said bluntly.

Shannon gave Whip a shuttered glance.

"Either way, it's not your worry," she said. "It's mine."

"I don't want you to love me," Whip said, biting off each word.

"I know."

"Love is a cage."

"Yes. I know that too. Now. Someday I'll thank you for teaching me how to build a cage of sunlight. But not today."

She put her forehead back on her knees, shutting Whip out.

"Shannon?"

"Go away, yondering man. You don't want my body, you don't want my love, you don't want anything but the sunrise you've never seen. Go chase it and leave me be."

11

Whip slammed the pick into rock and felt the shock wave all the way down his arms to his ankles. Stone splintered and sheared away from bedrock, showering him with biting pieces of grit in the process.

Nothing useful lay behind the rock Whip had hammered from the end of the short tunnel. The faint signs of gold he had been pursuing like a demon for the past two days weren't in evidence anymore. Nor could he guess where the faint trace of gold had gone. There were no visible faults, no layering of stone, no way to decide which was the best direction to dig—up, down, sideways, straight ahead, or not at all.

Reno might be able to make this sorry claim pay, but not me.

No wonder Silent John took to man-hunting. It's a damned sight more interesting than hammering on stone.

Despite Whip's sour thoughts, he kept on swinging the pick with all the power in him. He hoped if he worked long enough, hard enough, his body wouldn't stand up and howl every time he thought of Shannon crying out with hunger, opening herself to him, shivering with pleasure at his touch.

Sun-warmed honey in my hands.

Steel pick slammed into the mountain of stone.

A virgin.

Whip swung harder. Rock chips exploded.

Hotter, sweeter, wilder than any woman I've ever known.

Steel met stone and rang like a bell.

A goddamned virgin!

Whip tried to drown out the endless circling of his thoughts with the sound of steel hammering into rock, but it was impossible. He hadn't been in control of his own mind since two days before, when he had knelt between a virgin's legs and learned more about sensuality than he had since he was a man-sized fourteen and a widow woman had hired him to make repairs on her hayloft.

The pick struck, stone shattered, and new rock surfaces appeared. They looked even less promising than the stone Whip had been hammering on.

With a weary curse, he stopped, wiped sweat

and rock dust from his face, and lifted the pick again. He didn't want to go back to Shannon with more bad news about Silent John's useless gold claim. He didn't want to watch her trying to hide her fear of being alone and broke. He didn't want to fight himself not to take her in his arms, comfort her, kiss her until cold fear became wild, searing oblivion. . . .

Rock chips exploded, scoring Whip's skin. He barely noticed. He was too busy wrestling with his conscience and his body's driving need for a virgin widow who would give him everything he asked for as a man and take from him everything he had to give to a woman.

And never ask for more.

That was what was riding Whip with long spurs, digging into his pride and conscience. If Shannon had played the age-old feminine game of baiting the marriage trap with her own honeyed body, Whip could have played the age-old masculine game of stealing the honey without being caught in the trap.

The pick whistled down, sliced through air and slammed into the unyielding stone. The shock of the impact rang in the silence and traveled up through the hickory handle with numbing force.

Whip barely noticed. Whatever punishment the mountain delivered was lost in the larger punishment of the vise of hunger and conscience that was squeezing him mercilessly with every breath, every heartbeat.

He knew that Shannon wasn't playing the marriage game of tease and retreat and leave the quarry wild with hunger. She didn't expect—and no longer even wanted—marriage with the man called Whip Moran.

What possible use is a man who puts a baby in you and then flits off around the earth until it's time to come back and put another baby in?

I will never marry a man who wants me less than he wants a sunrise he's never seen.

Whip believed Shannon's words. He had seen the pain and bafflement in her beautiful eyes as she spoke, a darkness that couldn't be faked by even the most accomplished coquette.

And Shannon was far from a coquette. Her honesty was as unflinching as the land itself.

Someday I'll thank you for teaching me how to build a cage of sunlight. But not today.

Shannon might not understand why Whip would leave her, but she knew that he would. The knowledge was there in her eyes, in her words, in the fine trembling of her hands when she spoke about it.

Whip didn't want Shannon to love him, but she did.

Now she didn't want to love him, either.

Go away, yondering man. You don't want my body, you don't want my love, you don't want anything but the sunrise you've never seen. Go chase it and leave me be.

Whip planned to do just that. But first he had to be certain of Shannon's safety after he left.

The pick attacked cold stone, rang harshly, and retreated only to return again, even more violently. Yet no matter how hard Whip worked, no matter how much solid rock he reduced to rubble, the Rifle Sight claim showed about as much hope of gold as a mule's hind end.

With a searing word of disgust, Whip stopped hammering and leaned on the pick handle. He talked to the ungiving stone the way a teamster talks to his animals, describing in harsh, profane, and inventive detail just how aggravated and disappointed he was with life in general and this chunk of mountain in particular.

When Whip ran out of breath, he wiped his forehead, set aside the pick in favor of his rifle, and headed back to camp even though there was still plenty of sun in the sky. He was tired of wearing himself out on a claim that a blind man could see was as useless as teats on a boar hog.

Rifle on one shoulder and coiled lash on the other, Whip strode down out of the grim, cold notch where meltwater collected and ran down to Grizzly Meadow. He couldn't see the meadow from where he was, but he knew it was there.

Just as Whip knew Shannon would be there, waiting for him. She would heat water for him and he would bathe and pull on the shirt she had cleaned for him yesterday. The cloth would be warm from the sun and sweet from washing, but sweetest of all would be the mixture of caring and womanly hunger and approval in Shannon's eyes when she watched him.

As Whip hurriedly descended the rubble slope at the mouth of the ravine, rocks still cold with winter gave way to unexpected beauty. Willow, stunted aspen, and wind-harried spruce clung in shades of green to every pocket of soil and warmth. The icy rill that flowed from the ravine was joined by other ribbons of meltwater until they became a small creek flowing into Grizzly Meadow. Wild-flowers bloomed in scarlet and purple and yellow and white as rocky slopes gentled into a high mountain meadow.

Smiling, Whip emerged from shadow into the meadow's pouring sunlight, expecting to hear

Shannon's voice raised in welcome when she saw him. But no cry of recognition and delight came. Frowning, he walked even more quickly.

I'm coming in early, but Shannon should be here. Hell, where else would she be?

Unless something went wrong. Another grizzly or . . .

A cold that had nothing to do with sweaty clothing went through Whip. Eyes as clear and icy as meltwater probed every shadow of the meadow.

Whip wasn't even aware of moving until he felt the worn, hard butt of the bullwhip nestled in his left hand and heard the restless seething of the lash at his feet. His right hand was closed around the rifle, his finger was on the trigger, and his eyes were looking for a target. If he found one, he wouldn't have to switch hands. He had learned long ago the value of being able to shoot with either hand.

There. At the far end of the meadow. Movement.

Smoothly Whip pivoted to face whatever was coming toward him.

Feminine laughter rippled through the quiet summer meadow, laughter bubbling as clearly as the creek itself. Suddenly Shannon darted out of the aspens with Prettyface hard on her heels. The huge hound caught up in three bounds and put himself squarely across Shannon's path, forcing her to stop. Quick as a deer she turned and raced toward the aspens again. Prettyface followed, blocked her before she reached the trees, and chased her when she spun aside once more.

The game continued until Shannon was too breathless with laughter to run any longer. She leaned on Prettyface and petted him and praised him and hugged him until her breath came back. Then she told him to stay and tiptoed off into the aspens. Panting, his tongue lolling out in silent canine laughter, Prettyface stayed put and watched with alert wolf's eyes while Shannon vanished into the trees.

Whip watched too, motionless, aching with feelings he couldn't name.

A rock arched out of the aspens to land with a soft thump at Prettyface's side. It must have been the signal for the game to resume, because the hound leaped forward, nose to the ground, tracking his mistress at a lope. Soon Prettyface vanished into the aspens.

Whip waited, smiling, guessing what was going to happen next; the stalk and the laughter stifled into silence, and then the instant of discovery.

A few minutes later he heard laughter and saw flashes of movement in the aspen grove. Shannon burst into the meadow at a dead run, her long legs moving so quickly that they blurred.

No wonder she got to me so fast when that grizzly cornered me. She and that hellhound of hers keep each other sharp.

Despite Shannon's speed, she was no match for Prettyface. The hound caught her in ten strides, barred her way into the meadow, and leaped after her when she took off in another direction.

Whip laughed softly as he uncocked the rifle, coiled the long lash so that it could ride once again on his shoulder, and walked toward the girl and the savage mongrel that played like a puppy with her.

I'll bet Shannon and Willy would get along like a house afire. They both have grit and the gift of laughter no matter how bleak things really are.

Shannon could help with the kids and the cooking, and Cal could keep everyone safe. Even the Culpeppers aren't dumb enough to take on a man like Caleb Black.

And there's always Reno or Wolfe or both of them together if the fight gets too hard for Cal to handle alone. Shannon would be safe with them. She would have Willy and Jessi and Eve for company. Shannon wouldn't be at the mercy of strangers. She would be with . . . family.

I could go yondering again and not always be looking back, wondering if Shannon was hungry or tired or frightened or hurt, needing someone and no one was nearby.

Relief at the solution to his problem swept through Whip, loosening some of the tension that had ridden him without mercy since he had discovered just how innocent a widow Shannon Conner Smith really was. Smiling, he walked even faster into the meadow.

Shannon took one look at the man striding toward her and felt her heart leap with a joy she knew would end in heartbreak. Yet she could no more stop the joy than she could stop the sun from rising at dawn.

She had seen very little of Whip in the two days since he had discovered she was a virgin. When she awoke at dawn, he was already gone to Rifle Sight. He didn't come back until it was too dark to work any longer. By then he was too tired to do much more than bathe and eat and fall asleep.

"I'm glad you came back early," Shannon said.

Whip smiled. "You sure?"

She nodded almost shyly.

"Even though I've been less company to you than that beast?" he asked ruefully.

She nodded again and whispered, "Yes."

Whip looked at the heightened color of Shannon's cheeks, the sweet curve of her mouth, and the endless blue of her eyes. He realized anew how pleased he was to have found a solution to the problem of Shannon's future. A solution that didn't involve marriage.

To *any* man.

"Whip?"

"Mm?"

"What is it? You look as smug as a rooster with twenty hens."

Whip laughed and wished he could hug Shannon. Yet he knew he must not. Touching her would end up only one way—with her virginity gone and him so hard and deep inside her that it would be like tearing off their own skin when they finally separated.

But separate they would, for the undiscovered sunrise would call to him.

"I don't want to hurt you," Whip said, no vnger smiling.

Shannon's smile turned upside down. *Are you leaving? Is that why you came back early? Has that damned distant sunrise called your name?*

But Shannon didn't give voice to the questions that were tearing her apart. There was no purpose in speaking. Whip would go when he wished to. Knowing when he was leaving wouldn't make the remaining moments any better for her.

Knowing would make it worse. Knowing would cut out her heart and leave nothing but darkness in its place, an emptiness she couldn't hide from Whip no matter how hard she tried.

"I know you don't want to hurt me," Shannon said, balancing her voice as carefully as she would a pan of scalding water. "Don't worry about it, yondering man."

"Horse—"

"I'm fully of age," she interrupted, "and I've been warned more than once that you don't want ties. If I get hurt, it's on my head, not yours."

"But—"

"Come back to camp and wash up," Shannon interrupted again, determined not to talk about leaving. "That shirt must be about as comfortable as a handful of nettles. Do you want an early supper?"

"My shirt isn't what's nettling me," Whip retorted. "It's you. My conscience won't let me leave you at the mercy of the likes of the Culpeppers."

Then don't go!

But Shannon knew better than to voice the cry of her soul. Whip would go no matter what his conscience and her heart wanted. Nor did she want him to stay at the cost of his own happiness, his own heart and soul.

He loved the unseen sunrise more than he would ever love any woman.

"Tell your conscience that I got along just fine before I met you," Shannon said.

"But you didn't!"

"How do you know?" she asked reasonably. "You weren't here."

"Damn it, Shannon—"

"Yes. Damn it."

With that, she started walking to camp. Prettyface and Whip fell into step along either side.

"How did the digging go?" Shannon asked.

Whip grunted. "Worse than yesterday, better than tomorrow."

She tried to think of something encouraging to say. She couldn't. Fear for her own future was too strong. Yet if she talked about that, Whip would think she was building a cage for him, nailing him to the floor of her dreams while his own dreams called to him from the other side of the bars.

"I'm not going to find gold in Rifle Sight," Whip said bluntly. "Not tomorrow. Not the day after. Not ever."

Shannon stumbled, then righted her balance before Whip could touch her.

"There are other claims," she said through pale lips.

"You said Rifle Sight was the best one."

"Maybe I was wrong."

"Maybe. But I've got a better idea."

"What? Jump somebody's claim?" she asked bitterly.

"I'll leave that to the Culpeppers, and I'll leave robbing trains and banks to the James brothers."

Shannon smiled despite her unhappiness about the lack of gold on Silent John's claims.

"What's your idea?" she asked.

"The only real safety for a girl like you is in a nice town with picket fences around the houses and church bells ringing and a good, settled man for a husband. But—"

"I don't want to marry," she interrupted curtly.

"—there's no place like that in Colorado Territory," Whip continued.

"Thank God," Shannon muttered.

Whip ignored her. As he spoke, his original enthusiasm for the idea of sending Shannon to live with Caleb and Willow returned in full force.

"The next safest place for you would be Cal's ranch," Whip said firmly.

Shannon cut a sideways look at Whip and said not one word.

"The ranch lies beyond those peaks," Whip said, pointing to the west, "about a day's ride from your cabin on a good horse in good weather. Two days if you take Razorback. Four if you walk."

"And no time at all if you stay home," Shannon pointed out pleasantly.

Whip kept talking as though she hadn't said a word.

"Cal and Willy—my sister, remember?"

"Cal is your sister? I thought he was a man."

Whip shot Shannon a glittering glance.

She gave it right back.

"Willow is my sister. Caleb is her husband." Whip spoke slowly and clearly, as though to the town drunk. "They have a little boy and are expecting another baby before too long. All she has for help is Pig Iron's wife, and she only speaks Ute."

"They should send to Canyon City. Or Denver. Or maybe one of your other widows would want the job. I don't."

Whip made a frustrated sound and raked his fingers through his hair, dislodging his hat. He caught it with careless ease and pulled it firmly back into place. He wished his temper were as easy to get hold of and keep in hand.

"They wouldn't treat you like hired help,"

Whip said carefully. "You would be like . . . family."

"After my step-aunt, I'd rather be treated like hired help," Shannon said.

"Damn it! All I meant was you would have a safe place to live with good people around you and kids to enjoy and—"

"Their home, their children," Shannon said tightly. "Thank you, no. I'd rather have my own home and my own children to love."

The thought of Shannon having another man's children sent raw rage through Whip. The sheer violence of his reaction shocked him. He locked his jaw against the reckless words crowding his throat.

What business of mine is it whose kids she has, Whip asked himself savagely, *as long as they aren't mine*?

The rational, reasonable, logical question did nothing to cool Whip's elemental rage. Teeth clenched, he turned away from the girl who could trigger his temper—and his body—as no one else ever had.

That's the end of it, Whip told himself. *Time to pull up stakes and find another sunrise before she has me so hog-tied I can't even move.*

But first I have to see that the stubborn little witch is safe, whether she likes it or not.

Without a word Whip turned away from Shannon and strode toward his own camp.

Shannon let out a long breath, took in another one, and looked at her hands. They were trembling slightly. She knew she had come very close to making Whip lose his temper entirely.

But she didn't know what she had done to cause it.

"I wish you could talk, Prettyface. You're a male. Maybe you could tell me what I did."

The big, brindle hound nudged Shannon's hand. He didn't know what was wrong with his mistress, but he sensed something was.

"I thanked him very politely for his offer of a place in his sister's house," Shannon pointed out.

Prettyface's tongue lolled as he panted softly.

"Well, maybe not *very* politely," she conceded, "but I certainly wasn't rude. Not nearly as rude as he was."

The hound cocked his head to one side, ears erect, looking as though he were about to speak to Shannon.

"If only you could talk." She sighed deeply. "But you can't. So I guess I'll have to ask Whip why he got so furious when I said I wanted a home and children of my own. It's not like I was asking *him* to provide either one."

Unsettled, torn between anger and hurt, Shannon walked after Whip.

But when she got to his campsite, all her questions fled. Whip was quickly, efficiently, packing up his belongings.

No! Oh, Whip, don't leave me yet.

Shannon's short fingernails bit into her palms as she tried to stem the tears burning against her eyelids.

I won't cry. I knew it was coming. I just didn't think it would be like this. In anger.

Shannon started to speak, then thought better of it. She couldn't trust her voice not to reveal her hidden tears. Silently she turned away and went to her own campsite.

By the time Shannon heard Whip's big gray horse walking toward her campfire, she could trust herself to speak. Whip pulled the horse to a stop and dismounted without a word.

"Leaving?" she asked him evenly.

"I told you I was."

"Yes."

Shannon looked at her hands, took a deep, secret breath to calm herself, and smiled up at Whip.

"Thank you for all you've done, Whip. If you ever come back through here—oh, that's right. You never chase the same sunrise twice." She made a vague, jerky gesture with her right hand. "Well, thank you. Are you certain you won't take some pay? You've done so much and I do have a bit of gold left."

Whip looked at Shannon's pale face and trembling hands and wanted to comfort her and shake her at the same time. Silently he stalked past her and began packing up her camp.

"What are you doing?" Shannon asked after a minute.

"What does it look like?"

The tone of Whip's voice made Shannon flinch.

"It looks like you're packing my gear," she said.

"Do tell."

Whip rammed some dried food into a burlap bag and looked around for more.

There wasn't any.

That, too, irritated him. It reminded him of just how close to the edge Shannon had been before he came along, and how close to the edge she would soon be after he left.

Unless she took a job with Willow.

"Why are you packing my gear?" Shannon asked distinctly.

"Because you're coming with me."

Shannon's eyes closed. *I refuse to lose my temper over a yondering man who can't see love when it's right in front of him.*

When Shannon's eyes opened, they were as furious as Whip's. But her words weren't. They were well chosen, spoken in a low voice, and very distinct.

"You weren't listening very well," she said. "I'm not going anywhere except up to Rifle Sight to dig for gold."

"Oh? You going to eat grass while you dig?"

Shannon blinked. "No."

"Then you better ride as far as your cabin with me. There aren't enough supplies left up here to keep even a stubborn little idiot of a girl alive."

"Don't worry. There's no 'stubborn little idiot of a girl' around to eat the supplies. There is, however, a thick-shouldered, thickheaded, blind man with the appetite and disposition of a starving grizzly who—"

Abruptly Shannon remembered that she had promised herself not to lose her temper with this stubborn, blind mule of a man.

"There are enough supplies for a day of digging," she said with false calm.

Whip looked at the cloud-seething sky and then back to Shannon.

"By this time tomorrow, it will be storming fit to drown Noah," he said. "A smart little girl would get her rump moving down the hill to shelter."

"A smart little girl wouldn't be up here—"

"Amen."

"—with a rock-stubborn blind man!"

"Pack up," was all Whip said.

Shannon didn't move.

With a savage curse Whip turned to her.

"You calling me stubborn," he said coldly, "is like the pot yelling at the kettle for being black."

"Do I sense agreement on the subject of your stubbornness?"

"Right now we couldn't agree on water being wet, but that doesn't change the facts. There's no gold in Rifle Sight. There's a storm coming. There aren't enough supplies to see you through the storm."

Shannon wanted to dispute Whip's words, but she knew he was right. She had been so busy playing with Prettyface and arguing with Whip that she hadn't bothered to look at the sky.

She came to her feet in a graceful movement that belied her ragged men's clothing.

"Fine," Shannon said grudgingly. "I'll ride with you as far as my cabin."

"Don't do me any favors."

"Don't worry, yondering man."

Despite their mutual ill temper, Whip and Shannon worked side by side breaking the camp, understanding what must be done without discussion.

By the time Crowbait was packed and Razorback was saddled, much of Shannon's anger had bled away into a numbing kind of sadness. She doubted it was the same for Whip. His face was still set and his eyes were still narrowed as he swung into Sugarfoot's saddle.

Prettyface ranged out around the horses and mule as they took to the vague trail down the mountain. The trip to the cabin was accomplished swiftly and in a silence that made Shannon's heart ache. Not until they were at the cabin door did Whip speak.

"Gather up some supplies while I check Crowbait. He's walking kind of light on his left forefoot."

Shannon dismounted and went into the cabin. There weren't many supplies left, but she didn't grudge a mouthful of them to Whip. He had bought the food, after all, and shot the game. She had done nothing but cook and eat.

She packed all but one day's worth of her supplies into a burlap bag and carried it out to Whip. He tied the bag onto Crowbait's pack with a few rawhide strings.

"All set?" he asked.

Numbly Shannon nodded.

Whip swung up into the saddle and looked down at Shannon. The pain in her was almost tangible.

"Hey, honey girl," Whip said gently, tilting her chin up to him with his left hand. "Turn that smile right side up. People as stubborn and hot-blooded as we are will argue from time to time. Nothing wrong with that."

Shannon gave Whip a trembling smile. She brushed her lips over the soft surface of his riding glove.

"Thank you," she said in a low voice.

"For what?"

"Not riding off in anger. I . . . I don't think I could have endured it . . . not knowing where you were, knowing only that you were angry when you left."

For an instant Whip could only think how good it would have felt if Shannon's lips had been against his skin instead of his glove. Then the implications of her words sank in.

"You'll know where I am," he said flatly. "You're coming with me."

Hope flared like lightning across Shannon's soul.

"I am?" she asked.

"Bet on it."

"Where are we going?"

"To Cal's ranch, just like I said."

Shannon closed her eyes and fought against the desire to take whatever Whip offered, just so long as she could be with him.

"No, thank you just the same," Shannon said quietly. "I've got claims to work and Cherokee to look after and game to hunt and—"

"Judas H. Priest, you do know how to push a man."

"—Prettyface wouldn't do well with strangers," Shannon finished in the same quiet voice. "I'm staying here, where I belong."

Whip looked down at the slender, determined girl. He couldn't help admiring her spirit even as it infuriated him.

"What's to keep me from picking you up, tying you to that old mule, and taking you wherever I want?" Whip asked.

"Common sense."

Whip hesitated, then let air hiss out between his teeth.

"You're going to fight me every step of the way, aren't you?" he asked.

"I'm not going anywhere with you, so I can't very well fight you every step of the way, can I?"

Shannon never even saw Whip move. Suddenly a hard arm was around her and she was jerked off her feet. Whip held her against his body with an ease that angered her even as it set her blood on fire.

It set his blood on fire, too. She could see it in the sudden dilation of his pupils, feel it in the hard tension of his body, taste it in the hot kiss that left her shaking and clinging to him, whispering her foolish love for a yondering man.

"It won't work," Whip said roughly, hating himself and the girl who watched him with love in her eyes. "I won't stay here. I won't love you."

"I never asked—"

"The hell you didn't," he interrupted savagely.

Whip put Shannon's feet back on the ground so quickly that she staggered. He jerked the packhorse's lead rope off Sugarfoot's saddle horn, freeing Crowbait.

"I want you like hell on fire, but I won't give up my soul to have you. That's what love is, honey girl. Giving up your soul."

He backed Sugarfoot away from Shannon, spun the horse on its hocks, and set out across the meadow at a fast canter.

"Whip!" Shannon called. "I didn't—I really didn't mean to ask for your love!"

Nothing came back to her but the fading drumroll of Sugarfoot's hooves.

Only when Whip was out of sight did Shannon notice that he had left his pack animal and all the supplies with her. She stared at Crowbait's patient brown eyes and fought not to cry out against the sadness that was sweeping over her like a cold wind.

Even though Whip was furious, he had thought of her welfare rather than his own.

"Whip!" Shannon called. "Come back! I can't

help loving you any more than you can help not loving me!"

Only silence answered Shannon, a silence that echoed with Whip's good-bye.

I want you like hell on fire, but I won't give up my soul to have you. That's what love is, honey girl. Giving up your soul.

12

Prettyface nudged Shannon and whined deep in his throat. The movement and the sound reminded her that she was standing in front of her cabin with tears cold on her face. Taking a deep breath, she concentrated on the long list of things that must be done if she was to get through the summer, much less the coming winter.

Crying definitely wasn't on the list.

She put one hand under Prettyface's big jaws and rubbed his head with her other hand. His shrewd wolf's eyes glazed with pleasure. She smiled slightly, smoothed thick fur back into pace, and put her cheek against his broad head.

"I'll be all right, Prettyface," she said. She straightened and released him. "Go rustle up your dinner while I unpack Crowbait and Razorback and picket them in the meadow."

Prettyface stood, head cocked, watching Shannon.

"Go on, boy. I know you're hungry. The pickings were pretty slim for you up in Grizzly Meadow. Go."

Waving her arm in the direction of the meadow

and forest beyond the cabin, Shannon repeated her soft command.

After a moment Prettyface turned and trotted off to the edge of the meadow. He put his nose to the ground and began quartering the area for scent of game.

Shannon turned to Crowbait and Razorback. She unsaddled the mule, switched bridle for halter, and turned to the packhorse. As she worked over the neat diamond hitches securing the supplies, she felt tears crowding her eyes again. It had been Whip's hands that had tied the knots, Whip's hands that had loaded the pack saddle, Whip's hands that had smoothed the blanket pad in place and adjusted the halter.

"Don't think about it," Shannon whispered. "There's too much to be done. Crying over a stubborn yondering man won't butter any biscuits."

Shannon tried not to, but her hands still lingered over the pack saddle and supplies, touching everything that Whip had touched, until finally everything was put away in its place. Numbly she led the animals into the meadow to picket them so that they could graze their fill of the sweet grasses.

Just as Shannon was driving in the second picket pin, she heard Prettyface break into savage barking. Her heart hesitated, then beat frantically.

Prettyface made that sound only when strangers came too close.

Motionless, cursing herself for being so addled by Whip's leaving that she had forgotten to carry the shotgun, Shannon scanned the meadow's edge for any sign of men.

Abruptly two long-legged mules appeared at the edge of the concealing forest and came swiftly toward Shannon. She leaped to her feet and spun toward the cabin, only to find two more Culpeppers between her and the shotgun she had stupidly left behind.

Shannon didn't waste any breath calling for help. There was no one around but Prettyface, and he had already warned her. She whirled away from the two-pronged attack and raced for the forest, praying that she had enough speed to make the cover of the trees ahead of the racing mules.

Before Shannon was halfway to the forest, the beating of hooves sounded louder and louder in her ears. Even as she strained to run faster, she knew she was losing the race. She simply wasn't quick enough to reach the trees before the Culpeppers caught her.

A long, wiry arm reached out and grabbed Shannon just beneath the rib cage. Darcy wasn't strong enough to lift his struggling prize into the saddle, but he hung on no matter how hard she clawed and bit and screamed.

"Clim was right," Darcy crowed, slowing his mule. "She's plumb full of piss and vinegar!"

Beau grunted. It had been the extent of his conversation ever since he had learned just how fast and accurate a bullwhip could be.

"Hold still, darlin'," Darcy said. "I'm just as ready for it as you are, but Beau gets firsts, him bein' the oldest and all. I get thirds, so save your fightin' till—*eeeiow*!"

The words ended in a cry of shock and fear as Prettyface came up on Darcy's blind side and leaped straight for his throat.

Darcy dropped Shannon in order to protect

himself. An instant later, one hundred and forty pounds of enraged dog slammed into Darcy's shoulder. The force of the attack knocked him right out of the saddle.

Prettyface followed Darcy down, snarling and snapping the whole way.

Shannon landed on hands and knees on the other side of the mule from the fight. No sooner did she hit the ground than she was on her feet and running again. As she ran, she yelled at Prettyface to break off the attack and flee, for she knew the Culpeppers would have no mercy in them for the loyal hound.

Just as Shannon reached the forest, she glanced back. There was a snarling, swearing tangle of flesh and fur on the ground. Beau was still in the saddle. His six-gun was drawn. The barrel tracked the fight, waiting for an opening.

Inevitably, it would come.

Tears streaming down her face, her breath tearing at her lungs, Shannon raced into the forest, taking the chance Prettyface had given her to escape. And as she ran, she prayed that she could circle back up the mountainside, sneak into the cabin through the cave and grab the shotgun before it was too late to help Prettyface.

Shannon was only partway up the mountainside behind the cabin when Beau's six-gun opened fire.

Whip reined Sugarfoot to an abrupt halt at the edge of one of the trail's many crossings of Avalanche Creek. The horse chewed unhappily at the bit, but was otherwise quiet.

Listening intently, motionless but for his eyes, Whip probed the shadows and forest in all directions. He neither saw nor heard anything to explain his deep unease.

"You're imagining things," he muttered.

Yet still he heard Shannon's voice calling his name with every shift of the wind, every stirring of the forest, every swirl of water over rocks.

Whip, I really didn't mean to ask for your love.

His big hands clenched into fists.

"Damn you, Shannon. You're tying me in knots."

I love you, yondering man.

Whip closed his eyes. His fingers were so tightly clenched that the reins cut even through his riding gloves.

"I don't want your love," he said through his teeth. "I don't want to feel beholden. I can't stay in just one place, honey girl."

Suddenly Sugarfoot's ears pricked and his elegant gray head whipped around to watch the trail behind him.

His rider heard the sounds, too.

Back toward Shannon's cabin, someone had opened fire with a six-gun. Shannon didn't own a weapon like that.

But the Culpeppers did.

Whip spun Sugarfoot around and spurred him. As the horse leaped forward, Whip checked that his repeating rifle was safe in its scabbard. There were times when a bullwhip just wouldn't get the job done. Whip was certain this was one of those times.

Bending low over his mount's neck, Whip urged the horse to a reckless pace. Rocks and trees raced by, but it seemed to him that he was nailed to the ground, moving at a snail's space, slow as dawn on the longest night of winter.

He would have sold his soul to be able to reach Shannon before the Culpeppers hurt her.

Sugarfoot pounded back up the Avalanche Creek path, taking the fork in the trail at a dead run, leaping rocks and rotting logs without a break in stride. When the forest thickened again, Sugarfoot slowed just enough to be able to avoid or jump over the natural obstacles that were strewn across the trail. Small runoff channels and big boulders, freshly fallen trees and trees that had long ago fallen, all of them flashed beneath the hooves of the hard-running horse.

Whip rode Sugarfoot like a big cat, never coming loose no matter which way the horse jumped, always ready with a steady pressure on the reins to help Sugarfoot gather himself after a difficult jump.

As Sugarfoot hurtled yet another log, more shots came from up ahead. The sounds were much closer now. There was no doubt that it was a six-gun. Several six-guns, in fact.

No rifle answered.

No shotgun boomed.

"Run, you big gray bastard," Whip said through his teeth. *"Run!"*

Spurs reinforced Whip's command. Sugarfoot flattened out and gave everything he had. Nose stretched into the wind, tail streaming behind, the horse tore through the forest at a flatly dangerous speed. One misstep, one mistake, and both man and horse would go down in a tangle of broken limbs.

Whip knew it but didn't care. In his mind was the memory of how the Culpeppers had watched Shannon with eyes that were even more lewd than their words.

And now she was at their mercy.

The trees ahead thinned, telling Whip that the meadow was immediately ahead. As much as he wanted to gallop right up to the cabin, he knew it would be stupid. He wouldn't be much good to Shannon if he got cut down in a Culpepper cross-fire .

And he had no doubt it was the Culpeppers who were after Shannon.

Whip pulled hard on the reins. Sugarfoot sat on his hocks and slid to a stop in a turmoil of dirt and forest debris. The meadow was only thirty feet ahead. Rifle in hand, bullwhip over his shoulder, Whip kicked his feet free of the stirrups and jumped off. He landed on his feet, running hard.

Before he reached the edge of the trees, a rope shot out of the shadows and tangled around his feet. He rolled as he fell, yanking free of the rope and regaining his balance with a feline twist of his body.

But it was already too late.

When Whip stood, he was looking right up the barrel of Floyd Culpepper's six-gun. Whip could tell the man was Floyd because he was holding his gun in his left hand. His right wrist was wrapped tightly in rags that might have been clean once, but no longer were.

Pale blue eyes watched Whip with an expression somewhere between malice and glee.

"Lookee here, Clim. Darcy was right about this ol' boy hotfooting it back here if'n he heard shots."

Clim turned aside and spat a brown stream of tobacco juice.

"And here you thought Darcy was just trying

to cut me out of my rightful turn in that little widow's saddle," Clim added.

Rage and something more gripped Whip, a feeling as though his guts had been cut out and were falling away, leaving him cold all the way to his soul.

"Whoever touches Shannon is a dead man walking," Whip said.

Floyd's smile revealed sharp, uneven teeth.

"Right fine sentiments," Floyd said mockingly, "but you ain't in no position to be making no brags. Drop that long gun, boy. And that bullwhip, too."

Whip obeyed, but his gray eyes never stopped measuring the distances between himself and Floyd's drawn gun and Clim's holstered weapon.

"You see a knife, Clim?"

"Nah. 'Sides, no thick-chested West Virginia boy can hold a candle to me in a knife fight."

"Walk," Floyd said to Whip, gesturing with his bandaged wrist toward the meadow. "You try to get away and I'll kill you quick as a rabbit."

Whip didn't doubt it.

"Give the signal," Floyd said to Clim.

Clim whistled shrilly, three short blasts of sound followed by silence.

After a few moments, a whistle answered.

"Move it, boy," Floyd said to Whip. "They're waiting for us, and Beau ain't a waiting kind of man."

When Whip moved forward it was with a peculiar, gliding grace. His weight was always poised on the balls of his feet, ready to jump or lash out in any direction at the first sign of carelessness from his captors. He held his hands oddly, just away from his sides, his fingers slightly curved as though in relaxation.

"Told ya," Floyd said to Clim after a few steps.

"Told me what?"

"This here ol' boy ain't much account without his bullwhip and rifle. He's as heedful as a well-trained hound."

Clim grunted. "Damn big hound. Even bigger than the one Beau shot. We'd of had that gal if'n that cur hadn't jumped Darcy when he grabbed her."

Hope stabbed through Whip. It sounded like Shannon might have gotten away.

"Don't git yer water hot," Floyd said to Clim. "Beau ain't much on talkin' lately, but he can still track slick as sin. He'll get the widow 'fore she gets too far. Hell, ain't no place for her to go to anyways."

Clim eyed the big man walking in front of him. Despite Whip's surrender, the coiled ease of his stride made Clim nervous.

"Why don't you just shoot him and get done with it?" Clim asked.

"Beau," Floyd said succinctly. "He's got a bone to pick with this ol' boy. You want to be the one to tell Beau he can't have no fun 'cause you done gone and killed him?"

Whatever Clim said was too guttural to understand.

Whip walked from the shadows of the trees into the full sunlight of the meadow.

To the girl hiding and catching her breath after a reckless scramble down through Silent John's bolthole to the cave and from there into the cabin, Whip's appearance was dream and nightmare combined.

It can't be Whip! He rode away.

Seeing Whip captive to the Culpeppers wrenched Shannon's mind away from her fear for Prettyface, forcing her to concentrate on saving herself, for only then could she save Whip.

Still unable to believe that Whip had come back, Shannon leaned forward and peered through the ill-fitting shutters again.

There was no mistake. Sunlight flashed on hair as pale as corn silk. Sunlight outlined clean, powerful limbs and wide shoulders. And sunlight showed that Whip's hands were empty of weapons.

Nor did the bullwhip lie in quiet coils on his shoulder.

Shannon bit her lip against a hunger to cry out to Whip, to tell him that he wasn't alone, that she would help him. But crying out would be as foolish as walking barefoot through a campfire.

Quickly Shannon turned away from the shutters, went to the front door, and lifted the shotgun down from its pegs. As she reached to open the door, she heard a voice call from just beyond her cabin.

"Told ya you'd get him!"

"Yah. Easy as shootin' a hen on a nest," called someone from the meadow.

Heart beating wildly, Shannon shifted the shotgun and lowered the heavy bar into place across the door. She tiptoed back to the shutter and peered out again.

Whip was walking across the meadow toward the cabin. Behind him rode two men on mules. Another man stood ten feet from the cabin door, watching the three men approach. The ripped state of the nearest man's clothes—and the bloody marks on his face and arms—told Shannon that this was the Culpepper who had grabbed her, only to go down beneath Prettyface's attack.

Shannon's hands tightened on the shotgun as she thought of her loyal dog. Then she forced herself to think of here and now, and the danger to Whip and herself.

There was no time to claw her way back out the bolthole and down the mountainside to surprise the Culpeppers. Whatever she did would have to be done from here.

And soon.

I could open the cabin door, aim at the man closest to me, and let fly with both barrels of buckshot.

Frowning, Shannon thought about it. She would certainly take one man out of the fight that way, but it would leave Whip still captive to the other Culpeppers, who would likely shoot him out of hand before she could reload her own shotgun.

Then there was the fourth Culpepper to worry about. He had to be around somewhere. Probably he was still in the forest trying to figure out which way she had gone. If he heard shots, he would come on the run.

Maybe I only need one barrel on the closest Culpepper. Then I could fire the second barrel at the other two.

After a moment Shannon decided that was her best bet. She would wait until the other two Culpeppers were within range, and then she would tell them to let Whip go. If it came to shooting, surely Whip would have enough sense to drop to the ground. Knowing his quickness and size, he probably would take a Culpepper down with him.

White-knuckled, Shannon stood by the shutters and watched her front yard with the intensity of a cat at a mouse hole, counting each step Whip and his captors took toward the cabin. If she were really lucky, Whip would manage to separate himself from the group somehow. That way she wouldn't have to worry about wounding him when the buckshot spread out in its characteristic deadly pattern after it left the barrel.

Slowly, carefully, moving by fractions of inches, Shannon opened the shutters enough to rest the shotgun on the windowsill. She cocked the hammer on one barrel, settled her finger lightly around one of the two triggers, and waited, watching the man who held a gun on Whip.

"Any sign of the gal?" Clim asked, dismounting.

Darcy shook his head. "She took off into the forest."

Beneath Whip's predatory readiness, relief spread through him, warming the soul-deep cold that had begun when he thought of Shannon's fate at the hands of the Culpeppers.

"But we'll get her, just like we got her damned hound," Darcy added. "Beau's tracking her now."

"Looks more like Prettyface got you," Whip said. "Chewed you up and spit you right out. No hound likes the taste of skunk."

Darcy shifted his cud of tobacco from one side of his mouth to the other and measured Whip for a grave.

"It was the last thing that damned hound did," Floyd said. "Beau shot him."

"I should have killed Beau back at Holler Creek," Whip said. "Live and learn. Or in your case, boys, live and die ignorant."

Darcy spat a stream of tobacco juice onto Whip's boots.

Whip just looked at him and wondered what kind of insults it would take to distract Floyd long enough for Whip to grab his six-gun. Then Whip would feed the gun to Darcy. Sideways.

"What do we do now?" Floyd asked.

"Wait for Beau."

"I need whiskey. Goddam wrist is paining me something fierce," Floyd muttered, eyeing his right arm in disgust. "Every time my mule takes a step it feels like somebody's a-hammerin' on my arm."

Whip smiled. "It doesn't look too good, Floyd. All those red streaks. And the smell. Lord above. I'm surprised you can stand it."

Darcy and Floyd ignored Whip.

"You'll have to wait," Darcy said to Floyd. "Beau's got the tanglefoot with him."

Behind Whip, Floyd's mule shifted and stamped its right foreleg, dislodging a deerfly.

"Goddam," Floyd groaned. "Hurts."

"Then get down and quit your bellyaching," Darcy said. "I'm still bleeding from that damned hound and you don't hear me whining, do ya?"

A saddle creaked as Floyd prepared to dismount.

Adrenaline went through Whip. It was the moment he had been waiting for. From the corner of his eye he could see Floyd's shadow sliding along the ground as he moved.

He was still holding the six-gun in his left hand, keeping the barrel trained on Whip. Floyd's natural grip was right-handed. As he dismounted the barrel of the six-gun wavered from its target. It was just for an instant, but an instant was all that Whip had been waiting for.

In a blur of motion, Whip spun around and simultaneously kicked outward. His boot connected with Floyd's injured wrist. Floyd made an odd sound and forgot all about the six-gun. Pain knocked him senseless.

Whip struck the gun from Floyd's loose fingers and whirled around again. The side of Whip's left hand connected with Darcy's neck.

The sound of the impact was lost in Clim's bellow of rage. He drew a long knife and lunged for Whip's back.

But Whip was no longer there. He spun aside so suddenly that Clim went staggering past Whip, off-balance, knife slicing uselessly at air. A flashing movement of Whip's hands added to Clim's forward momentum.

Clim went head over heels and landed flat on his back. When he rolled to his feet and lunged again, Whip slipped the knife attack as he had before, grabbed Clim on the way by, and launched him headfirst into the side of the cabin. Clim hit with a force that shook the logs . . . and then he slid down onto the ground and lay very still.

Just as Whip bent over to check Clim, Shannon screamed from inside the cabin. Her high cry was cut off by the thunder of a shotgun blast.

The window was closer to Whip than the door. He kicked the partially open shutters aside as he vaulted over the windowsill, counting on surprise to help him against whatever he found inside.

Shannon spun toward him, her face pale and her hand frantically cocking the shotgun.

"Easy, honey girl. It's just me."

Shannon made a small sound and stood, swaying, her eyes huge in her bloodless face.

"I—" she said. Her voice broke. "A Cul-Culpepper—the cave—he—"

Whip saw the open cupboard door behind Shannon. A man's boots stuck out into the room, toes up. There was blood on them.

Shannon started to turn back toward the cupboard. Before she could finish turning, Whip took the shotgun from her hands and stepped between her and the fallen man, blocking her view.

"You did what you had to," Whip said gently. "I'll take care of it now. You go outside and make sure that Floyd doesn't get into mischief."

"F-Floyd?"

"The one with the bandaged wrist."

"What about the other t-two?"

"I don't think they'll be much trouble," Whip said neutrally. He handed Shannon the shotgun again. "Go on, honey girl. I'll be out real soon to collect their weapons."

Whip unbarred the front door and watched closely as Shannon walked by him. Her eyes were too dark and her skin was much too pale, but her hands were steady on the shotgun. She kept walking until she was in a place where she could watch all three Culpeppers at once.

"You'll do, Shannon Conner Smith," Whip said beneath his breath. "You've got real sand."

Whip turned and went to the cupboard. He lit the lantern and held it above Beau Culpepper.

After a single look Whip blew the lantern out and went to Shannon.

"Is he dead?" she asked starkly.

"Yes."

Shannon closed her eyes for an instant. A tremor ripped through her, but her grip on the shotgun didn't loosen.

"He had a knife in one hand," Whip said, "and a six-gun in the other. Don't feel bad for him. He's had it coming for a long, long time. It's just too bad you had to be the one to deliver it."

Shannon took a steadying breath. "Prettyface—"

She could say no more.

"I'll look for him," Whip said. "But first, I'd better see to these boys."

To Whip's surprise, Clim was still alive, but only barely. Darcy hadn't been so lucky. Floyd was already coming back to his senses, moaning and complaining every breath of the way.

Talking softly, Whip went to one of the mules.

The animal eyed him warily but made no attempt to flee; obviously the Culpeppers had trained their mounts not to be upset by a little gunfire and blood. With a few quick motions, Whip untied the blanket roll behind a saddle.

"I've never seen a man fight like you did," Shannon said, watching Whip and remembering his flashing, always unexpected movements. "Did you learn that in West Virginia?"

"China."

With one hand Whip removed Darcy's weapons. With the other, he shook out a blanket and covered the dead man. Then Whip turned to the other Culpeppers.

"The Chinese have tricks that made what I did look like child's play," Whip added.

Shannon made a disbelieving sound.

"It's true," Whip said. "The man who taught me didn't come up to my breastbone and weighed less than you. But he could lay me out like a fish for filleting in about five seconds flat. Damnedest wrestling tricks you ever saw."

While Whip spoke, he stripped away guns and knives from the fallen men, retrieved his own bullwhip, and put it on his shoulder. Then he bound Clim's wrists and knees together with rawhide thongs. He did the same for Floyd, ignoring the groans.

"Where did they jump you?" Whip asked Shannon as he stood up.

"Halfway between here and the big stump on the far side of the meadow."

Whip went to Shannon, tilted her chin up with his hand, kissed her lips lightly, and released her.

"You keep an eye on things here," he said. "I'll bring Prettyface back to you."

For a moment Shannon looked at Whip with haunted blue eyes. Then she nodded and turned back to watching Culpeppers.

Whip swung up onto a mule and headed out into the meadow. When he neared the place Shannon had described, he began quartering the tall grass and wildflowers. It didn't take him long to find the big hound.

Cursing under his breath, Whip looked down at Prettyface. Bloody cloth was still gripped in his jaws. A shallow scarlet groove went across his skull, just above the glazed, half-open eyes. Another wound left a bright strip of blood across his brindle chest. A third bullet had clipped his haunch.

Blood welled slowly from the wounds.

Whip made a startled sound and dismounted in a single rushing movement. An instant later he was kneeling by Prettyface's side. The hound's flank rose and fell slightly, steadily, as much a proof of life as the fact that his wounds still bled.

"You're a tough son, aren't you?" Whip said in a low voice.

Gently, thoroughly, he went over the big brindle body. Prettyface flinched once and made a high sound.

"Easy there," Whip said soothingly. "Looks like you got kicked pretty good, and you're bleeding in three or four places, and knocked sillier than a squirrel from that crease on your skull, but you're young and strong. You'll live to play with your mistress in the flowers again."

Before Prettyface could regain his senses completely, Whip eased the big hound into his arms, stood up, and grabbed the mule's rein. The dog whined, but made no other protest as he was carried across the meadow to the cabin with the mule following along behind.

The first thing Whip saw as he approached the cabin was a big stranger standing off to one side of the yard, watching him with eyes the color of gunmetal.

Damnation, Whip thought grimly. *I sure to God hope that man's name isn't Culpepper.*

"Shannon?" Whip called.

"If you mean the girl with the shotgun, she's inside the cabin, fixing to ventilate my spine if I do something foolish."

Whip looked past the man to the window. Sure

enough, the barrel of the shotgun was poked through the window, plainly tracking the stranger's every breath.

Prudently, Whip stepped to the side.

The dark-haired stranger nodded slightly, understanding Whip's move. If the shotgun went off, Whip wouldn't be in the way of any stray buckshot.

"Take care of your hound," the man said, looking at Prettyface with sympathy. "I'll keep."

Then the man's eyes changed, becoming as hard as flint when he glanced at the three Culpeppers on the ground.

Whip knelt and lowered Prettyface gently to the grass. As Whip stood again, the long lash dropped from his shoulder. The butt of the bull-whip came into his left hand as though summoned. Leather coils seethed and rippled restlessly at his feet.

"Come on out, Shannon," Whip said clearly. "Prettyface is cut up some, but he'll live."

The shotgun barrel vanished from the window. The cabin door opened and banged shut as Shannon ran out, hope and fear clear in her face.

"Prettyface?" she asked huskily.

"Right behind me. Watch that shotgun, now."

Shannon didn't bother to answer Whip. She had already uncocked the shotgun and was kneeling by her dog, making soft, happy noises.

Whip never took his eyes off the tall, long-boned stranger whose riding cape, trousers, and boots had once been part of a Confederate uniform.

"You know these boys?" Whip asked.

"Culpeppers, from the look of their mules."

"Friends of yours?"

"I've been hunting them ever since Appomattox. All eleven of them."

"Any particular reason?" Whip asked mildly.

"They're wanted, dead or alive, in Texas. During the War Between the States, they murdered three young Texas women and sold their children to the Comancheros. By the time the fathers came home from the war, found out what had happened, and went to rescue their children, it was too late. Every last child was dead."

Whip didn't ask any more questions. He didn't need to. The man was obviously a former Confederate officer. Whip suspected that the man's wife had been one of the three young women murdered by Culpeppers.

As for the rest, Whip had only to look at the man's bleak eyes to know that his children had been among the missing.

"Hunting Culpeppers, huh?" Whip asked softly. "Well, this is your lucky day, my friend. Those three are Clim, Darcy, and Floyd."

"Dead?"

"Darcy is. Clim and Floyd are alive for the time being. Wouldn't bet a Confederate dollar on their chances, though. Clim's back is broken and Floyd's wrist smells like it's gone bad."

"Gangrene?"

Whip nodded.

"From the fight in Holler Creek?" the stranger asked.

"Wasn't much of a fight. I took them by surprise and just kept at it until the job was done."

If one corner of a mouth lifting slightly could be called a smile, the stranger smiled.

"Thought it might be you," the man said,

looking at the long, restless lash. "Whip, isn't it?"

"That's what they call me."

"I'm called Hunter since the war."

"Hunter," Whip said neutrally, nodding.

"Heard Beau was with them," Hunter said, gesturing to the Culpeppers.

"He was."

"Then he got away again," Hunter said savagely. "Damn his slippery hide! Excuse me, ma'am."

"Don't apologize," Shannon said without looking up from Prettyface. "I'm no gentle Southern lady. I just killed a man."

Hunter's black eyebrows rose. "A Culpepper?"

Shannon nodded curtly.

"Well, ma'am, some folks would argue that a Culpepper doesn't count as a man," Hunter said. "Especially the folks who buried what was left of those three young women."

Hunter turned back to Whip.

"Which way did Beau go?" Hunter asked.

"Straight to hell, I imagine."

"He's dead?" Hunter asked, looking around again.

Whip nodded. "In the cabin."

Hunter gestured with his head toward Shannon, asking a silent question.

Again, Whip nodded.

Some of the fierce tension left Hunter's body. Not until he began to relax did Whip realize just how poised for battle Hunter had been.

"I owe you," Hunter said simply. "There was five hundred dollars on Beau's head, two hundred on Floyd and Darcy, and one hundred on Clim. I'll see that you get it."

"No," Shannon said fiercely. "No blood money. We wouldn't have killed them if we had a choice."

Hunter looked at Whip. Again, the left corner of Hunter's mouth turned up very slightly, not even enough to disturb his black mustache.

Though he didn't say a word, Whip knew that Hunter understood what Shannon hadn't yet realized: once the Culpeppers had grabbed Shannon, they had signed their own death warrants as far as Whip was concerned.

"If you'll help me load the Culpeppers on two mules," Hunter said, "I'll give them to the first bounty hunter I find."

"You're not taking them in yourself?"

"Abner, Horace, Gaylord, Erasmus, and Jeremiah are still alive. Erasmus and Jeremiah are rumored to be on their way to Virginia City. I'll be looking for the other three now that these boys are taken care of."

"What about the rest?"

"My brother Case is tracking Erasmus and Jeremiah. When the Culpeppers split up, we split up, too. Case drew the short straw, so he only got to chase two of the sons of bitches. He'll make up for it, though. I expect he might beat me to Virginia City."

"Eleven, you said," Whip muttered. "Is that all of them?"

"All there is to speak of," Hunter said dryly. "But Pappy Culpepper was a tireless old goat. I expect he left quite a few eggs in other nests before my daddy shot him."

"Eleven. Damnation. What about the rest of the alphabet? Am I likely to meet them any time soon?"

"Not likely. They're buried back Texas way."

Whip didn't have to ask who had done the burying. Hunter had a look about him that reminded Whip of Caleb Black; a good man, but hard as flint.

The kind who made a very bad enemy.

"Hope you get the last of them," Whip said.

"We will. You can count on it."

Whip smiled slightly, glad that his name wasn't Culpepper.

"Get on one of those racing mules and fetch that shaman," Whip said, turning to Shannon. "He can nurse Prettyface while we're gone."

Shannon's head snapped up. "Where are you going?"

"We," Whip corrected. "We're going to my sister's ranch."

Shannon opened her mouth.

"No," Whip said, cutting across whatever she had been going to say. "Common sense be damned. You're going with me this time if I have to tie you to the saddle."

13

Shannon awoke with a start and looked around wildly, heart pounding. It was first light, with stars fading in the east. She was in a small bedroom. A man was calling in a low voice from the porch to the corral. Another voice answered.

Whip's voice calling.

Caleb Black's voice answering.

That was what had awakened Shannon. The

sound of men's voices. Even three days after the brutal fight at her cabin, she was jumpy, flinching at sounds, looking over her shoulder to make certain she wasn't being followed.

Shannon drew a ragged breath. The scent of coffee and biscuits and bacon curled against her nostrils. Her stomach growled in instant response. She and Whip had arrived at such a late hour the previous night that Willow had done little more than greet them before going to bed. The trip had taken so long because Shannon refused to ride either of the two racing mules Hunter had left for her.

Hurriedly Shannon got out of bed and dressed, not wanting to lie abed while others were up and working. From what Whip had told her, Willow had her hands full with her young son, her pregnancy, and cooking for all of the ranch hands. Not to mention sewing, mending, knitting, cleaning, washing clothes, ironing them, tending the kitchen garden, feeding the chickens, collecting eggs, and the hundred other small jobs that added up to a mountain of work.

It was no easier for Caleb, who had the cattle and horses to tend, wood to chop, fences to build and mend, outbuildings to construct and maintain, waterholes and troughs to keep clean, horses to shoe, barns and corrals to muck out, calves to brand, horses to break, furniture to make . . . the list was endless.

With quick steps Shannon went down the wooden stairs from the attic loft where she had slept. She hurried through the house to the kitchen.

Willow was working over the wood stove, frying bacon and making biscuits and stirring a pot of stewed fruit. Her hair was heaped in gleaming golden coils on her head. If the sunlight color of Willow's hair hadn't told Shannon that this was Whip's sister, the catlike tilt of her wide hazel eyes would have.

"Good morning, Mrs. Black," Shannon said.

Willow turned and smiled. "Call me Willow, please. It's the western way to be informal."

"Willow," Shannon repeated, smiling in return. "Then you must call me Shannon."

"That's a pretty name," Willow said. "Has the West given you a nickname yet?"

Shannon didn't think honey girl qualified as a nickname. And even if it did, she wasn't about to mention it to Whip's little sister.

"Not yet," Shannon said.

Then she smiled slightly, looking at the pronounced curve of Willow's pregnancy pressing against her dress.

"It beats me how Whip can call you Willy," Shannon said.

"Whip?" Willow frowned, then smiled. "Oh, you mean Rafe."

"Tall, wide-shouldered, sun-haired, handsome as a fallen angel and thickheaded as a Missouri mule?"

Willow snickered. "That's Rafe. He calls me Willy because I used to follow my brothers around like a tomboy."

"How many brothers do you have?"

"Five. Matt lives less than a day's ride from here with his wife, Eve."

"Matt?" Shannon asked.

"You've probably heard him called Reno. That's the name the West gave him. Half the time I call him that, myself, just like I'm getting used to thinking of Rafe as Whip."

"Silent John mentioned Reno by that name," Shannon said. Then quickly, wanting to avoid the complex subject of the man who hadn't been quite her husband and was no longer alive in any case, Shannon asked, "Where are the other Moran brothers?"

"Scattered all over the world from Scotland to Burma to the Amazon jungle, last I heard. But that was years ago. They could be anywhere now."

"The yondering streak must run wide and deep in your family."

The haunted tone of Shannon's voice made Willow turn and look over her shoulder. A glance told Willow that her first impression of Shannon had been correct. The slender, edgy girl with the spectacular sapphire eyes was more than a little taken by Rafael "Whip" Moran.

"Yes, I suppose so," Willow said, turning back to the stove. "Even if we had been stay-at-homes, the war would have scattered us to the winds. There was no home to come back to."

"Yes," Shannon said simply.

"Sometimes I hear the gentle rhythms of the South in your voice," Willow said as she sifted flour.

"Virginia," Shannon said, "a long, long time ago."

"Is that why you came west? Did the war take your home from you?"

In another person the question would have been prying. But Willow's voice and gentle hazel eyes made it clear that sympathy rather than curiosity lay beneath the question.

Shannon closed her eyes for an instant, wondering how to tell this gentle Southern lady about the hell on earth that Shannon's life had been before Silent John had come and taken her to Colorado Territory.

"Never mind," Willow said quickly. "I didn't mean to pry. Would you like a cup of coffee, or do you prefer tea?"

"Do you really have tea?"

The wistful question told Willow a great deal.

"We always have tea. Jessi—Wolfe Lonetree's wife—was raised in Scotland and England. So was Wolfe, partly."

"Wolfe." Shannon frowned. "Whip has mentioned him."

"Not surprising. Rafe earned the nickname Whip the day some Canyon City toughs were talking indecently to Jessi because she married a man who is half Indian."

A vivid memory came to Shannon—the blurring speed of Whip's wrist, the harsh crack of the bullwhip, and the bright blood on Beau Culpepper's dirty mouth.

"That's how I met Whip," Shannon said.

Willow made an encouraging sound as she bent to remove a pan of biscuits from the oven. Though Willow hadn't asked, she was very interested in how her brother had come to be in the company of the wife—or, according to Whip, the *widow*—of one of the most notorious manhunters in the West.

"Some no-account claim jumpers name of Culpepper were in Holler Creek at the mercantile when I came in to buy supplies," Shannon said. "The Culpeppers started talking about me. I didn't like the vile things they were saying, but . . ." She shrugged.

"You were alone?" Willow asked as she deftly transferred biscuits to a napkin-lined basket.

"Yes," Shannon said. "I tried to keep Whip from mixing in. I was afraid he would get hurt, four armed men to his one, and Whip wasn't even carrying a gun. The Culpepper boys have an ugly reputation around Echo Basin."

Willow's breath caught at the thought of her beloved brother taking on four men.

"The Culpeppers kept on talking filth," Shannon said. "Then suddenly there was a sound like a shot and blood was on Beau's mouth and another sharp sound and another and Culpeppers were jumping and yelling like they had kicked over a hive of wasps. By the time I realized it was the bullwhip, the fight was nearly over."

Willow wiped her hands on her apron and let out a long breath.

"I've seen my brother do some fancy tricks with that bullwhip of his, but four armed men at once . . ." Willow said, shaking her head.

"They didn't expect it," Whip said from beyond the doorway. "That made it a whole lot easier."

Shannon spun around.

Behind Whip loomed Caleb Black.

"Don't do a damn fool thing like that again," Caleb advised dryly.

"I didn't exactly *plan* on doing it the first time," Whip retorted.

Caleb gave a crack of laughter, walked into the kitchen, and touched Willow's hair with a gentleness that astonished Shannon.

"How's my favorite girl?" he asked softly.

"Getting big enough to be two of your favorite girls."

Smiling, Caleb bent down and said something that only Willow could hear. The sudden pink on her cheeks and the smile on her generous mouth spoke eloquently of a woman who was well pleased with her man, and he with her.

"Is that biscuits I smell?" Whip asked.

"Nope," Caleb said quickly. "It's your imagination."

"Huh. Likely story."

Caleb picked up the basket of biscuits and pretended to conceal it beneath his work jacket.

Smiling, Whip held out his left hand. On his palm were two steaming biscuits.

Shannon made a startled sound. She hadn't even noticed Whip reaching for the biscuits, yet there they were in his hand.

"Thought you might feel that way," Whip said, "so I helped myself while you were whispering sweet nothings in my baby sister's ear."

Willow rolled her eyes and shook her head.

"You two," she said in mock disgust. "A body would think I made only one biscuit at a time and divided it crumb by crumb among all the help."

"I've been meaning to talk with you about that," Caleb said, bending down. "Among other things . . ."

Shannon blinked and tried not to stare. She was almost certain she had seen Caleb's lips skim across Willow's ear.

"Shoo," Willow said, laughing and pushing on her husband's broad back. "If you keep distracting me, I'll burn the bacon and put too much salt in the biscuit mix."

"You heard her," Whip said, grabbing Caleb's arm. "Move, man. You don't want to interfere with Willy's biscuits."

Laughing, struggling just enough to make Whip work a little, Caleb allowed himself to be led from the kitchen. Shannon watched them go with a look of wonder on her face.

"You look like somebody just hit you with a board," Willow said, trying not to smile.

"I feel like someone did," Shannon admitted. "Whip is so . . . different here. I mean, he smiled and sometimes laughed and such back in Echo Basin, but not like this. Not . . . playful."

"Whip knows that as long as he's here, he won't have to guard his back or his words or anything else. We're his family."

Shannon hoped her yearning didn't show, but she was afraid it did.

"Home for a yondering man," she whispered.

"That's my brother," Willow agreed, measuring out the salt. "A fiddlefoot and a wanderer. He's been like that since I was knee-high to a racing mule."

A child's fretful cry came to the kitchen. Willow looked at the flour and at the oven. Then she sighed, washed her hands in a basin, and wiped them on her apron.

"Excuse me," Willow said. "Ethan doesn't have his father's patience. If I don't fetch him out of that crib and nurse him, he'll yell down the house."

"Go ahead. I'll finish the biscuits for you. Have the hands eaten?"

"Pig Iron's wife cooks for them lately."

"Then we'll need four more pans of biscuits, right?"

Willow's honey-colored eyebrows rose. "How did you know?"

"Whip is good for two pans all by himself."

"So is Caleb."

Shannon smiled slightly. "Yes, I figured that from the size of him. Which leaves one batch of biscuits for us."

"If we're quick enough," Willow said, her voice dry.

"I'll stand over them with a loaded shotgun."

"The men?"

"The biscuits. The men are big enough to look out for themselves."

Laughing, Willow went to her son, whose cries were getting louder with each moment.

By the time everyone sat down to breakfast, Ethan had been fed, bathed, and dressed in clothes Willow had made for him. He sat next to Willow in a highchair that Caleb had carved from an old fir tree. Shannon sat on the child's other side.

The habits learned while tending to her step-cousins quickly came back to Shannon. When Ethan became fretful for his mother's attention, Shannon gave him a bit of biscuit to mangle or a sip of warm milk from the small cup in front of him. Sometimes she dipped a spoon in the stewed fruit and let him lick the naturally sweet juices.

The kitchen was warm and rich with the scent of food. Small dishes of jam studded the wooden table like rubies. Whip had brought in bright yellow wildflowers and put them in a canning jar in the center of the table. Blue-and-white-checked napkins wrapped the biscuits and covered the laps of everyone but Ethan. The mugs for coffee and tea were a thick, cream-colored ceramic that held heat for a long time. The plates were of the same creamy ceramic, glazed to a high sheen. The knives and spoons and forks were all made from the same plain metal whose patina came from daily use and vigorous scrubbing.

"Shannon? Aren't you hungry?" Whip asked.

She started and looked at her plate. It was empty. Whip was patiently holding a basket of biscuits out to her.

"I was just trying to remember the last time I saw a matched set of dishes and flatware and napkins," Shannon said. "It all looks so pretty I almost hate to eat."

"Eat anyway. You're too thin."

"I've done nothing but eat ever since you showed up," she muttered.

"Good thing, too. When I first saw you, you were skinnier than a bitch nursing twelve pups."

"How could you tell?" she challenged. "I was wearing a man's jacket and trousers!"

"I could tell."

The raking, sideways look Whip gave Shannon ended the argument by stopping her breath in her throat. The silver smoldering of his eyes told her that his hunger for her hadn't abated one bit.

Caleb looked down at his plate, hiding his amusement. Clearly Whip had a powerful male interest in Shannon. It was equally clear that Whip hadn't bedded the slender girl who might or might not be a widow. They lacked the ease with one another that lovers enjoyed.

But they certainly didn't lack the fire. The air fairly burned when Whip watched Shannon with hungry silver eyes. It was the same when she looked at him, a hunger that was almost tangible.

Whip had told Caleb that he believed Silent John was dead. Shannon hadn't spoken of her missing husband at all.

Caleb hoped it wasn't lack of proof of Silent John's death that was keeping Whip and Shannon from the affair each plainly wanted. Many a man had died in the West with no one to know of his passing but God—particularly when the man was a loner and man-hunter like Silent John.

"Whip tells me you have a cabin up above Echo Basin," Caleb said.

"Yes, on the north fork of Avalanche Creek," Shannon said.

"I remember chasing Reno through there a few years back," Caleb said. "Pretty place, once you get used to the altitude."

Shannon smiled. "That's all I remember about the first month or two I lived there, being breathless and feeling like I was carrying a fifty-pound sack of flour around on my back."

"Hard to grow much food up there," Caleb said.

"It's worse than hard," she said. "Sometimes there are only six weeks from the last frost of spring to the first frost of winter."

"It must be lonely for you, being the only woman," Willow said.

Shannon hesitated, then continued spreading bright red jam on a biscuit.

"To be lonely," Shannon said slowly, "you have to have someone to miss. I didn't leave behind anyone I cared about when I came west."

"But you spend so much of your time alone," Willow said.

"I have Prettyface."

"Prettyface?" Willow asked.

"The biggest, meanest, ugliest quarter-breed wolf you've ever seen," Whip said dryly. "He was still healing up from indigestion, so we left him with the shaman."

Caleb snickered, for Whip had told him about the Culpeppers.

"Indigestion, huh?" Caleb asked mildly. "Is that what you call it?"

"Yeah," Whip said. "The Culpepper he tried to eat would have gagged a skunk."

"Honestly, Rafael," Willow said. "How can you make a joke out of it? They had you at gunpoint!"

"Not when I jumped them. They were no more expecting my Chinese fighting tricks than they had expected the bullwhip."

Shannon made an odd sound. "If you had seen Whip move, you wouldn't have worried about him. He had them down and out cold before I could blink."

"All the same, big brother," Willow muttered, "one of these days you're going to bite off more than you can chew all by yourself."

"He already did," Shannon said, "in a place called Grizzly Meadow."

Caleb turned swiftly toward Shannon. His uncanny speed had been one of the first things she had noticed about him. She had thought no man could be quicker with his hands than Whip, but she no longer doubted that Caleb was faster.

"What happened?" Caleb asked Shannon.

"Whip took on a grizzly with a bullwhip."

Caleb turned on Whip. "A grizzly? Judas Priest! I thought you had better sense!"

"It wasn't exactly my idea," Whip said wryly. "I was having a bath quiet as you please, and then Prettyface went on the warpath and I turned around and there that damned bear was reared up on his hind legs. All I had was the bullwhip, so I used it."

"You drove off a grizzly with a bullwhip?" Caleb asked, astonished.

"No. Shannon came running up and shoved her rusty old shotgun—"

"My shotgun is cleaner than your bullwhip," Shannon cut in.

"—up against the grizzly's heart and let him have it with both barrels," Whip said, ignoring her interruption. "Killed him deader than a stone."

Caleb looked back at Shannon with new interest in his odd, whiskey-colored eyes.

"That took a lot of courage," Caleb said.

"Courage?" Shannon asked, and laughed curtly. "I was plain scared, but I'm such a bad shot I knew I had to get in close to do anything useful. Just wounding the grizzly would have been the death of us all."

"So you ran right up and blew that grizzly to kingdom come," Caleb said, watching her with unblinking amber eyes.

Shannon looked at Caleb rather warily.

"Are you going to yell at me too?" she asked.

Caleb smiled, making his black mustache shift and gleam in the lantern light.

It struck Shannon that in a dark, hard kind of way, Caleb was every bit as good-looking as Whip.

"Is that what Whip did?" Caleb asked. "Yell at you?"

"Yes."

"No," Whip said simultaneously. "I merely pointed out that Shannon was a triple-dyed idiot for racing in where she had no business and nearly getting herself killed. Prettyface and I about had that grizzly on the run."

Caleb snorted. "Did the grizzly know it?"

Whip shot his friend a hard look and then concentrated on demolishing the pile of biscuits on his plate. It still bothered him that Shannon had risked her life for him and never once had hinted that he owed her anything for it. Not even so much as a thank-you or a hug.

Instead of thanking her, he had yelled at her. That bothered him, too.

No surprise there, Whip thought sardonically. *Everything about that girl bothers me.*

"If my brother doesn't have the manners to thank you," Willow said, "I do. You're welcome to come to our ranch anytime, and to stay for as long as you like."

"Amen," Caleb said. "Much as I hate to admit it, I'd miss the sound of Whip's flute calling up the dawn when he comes visiting."

"And just who accused me of stampeding the cattle with my 'spirit pipes'?" Whip asked instantly, grateful for the change of subject.

"Must have been Wolfe," Caleb said.

"Huh," was all Whip said.

Shannon hid her smile. She also tried to hide her longing as she glanced sideways at Whip. She doubted that she was successful.

She had quickly learned that not much got past Caleb's amber eyes.

After everyone had eaten, Caleb and Whip went out to check on the ranch animals. Willow went about her chores, which Shannon insisted on going alongside her.

The first day set the pattern for the days that followed. Shannon worked as Willow did, whether it was cooking or sewing or cleaning. When Willow protested that Shannon was doing too much, Shannon simply laughed and said it was much easier than what she would be doing if she was in Echo Basin.

After supper on the fourth day that Shannon and Whip had been at the ranch, Willow coaxed Caleb to get out his harmonica and play some of her favorite songs.

Soon the haunting strains of a waltz were floating through the house. Lanterns glowed in shades of sun-bright gold throughout the main room of the house, softening everything their light touched. The spare lines of furniture and hand-made rugs were transformed into solid, gracious forms.

Smiling, Whip went up to Willow, bowed with polished grace, and held out his hand to her.

"Madam," Whip said gravely, "as hostess, the first dance of the evening is yours."

"I'm not as graceful as I was the last time we danced," she warned.

Whip's smile was haunting, almost wistful.

"You're a beautiful woman, Willow, and never more so than when you're carrying the child of the love you and Caleb share."

Willow flushed and smiled and allowed her older brother to help her to her feet. She curtsied with the ease of a woman who had been raised with all the refinements wealth and natural elegance could provide.

When Willow stepped into Whip's

outstretched arms, he held his sister as though she were made of fine, very fragile crystal. Their hair was as bright and golden as candle flames, their eyes gleamed with pleasure, and their steps blended smoothly. Together Willow and Whip glided and turned gracefully through the room while Caleb's harmonica transformed the night with music.

Shannon watched brother and sister dance with a feeling close to envy. She, too, had once known what it was to attend balls, if only by peeking through the second-floor balustrade and watching the swirls of silk and satin and music below. Too young to dance and too old to be sleepy, she had passed many an hour dreaming about the time when she would be of an age to join the laughing, silken dancers.

But before that time had come, the world had changed. Silks and gowns and balls vanished from Shannon's life before she could enjoy them first-hand.

The final notes of the waltz quivered through the air. Shannon sighed and turned to Caleb.

"I didn't know a harmonica could make such beautiful music," she said in a husky voice.

Caleb smiled slightly. "You've lived way off in Echo Basin too long. The only music you have to compare with my harmonica is the howling of the wolves."

"Would it surprise you to know that I enjoy the wolves' music—as long as I'm safely inside the cabin?"

"Nothing about a girl who charged a grizzly with an antique shotgun would surprise me."

The approval in Caleb's eyes made Shannon flush and smile shyly up at him at the same time.

"If you can spare time from flirting with my brother-in-law," Whip said coolly, "we could rest Willow's feet and dance together."

"I don't know how to dance and I wasn't flir—" Shannon began.

Her words stopped abruptly. The anger she saw in Whip's eyes made her mouth too dry to speak.

"Rafael!" Willow said, shocked. "Where are your manners?"

"In his watch pocket," Caleb suggested dryly, "along with his brains."

Whip shot him a savage look.

Caleb smiled thinly.

"Save it for Reno," Caleb suggested. "He's been waiting for a chance to get even ever since you dumped him on his butt with your Chinese wrestling tricks and then took strips out of his hide for the way he was treating Eve."

"He had it coming," Whip said. "He was being a damn fool about not marrying her. Anybody could see it."

"Except the damn fool involved," Caleb pointed out. "You might think on that. You might think on it real hard. Then you can apologize to Shannon by teaching her how to waltz."

With that, Caleb winked at Willow and picked up his harmonica. Soon haunting harmonies once again filled the room.

Shannon looked everywhere but at Whip. Her cheeks were still stained red from his accusation. And from her own anger. She had done nothing to earn the sharp edge of Whip's tongue.

Whip's large hand appeared in front of Shannon's eyes. His fingers were long, tanned, oddly elegant for all their strength. The nails were clean and closely trimmed.

He smelled of peppermint.

Whip saw the accusation in Shannon's blue eyes when she looked up at him, then the sudden flaring of her nostrils, and then her surprise.

"Peppermint," she said.

"Willow has it planted out back. I picked some for your room while you and Willow were clearing the dinner table."

"I—thank you," Shannon stammered. "That was very kind of you."

Whip held out his other hand and said softly, "Dance with me."

Honey girl.

Though Whip didn't say the words aloud, they were there in the silver blaze of his eyes as he looked at her.

"I d-don't know how," Shannon said.

"I'll teach you, if you'll let me. Will you let me, Shannon?"

A shiver lanced through her.

"Yes," she whispered.

"Then come to me," he whispered in return.

When Shannon stood up, Whip took her left hand and led her to the center of the living room floor. There he turned and faced her, lifting her hand as he did. If they had been alone, he would have kissed the center of her palm. Instead, he circled it with his thumb before pressing lightly in the very center.

Shannon felt as though her palm had been kissed. Her breath shortened and her eyes widened to luminous pools of blue.

"Put your left hand on my shoulder," Whip said in a deep voice.

"Like this?"

"Yes. Now, rest your right hand in mine."

A betraying shiver went through Shannon when her palm brushed over Whip's. He shifted his hand until he could grip hers lightly with his fingers.

"Can you hear the beats of the music?" Whip asked.

Shannon cocked her head, listening despite her nearly overwhelming awareness of Whip's body close to hers, their breaths mingling, the strong surge of the pulse in his neck. After the space of a few breaths, she heard the rhythms Whip was counting. She began counting with him, softly.

"That's it," Whip said. "Now, beginning with your right foot, follow my lead."

Whip's grip on Shannon changed, becoming more secure, guiding her at all times and supporting her if she wavered. He began with simple steps, but quickly went on to more intricate ones as it became clear that Shannon was capable of more than schoolroom exercises.

"Are you certain you don't know how to waltz?" Whip asked, turning swiftly, taking Shannon with him.

She laughed and hung on to Whip, trusting him to lead her through the dance. His strength and confidence made learning easy for her.

"I've dreamed of dancing like this," Shannon said softly to Whip, "but I never did it. The closest I came was huddling behind the potted plants and peeking through the balustrade at all the lovely, swirling dancers."

"How old were you?"

"Five or six or seven. It was a long, long time ago," Shannon said absently, counting the beat, "before Papa deserted us and Mama took to laudanum."

Whip was shocked, but he didn't pursue the subject. He wanted to erase the shadows from Shannon's magnificent eyes, not create more darkness by recalling unhappy memories.

"I think she's ready for a polka," Whip said, looking over Shannon's head to Caleb.

Immediately the harmonica's music went from stately to raucous, with rollicking refrains that made Willow laugh out loud and tap her foot to the driving, infectious rhythm.

"Hear the beat?" Whip asked Shannon.

"I'd have to be dead not to!"

"Or dead drunk," he said. "I suspect the Germans invented this dance as a way to get thirsty enough to drink beer all night long."

Whip took Shannon's hands and placed them on his shoulders. By now her foot was tapping along with Willow's.

"Ready?" he asked.

"For what?"

"To romp with me like I was Prettyface and we were in a high-mountain meadow with nothing around but wildflowers and the sun."

The thought of romping like that with Whip charmed Shannon. Laughter gleamed in her eyes and curved her lips into a dazzling smile.

Then laughter fled in a hot rush as Whip put his hands on her hips. His fingers flexed subtly, savoring the feminine flesh just beneath the worn cloth trousers. The smile he gave her was as reckless and sexy as the glittering light in his eyes.

With no more warning than that, Whip began the polka, counting out the measure as he had the waltz. But this time his voice was nearly a shout rather than a murmur. Shannon caught on quickly, for the polka was much more simple than the waltz. Whatever lack of experience she had was more than made up for by Whip's sheer strength. If Shannon faltered, Whip simply lifted her right off her feet.

Soon the two of them were romping and stomping from the living room to the kitchen and down the hall and back again. Every few steps Whip would lift Shannon entirely off her feet, whirl her around, then set her down and head off in another direction.

Cheeks flushed, eyes alight, laughing, Shannon gave herself to the music and to the man who laughed and danced with her. Finally, on the tenth trip from living room to kitchen, she was breathless from laughter and from the polka itself. She clung to Whip and begged for mercy. He whirled her around once more, feet off the ground, and hugged her close, for they were in the kitchen where there was no one to see.

"I know you weren't flirting with Cal," Whip said softly. "But if you had smiled like that at me, I'd have wanted to do . . . *this.*"

As he spoke, the humor in Whip's eyes gave way to the passion he no longer could conceal. He bent his head and took Shannon's mouth in a quick, deep, hungry kiss.

"And then I would have wanted more, so damned much more," Whip said softly, breathing hard, holding Shannon against him. "*I want you, honey girl.* Virgin or widow or wife, heaven or hell or everything between, I want all of it."

With a low sound, Whip let Shannon slide down his body, making no attempt to conceal his arousal from her.

Her breath fragmented over his name.
"Tell Cal and Willy that I went to check on Sugarfoot," Whip said hoarsely.
The back door banged, leaving Shannon alone in the kitchen with her heart beating frantically and the taste of Whip in her mouth like wine.

14

The next morning a wind howled down the peaks, herding brief, wild thunderstorms down the long green valley where Caleb and Willow had built their home. As Whip came inside, he held the doorknob carefully, making sure the front door didn't slip from his grasp and slam shut behind him.

Shannon was in the living room, sitting by a window in one of the chairs Caleb had made. In her hands was one of Willow's gingham blouses. Shannon was making tiny, neat stitches in the sleeve where the seam had given way.

"Where's Willy?" Whip asked.

"She's taking a nap with Ethan."

Whip smiled almost sheepishly. "Cal told me that we woke Ethan up with our dancing last night."

Pink brightened Shannon's cheeks, put there by the memory of Whip's hard kiss and even harder body.

"Ethan wasn't awake for long," Shannon said. "He went right back to sleep when Willow sang to him. She has such a beautiful voice."

"You should hear her sing with Reno and

Eve," Whip said, smiling. "Together they have the kind of harmony that would make angels weep with envy. Christmas was a special time last year, with all of us being together and the carols being so beautifully sung."

"It must have been wonderful," Shannon said, her voice wistful.

Whip looked at Shannon. Her face looked less drawn now than it had a week ago. So did her body. Sitting in the sturdy house with mending in her hands and a glass window nearby with sunlight shining through, she was as relaxed as a cat lying next to a warm hearth.

"You like it here, don't you?" Whip asked.

"It would be hard not to. Caleb and Willow are generous with their hearts and their home. Seeing them makes me realize how much my parents missed in their marriage."

"Reno and Eve are the same as Cal and Willy. So are Wolfe and Jessi. Must be something in the western air."

Shannon glanced away from Whip, not wanting him to see the emotion in her eyes when she looked at him and thought of a home, a marriage, a sharing of life and love and children with Whip.

But that wouldn't happen. Shannon knew it as surely as she knew that Whip was a yondering man. Yet she couldn't stop loving him.

So she looked away from what she knew she couldn't have.

But Shannon didn't turn aside quickly enough. Whip had already seen her dreams. He had seen the hope she couldn't deny, and the love, and the sadness of knowing that someday he would leave her. The fact that Shannon didn't scold him or demand his love in return made Whip feel more trapped and restless than ever—and at the same time, it made him want her until every muscle in his body was flexed in the brutal tug-of-war between restraint and consummation.

Whip glanced quickly at the hallway that led to the bedrooms. The door to the nursery was closed. So was the door to Willow and Caleb's bedroom.

Knowing he shouldn't, unable to stop himself, Whip crossed the living room with a few swift strides, took the mending from Shannon's hands, and lifted her without warning into his arms. He was rougher than he meant to be, because he was hungrier than he had known.

"Whip?" Shannon asked, startled.

"Don't fight me. Kiss me and let me kiss you. Let me have you, even if only in this way."

Shannon's lips were still parted in surprise when Whip took her mouth. His tongue shot between her teeth and he groaned when he tasted the minty flavor and sultry textures of her tongue. She made a small sound in response and lifted herself toward Whip's kiss, giving her mouth to him with a hot sensual honesty that made him ache.

Whip pushed deeper and deeper into Shannon's sweet mouth, wanting all of her, wanting it here and now, hot and wild, burning him all the way to his soul. The sounds she made deep in her throat, the eager glide of her tongue against his, and the hungry arc of her body pressed against his erect flesh all told Whip that Shannon wanted him the same way he wanted her; hot and wild, here and now, no promises and no regrets, nothing but the driving rhythms of their bodies locked together in elemental hunger . . . honey and ecstasy and flames twisting together, burning.

With a low cry Whip tore his mouth free of Shannon's, knowing that kissing her any more was like throwing alcohol on a raging fire. But it was too late to stop the blaze that had been ignited. Already he was stretched upon a white-hot rack of desire. He was shaking, burning, control slipping from his grasp one savage heart-beat at a time.

"God, woman," Whip said roughly, muffling his voice against Shannon's neck. "You're driving me crazy."

"I didn't mean—"

"I know," he interrupted, his voice raw and low. "My fault. I should know by now that kissing you only makes it hurt worse. But when I'm not kissing you I can't believe that anything can hurt worse than that."

Shannon felt the raking shudder that went through Whip. She caught his tormented face between her hands and kissed him lightly, gently, repeatedly, wanting to take the pain and darkness from his face, from his body.

Whip shuddered again, fighting for control.

"Every time I look across the room and see your eyes watching me," he said in a low, uneven voice, "I know what you're thinking, what you're remembering, what you're feeling. Your eyes tell me that you would lie down and hold out your arms and give me everything I need. And I need you, Shannon. I need you until I wake up sweating and hard and aching from forehead to heels. But I can't take you and I can't stop wanting you and I'm on fire!"

"Hush," Shannon murmured between tender kisses. "It's all right, yondering man. It's all right. You can take me and end the aching and not have to give up the sunrise you've never seen."

Shannon's brushing kisses, like her words, were both gentle and deeply beautiful to Whip, a stark temptation and an equally stark admission of her love. He knew he should stop the words and the kisses and the promises that could not, must not, be kept.

But Whip could no more turn away from the gentle, terrifying beauty of Shannon's caresses than he could turn away from a sunrise softly condensing out of winter's longest night, radiance calling his name in all the colors of love.

"Shannon," Whip whispered. "Honey girl. Stop. *You're tearing me apart.*"

"Then tell me what to do. I want to ease you, not hurt you more. Please, Whip. Tell me. Teach me."

The thought of it almost brought Whip to his knees. A bolt of violent desire transfixed his body and dragged a raw sound from deep in his chest. He closed his eyes and grappled with a kind of hunger he had never felt for a woman. Like Shannon's words and kisses, the depth of his hunger was an unimaginable lure and a shocking warning of his own frail hold on self-control.

"Whip?" Shannon whispered. "Please. Teach me."

With his last shreds of restraint, Whip reminded himself that he was in the living room of his sister's home. It was full daylight. Willow could awaken from her nap at any time and walk into the room.

"No," Whip said roughly, setting Shannon

abruptly away from him. "Don't ask me. Don't tempt me. Don't—"

"But you were the one who—"

"—tell me that you would let me open those men's trousers of yours and put my hand between your legs and feel your honey pooling in my hand like silky fire. Don't tell me it would be all right to unfastened my pants and push all my need and my aching and my hunger deep into you. Don't tell me you would let me take your maidenhead."

Shannon tried to speak but couldn't. The thought of having Whip so much a part of her made her feel hot and cold and shaking with a need she couldn't name.

And Whip saw it, all of it, the hunger and the need.

"Hell, you would *beg* me," he said, "because I can make you ache as much as I do right now. I can make the honey flow and the fire burn and—"

The sound of a door opening down the hallway cut off Whip's seething words. He flinched as though a lash had been laid across his shoulders.

"Caleb?" Willow called softly from the hall.

"Just me, Willy," Whip said, his voice low and rough.

Abruptly he moved so that Shannon was between him and the doorway where Willow would soon be.

"I was just talking to Shannon about that position you offered," he said.

Willow appeared at the entrance to the living room. Her hair was mussed by sleep. She was rubbing her eyes and trying not to yawn.

"Oh, good," Willow said, looking past Shannon to Whip. "Do you need anything?"

"No," Whip said, smiling through his clenched teeth.

Willow yawned behind her hand.

"Wonderful," she murmured. "I think I'll sneak off to the bathhouse before I start dinner. Would you mind watching Ethan while I'm outside?"

"Not at all," Shannon said quickly.

"Thank you," Willow said, covering a yawn again. "I'll hurry."

"No need," Shannon said. "I started the stew while you slept. If Ethan wakes up, I'll hold him at bay with some cow's milk from the well house."

"You're an angel."

Shannon thought of what Whip had been saying to her and how she not only had listened, but had felt her bones turn to fire at his words. She had never wanted to feel a man's body locked deep within her own until she met Whip.

Now she wanted nothing else.

"An angel?" Shannon asked with a bittersweet smile, looking with helpless hunger at Whip. "Hardly."

But Willow had already vanished back into her bedroom. She reappeared a few moments later with a change of clothes in her hand.

"I won't be long," Willow repeated.

"Don't rush," Shannon said. "There's nothing here that won't keep for a while, including your son."

Whip watched Willow leave, grateful that his sister was too sleepy and too hurried to notice the blunt ridge of his arousal thrusting against his trousers.

Thank God I've solved the problem of Shannon's safety, Whip told himself savagely. *I don't think I can keep my hands off her any longer.*

It's time and past time to find a sunrise that is more beautiful than Shannon's eyes when she looks at me.

"Don't worry about your things," Whip said abruptly to Shannon. "Cal or one of his men will help you fetch them when you go back for Prettyface. If you wait a week or two, that hard-headed son of a bitch will be able to walk on his own rather than being slung over your saddle."

Shannon blinked and shook her head, feeling as if she had just awakened into someone else's dream.

"What are you talking about?" she asked. "Even if we wait a fortnight to go back to my cabin, I don't need any more clothes."

What Shannon didn't say was that there weren't any more clothes at the cabin, whether or not she needed them.

"And why would I bring Prettyface here anyway?" she added, perplexed.

"I thought you'd want to keep him," Whip said. "Cal and Willy say it's fine with them. They've been trying to get a dog that was big enough and tough enough to survive the wolves and Texas longhorns and winter winds, but they haven't had much luck."

"Of course I'm going to keep Prettyface! What on earth are you talking about?"

"I'm talking about you coming here to help Willy out. She needs it and the two of you get along better than sisters and—"

"No."

"—you can't keep living in that goddamn

rickety shack off in the back end of nowhere and we both know it!"

"No."

"It's not safe!" Whip said savagely. "You have to—"

"No."

"—leave!"

"No."

Whip reached for Shannon with stunning speed. Before she knew what had happened, she was jerked off her feet and brought to Whip's eye level.

It wasn't a comforting place to be. His eyes were pale, glittering, dilated with rage, the eyes of a trapped animal.

"Yes," Whip snarled.

Shannon flinched but didn't back down.

"No."

The word was soft, final. The words that followed were equally soft, equally final.

"I have a right to live as I want to," she said.

"Or die," Whip shot back.

"Or die," she agreed.

His hands tightened harshly on Shannon's arms, but she didn't protest. Whatever pain she felt was nothing compared to the anguished fury driving Whip.

"You're trying to tie me down," he said through his teeth. "You think I won't leave until I know you're safe."

"No," Shannon said quietly. "You're trying to tie *me* down and make me live the way *you* want me to."

"Damn it, you're twisting my words!"

"Am I? I know you'll leave me, Whip. I've known it from the first time I heard you talking about the sunrise you've never seen. 'Nothing is more beautiful. Nothing is more compelling.'"

"Shannon, honey girl, I—"

"No," she whispered, stopping his words by brushing her lips just once over his. "I believed you then. I believe you now. You will leave. And I will stay in my cabin."

"I won't let you."

"Yondering man, you can't stop me."

Whip closed his eyes. His mouth was flattened, his lips pale.

"You're tearing me apart," he said in an anguished whisper.

"I'm just—"

Whip talked over Shannon's words, trying to make her understand.

"I want you. I want you like I've never wanted anything—*except the sunrise I've never seen.* I can have one or I can have the other. Do you know how it feels to be torn apart like that?" he demanded in despair and rage. "I would tear the soul out of my body if it meant an end to this pain!"

Tears burned behind Shannon's eyes, gathered in her lashes, and slid hotly down her cheeks.

"I would do the same," she whispered. "But you can have what you want most, Whip. Freedom. I'm not baiting any traps or building any cages with you in mind."

"The hell you aren't," he said roughly. *"I have to know you're safe."*

"And I have to know I'm free! Like you, yondering man. Free as the sunrise."

"You can't be. It's not the same for a woman."

"Not for a married woman, no. But I'm not married."

Whip opened his eyes and saw the tears in Shannon's.

"Honey girl, don't cry. I never meant to hurt you."

"And I never meant to tear you apart," Shannon whispered. "All I ever asked you to do was dig gold for me. Since that's too much tying down for you to live with, just ride on and find that sunrise you hunger for so much. Ride on and leave me be."

"I can't," he said simply. "Not until I know you're safe."

"You have to."

"Shannon—"

"If you stay, you'll hate me," she interrupted starkly. "I'd rather die, Whip."

"And that's just what you'll do if you go back to that damned shack!"

"My choice, Whip. Not yours."

Slowly Whip lowered Shannon to the floor. Then he removed his hands from her arms, turned his back, and went out the front door without another word.

Shannon looked over the dinner table, checking that everything was where it should be. Normally she wouldn't have worried, but normally she wouldn't be feeling used up and wrung out like an old rag. Already she had dropped a spoon, spilled coffee, and scorched her fingers adding wood to the fire.

"Thunderation," she muttered, using one of Cherokee's favorite phrases. "I forgot the plates."

If Willow noticed Shannon's unexpected clumsiness, nothing was said about it. But Willow had her hands full with Ethan at the moment. He was hollering from his crib, outraged that his mother wouldn't let him polish his walking skills in the kitchen, careening from sink to table and back again, with a heart-stopping run at the wood stove in between.

"Blazes, but that boy is quick," Willow said, coming back into the kitchen.

"He has Caleb's speed," Shannon agreed. "Along with his amber eyes. And a dimple at the corner of his smile that is just like Whip's."

Willow smiled. "If Ethan grows up one half as handsome as his daddy or his uncle, all the girls in Colorado Territory will beat a path to our door. How is the stew coming along?"

"It's ready."

"Good. I saw Caleb walking in from the barn when I put Ethan in his crib."

"Was Whip with him?"

"No, but he won't be far behind. In case you hadn't noticed, my brother likes home cooking."

Shannon ducked her head so that Willow couldn't see the sudden gleam of tears.

What's wrong with me? Shannon asked herself grimly. *I know better than to cry. It's a waste of salt and effort.*

"I noticed," Shannon said in a muffled voice. "So long as it isn't *his* home, of course. Is the bread cool enough to slice yet?"

"Should be. Mark my words, though. Whip will complain that there aren't any biscuits."

"No, he won't," Caleb said, closing the kitchen door behind him. "He left a few hours ago."

Shannon went very still.

"Left?" Willow asked, turning away from the stove. "Where did he go?"

"To see Reno."

"Oh." Willow frowned and went back to spooning stew into a big wooden serving bowl. "Odd that he didn't say anything to me. That's not like him."

Caleb's whiskey-colored eyes focused on the slender girl whose hair was the color of autumn.

"Did he say anything to you?" Caleb asked Shannon bluntly.

"No. But then, he's a yondering man."

"That doesn't excuse bad manners," Willow said. "I declare, for all the customs in all the countries of the world Whip has learned, he should know better."

Caleb hadn't stopped looking at Shannon. There was the same tension around her mouth, the same darkness in her eyes, that there had been in Whip's. Caleb had spent several hours thinking about how Whip had looked, and whether anything should be said about it.

He had decided it should.

"I understand Whip did some digging on your gold claims," Caleb said.

Shannon nodded.

"Any luck?" Caleb asked.

Willow shot him a surprised look. "Caleb, that's none of our business."

He turned toward her with startling swiftness. "Not usually, no. But this isn't usual."

Willow gave her husband a long look, said something under her breath, and went back to spooning stew.

"Any luck finding gold?" Caleb asked again, turning to Shannon once more.

"No. Whip said he lost the drift, whatever that is."

Caleb grunted. "The drift is the direction the

vein of gold takes in the bedrock. When you lose it, all you're doing is hammering stone."

"Whip did a lot of that. He came back every day covered in rock grit and sweat."

"Did he? Why? He hates gold mining almost as much as I do, and he hates working for wages even worse."

"Whip was worried about me," Shannon said. "Winters are long in Echo Basin, and supplies in Holler Creek are very dear. He was worried that I wouldn't have enough to eat unless the claims paid for it."

"There's always hunting," Caleb said. Then he smiled slightly, remembering the story of the grizzly. "But you're not much of a shot, are you?"

"Ammunition is too expensive to waste practicing," Shannon said, "so I just have to sneak up on game and do the best I can."

"I'm surprised Silent John didn't make his own bullets. Most men like him do."

"He did. But he never trusted me enough to teach me how. He was mighty particular about the weight of his bullets. He counted each grain of powder."

"I'll just bet he did," Caleb said, thinking of Silent John's reputation with a .50-caliber buffalo gun. "Do you think he's still alive?"

"No. But please don't tell anyone."

"Why?"

"I don't want two-legged wolves howling around the cabin each time they get a skin full of rotgut," Shannon said bluntly. "Silent John put the fear of God in the men around Echo Basin. I want it to stay that way."

Caleb nodded, unsurprised. "What about Whip?"

"Whip?" Shannon asked. She smiled sadly. "He can howl around my cabin any time he takes the notion."

Caleb laughed softly, even as he understood the pain in Shannon's smile.

"Does Whip think Silent John is dead?" Caleb asked.

"Yes."

"Then what's the problem?"

"I beg your pardon?" Shannon asked.

"Why did Whip light out of here like his heels were on fire?"

"He wants me to stay with you and Willow."

"So do we," Willow said from the stove.

"I . . . thank you," Shannon said. "But I can't."

"Can't or won't?" Caleb asked in a clipped voice.

"Caleb," Willow said. "We have no right."

"Did you see your brother when he rode out?" Caleb asked curtly.

"No."

"I did. When someone you care about looks the way Whip did, you start asking questions. And you get answers."

As Shannon looked at Caleb's face, she remembered what Whip had once called him—a dark angel of vengeance who had followed a man for years to avenge the seduction, betrayal, and death of his sister. It reminded her of the man called Hunter, another dark angel moving over the face of the lawless land.

Shannon closed her eyes and laced her fingers together until they ached. When she opened her eyes, Caleb was watching her with both compassion and determination.

He knew his questions were painful for her. But he was going to have answers anyway, for Whip, too, was hurting.

"If I thought you didn't care for Whip," Caleb said calmly, "I wouldn't have said a word about any of this to you. But I've seen you watching him. It's the way Eve watches Reno, the way Jessi watches Wolfe, the—"

"—way Willow watches you," Shannon finished for Caleb. "I'm sorry. I don't have much practice at hiding my feelings."

"There's no need," Willow said, putting the bowl of stew on the table. "You're among friends, here. You know that, don't you?"

Shannon nodded and tried to speak. Tears threatened to overflow her long, dark lashes.

Willow put her arms around Shannon and hugged her like a child.

"Then why can't you stay with us?" Willow asked softly.

Shannon hugged Willow in return, took a deep, broken breath, and tried to make Whip's sister understand.

"How would you feel," Shannon asked, "if you loved Caleb and he wanted something more than he wanted you and he left you?"

Willow's breath came in swiftly. She stepped back, wanting to see Shannon's eyes. Then she wished she hadn't.

"How would you feel," Shannon said painfully, "if, after Caleb left, you lived in his sister's house, saw Caleb in his sister's sun-bright hair and catlike eyes, saw Caleb in his sister's child, a dimple in one corner of the baby's smile . . .

you saw all this and you knew every day, every breath, every heartbeat, that there would be no baby for you, no home, no mate to share your life?"

"I couldn't bear it," Willow said. "Loving Caleb, knowing he didn't love me, being reminded of it everywhere I looked. . . . It would kill me."

"Yes," Shannon whispered.

She turned to Caleb, who was watching her with troubled eyes while his big hand stroked Willow's hair in silent love.

"That's why I can't stay," Shannon said to him.

"Is that what you told Whip?" he asked. "Is that why he looked like he had a knife in his guts?"

Shannon shook her head slowly, sending veils of autumn-colored hair sliding over her shoulders.

"No," she said in a husky voice. "That's not what I told him."

"Why not?" Caleb asked.

"It would have been like asking him to stay . . . begging him. I won't do that."

"Too proud?"

Caleb's voice was gentle but his eyes were the unflinching amber of a bird of prey.

He didn't have all of his answers yet.

"Too practical," Shannon corrected with a bittersweet smile. "Watching my mama and papa taught me how bad things can get when a man wants one thing and a woman wants another. He left and she took laudanum for the pain. For the first time, I understand why she did it. And I hope it worked."

"Does that mean I have to lock up the laudanum?" Caleb asked dryly.

"No."

"I didn't think so. You're tougher than your mama was, aren't you?"

"I had to be. I took care of her at the end."

"What did you tell Whip?" Caleb asked again.

"The other half of the truth. That I don't want to be obliged to anyone, no matter how kind they are, for my bread and salt. I want to be free."

"But you're a—"

"Woman," Shannon finished curtly. "Yes. I had noticed that very thing."

"So does every other man who sees you walk by," Caleb retorted.

"Caleb!" Willow said in exasperation. "Honestly!"

"Well, honey, it's the truth, and all the talking about freedom and such won't change the way Shannon walks."

"I don't do it on purpose," Shannon said tightly.

"Hell's fire, I know that," Caleb said. "You're no more a flirt or a tease than Willow is. That's not the point. The point is that males are going to notice you're female. The decent ones will strike up a conversation and come calling with candy in one hand, flowers in the other, and a gleam in their eye. If you aren't interested, they'll ride off and not come back. But not all men are decent."

"I know that better than most women," Shannon said.

"But you're still insisting on going back?" Caleb asked.

"Yes. I'll leave tomorrow."

"Aren't you going to wait for Whip to go with you?" Willow asked, surprised.

"What makes you think he's coming back?" Shannon asked.

"Did he say good-bye to you?" Willow countered.

"No."

"Then he'll be back."

Shannon only shook her head, remembering the anger and anguish in Whip when he rode away.

"Rafael isn't that unkind, no matter how hard the wanderlust is riding him," Willow said. "He'll be back."

"Will he?" Shannon said. "Some men love gold, some men love the sea, and some love only the horizon they've never seen. Whip is hearing that sunrise calling him."

"All he mentioned to me," Caleb said, "was getting gold out of a hard rock mine. He was hell-bent on it. He went to Reno for advice."

"Yondering requires money," Shannon pointed out. "Whip probably needs some. He refused to take wages from me."

"Whip has more gold than he knows what to do with," Willow said. "Ingots of Spanish gold so pure you can mark it with your fingernail."

Shannon looked startled. "I didn't know that. Then why is he going to Reno to find out how to dig more gold?"

"If Whip offered you his own gold to buy supplies or a home in a safer place than Echo Basin, would you accept it?" Caleb asked.

"Never," Shannon said softly. "I'm a widow, not a harlot to be bought by any man with an itch in one pocket and gold in the other."

Caleb smiled slightly and nodded, unsurprised.

"Why don't you stick around until Whip comes back?" he asked. "You shouldn't ride all the way to the basin alone."

"No, thank you. My dog was injured defending me from the Culpeppers. I should have gone back days ago."

"Stay," Willow said quickly. "Whip has . . . tenderness toward you. He might . . ."

"Settle down?" Shannon whispered, shaking her head and smiling sadly. "Only love could hold Whip, and Whip loves only the sunrise he hasn't seen."

15

Whip rode up to the small home whose finishing touches were still being completed. When he reined in his tired horse, a young woman with hair and eyes the color of pure gold came running out of the kitchen. She leaped lightly off the low porch that ran the length of the house and smiled up at Whip.

"It *is* you! What a lovely surprise! Reno thought the yondering urge must have come over you again and taken you to the far side of the earth."

"Not yet, Eve. I've got some gold to dig, first."

"You? Gold?"

The startled look on Eve's face made Whip smile despite the bleak emotions knotting his gut. The long ride from his sister's ranch hadn't eased his temper or his pain one bit.

"I thought you hated gold mining even worse than Caleb does," Eve said.

"I do," Whip said as he dismounted.

"Then why—"

Eve's breath broke when Whip turned toward her and she got a close look at his face.

"What's wrong?" Eve demanded anxiously. "It's not Willow, is it? Or the baby? Is—"

"Everything's fine at the Black ranch," Whip interrupted.

"Then what has you looking so grim around the mouth?"

"Nothing some gold won't fix. Where's Reno?"

"Right behind you," Reno said.

"Yeah, I thought so," Whip said, turning around. "Someone has been watching me ever since I forded the river."

Reno smiled. "Great view we have from our house. Saw you coming from a long way off."

"Nice of you not to shoot."

"Once I got that bullwhip in my sights, it was tempting," Reno agreed, deadpan. "But then I got to thinking you might be bringing some of Willy's biscuits to share around."

"All I'm bringing is an empty belly and a favor to ask of you," Whip said bluntly.

"That explains the look on your face. You always did look about as friendly as a wounded grizzly when you were hungry."

While Reno spoke, he glanced at Sugarfoot through narrowed green eyes. The horse's coat showed signs of having sweated and dried several times since the animal was last curried. The way the gelding tugged at the reins, trying to get close to grass, said that the horse was as hungry as its rider. And as tired.

"You and Sugarfoot both look like you've been rode hard and put away wet," Reno said.

"I left Cal's ranch just before supper yesterday."

Reno's black eyebrows shot up. "You must have ridden most of the night."

Whip shrugged.

"I'll help you see to Sugarfoot," Reno said, "while Eve makes something for you to eat."

As soon as the two brothers reached the pole corral, Reno turned to Whip.

"All right. Let's have it," Reno said bluntly. "What's wrong?"

"Like I told Eve. Nothing that some gold won't cure."

"One of those Spanish bars is buried right under your feet. If I dig it up, will it put the light back in your eyes?"

Whip said something terrible beneath his breath, lifted his hat, raked his fingers through his hair, and yanked his hat back into place.

Without a word or a glance toward his brother, Whip turned to Sugarfoot and uncinched the saddle. With one hand he lifted the heavy saddle and flipped it onto the highest rail of the corral. With his other hand he took the saddle blanket, turned it over, and laid it out to dry on top of the saddle.

Bending swiftly, Whip hobbled the gelding and turned him out to graze. Sugarfoot went forward eagerly, for the margin of the river that ran within a hundred feet of Reno and Eve's home was lush with grass.

Reno watched Whip with green eyes that

missed nothing, especially the ease of his brother's movements. Seeing Whip's muscular grace made some of the tension in Reno loosen; he had feared that Whip had some injury or illness he was trying to conceal.

"Cal and Willy and Ethan are all right," Reno said.

It wasn't exactly a question, but Whip nodded.

"You're as fit as a cougar, despite a ride that took the starch out of that tough gelding of yours," Reno said.

Whip shrugged.

"You haven't had bad news about any of our brothers?" Reno pressed.

"No."

Reno waited.

Whip said nothing more.

"Well, that cinches it," Reno said, smiling slightly. "It must be woman trouble."

"What the hell are you talking about?" Whip asked, nettled.

"The lines around your mouth and the look in your eyes that says you'd like to kill something, and God help anyone who gives you the excuse."

Whip flexed hands that kept wanting to become fists. He had come to talk about gold, not about a woman he shouldn't take and couldn't leave alone.

"Are you going to talk," Reno asked mildly, "or would you rather fight first?"

"Hell," Whip said in disgust. "I came here to ask a favor, not to fight you."

"Sometimes a fight *is* a favor."

Whip made a low sound that could have been a curse or laughter or both combined. Then he looked up, straight up. The sky was as deep and blue as Shannon's eyes.

"Have you ever wanted two things," Whip said slowly, "even though having one of them means giving up the other, and you can't give up either one, because you really want both of them, so you keep turning in tighter and tighter circles like a dog chasing its own tail until finally you don't know which end is up?"

Reno's smile was oddly gentle for a man who looked as hard as he did.

"Of course I have," Reno said softly to his brother. "It's called being human. Stupid, but human."

"What did you do?" Whip asked curiously.

"When you finished tearing strips off me, I figured out what was important. Then I married her."

Whip's mouth turned down. "I'd make a piss-poor husband. I'd always be looking over the fence and pacing like a mustang fresh off the range."

"Still chasing sunrises?"

"I can no more help my yondering streak than you can help being left-handed and hell on wheels with that six-gun of yours," Whip said flatly.

"Probably, but you never know."

"What does that mean?"

"When you started yondering," Reno said slowly, thinking as he spoke, "you were hardly more than a kid. Like me, you left home as much because our older brothers were restless—and Pa had a heavy hand with the belt on our backsides—as for any wanderlust of your own."

"Was that it?" Whip shrugged. "It's so long ago now, and I've seen so many places and done so many things since then, it's hard to remember what started me yondering."

"But you don't want to give it up."

"How do you give up your soul?" Whip asked simply, his eyes haunted.

Reno had no answer except the quick, hard embrace he gave his brother.

"Come on," Reno said after a moment. "Eve will be fretting about what's wrong with you. It galls me to admit that she has such poor taste, but she cares about you almost as much as she does about me."

Whip smiled slightly. "I doubt that. But I have a real fondness for her. She has the kind of laughter and sheer courage that I admire in anyone, especially a woman. Eve is solid gold. What she ever saw in you I'll never know."

A crack of laughter and a slap on the shoulder was Reno's answer. Side by side, the two brothers walked toward the house with long strides. When they reached the back door, Whip looked dubiously at his boots, and then at Reno's.

"Something wrong?" Reno asked.

"There are parts of this world where you would be insulting your host and hostess by wearing your boots across the threshold of their home," Whip said. "Especially boots like these and a new home like yours."

"Eve must have been to those same places," Reno admitted. "She leaves a pair of moccasins next to the door for me to swap for my boots."

Reno's smile was wry and amused at the same time. Eve's pleasure in having a home of her own had been a keen satisfaction to him.

"What about my boots?" Whip asked. "Will she settle for stocking feet?"

"She'll think of something. She protects this house like a tigress with only one cub."

"Can you blame her? An orphanage like she was raised in would make a body crave a home of their own."

Reno and Whip washed up at a small bench Reno had built at the back of the house. The water waiting for them was warm and scented with lilac.

As cheerful as the scent was, Whip couldn't help remembering the spearmint freshness that he associated with Shannon, and the small ritual of handling him a towel and inspecting his face so carefully for any speck of lather.

Stop thinking about those beautiful blue eyes and that sweet mouth smiling up at you, Whip advised himself grimly. *It isn't fair to either one of us.*

Do what you have to do.

Get Reno. Get gold.

Get out.

The thought didn't have as much appeal as it should have.

"Well, don't take all day," Eve said, smiling at the men from the back doorway. "If I wait any longer to give you a hug, the biscuits will burn."

Grinning, Reno wiped his hands on a clean rag and held out his arms. Eve stepped into them and held on hard.

"Is everything all right?" she whispered very softly against Reno's ear.

"Nothing for us to worry about, sugar," Reno answered with equal softness.

He felt as much as heard his wife's sigh of relief.

"I smell burning biscuits," Whip said blandly.

Reno released Eve, who turned immediately to Whip and held out her arms.

"They'll be all right," she said, "but I'm pining for a hug from my second-favorite man in the whole world."

Whip bent slightly, gathered Eve in a big hug, and held her close.

Reno watched with an indulgent smile and no jealousy at all. He knew that his wife and brother had forged a special bond between them when both had risked their lives to dig Reno out from deep inside an ancient, dangerous mine.

With a final squeeze, Whip set Eve back on her feet.

"Come in and eat," Eve said, smiling widely. "I can hear your stomach growling all the way from here. I'll set your place while you change shoes. If you like, you can hang your bullwhip on one of the jacket pegs. Or you can wear it at the table. Suit yourself, so long as the hat stays here with the boots."

Reno and Whip exchanged a silent glance of amusement when they saw the pair of large, clean socks laid out beside Reno's moccasins. But neither man had the heart to tease Eve about her attempt to civilize one small part of the West. In truth, the men welcomed the gentle rituals and generous feminine warmth that made a home from a simple house.

While Whip ate, he told Reno and Eve about what he had been doing since they had seen him months ago. When he got around to talking about Echo Basin and Holler Creek, he passed lightly over the Culpeppers.

Even without explanations or embroidery, Eve understood what had happened in Murphy's mercantile. She had lived in some rough places before she met Reno. She knew exactly what stripe of male animal the Culpeppers bunch was.

What she didn't know was why Silent John's widow was at the Black ranch rather than with Whip.

"Why didn't you bring Mrs. Smith with you?" Eve asked Whip.

"Mrs. Smith?"

Eve saw the blank lack of comprehension in Whip's eyes and made an exasperated sound.

"The woman you brought from Echo Basin to the Black ranch," Eve said, speaking slowly, as though to a backward child. "The woman who was insulted by the Culpeppers. The woman whose modesty you defended with that lethal bullwhip of yours."

"Oh. You mean Shannon."

"Lord above, of course I do," Eve said, laughing. "Is your mind off woolgathering around the world again?"

Surprisingly, red stained Whip's cheekbones.

"I don't think of Shannon as Mrs. Smith," Whip said tersely.

Eve blinked, sweeping long lashes over her eyes, concealing the sudden speculation in them. She very much wanted to look at Reno, to see what he thought of Whip and the woman who might or might not be a widow, the woman Whip obviously didn't like to think about as married at all.

"I see," Eve murmured. "Was *Shannon* too tired after the ride down from Echo Basin to come here?"

"I left her with Willy and Cal. I was hoping Shannon would want to live with them and help Willy."

"That would be nice," Eve said. "Willow has been looking to hire a girl for—"

"Not as hired help," Whip interrupted roughly. "Not really. Sort of like a sister or a maiden aunt."

Eve cleared her throat rather than point out that a widow was nobody's maiden aunt. She knew the Moran men too well not to recognize the warning in Whip's clear, bleak eyes. He was a man caught between a rock and a hard place, unable to move.

Yet he had to move.

Yondering man.

Half of Eve's heart went out to Whip and his pain. The other half of her heart went out to Shannon, whom she suspected was caught in pain as Eve had once been caught, in love with a man who wasn't ready to love her. But in the end, Reno had come to love her.

Eve wondered if Shannon would be that lucky.

She looked at the big, blond-haired man whose eyes were clear as autumn ice. Whip could be gentle and loving, but God help anyone who tried to hold him when he would rather roam.

"A family kind of thing, room and board and a little egg money," Whip explained. "And safety. That most of all."

A sideways glance at Reno told Eve that her husband was both amused and bemused by his brother. The gentle curve of Reno's mouth told of his sympathy, as well.

"Is that what Shannon wants?" Eve asked, curious. "Safety and a little egg money?"

The line of Whip's mouth flattened even more. Put that way, it sounded like a paltry kind of existence for anyone, much less for a young woman like Shannon.

Silence stretched uncomfortably.

"If Shannon is half the woman you make her out to be," Eve said finally, her voice careful, "you won't need to worry about her for long. Some smart man will come down the road and give her a lot more than room and board and a little egg money."

Whip's head came up. His eyes were narrowed to splinters of glittering gray.

"He'll give her his name and his children and build a home for her," Eve said calmly. "She won't have to live on the kindness of others. She'll have her own home to enjoy, her own man to love, and her own children to raise. He will be her safety and she will be his refuge."

"No!"

Whip didn't know he had spoken aloud until he heard the echo of his own savage denial at the thought of Shannon bearing another man's child. Whip's hands gripped the edge of the table until his skin was white. He shouldn't feel this way about Shannon and another man.

But he did.

Eve's dark gold eyebrows raised in silent query at Whip's vehemence.

"She doesn't have to marry some man and have his kids to be safe," Whip said doggedly. "All she needs is . . ."

His voice died.

"I take it you don't want to marry her yourself," Eve said neutrally.

"It's nothing against Shannon." Whip's voice was raw. "It's me."

"Sugar," Reno said softly, "it would be no

kindness for Whip to marry Shannon. She might as well marry the wind."

"Does she know that?" Eve asked.

"She knows," Whip said flatly. "She told me she'd never marry a man who loved a sunrise he had never seen more than he loved her."

"Smart woman," Eve said.

"Stubborn woman," Whip shot back. "She won't leave the high country and it's not safe there for a woman alone."

"Why won't she leave?"

"Up there, she isn't beholden to anyone for her salt and bread."

"*Very* smart woman," Eve said.

"Very damned *stubborn* woman," Whip snarled. "I can't leave her at the mercy of those miners and I can't stay up there with her until she comes to her senses."

Eve made a sound that was sympathetic, questioning, and subtly goading.

"The only way out of the mess," Whip said, "is to find enough gold on those damned claims to buy her a place in Denver or back east or whatever, just so I know she's safe."

"And unmarried?" Eve suggested sardonically.

The bleak anger in Whip's eyes was all the answer she needed.

"Whip, for the love of heaven!" she said, exasperated. "If you don't want to marry Shannon, why should you get to upset at the idea that some other man—"

A nudge from Reno's foot under the table cut off Eve's words.

"Whip knows he's being unreasonable," Reno said. "That's why his temper is on a hair trigger.

If he needs a fight, I'll be the one to give it to him."

"Men," Eve said under her breath.

Then she sighed and tried another approach.

"Why don't you just give her some of your own gold from that Spanish mine?" Eve asked. "Lord knows you've barely touched it."

"In her place, would you take it?" Reno asked before Whip could speak.

"No. But I was in love with a man who was a fool for hunting gold."

"And Shannon," Reno said, "is in love with a man who is a fool for you—"

"She doesn't really love me!" Whip interrupted harshly.

"Is that what she says?" Eve retorted. "Or is it what you hope?"

"She's never been around anyone but a snakemean old man hunter, and a tough old hermit called Cherokee, and a bunch of young miners with the manners of rutting elks," Whip said. "Of course she would think the first man who treats her decently is special."

"In other words, she loves you," Eve summarized.

Whip grimaced and said nothing.

"Let's see if I have this straight," Eve said blandly. "You don't love Shannon, but you care about her safety. She doesn't want to be someone's hired girl. You don't want her to live alone in Echo Basin, and you don't want her marrying anyone, including you. So you've decided to find enough gold on her claims to save your conscience before you take off yondering again. Does that about cover it?"

Whip's eyelids flinched.

Reno's breath came out in a low rush of air. "Eve . . ."

She ignored him.

"If you were a man," Whip began, his voice uninflected.

"If I were a man you'd be beating the tar out of me," Eve said. "That's one of the reasons God made women, so that men would have to *think* as well as fight."

Whip's expression said he would rather fight.

Eve stood and went around the table to where Whip sat coiled and struggling within a cage of his own making. She stroked his sun-bright hair, so different from her husband's.

"I love you, Whip," Eve said softly. "You and Caleb and Willow and Wolfe and Jessi. You're the family I always wanted and thought I would never have. Be mad at me if it helps. Because I want to help you. I ache to see you so unhappy."

Whip closed his eyes. A visible tremor went through him. Then, slowly, his grip on the table loosened. He looked up at Eve and gave her a smile so sad that it brought tears to her eyes.

"You're like Willy," Whip said softly. "A handful of sunshine. I can't stay mad at either of you for more than a few minutes at a time."

Eve touched Whip's cheek and smiled in return.

"What do you find in all those foreign places?" she asked softly.

"I don't think I can put it into words."

"Will you try?"

Whip raked his fingers through his hair, then ran his fingertips over the soothing coils of the bullwhip on his shoulder. The gesture said much about his restlessness, as did the narrowness of his eyes and the bleak line of his mouth.

"It's exciting," Whip said finally.

"What is?" Eve asked. "New land? New languages? New cities? New women?"

Frowning, Whip pulled the long lash off his shoulder and began running the supple coils through his fingers, absently probing for frayed places.

"It's not the women," Whip said. "Oh, they're pretty, all right. Some of them are as exotic as anything you can imagine. But Shannon is a lot prettier to me than any girl I've seen across the ocean. It's not the kind of pretty that wears off, either. She just gets more beautiful every time I look at her."

Reno's black eyebrows went up, but he said not one word. Pointing out that Reno felt the same way about Eve would only make Whip's temper flash.

"The languages are kind of intriguing," Whip said after a moment. "Chinese is pure hell to get a handle on, but Portuguese isn't, and their explorers settled some far-flung ports. Between Portuguese and English, I can get by in most places around Asia, so long as I don't stray too far from the water.

"And Portuguese and Spanish aren't all that different, once you get the hang of how to pronounce the same words in a different way. I can go anywhere in South America and Mexico . . ."

Reno waited quietly, watching his brother wrestle with the roots of his own yondering urge.

Eve stood close by, touching Whip's shoulder from time to time, silently urging him to talk, to loosen the harsh tension that lay just beneath his surface.

"The cities . . ." Whip began.

Then he stopped and shifted restlessly, running the bullwhip through his fingers the whole time.

"The cities . . .?" Eve coaxed softly.

Whip's wrist made a lazy movement. The bullwhip uncoiled across the floor. The lash popped softly.

"It was the cities that lured me, at first," Whip said. "I couldn't get enough of them. Strange ways of putting together buildings, exotic faces, new smells and sounds and foods. Some of what I saw was good and some was plain awful, but it all was *different*."

Reno nodded and made an encouraging sound.

Eve waited.

"Funny thing," Whip said quietly, "but after a time, all that difference ends up feeling pretty much the same to me. I never thought about it until just now."

The bullwhip stilled, then resumed its whispering movements, popping softly, punctuating Whip's thoughts.

"As for the land itself," Whip said slowly, "that's a big part of it. This old world is plain incredible when it comes to putting rock and water together in new shapes."

"Yes," Reno said. "That's why I came back here. For my money, the Colorado Territory has some of the most extraordinary and curious shapes of land. Not to mention a lot of gold waiting to be found."

"Do you have your own favorite landscape," Eve asked Whip, "one you can't wait to get back to?"

Whip shook his head. "I never go to the same place twice."

"Then you haven't found what you're looking for yet, have you?" Eve asked simply.

Whip opened his mouth. No words came out.

He stood up and walked out of the house into the glorious Colorado day. As he moved, the bullwhip seethed around him, nipping delicately at the grass, snapping softly as a campfire.

"What do you think he's going to do?" Eve asked Reno in a quiet voice.

"What he has always done."

"Yondering."

"Yes," Reno said.

"Poor Shannon."

"Poor Whip. He's not exactly what I'd call happy."

"That's his choice," Eve said. "It's a choice Shannon didn't get to make."

"You sound like you wouldn't mind hammering on my brother's thick skull."

"One thick-skulled man at a time is all I can handle," she retorted.

"And I'm the one?"

Eve smiled slightly, went to Reno, and ruffled his midnight hair with her fingers.

"You're the one," she agreed.

Smiling, Reno pulled Eve onto his lap. For a long time there was no sound in the kitchen but that of soft words and kisses that started as gentle comfort and swiftly became smoldering promises that would be kept later, when they were alone in the big bed.

When Whip finally came back to the house, the long lash was once again riding quietly on his shoulder. Nothing was mentioned about Shannon or yondering.

Whip permitted talk only of gold—where it was found, how it was found, how to mine it. While Reno listened intently, Whip described the claim he had worked. Then they talked through sundown and well into the night.

At dawn the next day, the silence was broken by a drumroll of hooves. Horses, running hard.

Moments later Whip eased out the back door, rifle in one hand and bullwhip on his shoulder, and his pants only half fastened. Reno stood back from the front window, watching through narrowed eyes. Eve stood beside him, a shotgun in her hands.

There were two horses. Only one of them carried a rider. Reno identified that horse instantly. The redgold coat, flashing white stocking, and tail carried like a red silk banner could belong only to Willow's prize Arabian stallion.

"That's Ishmael," Reno said. "And that's Wolfe riding him!"

Reno whistled sharply, a signal left over from childhood. A few moments later, Whip appeared around the side of the house, saw who the visitor was, and ran out to greet Wolfe. Whip noted that both horses had been ridden hard and fast, which told him that Wolfe had come on the run, switching mounts to rest first one horse, and then the other. The second horse was tall, long-legged, with the lean lines of a racing horse and the stamina of a mustang.

"What happened?" Whip and Reno asked urgently as Wolfe reined to a stop in the yard.

"Cal galloped up to our house leading Ishmael,

handed me the bridle, and told me to find Whip and find him fast. Then he hightailed it back to Willow."

Whip looked up into Wolfe's dark face. Eyes the same blue-black as twilight looked back at him.

"You found me," Whip said. "Now spit it out."

"You have a woman called Shannon?" Wolfe asked.

Whip was too surprised to answer.

"Let me put it this way," Wolfe said sardonically. "If you *know* a woman called Shannon, she's not staying with Willow and Cal anymore."

"What? Where is she?"

Wolfe took off his hat, smoothed back his straight black hair, and settled the hat firmly into place once more. Whip had the look of a man on a hair trigger. Wolfe suspected that his next words would set his friend off.

"All Caleb said was the tracks went north and he couldn't leave Willow alone to follow them," Wolfe said. "Besides, Shannon wasn't lost. She knew where she was going."

Whip started swearing in a language none of the others had ever heard. But they knew it was cursing just the same. Whip didn't have the look of a man strewing blessings.

He ran toward the corral, cursing fit to burn stone at every step.

"Stop by our place on the way," Wolfe called out. "Jessi will give you a fresh horse to use along with your own."

Whip jammed the rifle into the saddle scabbard and grabbed his bridle and saddle from the corral rail. He walked swiftly toward the hobbled horses that were a hundred feet away, grazing at the river's edge.

Reno glanced at Wolfe. "Are you coming with us?"

"Do you need another gun?" Wolfe asked bluntly.

"Doubt it."

"Then I'll stay with Jessi." Wolfe's smile flashed, changing the predatory lines of his face to something much gentler. "She started losing her breakfast a week ago."

Reno's face lit up with an answering smile. "Congratulations! Other than losing her breakfast, how is Jessi taking it?"

"Just fine. Seeing Ethan born took away most of Jessi's fears about childbirth. My biggest problem is keeping her from dancing around so much with joy that she wears herself out."

Whip swung up onto Sugarfoot and cantered toward the house.

"Where should I meet up with you?" Reno asked.

"Avalanche Creek," Whip said curtly.

"Which fork?"

"East!"

With that, Whip set his heels in the big gelding and headed out at a dead run.

16

Shannon stood at the door to Cherokee's tiny cabin. Prettyface was by her side, looking almost as healthy as before the fight. Above Shannon the wild Colorado sky seethed with clouds in every color from pearl to pewter to a strangely radiant midnight. A freshening wind swept over peaks and forests alike, making narrow stone ravines sing eerily and trees shiver and bow.

"Nice-looking mule," Cherokee said from the doorway.

Shannon glanced back at the old woman. She was leaning on the cane she had carved to ease the burden on her ankle. Shannon suspected that the cane might become a permanent part of Cherokee's life. The thought made Shannon frown. It was Cherokee's stalking skills that had kept both of them alive the past winter, when snow had come early and stayed late.

"Last time I saw a mule like that was nigh onto two years ago," Cherokee said, "when I dusted a Culpepper's hat with two bullets from more than a thousand yards."

"They thought it was Silent John doing the shooting."

"Close enough. I used his long gun. Shoots true as a dying man's prayer. I was grateful. No need to waste a fine mule with bad shooting."

Shannon looked at the long-legged mule that was tied to a tree, waiting patiently while she visited with Cherokee.

"After the ride from the Black ranch, Razorback was too tired to go another foot," Shannon said. "I don't like riding a dead man's mule, but there wasn't much choice. Crowbait isn't broken to the saddle."

"Hell, gal, you been riding a dead man's mule for years. Time you face up to it and get on with your life."

Shannon winced. "Now that the Culpeppers

are gone, I suppose there's no real harm in folks knowing. Murphy is a weasel, but I can handle him."

"Sic Prettyface on that old boy. Bet Murphy's manners perk up something joyful."

Smiling, fondling the dog's big ears, Shannon glanced again at the wild sky. The wind rushed over her face, fresh and cold as ice water.

"I better ride soon," Shannon said. "It smells like snow."

"Won't be the first time she snowed in July," Cherokee agreed.

"A tracking snow would be a godsend."

Cherokee straightened, shifting her weight gingerly. Though she had wrapped her foot and applied every poultice she knew, her ankle was being stubborn about healing.

"Going hunting?" Cherokee asked.

"Sure am," Shannon said with a cheerfulness that went no farther than her smile.

The old woman grunted, turned, and limped back into the cabin. When she returned, she had a box of shotgun shells grasped in her gnarled fingers. She held out the box to Shannon.

"Go on, take 'em," Cherokee said impatiently. "I can't hunt for a bit and there's no sense in letting a good tracking snow go to waste. This way you won't have to get so close to the critter you could skin it with a knife same as shooting it."

"But I already owe you for doctoring Prettyface."

"Oh, horseshit. It's been share and share alike with us for nigh onto three years, and it was the same with Silent John and me for ten years before that. Take them shells and use as many as you need to bring back venison for us to eat."

"But—"

"Now don't go making me mad, gal. Prettyface wasn't no problem at all. Skull like granite and a body to match. He healed hisself without no help from me. Didn't you, you ornery mongrel?"

Prettyface looked at Cherokee, waved his tail, and turned back to Shannon. The bullet wounds on his body had shrunk to little more than healing scabs. It was the blood that had made the wounds look so awful at the time.

As for Prettyface's skull, Cherokee was right. Solid stone from ear to ear. Other than a furrow in the thick fur on the dog's head, there was little to show of the bullet that would have killed a less hardy and hard-skulled animal, or one not lucky enough to be cared for by a woman skilled with herbs.

"Thank you for taking such good care of Prettyface," Shannon said, rubbing the dog's muzzle gently. "He's all the family I have, except for you."

Cherokee's shrewd brown glance saw in Shannon's face everything that she had left unsaid, the dream of loving and belonging that had been stillborn in a yondering man's eyes.

"Well," Cherokee said, "I guess you won't be needing this after all, seeing as how you're alone again."

As Cherokee spoke, she pulled a stoppered jar from her jacket pocket. A small bag hung from the neck of the jar by a rawhide thong.

"What's that?" Shannon asked, curious.

"Oil of juniper and spearmint, mostly. The bag holds bits of dried sponge."

"I'll bet the oil smells wonderful. Why won't I be needing it?"

"Because Whip's a double-damned fool, that's why. Or did he become your man and then walk out on you?"

Shannon's face went pink and then very pale.

"Whip isn't anyone's man but his own," Shannon said through her teeth. "But, yes, he's gone."

"Is there any chance you're breeding?" Cherokee asked bluntly.

Shannon drew her breath in swiftly. "No."

"You dead sure?"

"Yes."

The old woman sighed and eased weight off her injured ankle.

"Well, I won't need to worry about bringing on your monthly bleeding then," Cherokee said, "any more than you'll need that bottle of oils and such to keep from getting a babe that won't have no pa to speak of."

"Is that what you give Clementine and—"

"No," Cherokee said, her voice curt. "Be a waste of time. If the oil's gonna get the job done, you got to apply it careful like and at the right time. But when them poor gals is working, they're drunk as skunks."

Shannon thought of the Culpeppers and other men like them and shuddered.

"I don't know how they survive it," Shannon said.

"Most of them don't," Cherokee said. "Not for long, anyways."

The wind howled around the tiny cabin, foretelling the storm to come.

"I'd better go," Shannon said.

She turned around—and saw a big man riding toward her out of the wild afternoon.

"Whip."

At Shannon's soft cry, Cherokee turned, saw the man riding up, and laughed out loud in triumph. Hurriedly she stuffed shotgun shells into one of Shannon's jacket pockets and the bottle of contraceptive oil and sponges into another.

Shannon didn't even notice. The lightning stroke of joy she felt on seeing Whip quickly turned to dismay. If he was happy to see her at all, it wasn't reflected in his face. He looked angry enough to eat lead and spit bullets.

"What are you doing here?" Shannon asked.

"What the hell do you think I'm doing?" Whip asked bitterly, reining in just short of Shannon's toes. "I'm chasing a girl who has no better sense than to leave a fine home and come back to a miserable shack where she'll like as not starve to death this winter, if she doesn't freeze first!"

"You left out the part where a grizzly eats her," Cherokee said dryly. "But since she'll be froze to death first, it don't make no never mind, do it?"

"That's not true," Shannon retorted. "I've lived alone here for—"

"Howdy, Whip," Cherokee called cheerfully, overwhelming Shannon's words. "Nice horse you got. Look of speed about him."

Whip didn't even look away from Shannon when he spoke. He did, however, scratch the ears of the hound that had put his front paws on Whip's thigh and was panting happily up into his face.

"I left Sugarfoot to graze around the damned

hovel Shannon calls home," Whip said. "This is one of Wolfe Lonetree's horses."

"Thought so. Get down and set awhile."

"Thank you, no," Whip said, still not looking away from Shannon. "Likely it will be snowing before we get back to Silent John's leaky old shack."

"It's not leaky," Shannon retorted.

"Only because I shoved half the mountainside into the cracks," Whip shot back.

Cherokee snickered. "Well, children, I'll leave you to it. My bones ain't up to the chill."

With that, Cherokee backed away and shut the cabin door against the cold, questing wind.

"Can Prettyface make it to your shack?" Whip asked.

"You're the man with all the answers, what do you think?" Shannon retorted.

"I think you're a damned fool."

"How quaint. Cherokee thinks the same of you. So do I. You've had a long ride for nothing, Whip Moran." Shannon's head came up, giving Whip a clear view of her eyes. "I'm not going back to the Black ranch."

Whip hissed a foreign word between his teeth. Not until he saw the anger in Shannon's eyes did he admit how much he had wanted to see joy because he was back.

Cherokee is right. I'm a damned fool.

"Get on the mule," Whip said curtly.

Shannon spun on her heel and stalked toward the mule she had named Cully. She mounted swiftly, unaware of her own grace.

Whip was aware of it. Just seeing her walk raised undiluted hell with his body.

Deliberately Whip looked away.

"If Prettyface starts limping, holler," Whip said curtly. "He can ride across my saddle. Moccasin won't mind. Wolfe breaks his horses to take anything in their stride."

Shannon reined Cully in behind Whip's horse. It was a lean, long-muscled chestnut with the look of a hard ride just behind it.

The man looked the same.

By the time they reached the cabin, Shannon was stiff from the cold wind and the emotions churning behind her expressionless face. She dismounted, stumbled, and reached out wildly.

Whip grabbed her. Though he was wearing gloves and Shannon was wearing heavy clothes, he swore he could feel her heat and sweetness radiating up to him, setting him on fire. Her eyelashes trembled, then opened fully, revealing eyes whose hunger and confusion matched his own.

But there was no confusion about one thing. Shannon was his. All Whip had to do was take her.

With a vicious word, Whip set Shannon on her feet and backed away even as she reached for him.

"No," he said coldly. "Don't touch me."

Stunned, she froze in place, her hands held out to him, the love she felt for him so clear in her that Whip couldn't bear looking at her. Nor could he force himself to stop.

"Whip?"

"I mean it," Whip said fiercely. "*Don't touch me*. I came here to dig gold, not to dig a deeper hole with you. When Reno and I find enough gold to see you through the winter, I'm gone. Do you hear me, Shannon? I'm gone! You can't hold me with your body. Don't even try."

Waves of hurt and humiliation swept through Shannon, making her cheeks alternately pale and flushed.

"Yes," Shannon whispered through trembling lips. "I hear you, Whip. You won't have to say it again. Ever. I'll hear you pushing me away until the day I die."

Whip closed his eyes against the humiliation he saw in Shannon's eyes, her face, her whole body. He hadn't meant to hurt her like that. He had just felt a cage door closing and had lashed out without thinking about the cost.

"Shannon," he whispered in agony. *"Shannon."*

There was no answer.

Whip opened his eyes. He was alone with the cold wind.

He told himself that it was better this way, for Shannon and for himself, better to hurt now than to spend a lifetime regretting a choice made because his blood was running hot and she didn't have enough sense to say no.

It's better this way.

It has to be.

Nothing else would be worth the pain I saw in her eyes.

Shannon awoke at the first unearthly notes of the panpipes. She had never heard the tune before, but she knew it was a lamentation. Grief resonated in the keening, minor key harmonies and shivering, wailing echoes, as though a man was breathing in pain and exhaling sorrow.

The haunting music closed Shannon's throat

and filled her eyes with tears. As remote and desolate as moonrise in hell, the music mourned for all that was untouchable, unspeakable, irrevocable.

"Damn you, Whip Moran," she whispered to the darkness. "What right have you to mourn? It was your choice, not mine."

There was no answer but a soulful cry of loss and damnation breathed into the night.

It was a long time before Shannon slept again, and she wept even in her sleep.

When Shannon awoke again it was still dark. There was nothing to hear but the peculiar hush of a fresh snowfall mantling the land in silence. Shivering, she went to the badly fitted shutters and peered out.

Beneath a clear sky and a waning moon, snow lay everywhere, soft and chill and moist. Too thin to survive the coming day, the layer of snow waited for its inevitable end in the rising heat of the sun.

But until that came, every twig, every leaf, everything touching the snow would leave a clear mark.

Especially the hooves of deer.

Hurriedly Shannon dressed, forcing herself to think only of the coming hunt. Thinking about yesterday would only make her hands shake and her stomach clench. If she was to have any chance at all of bringing down a deer, she would have to have steady hands and nerves.

Don't think about Whip. He's gone whether he's here or on the other side of the world.

He doesn't want me. He couldn't have made it any plainer if he had carved it on me with that bullwhip of his.

The unexpected weight of her jacket made Shannon check its pockets. The first thing she found was the shotgun shells. The second was the jar and its accompanying bag.

With a grimace of remembered humiliation, Shannon shoved the jar onto a cupboard shelf. The shotgun shells she kept, for she would have a use for them. Blindly, forcing herself not to think of anything but what must be done, Shannon shrugged into the jacket, grateful for its warmth. She felt cold all the way to her soul.

Shivering, she lifted down the shotgun from its pegs, checked it, and found it clean and dry and ready to fire. She grabbed a handful of jerked venison, drank a cupful of cold water from the bucket, and eased out of the cabin into the dense, featureless darkness that preceded dawn.

Breathing softly, Shannon stood just beyond the door and waited to see if Prettyface was going to object to being left alone. As much as she would appreciate his company, he still wasn't fully recovered. He tired too quickly and was a bit stiff in his hindquarters where he had been shot. Another week would see the dog entirely healed, but she couldn't wait that long to go hunting. A tracking snow such as this one was too good to pass up.

Prettyface whined at the door and began scratching to get outside.

"No," Shannon whispered.

Quickly she moved to the side of the house, where the wind couldn't carry her scent inside.

Prettyface's whining increased in volume and intensity. So did the scratching sounds.

Shannon knew Prettyface well enough to predict what would happen next. He would start to howl. That would awaken Whip, wherever his campsite was, and he would come investigating.

The thought of having to face Whip again made Shannon's skin clammy and her stomach churn.

Even if she could face Whip, he would pitch a fit about her taking off to hunt by herself. Yet that was exactly what she had to do. She had to hunt and hunt successfully, without depending on Cherokee. If Shannon couldn't manage that, she faced death in the coming winter or a lifetime of taking care of other people's homes, other people's children, other people's lives.

And never having her own.

Shannon wasn't certain which was worse, dying or never having lived in the first place.

"Quiet."

The low command stilled Prettyface for a few moments. Then he began a high whimpering that would soon escalate into true howling.

"Damnation," Shannon said beneath her breath.

She opened the door, grabbed Prettyface's muzzle with both hands, and clamped down.

"You can come with me, but you have to be quiet."

Prettyface quivered eagerly. And quietly. He knew the hunting ritual too well to make noise now that he was going to be included.

Silently Shannon and the big dog set out in the darkness. She knew that Whip could follow her tracks as easily as she hoped to find and follow deer, but it was several hours until daybreak.

In any case, Whip was going to be waiting around for his brother to show up, not looking for Shannon. Whip had made it savagely clear that he had no desire for more of her company.

With luck, Whip wouldn't even come to her cabin. Then he wouldn't even notice she was gone.

The sound of a shotgun being triggered woke Whip up. He lay beneath the tarpaulin and a layer of fresh snow and listened intently. Another shot came, sounding the same as the first.

One man. One shotgun.

No answering fire.

A hunter, probably, taking advantage of the tracking snow.

Whip lay half awake, half asleep, feeling worn out and used up, as though he had spent the night in hell rather than in a comfortable bedroll while snow fell softly, making another warm blanket for him to lie beneath. Through slitted eyes, he measured the peach-colored light in the eastern sky. True daybreak was two hours away, for the sun had to climb over some tall peaks before its brilliant rays could fall directly on Echo Basin.

A third shot came echoing through the cold air, quickly followed by another.

Whip smiled thinly.

Must be a miner. No other kind of hunter would take four shots to bring down a deer. Sounded like he was using both barrels, too.

No sooner had the thought come than Whip sat bolt upright in his bedroll, scattering snow in all directions.

She wouldn't!

But Whip knew that Shannon would. He had never met a girl more stubborn.

Whip crammed his feet into cold boots, adjusted his bullwhip on his shoulder, grabbed his rifle, and ran to the stony outcropping that overlooked the clearing.

There was no smoke coming from the cabin.

She could be asleep.

Then Whip saw the tracks leading away from the cabin. He began swearing under his breath.

A very short time later, Sugarfoot was saddled, bridled, and crow-hopping his way across the clearing. It was the horse's way of letting Whip know how much it resented a cold blanket and a colder saddle.

Whip rode out his mount's tantrum without really noticing it. He was still consumed by the knowledge that Shannon was out prowling the gray, icy predawn, hunting her next meal as though she had no other choice but to fend for herself.

Does she think I'm such a bastard that I won't hunt a winter's worth of game for her before I leave? Is that why she's walking around in worn-out boots and clothing that's fit only to be made into a rag rug?

The answer lay in the tracks showing starkly against the gleaming silver snow. Shannon obviously believed she had to hunt for her own winter supplies.

A harsh wind keened down from the peaks, stirred up by the rising sun. Whip shivered and swore and pulled the collar of his jacket higher against the icy fingers of wind.

She must be cold.

The thought only increased Whip's anger.

Why didn't she wait for me to hunt for her? I'm not so much a bastard that I wouldn't help her out. She must know that by now.

Christ, other men would have taken what she offered and never looked back when they left.

But Shannon hadn't offered herself to other men. Only to Whip.

And he had turned her down flat.

Remembering Shannon's pain and humiliation, Whip suddenly knew why Shannon was out hunting in the icy morning alone. She wouldn't take food from his hand if she was starving to death.

Grimly Whip followed the tracks, making the best speed that the land allowed—certainly much better speed than Shannon had made, for she was on foot.

She at least could have ridden one of the damned racing mules. They're hers, after all. Sure as hell the Culpeppers don't need them anymore, and Razorback will be lucky to make it through the winter.

Whip knew that Silent John's old mule wasn't the only creature that would be lucky to survive the coming winter. The thought of Shannon struggling against hunger and cold was like a splinter jammed deeply under Whip's thumbnail, aching with each heartbeat, painful no matter what was done to ease it.

She's too damned poor to be so proud. There would have been no shame for her in accepting a place with Cal and Willy. It's honest work. And they liked her.

But Whip didn't fool himself about his chances of getting Shannon to be practical and take the job with Caleb and Willow. After what Whip had said to Shannon yesterday, she wouldn't go anywhere near relatives of his.

It's for her own good. Surely she can see that. If only I had put it more gently. . . .

Just how many gentle ways are there to tell a girl not to touch you, especially when you would move heaven and earth and take on hell just to be touched by her?

The thought of being caressed by Shannon's warm and loving hands made Whip shift uncomfortably in the saddle. His own swift, pulsing arousal made him angry with himself, with her, with everything. He had never been this vulnerable to a woman in his entire life.

He didn't like it one damned bit.

Hurry up, Reno. Find the gold that will free Shannon from this place.

And me.

The tracks Whip was following veered abruptly. As soon as he looked up, he understood why. Off to the right was a small clearing. Through the screen of trees he could see that deer tracks circled the clearing partway and then dashed across the fresh snow in the center as though the deer had been startled into flight.

Whip reined Sugarfoot over to the edge of the clearing and confirmed what he had already guessed. Several deer had been browsing along the margin of forest and meadow. The wind must have been on Shannon's side, because she got within one hundred feet of them before they discovered her.

There was an area of trampled snow where Shannon had stood. Spent shotgun shells lay where they had been pulled out of the chambers and dropped as she reloaded.

A closer examination of the deer tracks gave a picture of animals eating shrubs one minute and running flat out the next. There was no sign of blood in the tracks.

Must have been a clean miss, Whip thought.

The rest of the tracks made it clear that

Shannon and Prettyface were in hard pursuit of their quarry. The deep, skidding impressions in the snow told of a girl running recklessly across the meadow and into the forest, leaping small obstacles and scrambling over larger ones. The tracks of a large canine ran alongside Shannon's. The raggedness of the dog's stride told Whip that Prettyface was favoring his wounded haunch.

Abruptly Whip flung his head up toward the peak looming above and listened with every sense in his body.

He heard only silence.

Uneasiness blossomed darkly in him. He had a clear, uncanny certainty that Shannon had just called his name.

He listened again with an intensity that made him ache. Nothing came to him but the increased wailing of the wind.

Grimly Whip forced his attention back to the tracks in the snow.

Shannon never should have taken Prettyface along. What was she thinking of? he asked himself bitterly.

Hell, if she was thinking at all, she never would have left the cabin.

But Whip was too late to do anything about that, just as he had been too late to prevent Shannon from setting off into the frigid morning in search of food he could have—and would have—hunted for her.

A tracking snow might be pretty as the devil's smile, but like the devil, it hides a lot of mischief.

The tracks led across a boulder-strewn creek where snow hid broken branches and logs slick with snow and water. Sugarfoot was a fine trail horse, but he had to pick his way with care.

Suddenly, spots of blood gleamed brightly among the tracks. The spots dogged one deer's tracks, sticking with them no matter what the terrain or where the other deer veered off to find cover.

Shannon didn't miss after all. Not completely.

When Whip saw clear signs that Shannon had slipped and fallen, his temper mounted. A bleak, unspeakable anxiety was pressing against his guts, chilling him.

He kept hearing Shannon calling his name with an urgency that was making him wild.

Yet he knew that the only sound in the landscape was that of the keening, ice-tipped wind.

The little fool. She could break an ankle running like that. A wounded deer can go for miles or days, depending on the wound. If she keeps running she'll sweat and when she stops running the sweat will freeze.

Whip didn't want to think about what would happen after that. He had found more than one man dead of cold or wandering around with no more brains than a bucket of sand, too numbed by cold even to think.

The reckless trail went on, crossing and recrossing the creek as the deer bounded ahead. The signs of blood became more pronounced and frequent. One deer was tiring, struggling to keep up with its companions.

The ravine gouged out by the creek became steeper and the way got more rough. Even the deer that weren't wounded had a hard time of it. Despite having four agile feet apiece, there were signs that the animals slipped on the rough, snowy terrain almost as often as Shannon and Prettyface did.

Abruptly Shannon's tracks shortened from a full running stride to a complete halt. Spent shotgun shells poked up from the snow, telling their own story.

Whip stood in the stirrups and looked around. He quickly spotted the remains of the deer. Shannon had dressed it out with an efficiency that told Whip this part of hunting wasn't new to her. What meat she couldn't carry, she had strung up on a rope over a high branch, keeping the venison beyond the reach of other predators.

Well, Silent John was good for something, I guess. The hide itself won't be worth much from all the buckshot holes, and a man will have to be real careful not to crack a tooth on stray chunks of lead, but the meat will fill an empty belly just fine.

Shannon's tracks aimed toward a notch just ahead, a side ravine that snaked up and over the shoulder of the mountain. Whip's past explorations told him that the notch would open out into a steep forested slope about half a mile from the cabin. Except for having to cross a fork of Avalanche Creek several times getting through the notch, the trail was a handy shortcut back to the cabin for someone on foot.

Whip wasn't on foot.

For a moment he was tempted to push as far up the notch as he could on horseback, just to ease the clammy fear in his gut that something had happened to Shannon.

Don't be a bigger fool than you already are, Whip advised himself harshly. *The trail ahead is no worse than the one behind. There's no point making Sugarfoot walk in ice water and take a chance of breaking a leg on those damned slippery rocks just to see Shannon's tracks heading up and out of the notch.*

Yet Whip wanted very much to do just that. The uneasiness that had begun shortly after he started tracking Shannon had grown into flat-out fear.

Common sense told Whip that Shannon was all right.

Instinct whispered a different message, her voice calling wildly to him in the silence.

Abruptly Whip reined Sugarfoot around and headed back down the ravine. Although he was savagely uneasy, he didn't hurry the big gelding as it picked its way over the uneven ground. He kept reminding himself that by the time he reached the cabin, Shannon would already be safe inside. There would be a cheerful fire and mint-scented water to wash in and fresh biscuits baking.

But not for Whip.

The thought did nothing to shorten the two miles back to the cabin.

When Whip arrived, there was no smoke coming from the chimney, no scent of biscuits baking—and no tracks coming in from the direction of the notch.

The uneasiness that had been riding Whip exploded into raw fear. He spun Sugarfoot around and examined the sparse, windswept forest where Shannon would have descended from the notch to the cabin.

Nothing was moving.

Whip yanked open the buckle on his saddlebags and pulled out a telescoping spyglass. He snapped it out to full length and held it up to his eye. Between spaces in the trees, snow gleamed whitely in the growing light.

Not a single track marred the perfect snow.

17

Whip was nearly all the way to the notch itself before he found Shannon. She was in ice water up above her knees, pushing hard on a branch stuck between boulders in the creek.

Suddenly there was a dry, cracking sound. The branch splintered and Shannon fell headlong into the small pool of water.

Only then did Whip see what was wrong. Prettyface had slipped while scrambling across the stony creek. Somehow the dog had managed to wedge a hind foot between two boulders. The boulders were too heavy for Shannon to shift aside even an inch.

From the looks of the broken branches thrown beyond the creek, she hadn't had much luck finding a sturdy lever to help her free Prettyface.

When Sugarfoot came to a plunging, snow-scattering stop near the stream, Shannon was pulling herself upright. Her motions were clumsy, as though she had little feeling in her hands and feet.

Whip dismounted in a rush.

"Get out of there before you freeze to death," he ordered curtly.

If Shannon heard Whip above the chatter and splash of the icy creek, she didn't respond. She simply picked up the longest of the discarded branches, jammed one end beneath the smaller boulder, and heaved upward with all her strength.

The branch broke.

Only Whip's quickness saved Shannon from another ice water bath. He grabbed her, lifted her high, and dumped her into Sugarfoot's saddle. With swift motions he peeled off his jacket and stuffed her into it.

"Stay right here," Whip commanded. "Do you hear me, you little fool? *Stay put.*"

"Pre-Pretty—"

"I'll get him out, but so help me God, if you move from that saddle I'm going to take you to the cabin and tie you to the bed before I help Prettyface. Hear me?"

Dazed by cold and fear for her dog, Shannon nodded jerkily. When Whip took her hands and wrapped them around the saddle horn, she hung on instinctively. He looked at her for a searching instant before he turned abruptly toward the dog who was standing three-legged in the rushing creek.

"Well, Prettyface," Whip said as he waded into the frigid meltwater, "you've landed yourself in a mighty cold kettle of fish."

The big dog waved his tale in greeting and watched Whip with clear wolf's eyes. Except for his legs, Prettyface was dry. If the dog was cold, he didn't show it. He wasn't even shivering.

Whip bent and ran his hands lightly over as much of the captive leg as he could reach. There were no swellings and only a few scraped places.

"You're better off than your mistress, aren't you?" Whip muttered. "Now all we have to do is get your foot out without banging it up any worse than it already is."

Whip rubbed the dog's head affectionately as he talked, but there was no gentleness in Whip's silver eyes as he measured the problem. He pushed against one of the boulders, then another, testing them.

Heavy, damned heavy, but not impossible, Whip told himself.

Prettyface whined softly as Whip tested the boulders again, trying to decide which might be easiest to lift.

"All right, boy. I hear you. I won't pinch you again."

Whip gathered up several of the broken branches and jammed them between the boulders as far down as he could on either side of the dog's captive paw. Then he picked up a water-rounded stone and hammered the branches down between the boulders until the heavy sticks would go no farther.

"That should keep the boulders off your paw," Whip said. "Now hang on tight, Prettyface. There's going to be some shoving and swearing."

With that Whip squatted, plunged his hands into the ice water, and groped around the base of the boulder he had chosen. There was a lot of gravel and smaller stones. He began raking the rubble away from the bottom of the boulder until he could get a better grip on it. He worked quickly, for he knew his hands would soon go numb from the icy water.

"We're in luck," Whip said, wrapping his arms around the boulder and straining upward. "There's a nice little ridge—near the bottom—to hang—on to."

The words were spoken through Whip's teeth as he straightened slowly, driving his body upward with his powerful legs while he gripped the base of the boulder. Stone gnashed over stone. Whip's feet slipped slightly, icy water sluiced over him, but he didn't let go.

Despite the freezing water, sweat stood on Whip's face. The pulse in his neck beat hard. His eyes were slitted and his teeth were clenched with effort as he poured his strength into shifting the heavy boulder enough to free Shannon's dog.

Suddenly Prettyface jerked aside and scrambled out of the creek with a happy yip.

Whip let go of the boulder and straightened, breathing hard and smiling widely. Prettyface was favoring the foot that had been caught, but otherwise was moving well.

"Go home, boy," Whip said, gesturing down the slope.

The big dog looked toward Shannon, who was slumped in Sugarfoot's saddle.

"Home," Whip commanded, wading out of the icy creek.

Prettyface turned and trotted unevenly down the slope toward the cabin.

Whip went to Shannon. He took one look at her dazed eyes and blue lips, and knew that only willpower was keeping her from succumbing to the cold.

Yet she was trying to dismount.

"What the hell do you think you're doing!" Whip demanded. "I told you to stay put."

Shannon tried to speak but her lips were too cold. She pointed with a hand that shook.

For the first time Whip noticed the ragged backpack and the haunch of venison that had been thrown aside in Shannon's rush to rescue Prettyface.

Whip was tempted to get up behind Shannon, ride to the cabin, and to hell with the venison.

Instead, he stalked over and picked up the backpack. The sheer determination Shannon had shown in hunting the deer moved Whip in ways he couldn't express; the venison meant survival to her in the most fundamental sense of all. Though it infuriated Whip that Shannon had gone after deer in the first place, he couldn't deny her the fruits of her hunt.

"Here," he said roughly.

Whip shoved the backpack into Shannon's lap and swung up behind her.

As soon as Whip put his arm around Shannon to take the reins, he realized that she was colder than he had thought.

Dangerously cold.

Beneath his heavy, loose jacket, Shannon's whole body was racked by convulsive shivering.

"Son of a *bitch*," Whip said harshly.

His other arm came around Shannon and he set his spurs to the big gray. Sugarfoot took off down the slope at a pace just short of reckless. As far as Whip was concerned, it was much too slow, but common sense told him otherwise.

It was only a few minutes until they reached the cabin, but Shannon's shivering was worse by then. If it hadn't been for Whip's strong arms holding her in the saddle, she wouldn't have been able to stay on.

Prettyface was waiting patiently by the cabin door.

Whip dismounted, lifted Shannon off, and carried her to the cabin. Despite her shivering, she hung on to the venison as though it was life itself.

"I wish to God you had as much sense as you

have sheer grit," Whip said as he kicked the cabin door open.

Prettyface shot through the opening. Shannon shivered violently and said nothing.

It was dead cold inside the cabin. A fire had been laid in the stove, waiting for a match to bring heat and life to the room.

Prettyface didn't mind the lack of warmth. He simply went to his corner and stretched out on a ragged saddle blanket with a groan of pleasure.

Whip put Shannon on her bed, threw the bearskin blanket over her, and went to light the fire in the stove. His hands were so cold that it took several tries before he could hold and strike a match without breaking it. Once touched by the match, flames caught and held very quickly.

That wasn't fast enough to suit Whip. He was bigger than Shannon, he hadn't been in the water as long as she had, and he was damned cold.

It took Whip five tries to light the lantern. When he turned toward the bed once more, his glance fell on the dry goods cupboard that led to the hot spring.

Without hesitation Whip went to the bed, scooped up Shannon, grabbed the lantern, and went through the cupboard to the darkness beyond. The warmth of the cave was like a benediction.

Whip set the lantern on the wooden box that served as a table. Golden light spilled over everything as Whip took off Shannon's soaked boots, the bearskin blanket, and the jacket he had wrapped her in. Ruthlessly he stripped off her clothes, ripping the old cloth in his haste to get her free of its icy folds.

Shannon neither spoke nor focused her eyes

on Whip while he undressed her. She simply shuddered convulsively, repeatedly.

"Shannon, can you hear me? Shannon!"

Slowly her eyes focused.

Whip let out a breath of relief.

"You're going to have a nice, warm bath," he said. "Then all the shivering will stop and you'll be fine. Do you understand?"

Shannon's head made a motion that could have been a nod. Her teeth chattered audibly until she clenched her jaw.

"That's it, honey girl. Keep on fighting the cold. Don't let it put you under."

As Whip spoke, he wrenched off his own soaked boots and clothing. Moments later he carried Shannon into the pool. The broad bench Silent John had chipped and hammered out of stone was too shallow for Whip to get warm water up as high as his breastbone, but it was just right for Shannon.

When Shannon was on his lap, the water came up to the hollow of her throat. The hot spring swirled gently around Shannon, engulfing her with heat.

Breath hissed through Whip's teeth at the touch of the water. Though he knew it wasn't really hot in this part of the pool, for the first few moments the water felt like fire against his chilled skin.

"Are you all right?" Whip asked. "Does this hurt you?"

Shannon shook her head.

For a time there was only the soft hiss of the lantern and the subtle currents of warmth drawing the chill from their bodies. Whip's arms surrounded Shannon, holding her upright against his chest while she shivered.

Whip could tell when Shannon's brain started to thaw out. Though she was still shivering, she stiffened and tried to draw away from him. His arms locked, holding her against his chest.

"P-Prettyface," she said.

"Prettyface is fine. Hell, he's better off than you are. No need to jump out and check on him. You're still cold enough to shiver icicles. Stay put until you're warm."

Shannon didn't argue. It was too much effort to speak. She simply nodded.

But she didn't rest against Whip's chest again, either. She was remembering all too clearly how he had pushed her away the last time she had been close. She wasn't going to put herself in that position again. It had hurt too much.

It still hurt.

Whip's mouth settled into a tight line that had nothing to do with being cold. He had liked the feeling of Shannon leaning on him. He had liked the gentle weight of her on his chest and the fragrant silk of her hair brushing against his shoulder with each shift of her body.

But when he tried to draw her close again, she stiffened and pushed away.

After a time the hot spring won out against the chill left by the icy meltwater. Shannon's shivering subsided and her body slowly relaxed.

Whip could tell the precise instant when Shannon's skin thawed out enough for her to recognize what he had known ever since he climbed into the pool with her—they were both naked.

"Let me g-go," Shannon said stiffly.

"You're still shivering."

A tremor went through her that had nothing to do with cold.

"I'm f-fine," she whispered.

"Good," Whip said coolly. "Then maybe you can tell me what the hell you were doing floundering around the countryside when you should have been snug and warm and *safe* in your bed?"

"Hunting."

"I figured that out. What I didn't figure out was why."

Shannon's head came up. For the first time she saw Whip's eyes. For all his outer calm, he was furious.

No news in that, Shannon told herself. *Seems like he's been furious with me ever since I admitted to loving him.*

"Why do people usually hunt?" Shannon asked.

"Do you think I'm such a bastard that I won't hunt for you?"

Shannon's surprise showed clearly in her wide sapphire eyes.

"Of course not," she said.

"If I hunted for you, would you take what I gave you?"

"Yes."

"Then why in the name of God were you out hunting?" Whip demanded.

"You won't always be here to hunt for me, so I have to learn to fend for myself."

"You would do one hell of a lot better fending for yourself with Cal and Willy."

"By your estimate, yes."

"But not by yours," he retorted.

"Not by mine," she agreed. "Besides, I can't just walk out on Cherokee and Prettyface."

"Prettyface would warm to the ranch."

"Cherokee wouldn't."

"How do you know?"

"I asked first thing after I got back."

It was Whip's turn to be surprised. "You did?"

Shannon nodded.

"I had a long time to think about how sad and angry you looked when you rode off," Shannon said simply. "I decided I could go back and—and try—try living someone else's life."

Whip's eyelids flinched at the pain in Shannon's voice.

"If—if it didn't work, the cabin would still be here," Shannon said, "but I couldn't go unless Cherokee was taken care of, too."

Relief coursed through Whip. The arms holding Shannon gentled. He brushed his lips lightly over her hair, so lightly that she couldn't feel the caress.

"That tough old boy has been taking care of himself twice as long as you've been alive," Whip said. "He'll do fine up here alone. You won't."

"Wrong," Shannon said succinctly. "*She* has been taking care of herself for a long time. *She* likes it that way. That's the way it's going to stay."

"She?"

"She," said Shannon. "Cherokee is a woman."

"Judas H. Priest." Whip shook his head in disbelief. "You sure?"

Shannon nodded.

"So stop worrying about me, yondering man," she said in a low voice. "A woman can make it just fine alone, even all the way up Avalanche Creek."

"No. You won't survive the winter alone."

There was no inflection in Whip's voice, simply an absolute certainty that said more than any shouted tirade could have.

"I survived last winter," Shannon said, "and the one before that, and the one before that."

Whip tried to speak, couldn't, and tried again.

"What do you mean?" he asked roughly.

"Silent John disappeared three winters ago."

For a moment Whip was motionless. Then he shook himself as though he had been hit with a board.

He felt like he had.

"You've wintered alone here three times?" Whip asked harshly.

"Yes."

Whip wanted to believe Shannon was lying, but he knew all the way to his soul that she wasn't.

"Then Silent John must be dead," Whip said.

Shannon nodded and closed her eyes. "He's buried in a landslide up Avalanche Creek."

"How long have you known?" Whip demanded angrily.

"I guessed he was probably dead the second winter. But I wasn't truly certain until just a bit ago, when Cherokee told me she had backtracked Razorback to a fresh landslide when Silent John didn't come back from the claims. His tracks went in, but none came out."

"Then nothing's holding you here but your own stubbornness," Whip said.

"There's nothing holding anyone to life but sheer stubbornness," Shannon said wearily.

"You're planning on staying here."

Shannon nodded.

"Damn you!" Whip said roughly. "You're trying to tie me down!"

"No! I'm just tell—"

"How can I leave you alone and helpless up here?" he asked, his eyes as hard as his voice. "I can't and you know it! You're counting on me to—"

"I'm not helpless!" Shannon interrupted. "I'm not counting on you for one damned thing! I don't need you!"

A turmoil of emotions twisted in Whip, tightening his throat, making it raw. The cold he had felt in the stream was nothing to the freezing emptiness that came to him when he thought of Shannon lying dead in the high country, her grave as unmarked as Silent John's.

"The hell you don't need me," Whip said in a low, savage voice. "You nearly died out there today."

For the space of two long breaths, Shannon looked at the man who was so close to her, yet so very far away. Lantern light made his hair burn like the sun and turned the icy clarity of his eyes into a quicksilver mystery. Nothing had ever called to Shannon the way Whip did. She would have given the blood from her body to see herself reflected in his eyes, in his heart, in his soul.

She would have sold her own soul to be a distant sunrise calling his name . . . and to hear him answer.

"Yes," Shannon said calmly. "I could have died. But so what? The stars would have come out tonight and the sun would have risen tomorrow morning. The only difference would be that I wouldn't see it." She smiled oddly. "Not much difference, really. About the same as this."

Shannon lifted her hand from the water. Liquid swirled and then flowed back as though her hand had never been there, never known the pool's warmth.

Whip looked at the dark water and felt a dull knife sawing through his soul, cutting him in two.

"See?" she asked softly. "No real difference. Now do what the water did, Whip. Let me go."

"You're still shivering."

"I'll be fine as soon as I get some clothes on."

"The water is warmer than those rags you wear."

The protectiveness of Whip's arms around Shannon said much more than his words did. He didn't love her, but he cared about her safety.

It was a heady feeling to be cared for, to be cherished, to know that she wasn't alone, if only for a time.

The temptation to give in and rest her head against Whip's chest undermined Shannon's determination to stand alone. She longed to lean against Whip's heat and strength, to pull him around her like a living blanket, to warm herself with his abundant fire.

And then she remembered what Whip had said the last time she reached out for him.

Don't touch me.

Echoes of shame and humiliation swept through Shannon in waves. Abruptly she pushed at Whip's arms, trying to get free of him.

"What the hell?" Whip asked. "Why are you fighting me? You act like I'm going to rape you!"

Shannon made a sound that was almost laughter and not quite a sob.

"You wouldn't have to rape me and you know it," she said bitterly.

A shudder went through Whip.

"Dangerous words, honey girl."

"Why? You don't want me. You can't even bear my touch."

The pain and shame in Shannon's voice shattered Whip's restraint. He moved suddenly, scattering water in all directions as he captured one of her hands. He dragged her hand below the warm surface of the water and pressed her fingers around the blunt, heavy proof of his hunger for her. His breath hissed in, then came out with a low groan.

"Now," Whip said through his teeth, "tell me again that I don't want you to touch me. *I'd kill to have you and you damn well know it.*"

Shocked sapphire eyes looked at Whip.

"Then why do you keep pushing me away?" Shannon asked raggedly. "I'm not asking you to love me. I'm not begging you to stay with me. I just want . . . I just want to be alive, really *alive*, before I die. I'm a widow who was never a bride, and if you don't take me I'll go to my grave without knowing what it is to give myself to the man I love."

Abruptly Whip dragged Shannon's hand free of his aching flesh and released her.

"I can't," he said.

Shannon gave a broken laugh and ran her hand back down Whip's body.

"You most certainly can," she said.

Whip's breath hissed as Shannon explored the rigid evidence of his capability.

"You're a virgin," he said through his teeth.

"I'm a widow."

"I could make you pregnant."

"I'd love to have your child."

"I couldn't leave if you were pregnant," Whip said. "Is that what you want? To force me to stay?"

"No. You would hate me."

"I'd hate *myself*. Oh, God . . . stop."

Gently, relentlessly, Whip recaptured Shannon's exploring hand and brought it to his lips. The kiss he gave her palm was fierce, edged with teeth. It sent a shaft of pure desire through Shannon's body.

"What did you do with your other widows?" she asked in a husky voice.

A tinge of red appeared on Whip's cheekbones. "Honey girl, you ask the damnedest questions."

"Were they all too old to get pregnant?" Shannon persisted.

Belatedly Whip realized that Shannon wasn't asking for a detailed description of how he coupled with women. He let out a sigh, half laughing and half on fire at Shannon's combination of innocence and breathtaking honesty.

"No, they weren't too old to get pregnant," Whip said. "They were old enough to know how *not* to get pregnant."

"Celibacy."

The disappointment in Shannon's voice made Whip ache with laughter and a reckless kind of passion he had never known before he met her.

"There are other ways," he said.

"Truly? What are they?"

"Not coupling."

"Sounds like celibacy to me."

Whip's smile was slow and very male. "Not

quite, honey girl. More like half a loaf. Like you under the tarpaulin with hail hammering down."

A shudder of memory and anticipation went through Shannon.

"Is that what you want?" she asked.

"It's a hell of a lot better than nothing."

"But . . ."

"But?" Whip asked, gathering Shannon closer.

"I want to touch you, too. I want to make the world catch fire around you," Shannon whispered, remembering how it had been for her. "I want to watch you burn. I want to pleasure you until you cry out and the world goes a hot kind of black that's shot through with all the colors of the rainbow."

Whip's heart kicked and blood slammed through his veins. He could barely force words past the heady rush of passion that was closing his throat.

"Did I make you feel like that, honey girl?"

"Yes," she said in a low voice. "Only better. I don't have words to tell you. Except . . ."

Whip nuzzled Shannon's hair and made a questioning sound.

"I wanted more," Shannon admitted. "I wanted to feel your body all hot and strong around me. I wanted . . ." Her voice faltered. "I don't know what I wanted. I just knew that there was something missing."

Every muscle in Whip's body clenched at Shannon's words. His breath wedged, then hissed out through his teeth.

He knew exactly what had been missing.

"Is that wrong of me?" Shannon asked when Whip didn't speak.

"No, it's not wrong," Whip said huskily. "It's

damned wonderful. Some women are happy just to be petted a bit from time to time, but men want more."

"Just a bit of petting? That's all the women wanted?"

Whip made a rumbling sound of agreement.

Shannon frowned. "All the time?"

Whip's teeth closed gently over the top of Shannon's ear. He savored the shiver of awareness that went through her.

"Well, it's certainly better than nothing," she said finally. "But if the, er, whole loaf is at hand, why be satisfied with less?"

Whip laughed silently and wondered if a man could die of desire while sitting naked in a hot spring with a virgin widow who was as curious as a kitten.

And as heedless.

"Women are more likely to get pregnant during certain times of the month," Whip said. "That's when the, um, whole loaf is best kept in the bread drawer. Or drawers."

"You're laughing at me."

"No, honey girl. I'm laughing, period."

"Why?"

"You delight me," Whip said against Shannon's ear. "I want to kiss you from head to heels and back again, but I don't trust myself not to take you."

Shannon shivered and looked into Whip's silver eyes. The heat and approval she saw made her heart stop.

"I'd like to kiss you the same way," she whispered, "all over, head to heels. You have such a beautiful body, all sleek and powerful and—"

Warm, wet fingers sealed Shannon's lips, shutting off the tumbling flow of her words.

"No more, honey girl. You're burning me alive."

Slowly Whip removed his fingers, caressing every curve of Shannon's lips as he did.

"I don't mean to burn you," she whispered. "I don't even know how. Will you teach me, Whip? Will you tell me how to turn the world into a glittering black rainbow for you?"

"No," Whip said roughly. "Don't you understand? *I can't.*"

18

Whip closed his eyes against the desire raking through his body, tormenting him with what he wanted more than breath—*and must not take.*

When his eyes opened, he saw the hurt and confusion in Shannon's.

"I want you too much to trust myself," Whip admitted, his voice raw. "That's a first. I never had any trouble protecting a woman before."

Shannon took a deep, shivering breath. "I don't understand."

"I can take a woman without making her pregnant," Whip said in a clipped voice. "All I have to do is hold back my own pleasure until I'm not inside her anymore."

"Oh." Shannon frowned thoughtfully. "I understand. I think."

Whip didn't know whether to laugh or curse at his earnest, innocent widow's expression.

"It's not foolproof," he added. "If a woman is in her fertile time, I don't risk it."

"What's her fertile time?"

Whip's eyelids lowered halfway, making his eyes a smoky silver gray against the heightened color of his face. His thick eyelashes were the same radiant gold as the lantern light itself.

"Didn't your mama tell you anything?" Whip asked when he could trust himself to speak.

"Such as?"

"Such as women are most likely to get pregnant about halfway through their monthly cycle."

A flush that had nothing to do with the hot spring's warmth crept up Shannon's body.

"Oh. Er, no," Shannon muttered. "She didn't say anything about that."

Whip waited.

Shannon said nothing.

"When did you last bleed?" he asked bluntly.

She swallowed and closed her eyes.

"First I have Silent John and now I have Talkative Whip," she muttered.

"When did you last bleed?" Whip repeated, his eyes level and his tone determined.

"It—it stopped last night," Shannon said in a rush.

Desire lanced through Whip, hotter than any steamy spring, tightening his body even more. Just the thought of pushing into Shannon's snug, sleek body was enough to take him to the edge of his self-control.

"Last night, huh?" Whip said huskily.

Shannon nodded and wondered if her face was as bright a red as she thought it was.

Whip smiled and nuzzled her ear with his tongue.

"I didn't know a woman could blush from her breasts to her forehead," he said huskily.

"It's the heat of the water," Shannon muttered.

Whip laughed very softly.

When Shannon shifted in embarrassment, she encountered the stark reminder of Whip's arousal. She stopped moving even as he groaned.

"I'm sorry," she said hurriedly. "I didn't mean to hurt you."

"You didn't."

"It sounded like I did."

"You made the same kind of sounds beneath the tarp. Was I hurting you?"

The sensual shiver of memory that went through Shannon was felt by Whip, too.

"No," she whispered. "You didn't hurt me. I didn't even know that kind of pleasure was possible. Can I truly make you feel like that?"

"Yes," Whip said simply.

"How?"

Closing his eyes, Whip took a deep breath . . . and a tighter rein on his own driving hunger.

"We'll start with a kiss," he said. "Would you like that?"

"Oh, yes. Would you?"

"It's a start," Whip said tightly, lowering his head.

An instant later. Shannon felt the velvet penetration of his tongue. The heat and textures of Whip's kiss rushed through her, making her dizzy.

With a soft whimper, she turned her face up and parted her lips even more, wanting to get as close as she could to Whip. Her arms slid around his neck and her fingers searched through his hair, holding him hard against her mouth while she tasted him as deeply as she could.

With a rough, throttled sound, Whip kissed Shannon in return, pressing into her mouth, thrusting against her tongue, devouring her as thoroughly as he could with just a kiss. Finally, shuddering, he pulled free.

"Whip?" she asked huskily. "Is something wrong? Why did you stop?"

"You make me too damned hot."

Shannon looked around the gently steaming pool. "Maybe we should get out of the water."

He laughed despite the agony of his unruly, unfulfilled desire.

"It's not the water," Whip said. "It's you. I feel like I've wanted you forever. You burn me even in my dreams."

The look in Whip's eyes made Shannon forget to breathe.

"Does that mean you'll let me pet you?" she whispered.

"Anytime. Anywhere. Any way you want."

And I'm a fool to even suggest it, Whip said silently to himself.

But he didn't say the words aloud. He wanted Shannon's hands on him too much to be wise.

Watching Whip's face, Shannon ran her hands over his shoulders and chest, luxuriating in the strength and resilience of his flesh. Slender fingers kneaded, discovered, and enjoyed every difference in texture from hair-roughened chest to the flat, surprisingly smooth male nipples.

Whip's eyelids lowered as waves of pleasure visibly swept through him.

Smiling, Shannon petted and stroked Whip from his forehead to his powerful thighs, loving the heightened color of his skin and the burning silver of his half-opened eyes. After a time she turned her head and touched the base of his neck with her tongue. The caress had a catlike delicacy and curiosity.

Whip's whole body shuddered, raked by passion. Shannon murmured and ran the tip of her tongue over the steely tendons in his neck. Then she gave in to an urge she didn't understand and tasted him thoroughly, savoring his skin with the sensitive surfaces of her tongue and lips.

"You're salty," Shannon said against Whip's skin. "I like that. It makes me want to lick more of you. Is that all right?"

Breath came from Whip in a harsh rush. One of his hands went to Shannon's head, caressing and pressing, encouraging her to more forceful explorations.

"Whip?"

"Your teeth," he said huskily. "Let me feel their sharp little edges."

A few minutes earlier Shannon would have hesitated, but not now. Now she wanted to give the primitive caress as much as Whip wanted to receive it. She lowered her head until her chin was barely above the steamy water. Slowly she opened her lips. Her teeth tested the pad of muscle that surrounded a nipple.

A thick, hungry sound was dragged from deep within Whip's chest.

"Whip?"

"Do it again, honey girl. Harder."

"Are you sure?"

Whip laughed, bent his head swiftly, and lifted Shannon up at the same time. With no warning he fitted his mouth to the base of her neck. Then his teeth tested her resilient flesh with a force just short of pain while his mouth tugged at her silky skin.

Fire burst in Shannon. Her eyes closed and she lifted herself against Whip's mouth. She twisted slowly, increasing the power of the fierce caress. Whip laughed low in his throat and gave her what she was asking for, branding her with his mouth until she cried out.

Instantly he released her.

"I'm sorry," Whip said. "I didn't mean to hurt you."

Shannon's eyes opened, luminous with fire.

"Hurt me?" She shook her head and laughed. "Oh, no."

Her mouth went to Whip's chest and returned the fierce love play, tasting and biting and branding Whip with her heat until he groaned. Slowly she lifted her head.

"Am I hurting you?" Shannon asked.

But her eyes said she already knew the answer.

"You're killing me," Whip said huskily, "but you're not hurting me one bit. Well, not most of me. One particular part of me is aching fit to die."

"Where?"

"Guess," he said succinctly.

"Oh. There."

"Yes. There."

Shannon's hand slid beneath the water and rubbed down the taut muscles of Whip's torso. Her fingers met a dense cushion of hair and a blunt, rigid thrust of flesh.

"Here?" she asked.

Breath hissed through Whip's clenched teeth.

"Does touching you make it worse?" Shannon asked anxiously.

"Depends."

"On what?"

"On where you touch me. And how."

Shannon bit her lip, looked away, and went very still.

"I don't know how," she said.

"Explore, honey girl. I'll survive."

"But—"

"Unless touching me offends you?"

Shannon's head came up in surprise. "How could it offend me? You feel wonderful."

Whip shrugged. "Some women don't like touching a man at all, much less where he's most a man."

"Truly? I've spent most of my time wishing I *could* touch you, even . . . there."

"You've got your wish."

She smiled despite the blush burning across her cheeks.

"Tell me if I hurt you," she said huskily. "Although how I could hurt anything so hard is beyond me."

Whip made a sound that was part laugh, part groan. The feel of Shannon's fingers exploring him beneath the surface of the hot spring was a pleasure so great it was almost pain. As she caressed his length several times from blunt tip to rigid base, blood hammered so fiercely through him that he was afraid he would burst.

"Shannon.".

Her hand froze. "Am I touching too much?"

"Not enough."

"I told you I didn't know how," she said unhappily.

Breath hissed between Whip's clenched teeth. When Shannon would have withdrawn her hand, his fingers closed around hers.

"Like this," he said hoarsely.

Shannon felt the circle of her hand being moved slowly over Whip's hard, silky length, felt the fierce beating of his life's blood beneath her palm, and savored the sleek combination of satin and steel that was uniquely male. She smiled and gave a shivery little sigh of pleasure at being permitted the freedom of Whip's body.

The knowledge that Shannon was truly enjoying his arousal almost undid Whip. As her fingers pressed firmly around him, measuring and pleasuring at the same time, his blood leaped wildly. He dragged at breath and self-control and found neither. Release surged through him, taking him by surprise, for he had never been so quick off the mark before.

But then, he had never had a virgin widow looking at him before, watching his eyes and enjoying his flesh like a cat discovering catnip for the first time.

"You're shivering," Shannon said after a time. "Are you all right?"

"Much better."

She smiled and stroked all of Whip's body slowly, soothingly, for she could feel that some of the tension had left him. As she caressed him, she looked down at the swirling surface of the pool, where streaks of golden lantern light intertwined with black water.

"I wish I could see as much of you as I can feel," Shannon said, trailing her fingertips down over Whip. "I'd like to see how you change when you want me."

Whip's heartbeat kicked hard as hunger rushed through him once more.

"Honey girl, you're going to be the death of me."

She looked at him, startled. "What do you mean?"

"I'm not sure I can tell you, but I'm damn sure I can show you."

With that, Whip captured Shannon's caressing hand and lifted it to his neck. Then he bent his head and took Shannon's mouth, consuming it, making it completely his.

While he kissed her, his fingers stroked from Shannon's neck to her knees. He teased her breasts, drawing their peaks into tight velvet crowns. When he tugged on one nipple, twisting it with great care, she arched and cried out.

The sound was lost in Whip's mouth, but Shannon didn't notice. A radiant darkness was swirling around her, glittering with the possibility of ecstasy, calling to her in all the colors of the rainbow.

One of Whip's hands slid slowly up between Shannon's thighs until he could go no higher. Long fingers curled around her softness. He probed lightly, felt a sultry welcome that owed nothing to the hot spring, and eased deeply into her clinging heat.

Shannon flinched and stiffened as though he had taken a lash to her.

"What's wrong?" Whip murmured against her lips. "We've done this before."

"And then you raged at me and wouldn't touch me again."

"Not this time. This time I know you're a

virgin. This time I'm going to touch you every way I can, but one."

Whip's hand moved swiftly, hungrily. A ripple of tension went through Shannon's whole body, making it impossible for her to speak.

"I—" she said raggedly. "I—"

His thumb circled the knot of swollen flesh he had drawn from her softness. Shannon's arms tightened around his neck as another fierce shiver took her. She tried to speak but could make only a choked sound.

Concerned, Whip reluctantly withdrew from Shannon's body. His fingertips caressed the full, soft folds with great gentleness.

"What?" Whip murmured. "What is it?"

"I feel so strange," she said raggedly.

"But do you like it?"

A long finger eased into Shannon as Whip spoke.

"Yes," she whispered. *"Yes."*

Even more than Shannon's words, her body told Whip that she enjoyed the intimate caress. Hotter than the pool, her response spilled over him. Slowly he withdrew from her, his own body taut with the certainty that she could take him with only brief pain when her maidenhead was breached. She was sleek and sultry, made to hold him within her loving heat.

No, Whip told himself savagely. *I can't risk it.*

What risk? came his own instant retort. *There will never be a safer time of month for her. It will never be easier for me to control my own release than it is right now, when she has just given me such a sweet easing.*

There were more arguments in Whip's mind against taking Shannon, but he wasn't listening to them. He was listening to the swift breaking of Shannon's breath as he caressed her softness once more, slowly, deeply.

"Did you mean it?" Whip asked when he could go no farther into her.

"What?" she asked, dazed.

"That you wanted to see me?"

"Yes."

"Good. Because I sure as hell want to see you. I've been dreaming of watching you again, all honey and cream and fire. I've dreamed some other things, too."

"What?"

"When I show you, you'll blush all over." He laughed softly. "But you'll love it."

Whip stood up and walked out of the pool with Shannon in his arms. He got only as far as the heavy bearskin blanket before he stopped and looked down at the girl who was lying so trustingly in his arms, watching his eyes.

Steam lifted in silver wisps from Shannon's skin. Water gleamed on her shoulders and slid in golden rivulets between her breasts. Taut nipples glistened with liquid diamonds. The desire to lick up each shining drop nearly brought Whip to his knees.

"The cabin will be cold," he said huskily. "And it's too far."

"It's just a few steps."

"Like I said. Too far."

Shannon smiled and watched steam lift from Whip's body, first revealing and then concealing the power of his shoulders. Silver lines of water tangled in the thatch of dark gold hair on his chest. Captive drops glistened and winked at her as though they knew how much she wanted to sip them from his skin.

"Shannon?"

"Whatever you want," she said huskily. "However you want it."

Whip looked from Shannon's mouth to her breasts and then to the sleek, dark pelt concealing her softness.

"Don't tempt me, honey girl. I want you in ways that would make you blush to the soles of your pretty feet."

Shannon's glance lifted lazily from Whip's chest to his burning quicksilver eyes.

"Do you?" she asked. "What are they?"

Whip opened his mouth. No words came out. He lowered Shannon to the thick, furry blanket. Then he sat on his heels and looked at her, simply looked at her, until she trembled.

For she was looking at him, too. The blunt, heavy flesh she had so recently measured with her hand looked very intimidating.

Whip put his fingers beneath Shannon's chin, lifting her face, forcing her to look away from the stark evidence of his renewed arousal.

"Don't be afraid," Whip said simply. "I won't take you that way."

"I—but—" Shannon swallowed and tried again. "It's all right. It just—"

Whip waited.

"Well, damn," she muttered. "It didn't feel as—as unsettling—as it looks."

"Then close your eyes."

With a small sound Shannon did as Whip asked.

"Give me your hand," he said.

She held out shaking fingers to Whip. He took

them, kissed them gently, and put them around flesh that ached as though it had known no ease in months, rather than in mere minutes.

Shannon let out a long, ragged breath. After another breath she began to caress Whip with slow, tentative movements.

"See?" he asked deeply. "No teeth."

Helplessly Shannon laughed. When she opened her eyes, Whip was smiling down at her. His eyes blazed with an odd combination of tenderness and raw desire.

"I won't take you that way," Whip said again. "Not unless you ask me to just as plain as the sun rising."

"Will it hurt?" Shannon asked.

"A little. But only a little, and only the first time. You were made for me, honey girl. I'll fill you perfectly and you'll fit me just the same."

"Are you sure?"

Whip's eyelids lowered. Watching Shannon, he caressed the soft nest between her thighs, then parted her, sliding deeply within. She gasped as pleasure washed through her, licking over him hotly in turn.

"I'm sure," Whip said, his voice thick. "And so is your body. It kisses me in the sweetest way."

With a swift, controlled movement, Whip moved between Shannon's legs, urging them apart.

"W-Whip?"

"It's all right. I'm just going to return the favor."

"What?"

"I'm going to kiss your body in the sweetest way."

At first Shannon didn't understand. Then

Whip bent and nuzzled the tender skin of her inner thighs. His tongue flicked out just as his lips brushed over her softest skin.

Shannon gasped Whip's name as she understood.

"You told me whatever I wanted, however I wanted it," Whip said, nuzzling her. "Right now, this is how I want it. Does it hurt you?"

"N-no."

"Do you like it?"

Shannon's breath came in with a ripping sound as Whip caressed her lovingly. He smiled, repeated the intimate touch, and felt her response all hot and sleek around him. The scent of her pleasure was a primitive perfume, telling Whip what he already knew. The virgin widow was his—whatever he wanted, however he wanted it.

And he wanted it all.

"There are some other things I learned in odd places around the world," Whip said, biting Shannon with great delicacy.

A hoarse sound came from Shannon's throat. Her back arched like a bow drawn by a master archer. Lightning strokes of pleasure surged through her with each touch of Whip's mouth. As he pleasured her, his hands pressed against her inner thighs, opening her to his unexpected, consuming caresses.

"Seems there are as many ways of loving as there are of fighting," Whip said against Shannon's sultry skin.

Distantly Shannon realized that she was in a position of total vulnerability, utter abandon. Yet she could do nothing about it, for a net of wild, glittering lightning held her enthralled and shivering between her lover's hands.

"I had no problem finding partners to hone my fighting skills on," Whip said between tender, probing kisses. "But I never got around to finding a partner for this kind of play. So be patient with me while I get the hang of it."

Whip's tongue discovered the tight knot passion had drawn from Shannon's soft, sultry flesh. Intrigued, he swirled around the knot teasingly.

Shannon gasped as tension and pleasure spiraled up swiftly, driving her higher and higher with each moment.

"Do you like that?" he murmured. "I do. I know how delicate you are there, so I'll take only a tiny little bite."

A high, rippling cry came from Shannon as the world became a glittering kind of black and then exploded into a thousand rainbow shards.

Smiling darkly, Whip felt ecstasy take Shannon, shaking her like a leaf in a fierce storm. He knew he should release her untried flesh, but he couldn't force himself to do it. He kept on caressing her, tasting her lightly, biting her tenderly, loving her in a silence broken only by her wild cries.

Finally, reluctantly, Whip released Shannon from the thrall of his sensuality. He stretched out beside her, stroked her hair, and kissed the passionate tears from her eyes.

Blindly Shannon reached out to hold on to Whip, needing him in ways she didn't understand. When he gathered her against his body, his rigid flesh nuzzled the apex of her thighs. She was soft, hot, flushed from his caresses and her own response.

The intimacy of their position made Whip's

heart stop, then beat with redoubled force. Reflexively his hips moved, probing the sultry nest with his blunt, unbending flesh. Silky heat curled out to meet him, inviting a deeper exploration. Knowing he shouldn't, not able to stop himself, Whip caressed her with slow movements of his hips.

Instinctively Shannon's own hips stirred. The motion slid Whip more firmly against her softness. A thrill of pleasure radiated up through her body at the slight penetration. She moved again, and was rewarded again by the sweet, unexpected pressure that caressed and stretched her in the same motion.

Whip groaned when Shannon's helpless response licked over him as hotly as his mouth had moved over her a few minutes before. Then he felt her shift closer to him, her hips moving, her sultry core opening to him, weeping for him.

"Honey girl," Whip said almost roughly. "Do you know what you're asking for?"

Slowly Shannon opened her eyes. They were changed by passion until all that remained was a smoldering sapphire rim around each dilated pupil.

"What?" she asked, her voice husky.

"Look down."

She did. Her eyes widened. She moved experimentally, then smiled a smile as old as Eve.

"I thought you said it would hurt," Shannon said.

"You keep moving your hips like that and it will."

"You mean . . .?"

"I mean you're still a virgin," Whip said bluntly, "but if you keep kissing me like that with your hot little mouth, I'm going to slide in you so deep you won't know where I end and you begin."

Shannon's glance traveled down Whip's powerful body to the place where they were almost joined. She moved again, testing him and herself at the same time.

"I don't think so," she said.

Disappointment sleeted through Whip. His body tightened in savage rebellion at being denied what it needed more than breath.

"We're already as close as we can get," Shannon said. "I push and it feels good but we don't get any, um, closer."

Whip let out a long, breaking breath as he realized that Shannon wasn't turning away from him. She just didn't understand how to accomplish the deeper interlocking that their bodies desired.

"Do you want to join with me, Shannon?" Whip asked softly. "Do you want to get as close to me as a woman can get to a man?"

Shannon looked up into Whip's eyes and felt her heart turn over with love.

"Yes," she said huskily. "I want that. I want *you.*"

Slowly Whip shifted until he was lying between Shannon's legs once more.

Shannon's breath broke. She could feel him more clearly now. The sensation was delicious. Bubbles of pleasure expanded through her. When they burst, they caressed him with loving warmth.

Whip smiled and fought against the harsh urgency that was driving him. He hadn't expected Shannon to want him after he had given her one kind of fulfillment.

But she did want him. The honeyed proof of

it was licking over him right now, calling to him, telling him how easy it would be to push into her untried body.

And how hot.

"Wrap your legs around my hips," he said huskily.

When Shannon did, her breath broke. She felt Whip between her legs with stark clarity. It was disturbing . . . and profoundly arousing.

A shudder of pleasure and anticipation rippled through her.

"All right?" Whip asked.

"Yes," she whispered.

Whip pressed into Shannon until he knew he would forever change her if he went any farther. He retreated, then returned, then retreated.

"Still all right?" he asked, his voice strained.

Shannon didn't notice the roughness of Whip's voice or the sweat standing on his skin. She was consumed by sensations that taunted her as much as they pleasured her. She twisted hungrily beneath his powerful body, seeking to increase the sensuous pressure of his presence within her.

Whip froze.

"Is it too much?" he asked, withdrawing.

"I want more, not less," Shannon said raggedly. "I want everything you have to give me!"

Whip's eyelids lowered for an instant as a shudder racked his body and soul. Then he looked straight into Shannon's eyes and began rocking slowly, carefully. Her hips lifted insistently, demanding a more thorough kind of movement.

"Not yet," Whip said, laughing, retreating.

"When . . .?" she cried.

"When your body is shivering and you're all around me like hot, wild honey. Then I'll take you, Shannon. And we'll both scream with the pleasure of it."

One of Whip's hands moved down Shannon's body, caressing her breasts and belly and hips. Then he found the satin knot of her desire once more. It was the same as she was—hot, slick, hungry. He teased her until she cried out and sought him even more urgently, her body coiling beneath his as forerunners of ecstasy raked through her.

Whip's hand slid beneath Shannon's hips, testing and caressing her resilient flesh. Then his arm moved fully around her bottom and he dragged her upward, lifting her, opening her completely to him, wondering if she would like it that way.

She did. He knew, because he felt the sultry pulses of her pleasure caressing his hungry flesh. The world darkened around him as desire coiled violently, pulling him down into the hot center of Shannon's being.

"Shannon," Whip said urgently. "Look at me!"

Dazed, shivering, Shannon opened her eyes. Whip was poised above her, his face dark with passion and his eyes like twin silver flames, burning.

"Now, honey girl. *Now.*"

He took her with a smooth, powerful thrust, not stopping until their bodies were as deeply joined as it was possible for a man and woman to be.

Shannon stiffened and gave a keening cry.

Instantly Whip froze, hoping that her body would adjust to his presence if he didn't move.

Then he felt the secret, deep pulses within Shannon and knew that she was transfixed by pleasure rather than pain. With a hoarse sound he began moving, no longer fighting the dark, elemental passion that called to him from her body. He drove into her tight satin depths, felt the honeyed kisses of her climax licking over him, and pulled her hips even more tightly against him.

Whip's last thought was that he hoped Shannon meant what she had said about wanting everything he had to give, because he had just discovered it was too late for him to hold back anything at all. Life had become a hot, radiant darkness with neither beginning nor end; and its heartbeat was the hard, silken pulses of his release spilling into her welcoming body.

19

Reno rode up to Shannon's cabin in a blaze of summer heat that made the snowstorm of three days ago seem impossible. Pearly wisps of clouds trailed from the highest peaks. The rest of the sky was as clear and blue as Shannon's eyes. The smell of evergreens and meadow grass gave the air an extraordinary savor.

But whatever birdsongs the meadow and forest might have had to offer were being drowned out by Prettyface's savage barking.

"That's enough, Prettyface!" Whip said,

walking out of the cabin. "Reno is a friend. Friend!"

Prettyface didn't think so, but he subsided into snarls and then a grumbling kind of silence.

Reno's green eyes looked at the dog with deceptive laziness. His left hand wasn't exactly on the butt of his revolver, but it wasn't very far away, either.

"Real sociable type," Reno said dryly.

"He'll warm to you," Whip said.

"I'll hold you to that."

"Just don't try to come here when I'm gone."

"When will that be?" Reno asked coolly.

Whip didn't answer.

Reno glanced from Prettyface to his brother, wondering if Whip was any closer to solving the problem of his conflicting passions for a distant sunrise and a pretty widow lady.

Then the cabin door opened and a woman with a walk as sultry as the summer day came toward Reno.

"Judas Priest," Reno said beneath his breath as he dismounted in a fluid rush. "No wonder you're between a rock and a hard place."

Whip said nothing, simply watched Shannon with haunted, quicksilver eyes. Then he held out his hand to her and smiled gently. When she laced her fingers through his, he pulled her close, tucking her against his body.

Reno watched all of it, his brother's tender smile and sheltering arm, Shannon's loving blue eyes and equally loving smile. But most telling of all to Reno was their physical ease with one another.

Shannon and Whip had become lovers. Reno had no doubt of it. If the radiance of Shannon's eyes hadn't told Reno, the shadows in Whip's would have.

Reno touched the rim of his hat to Shannon in silent greeting.

"Shannon," Whip said, "this is my brother Matt Moran, but we all call him Reno. Reno, this is Shannon Conner Smith."

My woman.

Though the words weren't said aloud, Reno sensed them very clearly.

So did Shannon. Red tinged her cheekbones for a few moments. She held out her hand and searched Reno's vivid green eyes anxiously, wondering if he would condemn her.

Reno's hard fingers lifted Shannon's hand to his lips. He bowed as elegantly as though he were in a Paris ballroom rather than in a wild mountain meadow.

Shannon startled both men by sinking into a deep, graceful curtsy, as though she were wearing yards of silk and crinolines rather than ragged men's clothing. Then she peeked up at Whip's dark, startlingly handsome brother with laughter and relief in her beautiful eyes.

"A pleasure, Mr. Moran," she murmured, rising.

"Reno, Mrs. Smith," he corrected gently, holding Shannon's hand between both of his. "I left Mr. Moran behind a long, long time ago."

"Then you must call me Shannon. I never was truly Mrs. Smith. Silent John was my great-uncle."

For an instant Reno's dense black eyelashes shuttered his reaction.

No wonder Whip is having such a wrestling match

with his conscience, Reno told himself silently. *Shannon is a virgin*.

Or was.

"In any case, Silent John is dead," Shannon said clearly.

"A lot of men will be relieved to hear that," Reno said beneath his breath as he released Shannon's hand.

"I beg your pardon?" she said.

"Silent John was, um, well-known around Colorado Territory," Reno said.

"His reputation—and Prettyface—went a long way toward keeping me safe while he was gone," Shannon said.

"Prettyface," Reno said, glancing toward the huge brindle hound. "Hell of a name for something that, um . . ."

Tactfully, Reno didn't finish the sentence.

"Maybe you'd like to be the one to call him ugly," Whip offered, smiling as he remembered Shannon's saying something similar to him.

Shannon snickered.

"No, thank you," Reno said promptly. "My mama didn't raise any dumb ones."

Whip laughed out loud.

"Come on inside," Whip said. "We were just sitting down to lunch."

"Only if you'll let me put something on the table. Eve packed enough food for two."

"Why?"

"She wanted to come along, but when we got to Cal's place, Ethan was feeling puny and so was Willow."

"Are they all right?" Whip and Shannon asked simultaneously.

"They're fine. Just a summer cold. I told Eve

I could look the claims over by myself. If nothing looks good, I'll go and bring her back up here. If there's gold here, the two of us will find it."

What Reno didn't say was that he doubted there was any gold worth mentioning up Avalanche Creek, which was why he had brought Eve along in the first place. He had prospected Avalanche Creek's high, dangerous reaches years ago and found mostly chilblains and bruises for his efforts.

"Did you bring the Spanish needles?" Whip asked.

"In my saddlebags," Reno said. "They don't work worth a tinker's damn without Eve, though."

"What are Spanish needles?" Shannon asked.

"Dowsing rods made of metal," Reno said. "They respond to gold or silver rather than to water. The Jesuit priests brought them to the New World hundreds of years ago."

"Do they really work?" Shannon asked him.

"Count on it."

"But only for Reno and Eve," Whip put in. "Damnedest thing you ever saw. If any other people hold the needles together, they're just so much junk."

"Truly?" she asked.

"As ever was. Makes the hair on your arms stand straight up to watch Reno and Eve using those needles."

"Then you found gold?" she asked Reno.

"Yes. Way up in the Abajos, in a crumbling old mine that had been dug by Indian slaves for Jesuit priests. There were ingots of pure gold so heavy Eve could hardly lift more than one at a time."

"Oh, my," Shannon said. "Those needles must be something!"

"They were a doorway to hell," Whip said curtly.

Shannon looked at Whip, shocked.

"The mine came down around my ears," Reno explained. "Eve and Whip damn near died digging me out."

Shannon went pale. She touched Whip's sun-bright hair with fingers that trembled.

"I don't want gold that much," she said starkly.

"It's all right, honey girl," Whip said, brushing his lips over her hand.

"A cave-in won't be a problem up Avalanche Creek," Reno said. "It's hard rock all the way. The old Spanish mine wasn't."

"How do you know about Avalanche Creek?" Shannon asked.

"Silent John wasn't the first man to see a gleam of gold dust in the creek and follow it back up the peak."

"Did you find gold?" she asked eagerly.

Reno made a neutral sound. "Some."

"How much is 'some'?" Shannon persisted.

"Not much," Whip said succinctly. "Otherwise Reno wouldn't have risked his butt in the Spanish mine."

"Oh," Shannon said, disappointed.

"But I wasn't looking all that hard," Reno said kindly.

"This time will be different," Whip said.

Reno raised his eyebrows at the certainty in Whip's voice. A look at his brother's pale silver eyes told Reno that questions wouldn't be appreciated.

Gold was the subject during the quick lunch the three of them ate, and gold was discussed at every opportunity along the trail to Rifle Sight claim. Sweat gleamed on the horses and mules, for Whip was holding to a very hard pace.

Sunlight followed them every step of the way, its blazing warmth as golden as the metal they pursued. Grizzly Meadow was hot. It brimmed with wildflowers and the songs of hidden birds. Both men examined the area carefully, but found no fresh evidence that a grizzly had been there. Relieved, they quickly set up camp.

"Plenty of deer sign around," Reno said. "If there's any light left after you show me the claim, why don't you hunt? Winters are long up here."

Whip heard what Reno didn't say—Shannon would need every bit of meat she could get in order to survive the season of storm and ice.

While Shannon began preparing supper, the two men went quickly to the claim. The sky was already turning color, hinting at the glorious sunset to come.

It didn't take Reno long to look over the mine. There was little to look at.

"Any other tunnels?" Reno asked as he emerged from the shallow hole in the mountain, a lantern in his hand.

"Not that I've found," Whip said. "And yes, I looked carefully."

"I believe you. A man looking for freedom is real careful."

Whip's mouth flattened, but he didn't deny what Reno was saying.

"The gold is for Shannon," Whip said.

"Uh huh. Regular little gold digger, that one."

"Damn it, Reno—"

"Put your ruff down," Reno interrupted calmly. "We both know the gold is as much for your freedom as for Shannon's security. If you can't stand hearing the truth, then maybe you better take a long look at what you're doing."

Whip gave his brother a cold, level stare. "I know what I'm doing."

Reno shrugged. "I thought I did, too, last autumn. Then you dumped a saddlebag full of pure gold bars at my feet and told me I was a goddamned fool."

"And you're thinking I'm the fool now, is that it?"

"I'm thinking that's one fine woman whose heart you're going to break. Too bad she was a virgin. That will make it harder when—"

"It's none of your business," Whip interrupted, his voice flat, dangerous.

"The hell you say. I'm the one finding gold so you can pay off your conscience and go back to chasing sunrises."

Whip shifted his stance slightly, menacingly.

Reno's answering smile was as narrow as his eyes.

"That's it," Reno goaded. "Jump me. Maybe I can pound some sense into your thick skull. Sure as hell someone should."

"Pound rock. It's softer."

"Smarter, too."

Abruptly Reno turned away, cutting off whatever Whip had been about to say.

"Three days ago I would have given you the fight you want," Reno said over his shoulder.

"But I'm slam out of patience at the moment. I'm going back to camp before I lay my revolver along your thick skull. Shannon doesn't need a bloodied, banged-up yondering idiot to worry about. Her worry plate is plumb full as it is."

When Shannon awoke, the stars were just fading from the sky. In the distance she heard the murmur of male voices. There was no crackle of campfire or smell of coffee in the crisp air.

"Whip? Reno?" she called. "Do you want breakfast?"

"Go back to sleep," Whip called. "Reno and I are just talking about the claims. I'll wake you when it's time to start back to the cabin."

Sighing, Shannon rolled over and pulled the blankets up to her eyebrows. Nights were always chilly in the high country. More than once during the darkness she had wished for the warmth and comfort of Whip holding her close while she slept. It had been so easy to get used to the luxury of his presence.

Whip had set up his bedroll across the campfire, where his brother slept. Prettyface had kept Shannon company, but not for long. The dog preferred not to sleep near the campfire, as though the bright flames and pungent smoke dulled his canine senses. He kept to the perimeter of the camp, well away from the people he guarded so carefully.

When Whip walked past Prettyface on the way back to camp, the dog lifted his huge, blunt head and thumped his tail against the ground several times in silent greeting.

"Your mistress is still sleeping, isn't she?" Whip asked softly. "Good. I could use a little rest myself. Didn't sleep worth a damn last night. Stay here and guard us."

Soundlessly Whip went to the place where Shannon was. He took off his heavy jacket and slid beneath the blankets, stretching out next to her. Shannon murmured sleepily and turned toward him, burrowing into his warmth, nuzzling against him, sighing.

At first Whip thought that she had awakened. Then he felt the utter relaxation of her body and knew that she was deeply asleep. The realization that Shannon turned toward him even when she was asleep was like a silver needle of emotion stitching through Whip's soul, pain and pleasure combined.

Shannon, don't love me. I don't want to hurt you, honey girl.

The only answer that came was the smell of spearmint and woman combined.

Whip's heart turned over and his body hardened in a savage rush. He knew he couldn't stay with Shannon for much longer . . . but he could make a lifetime of every moment they had together.

Slowly Whip eased beneath the blankets, breathing deeply of warm, woman-scented air.

I would love to kiss those sweet breasts, but I shouldn't wake her.

Even as Whip told himself that Shannon needed sleep more than she needed loving, his hands were moving over her old, painfully clean shirt.

Silk and lace lay warmly beneath, shocking in their femininity after the man's shirt.

What the hell . . . ! Where did she get this?

Long fingers untied silk bows one by one. But

it was Whip's mouth rather than his hands that moved the silk aside, discovering the even softer silk of Shannon's skin.

Shannon murmured and sighed and shifted, lifting herself to his kisses.

Whip hesitated and asked very softly. "Shannon?"

Her only answer was a sigh. Except for the subtle tightening of her nipples beneath his lips, her body was still completely relaxed, trusting him in a way no one ever had.

Even himself.

Honey girl, how am I going to live without you?

His tongue touched the tip of each breast. The velvety hardness of Shannon's nipples teased his lips, silently asking for another kind of caress. He gave it to her softly, delicately, holding her within his warmth even as he tugged her nipples to hard peaks with his mouth.

Shannon's body moved languidly, held between the heat of Whip's caresses and the growing heat of her dreams.

Don't wake up yet, sweet woman. Let me taste your dreams.

Long fingers found and unfastened Shannon's pants, pushing the loose fabric down her legs and over her feet. She stirred restlessly, then calmed when Whip held her close.

"It's just me, honey girl," he murmured against her ear.

Shannon made a sleepy sound and cuddled even more closely against Whip.

He lay very still, trying to slow the savage hammering of his heart that had begun when his fingers encountered the silky underwear. He wanted to look at Shannon wearing only that bit of softness and lace. He wanted it until sweat gathered in the small of his back.

But he wanted to touch her sleeping dreams even more.

Whip knew if he cast off the covers so that the swelling light of dawn could bathe Shannon, she would awaken. So he held her until she lay relaxed in his arms once more. Then he eased slowly down her body beneath the blankets, his mouth following the opening in the chemise, tracing the margin between silk underwear and satin skin.

Shannon stirred as heat flushed her body, a seething warmth that was summoned by Whip's slow, thorough loving. She sighed and her hips moved in the languid rhythms of his caresses.

Her sensuous response consumed Whip as softly and completely as he was consuming her. The world became infused with heat and the elemental perfume of a woman's desire.

Honey girl, Whip groaned silently. *God*, *I could die trying to get enough of you.*

A tiny, shuddering sound escaped Shannon's lips. It was Whip's name, called as much in dream as in waking.

He answered with a silky movement of his mouth and her name whispered into the seething darkness beneath the blankets.

For a time Shannon could find no difference between her dream and the hot awakening that flushed her skin. Then pleasure speared softly through her, stopping her breath. When the sweet, pulsing sensations passed, she moaned, wanting more.

Whip felt the difference in the tension of Shannon's body and knew that he had awakened her into ecstasy. He could feel its heat all around him and taste its sultry mystery. When he caressed her again, he sensed the rhythmic pulses deep within her.

Sweat bathed Whip from his forehead to the soles of his feet. He wanted to be within Shannon's ecstasy so much that he felt as though he were being torn apart.

He didn't know that he had called her name in his need, until her hands buried themselves in his hair and tugged at him, pulling him back up her body. As he moved, her hands went to his shirt, his pants, unfastening everything, seeking him blindly.

Whip captured Shannon's hands beneath one of his own, holding them against the rigid ache of his arousal.

"Whip . . .?" she murmured questioningly, moving her hips, trying to capture him.

"No, honey girl. Not that way."

"Why?" she murmured, eyes closed.

"I don't trust myself not to get you pregnant."

Shannon shivered and threw off the last of her sultry dreams. But reality was no less hot. She could feel the hard beating of Whip's pulse beneath her captive hands.

"Yesterday and the day before—" she began.

"And the day before that," Whip interrupted tautly. "Each day is closer to the time when you're fertile."

"But from what you said, it should be safe for at least five days, maybe more."

Whip's breath hissed out through his teeth.

"Should be isn't good enough," he said flatly. "You're too damned addictive, honey girl. Each time I slide into you I want you more. Deeper. Hotter. Harder. I can't trust myself to hold back long enough to protect you. Hell, I'm all but out of control right now, just thinking about how it is when we're locked together."

Shannon looked at the smoky silver of Whip's eyes. They gleamed like a cat's in the rising light of dawn. She lifted her mouth to Whip's, tasted him and herself and passion, and let out a long, broken sigh.

"I love feeling your pleasure so deep inside me," she said, moving slowly against him. "I love feeling the weight and strength of you. I love the feel of your hunger in my hands, in my body."

"Shannon," Whip whispered. "I—"

Then he could say no more, for she had moved suddenly. His hot, sensitive flesh was sliding against the entrance to her sultry core.

"I love you, Whip. Love me in the only way you can, for whatever time we have left."

With a sound of a man in torment, Whip allowed Shannon to take him. The hot, slick ease of the joining almost undid him. He clenched his whole body, fighting for control.

Then Whip felt the butterfly wings of Shannon's ecstasy caressing him. He cried out as the exquisite, delicate touches hurled him into a pleasure so great he could only surrender himself to it, and to the woman whose cries echoed his.

The second time Shannon woke up, Whip was watching her with haunted gray eyes. He was fully dressed and held a rifle in his hands. Prettyface was dancing impatiently around Shannon's bedroll, eager to be off hunting.

"I'm going up to see how Reno is doing," Whip

said tightly. "Then I'll go with you back to the cabin."

"And then?" Shannon asked, uneasy at what she saw in Whip's eyes.

"Then I'll come back and help Reno."

"He didn't look like he needed any help."

"The sooner he finds gold, the safer you'll be," Whip said.

"Safer?"

"The sooner I leave, the less chance there is of making you pregnant," Whip said savagely.

"I see."

"I shouldn't have taken you!"

"You didn't," she retorted. "I took you."

Whip's mouth flattened. "Either way, honey girl, only one of us will get pregnant."

"Do tell."

"I'm trying, but you aren't listening. I can't keep my pants fastened around you and I'm damned if I'll be tied down, so—"

"You'll leave as soon as you can," Shannon interrupted, her voice as flat as the line of Whip's mouth. Though tears stood in her eyes, her voice was steady. "Old territory, Whip. We've been over it fifty times by now. Tell me something I don't know."

"Be ready to leave by the time the sun is full overhead," Whip said.

He turned and stalked off. Prettyface followed, only to be sent back to Shannon with a curt word.

Whip took the trail to Rifle Sight claim with long, punishing strides. He hoped it would take the starch out of his relentless hunger for the girl with autumn hair and eyes as deep as the mountain sky.

But he knew it wouldn't.

Nothing could compete with Shannon except the sunrise he hadn't seen—the vast distance calling his name, promising him the freedom of the world and the mysteries of a thousand Edens.

And Whip had just thought of a way to be certain of keeping that promise.

By the time Whip reached the claim, he was somewhat calmer. Even so, Reno gave his brother a wary look when he saw Whip waiting for him just beyond the entrance to the mine. The look in Whip's eyes would have done credit to a trapped wolf.

"Lose something?" Reno asked mildly.

"No. I found it."

Reno's green eyes asked a silent question.

"Gold," Whip said succinctly.

"Where?"

"In your corral."

"If I wait long enough, I suppose I'll hear something that makes sense," Reno said.

"How much chance do you think there is of finding gold on Silent John's claims?"

"Real gold? The kind that buys bacon and beans and freedom for dumb yondering men?"

"Yes," Whip said savagely.

"About a snowball's chance in hell."

"That much?" Whip retorted. "I would have put the odds a lot lower, myself."

Reno smiled despite his irritation with his thick-headed brother.

"I was trying to let you down easy," Reno said. "Truth is, horseshit has more gold in it than this mine."

Whip gave a crack of laughter that was almost painful.

"Yeah, that's what I thought," Whip said. "Yet

Shannon talked about Silent John bringing pieces of ore down the mountain that were so rotten with gold they came apart in your hands."

"Then Silent John must have had God's own claim. But it isn't on Avalanche Creek," Reno added with certainty.

"Shannon doesn't know that."

"She will when I tell her."

"Don't." Whip's voice was curt, final.

Reno waited.

"Do you still have nuggets and dust stashed around from your old claims?" Whip asked.

Reno nodded.

"Dig up one of those ingots of Spanish gold Eve gave me," Whip said. "Swap it for nuggets and dust."

"Hold it. I don't have that much loose stuff."

"Make up the difference with my gold. Shave it or melt it and pour it into the dust or put dynamite under it and blow it to hell and back. Just get that damned gold up here in pieces."

Reno's black eyebrows rose.

"Bring Eve," Whip continued relentlessly. "Salt that damned useless mine. Put on a show with the Spanish needles. Do whatever you have to, *but make sure Shannon believes the gold came from Silent John's claim*."

"If I do what you say, I'll end up with at least three kinds of loose gold—placer, dust, and shotgunned into the rock," Reno said. "In addition, the gold will be different colors from what is found up here. Some of my gold has more copper, some has more silver. Hell, some of it is placer gold, worn smooth as a baby's bottom."

"So?"

"So it wouldn't fool a miner who knows Echo Basin gold mines," Reno said impatiently.

"That's not a problem. Shannon doesn't know gold from granite."

Reno took off his hat and slapped it against his thigh. Rock dust rose.

Warily, Whip waited.

Reno whacked the hat a few more times and put it back on his head with a smooth, quick motion.

"All right," Reno said. "I'll be back in six days with Eve and enough gold so that Shannon can be free of Echo Basin—and you can be free of her."

Whip's eyelids flinched in silent pain, but he said nothing. With hungry eyes he watched the arc of the sun across the sky.

"Make it four days," Whip said flatly.

"Judas Priest. If you're that restless, just leave. I'll take care of things here."

Slowly Whip shook his head. "It's not that. It's just that the longer I stay with her . . ."

Whip turned and walked away without saying any more. He didn't know how to explain that each day spent with Shannon made it harder to leave her.

And each day made it more certain that the pain of parting would be deeper.

I never meant to hurt you, honey girl.

Yet Whip would, and he knew it.

20

Torn between hope the gold hunt would succeed and certainty that success meant the end of her time with Whip, Shannon watched Reno work the valley next to a slender woman whose hair was the color of gold dust. Their movements were smooth and elegant, in complete harmony.

As Reno and Eve turned, Shannon could see that each held a Spanish needle between one thumb and palm. The forked end of the needles rested against each other, interlocking gently.

There was no pressure from either Reno or Eve that forced the needles into contact. Nor was there any attempt to keep the needles touching. In truth, there was no visible reason for the dowsing needles to remain interlocked while Reno and Eve walked over the rugged land.

Yet the needles did.

"It's . . . incredible," Shannon said.

Her voice was a whisper, though there was no chance of being overheard.

"The needles?" Whip asked.

"The way Reno and Eve move together. As though the Spanish needles were connecting them rather than the opposite."

"Reno once told me that if moonlight were water flowing, the feel of its currents would be like the needles when he and Eve use them. Ghostly, but very real."

"Like the feeling that comes when I remember

how we . . ." Shannon's voice died as a flush climbed her cheeks.

The quicksilver gleam of Whip's eyes told her that he knew what she was thinking.

"Just like that, honey girl. Interlocking, moving, rocking. Only with us, it's more like currents from the sun than the moon."

Shannon smiled and took a shivery kind of breath. "Yes."

The back of Whip's fingers brushed lightly down Shannon's hot cheek. His thumb slid lower, caressing first her lips and then the race of her pulse in her neck.

"Time to go," Whip said, his voice unusually deep. "Crowbait is packed and ready for the trail."

Shannon spun to face Whip fully. Pain made her features bleak and her voice raw.

"But I thought you wouldn't leave until they found gold," she protested shakily.

Whip gathered Shannon close, wrapping his arms around her, feeling her pain as though it was his own.

"Shannon," he whispered against her hair. "I wasn't talking about leaving alone. I was talking about taking you back to the cabin and doing some deer hunting."

For an instant Shannon's arms tightened almost harshly around Whip. Then she pulled back and forced a smile onto lips that would rather have done anything else.

"Of course," she said, looking away from Whip's too-knowing eyes. "Silly of me. I don't know what I was thinking of."

Whip's eyelids flinched. He knew exactly what Shannon had been thinking of. The fact that he would leave her soon had been haunting him, too.

I don't want to hurt her.

I can't stay.

God, why did I ever come to Echo Basin in the first place? Before now I never guessed how much a man could hurt and never show a wound.

Nor how much a woman could cry and never make a sound. Looking at Shannon's sad eyes is tearing my heart out.

But all Whip said aloud was, "You've learned a lot about tracking and stalking in the last few days. By the time deer and elk start coming down out of the high country, you'll be a good hunter."

Not that she needed to be. Whip had shot enough game for Shannon, Cherokee, and a starving bear to winter on. Most of it was at Cherokee's cabin right now, curing over slow fires.

"Hunting. Of course," Shannon said distantly, her voice as empty as her smile. "Well, we'd better get cracking, hadn't we? Should I say good-bye to Reno and Eve now, or will they come by the cabin before the three of you leave for good?"

"Shannon . . ." Whip's voice dried up.

He swallowed hard, trying to banish the emotion that kept ambushing him without warning.

"Reno and Eve like you a lot," Whip said finally. "They would be happy to have you visit them."

"Of course," Shannon said for the third time.

And for the third time, the words meant nothing.

"Will you?" Whip pressed.

"Will I what?"

"Visit Reno and Eve."

"Don't worry," Shannon said, her voice neutral. "You won't trip over me if you come back from yondering and want to see your own family."

"That's not what I meant!"

"Isn't it? Well, in any case, it's what I meant."

"What about Caleb and Willow?" Whip demanded. "Are you just going to walk away from them, too?"

Shannon gave Whip a look from narrowed blue eyes.

"They're your family, not mine," she said distinctly. "I'm not walking away to anywhere but home, yondering man."

"Damn it, that shack isn't a home," Whip said between his teeth.

"It is to me. Nothing you can say or do will change that. Accept it. Just as I've accepted that you'll leave me as soon as your conscience lets you."

Shannon turned away from Whip. In silence she watched the two people who moved as one over the rough slope. Just beyond Reno and Eve the mine's mouth opened like a black, empty eye. They began quartering the area carefully, walking out from the mine's entrance.

Whip watched, too. A muscle at the side of his jaw worked visibly as he fought to control his temper at Shannon's maddening, stubborn insistence that she would keep on living in a place he didn't believe was safe for her.

But there was nothing he could do about that, any more than he could take the darkness from Shannon's beautiful eyes and replace it with light.

"It's getting late," Whip said finally.

Shannon nodded without looking away from the intricate dance of Spanish needles, woman, and man.

And love.

Shannon felt Eve's and Reno's love for one another like a knife turning in her soul. She would never have its like. When Whip left, he would take her love with him.

And he wouldn't come back.

I never go to the same place twice.

"It takes time to find gold," Whip said, keeping his voice level. "We have better things to do than watch Reno and Eve working."

"How long does it take?"

For a moment Whip didn't answer. He was too shocked by the flatness in Shannon's voice. Where laughter and hope and love had once been, there now were only harshly controlled syllables and no life at all.

"It could be days," Whip said. "The needles are tricky and tiring to use."

"Days."

The word was almost a ragged sigh, telling Whip that Shannon had hoped the answer would be weeks, perhaps months.

Perhaps even until the snows came, closing the trail to Avalanche Creek's highest reaches.

"Then you're right," Shannon said. "We can't waste any more time stalking sunlight through the forest, or picking flowers, or playing with Prettyface, or holding hands and watching sunset and moonrise, or lying together at night and pretending that tomorrow will never come."

"Shannon—"

"No," she said, speaking over Whip's interruption. "You're right. It's time to move on."

"Damn it! You make it sound like I'm saying good-bye right now. I'm not!"

"You should be. It might be easier that way."

"Is that what you want? For me to walk away right now?"

"What I want?" Shannon laughed oddly. "What in God's name does what I want have to do with it?"

Tears flashed unhappily in her eyes.

"Shannon," Whip whispered. He reached for her. "Honey girl, don't cry."

"No."

Shannon stepped back from Whip so quickly that she almost tripped.

"Don't touch me."

Her voice was raw from the fierce grip she had on her emotions.

"But—"

"If you touch me," Shannon said over Whip's voice, "I'll really cry and that won't do any good at all."

Whip moved with alarming speed and strength, yet his hands were gentle when he pulled Shannon into his arms and wrapped her close against his body.

"I m-meant it," Shannon said brokenly, refusing to meet Whip's eyes.

"I believe you."

He bent and kissed her eyelashes where silver tears already glittered.

"Go ahead and cry, honey girl. Cry hard and long. For both of us."

A shudder went through Shannon as she fought against herself and the man who held her, cherished her, protected her, wanted her . . . but loved only the sunrise he had never seen.

Then she looked up at Whip's eyes and saw her own helpless pain reflected there, an anguish that was all the more intense because he had never expected to feel it.

Cry hard and long. For both of us.

The fierce tension in Shannon's body broke. She pressed her face against Whip's neck and wept as though everything of life had been taken from her except pain itself.

Eyes closed, jaw clenched, Whip held Shannon, rocking her slowly, trying to ease the anguish that came from a hurt he had never meant to give, an agony that sprang from what he was and didn't know how to change.

Yondering man.

After a time Whip carried Shannon to his horse, for he couldn't force himself to let go of her. They rode down the mountain together, followed by a long-legged mule and a packhorse, with a huge hound trotting alongside.

Somewhere between Rifle Sight's dreams of gold and the cabin's lonely reality, Shannon's tears finally stopped. Even then, Whip didn't release her. He simply held her against his chest, his arms close around her as though he expected her to be taken from him without warning.

When they reached the cabin, Whip carried Shannon inside and put her on the bunk. Despite the heat of the day, the cabin was chilly, for no fire had been lit for many nights. He pulled the thick bearskin blanket over her and tucked it beneath her chin.

"I'll be back as soon as I've taken care of the animals," Whip said.

Shannon started to protest, then simply nodded agreement. She had never felt so tired in her life, or so cold. Not even after she had tried to dig Prettyface out of the creek's icy trap.

When Whip returned he found Shannon curled beneath the heavy, furry blanket, staring at the rich sunset colors that were seeping through the ill-fitting shutters. A narrow shaft of red-gold light lay across her eyes, transforming them into an orchid color that was as exotic as anything Whip had ever seen in his years of yondering.

Then Shannon turned and looked at Whip. The grief in her eyes hit him like a blow.

"Honey girl," he said roughly, kneeling beside her bed. "Oh, God, I wish I were a different man!"

"I don't." Shannon touched Whip's sun-bright hair with fingers that trembled. "I wouldn't have loved a different man."

"I'll stay."

For an instant joy blazed in Shannon, burning away the desolate shadows. Then Whip's eyelashes lifted and she saw the metallic sheen of his eyes. He had the fierce, hunted look of a wolf brought to bay.

"It wouldn't work." Shannon smiled with trembling lips. "But thank you for offering."

"I'll make it work."

"How?" she asked simply. "Will you stop playing your flute at dawn, calling to the sunrise you've never seen? Will you stop looking into the clouds at sunset with hunger in your eyes for a different land, a different language, a different life? Will you stop yearning for something that has no name, no description, simply your soul-deep belief that such a thing exists somewhere on the face of the earth, waiting for you to discover it?"

Whip's breath caught. He hadn't realized that Shannon understood him so well.

Better than he understood himself.

"I want you," he said starkly.

"I know," Shannon said. "But you'll leave anyway. Desire isn't enough to satisfy your yearning, yondering soul. Only love could do that."

Abruptly Whip closed his eyes. "I'll come back to you, honey girl."

"Don't," Shannon whispered, stroking the fierce lines of Whip's face. "The pain would be too much when you left again. For both of us."

"Shannon—God, I'm so sorry—"

Whip's voice broke. Tears glittered wildly in his eyes.

"It's all right, yondering man," she whispered. "It's all right."

She kissed Whip's eyelids, his cheeks, the corners of his mouth.

"I never should have touched you," Whip said, shivering beneath the delicate caresses.

"You never lied to me," Shannon said, kissing him gently, repeatedly. "You warned me every step of the way that you were a yondering man. I didn't understand at first. Then I didn't believe. But I do now."

"I should be horsewhipped for taking your innocence," Whip said roughly. "No decent man would have."

"I wanted you. You were kind and gentle when other men were savage and crude. I couldn't have asked for a more decent man to teach me passion."

"I didn't want you to love me," Whip whispered, for his throat was closed around emotions he refused to release. "I didn't want to hurt you."

Shannon smiled sadly. "I can hardly be the first widow who watched you leave with love in her eyes."

"You're the first one whose sorrow cut me until I bled and just kept on bleeding."

There was pain in Whip's tone, and accusation, and bafflement.

"You can no more change my loving you than I can change your not loving me," Shannon said. "It's just the way it is, like a river running down to the sea or smoke rising into the sky or the earth turning, carrying you away from me toward the sunrise you've never seen."

Shannon's name came from Whip's mouth in a broken rush that was nearly a cry.

"Whip," she whispered. "Let's not waste any more breath on what can't be changed. Love me in the only way you can while you're here. Join your body with mine and take me to the sun. We have so little time left. . . ."

Whip's breath came in with a swift, ripping sound as Shannon's hands slid down his body and cradled his very different, very aroused flesh.

"No," he said thickly. "It's too dangerous. Too many days have gone by."

"Then at least let me bring you ease."

With an anguished sound, Whip dragged Shannon's hands back up his body.

"No," he said curtly. "Don't you understand? *I don't trust myself.* I start out telling myself that we'll just pet each other a bit, no more. Just mutual ease and comfort. Then your breath begins to break and you tremble and I feel the honey and fire between your legs and all I want to do is bury myself in you.

Shannon's breath caught.

"And that's just what I do each time," Whip said bitterly. "I lock myself inside you and the honey flows and the fire burns and nothing else is real. No sorrow, no pain, no thought, nothing but you and me and the kind of white-hot pleasure I'll die remembering."

"It's the same for me," Shannon said against Whip's mouth. "Be a part of me, Whip. I love the way it feels when you're deep inside me."

"Haven't you been listening? It's not safe! I don't trust myself not to make you pregnant!"

A shudder went through Shannon, hunger and grief combined.

A baby.

God, I want Whip's child. But he doesn't want to leave that much of himself behind.

Then Shannon remembered Cherokee's odd gift.

"Cherokee gave me something so I wouldn't conceive," Shannon said huskily.

"What?" Whip asked, startled.

"Over there." Shannon pointed. "On the shelf. The vial and the little bag."

Whip gave her a strange look. Then he stood with swift grace and went to the shelf. Carefully he opened the bag and tipped it over his open hand. Tiny scraps of sponge rustled onto his palm. He took the stopper out of the vial and sniffed. His eyes widened as he smelled juniper and spearmint combined, plus a whiff of something sharp he couldn't name.

"I'll be damned," he said.

"But I don't know what to do with any of it," Shannon said. "Do you?"

He nodded.

"Oh, good," she said, relieved. "What do I do?"

Whip selected a sponge, doused it thoroughly with the pungent oil and turned toward Shannon with a lazy, very male smile.

"I'll show you," he said.

She blinked, startled by Whip's transformation. Gone was the wildness of an animal brought to bay. His elemental hunger and his certainty of ecstasy were all but tangible.

"Don't be nervous, honey girl. You'll love learning how to use this. And I'll love showing you."

"Whip?" Shannon called up the ridge from the cabin doorway. "Lunch is ready. Are you finished dressing out that elk yet?"

Prettyface's head appeared from the corner of the meadow where he had been dining on scraps from Whip's latest hunt. She had heard Prettyface bark wildly earlier, followed by Whip's stern command for silence.

"Go on," Shannon called, waving her hand at the dog. "It's Whip I'm looking for, not you."

Prettyface vanished back into the tall meadow grass.

"Whip? Where are you?"

No answer came from the meadow, where three hobbled mules grazed. No answer came from the woodpile, which now held little but chips. No answer came from the lean-to, where strips of venison and fish cured over a slow, smoky fire. No answer came from the ridgeline, where trees stood tall and windswept, lifting green arms to the sky.

Abruptly Shannon spun back toward the meadow, finally realizing what was wrong.

Whip's horses weren't there.

"Whip can't have gone," Shannon whispered. "It's been only four days since we left Reno and Eve at the mine. They haven't come back with news of gold."

Surely Whip hasn't left.

Oh, God, not yet. Not yet!

Shannon leaned against the door frame as her bones turned to sand and her skin went cold. Her hands clutched at the ragged hem of the shirt she wore. The worn cloth gave way beneath the pressure of her fingers, ripping with a muted sound.

"Whip, where are you?"

The ghostly keening of panpipes breathed over Shannon, whispering to her of exotic mysteries, distant sunrises and the unbound soul of a yondering man.

The haunting music came from behind Shannon. Inside the cabin.

She drew a swift breath and spun around.

There was no one behind her.

"Whip? Where are you?"

The trembling harmony of the pipes curled around Shannon like an invisible leash, pulling her toward the cupboard that opened into the cave.

Of course, Shannon thought in relief. *Whip just came in the back way after dressing out that last elk. He's probably washing off in the hot spring pool right now.*

Quickly Shannon shut and barred the cabin

door. When she opened the cupboard passage, light from a single candle danced in silent welcome. As she closed the cupboard behind her, the husky keening of the panpipes faded into a spectral whisper, then into silence.

Shannon searched darkness that seethed with mist from the hot spring. She couldn't see Whip. Impatiently she kicked off her boots and socks and tugged off the leather belt that held up her worn men's pants.

"Whip, are you in the pool?"

There was a hissing whisper as a long lash curled out of the darkness. Shannon felt a tug at her shirt and heard a soft tearing sound. Before she could do more than gasp, she sensed another swift movement, another tug, then another and another. Very quickly her old flannel shirt vanished, floating to the rocky floor in uneven ribbons.

Shannon made a surprised sound as the bull-whip's supple lash licked over her trousers. There was a soft pop followed by a metallic clink as the single button on her pants hit the ground.

She looked around and saw nothing but twists of steam and the dark curl of the lash returning. Though she saw it coming, she still made a startled noise when the leather whip delicately, precisely, sheared cloth away from her body without touching her skin at all.

She shivered as the remnants of her trousers fell to the stone floor, leaving her wearing the shabby pantalets that were her only underwear.

"W-Whip?"

"I wanted to do this the first time I saw you dressed in ragpicker's clothes that were an insult to your beauty. But I knew the bullwhip would frighten you then. Does it frighten you now?"

Shannon closed her eyes as a delicious shiver of anticipation went through her.

"No," she whispered. "Nothing you do could frighten me, Whip."

The lash curled, tugged, and the worn ribbon came untied, leaving nothing to hold up the pantalets. They slid to the floor. Shannon stood motionless, wearing only candlelight and the seething mist rising from the hot spring.

"You're like the sun, honey girl. Beautiful. Perfect."

Whip's voice was as dark and sultry as the cave itself.

"I've seen myself in your shaving mirror," Shannon said. "I'm not perfect or beautiful."

"You are to me."

The truth in Whip's voice was another kind of caress licking over Shannon as softly as the mist, as gently as the smooth leather kissing her cheek, her shoulder, the swell of a breast, the full curve of one hip, the sensitive skin behind one knee. The cool, delicate touches were swift, always unexpected, shockingly arousing in their restraint and sensual promise.

Shannon whimpered Whip's name as her body shimmered and caught fire. She captured the teasing, flicking lash and tugged hard, only to find herself pulled in turn toward the steamy darkness where Whip waited. Beneath her feet cool stone gave way to the soft, thick blankets Whip had spread near the edge of the hot spring.

There was a swirl of water and the secret rush of drops onto stone as Whip came out of the seething pool. Wearing only coils of steam and a glistening sheen of water, Whip loomed in front of Shannon.

He was as beautiful to her as a pagan god, but the shadows haunting his eyes were those of a man whose powers were merely human.

I wish I were a different man!

Don't love me, *Shannon. Please. Don't. It hurts too much.*

An eerie stillness wrapped around Shannon's heart, making it stop. She knew in an instant of total silence that Whip would leave her soon.

Very soon.

Shannon's heart turned over and beat frantically. She bit back a cry of protest at all that could have been and now never would be, shared laughter and intertwined lives, building a home and holding babies, children with his eyes and her smile and their love like a sunrise bringing light to the landscape of their lives. . . .

But it was not to be.

All Shannon had was this moment when she would share her body and soul with Whip for the last time.

As graceful as candlelight and mist, Shannon walked to Whip. And like candlelight and mist she flowed over him, touching him, tasting him, learning every bit of his body in a rage of silence that left Whip shaken.

"Honey girl," he said through his teeth. *"My God."*

Shannon's answer was a delicate movement of her tongue over the blind eye of his passion.

"Stop," he said hoarsely.

"Not yet," she whispered, touching him tenderly again. "I haven't memorized all of you yet. Let me . . . memorize you."

Whip didn't know what to say, nor did he have any breath left to speak. Shannon was a living warmth enfolding him, a sigh and a caress and a tender, searching flame that set his body afire. Softly, wildly, she surrounded him, knowing him in ways he had never expected. Her loving was a sunrise sweeping across his very soul, illuminating more of himself than he could bear to see.

Whip shuddered and fought for control when he realized that Shannon was making love to him as though it were the last time.

She knows, Whip thought bleakly. *Somehow she knows*.

Shannon's name was dragged from his lips, but the word was unrecognizable. A sudden, violent ecstasy was raking Whip with claws of fire. He fought it even as he desired it, shaking with the wanting.

When Whip could endure no more, he took Shannon down onto the rumpled blanket and buried himself inside her, trying to ease the bittersweet agony of her love for him. Yet even as he spent himself deep within her clinging heat, Whip wasn't free of pain or knowledge. When he looked into her eyes he saw the desolate future; and when he kissed her, he tasted her intimate knowledge of him, a knowledge no other woman had ever wanted.

Whip tried to speak but could not force words past the anguish and passion constricting his throat. He bent and began kissing Shannon's hair, her forehead, her eyebrows, the curves of her ears, her cheekbones, her trembling lips. As he kissed her, he rocked gently within her, caressing her, leading her toward ecstasy, knowing her in a silence that seethed with all that had been and would not be again.

With a rippling cry, Shannon gave herself to the ecstasy Whip had summoned. He smiled to feel the tender shuddering of her flesh around his . . . and he kept rocking against her. Gently, relentlessly, he moved within her even as ecstasy itself did, driving her higher with every powerful, restrained movement of his body.

Shannon's eyes widened as unexpected, intense pleasure speared through her. He moved again and again, rocking against her in primal rhythms, and each time he moved, her body answered with frightening intensity.

A hoarse cry was dragged from Shannon's throat and her nails dug into the rigid muscles of Whip's back. Her body arched helplessly, shuddering with the violence of her release.

Whip laughed and kept driving rhythmically into Shannon. His motions were both measured and fierce, demanding everything she had to give as a woman. Her whole body arched once more. Sharp, wild lightning surged through her until she cried out and simply clung to Whip, shaken by savage waves of ecstasy.

Holding her, sheltering her, Whip took Shannon's mouth as completely as he had taken her body, trembling even as she did, sharing the sweet fury of her release. When Shannon no longer shuddered with each breath, Whip began to move within her again.

And again lightning raked her violently sensitive flesh.

"Whip?" she asked, dazed, almost frightened.

"It's all right, honey girl. I just have to know."

"W-what?"

"How high you can take me. Each time higher and then higher again."

"Me?" Shannon laughed brokenly. "You're the one who—"

Her words became a hoarse cry of pleasure as Whip put his arms behind her legs and surged forward, opening her to the full power of his body. Then he began to move deep within her, where ecstasy welled up hotly, endlessly.

Whip's name came from Shannon's lips with every broken breath, every wild cry, every shattering wave of pleasure driving through her, consuming her utterly.

Deeply sealed within her, Whip held Shannon shivering and wild, letting her sink into him, through him, caressing him body and soul; and then an endless, rippling release raged through him, fusing him to her in an elemental union unlike anything he had ever known.

Finally, slowly, Whip pulled away from Shannon. Saying nothing, he struck a match and lit the lantern that sat on a wooden box nearby.

The sudden blossoming of light revealed two heavy saddlebags. A ragged tongue of gold spilled from one of them.

Shannon looked, and knew without any doubt that she had lost Whip to the sunrise he had never seen.

"Shannon, honey girl, I . . ."

She shook her head, touched Whip's mouth with her fingers, and watched him with eyes that held no tears. Tears come from hope, and she had none left.

"I will always love you," Shannon whispered. "Now ride on, my sweet yondering man. Just . . . ride on."

21

Shannon walked into Murphy's mercantile with Cherokee's six-gun shoved into a belt at her waist and an irritated Prettyface at her side. She didn't know how much time had passed since Whip left. She knew only that the aspens had been a vivid, living green while he was here and had turned to beautiful, unliving gold since he left.

She felt the same as the leaves. There had been a time of pouring sunshine and growth and beauty; and then the world had turned and everything had changed.

A pity that I'm not like those bright, lifeless leaves, able to lift on the wind and be whirled away forever.

But I'm a woman, not a leaf, and Cherokee needs me. That ankle of hers will never be the same.

Maybe one day I'll get used to Whip's loss the same way Cherokee is getting used to her change ankle. Maybe one day the pain will no longer surprise me, making me feel as though it has just happened all over again for the first time.

As Shannon quietly looked over the merchandise, a miner she had never seen before started arguing with Murphy over the weight of the slab of bacon he had on the scales.

"Five pounds?" scoffed the miner. "Hell's fire, man, back home I have me a redbone hound what whelps bigger pups than that there miserable hunk of bacon."

"Then maybe you oughta go back and smoke one of them pups to et with your beans, rather than waste my time with all yer whining and—"

Murphy's words stopped cold when Prettyface walked out from behind a stack of dried goods near the front door. The storekeeper stepped back from the counter so quickly that the scales jumped, rattled and settled into a new weight.

"Three pounds and some for good measure," the miner said with satisfaction. "That's more like it. Folks in Canyon City tell me you're a real cheeseparing son of a bitch, but I guess they was thinking of some other Murphy."

The storekeeper grunted unhappily, took the miner's money, and sacked up the remaining supplies without another word. When the miner turned around with his supplies in hand, he spotted Shannon.

"Well, Lordy me, would you look at this sweet little thing," he said, walking toward Shannon. "You Clementine or Betsy?"

"Neither," she said tightly. "I'm Silent John's . . . widow."

Murphy's eyebrows shot up but he kept quiet.

The miner halted. He looked chagrined at his error, but was no less eager to talk to Shannon.

"Sorry, ma'am," said the miner. "Mean no insult. No one told me there was more than two women loose in Echo Basin. Can I make it up to you over supper?"

"Thank you, no."

"Can I come calling?" he asked, walking forward again.

Prettyface's upper lip lifted in a rippling, gleaming snarl.

The miner stopped dead.

"There would be no purpose in calling on me,"

Shannon said neutrally. "I will never offer the kind of companionship you're seeking."

"And if you're of a mind to just help yourself anyway," Murphy said from behind the counter, "this here gal belongs to a man called Whip Moran. He told me that most particularly, just 'fore he went off looking for gold. He been gone a month or two, but he be comin' back soon enough, and there be pure fiery hell to pay if'n his woman is bothered."

Shannon wanted to object that she was no longer Whip's woman, he wasn't off looking for gold, and he wouldn't be back at all. But she kept her mouth tightly shut. For a time, at least, Whip's reputation would help to protect her in the same way Silent John's had.

"Whip?" asked the miner unhappily. "Be that the one what sent them four Culpeppers straight to hell?"

"Yeah," Murphy said with malicious pleasure. "And if that ain't enough to take the starch out of your pecker, Whip's brother is a gunfighter called Reno."

The miner looked even less happy.

"And Whip told me right forcefully," Murphy continued, "that Caleb Black and Wolfe Lonetree think of this little gal as one of the family. Any man goes to botherin' her will answer to them. And her dog ain't no bargain, neither."

Shannon gave Murphy a shuttered look and wondered just how "forcefully" Whip had presented his arguments to the storekeeper. Whatever had been said or done, the result was a remarkable improvement. It was clear that Murphy wouldn't be acting anything but respectful toward Shannon.

The thought of Whip trying to see to her welfare from afar was another knife turning deep in Shannon's soul. Whip had left the larder full of store-bought supplies, Cherokee's smokehouse full of venison and fish and grouse, and firewood stacked to the eaves all around both cabins. Reno had found enough gold that Shannon could leave Echo Basin and live in comfort anywhere she wished.

There was no doubt that Whip had cared for her very much.

But not enough to stay.

May God keep you, yondering man, Shannon prayed silently as she had many, many times in long, painful weeks since Whip had left. *May you someday find what you want.*

And may it want you in return.

"Excuse me, ma'am," the miner said politely. "I'll be getting along, now."

Shannon tore her thoughts from Whip to the miner, who was standing with his arms full of supplies and watching Prettyface with wary eyes.

"The dog is betwixt me and the door," the miner explained.

"Prettyface," Shannon said, stepping to the side. "Come here and be quiet."

After another seething snarl, Prettyface subsided. When Shannon walked toward the counter, the dog followed. But he never took his wolf's eyes off the miner.

The front door of the mercantile slammed shut behind the miner, shoved by a gust of cold September wind.

Shannon felt the chill and pulled her worn jacket more closely around her body. September had been filled with storms and wild, icy winds.

Elk and deer had already left the high country, sensing that the first heavy snows of the season could come at any time.

That was what had forced Shannon to come into town. She needed to buy warm clothes for herself and supplies for Cherokee. The old woman was in no shape to make the trip herself . . . although Shannon suspected that Cherokee was lying in ambush somewhere back up the trail as Silent John often had, making sure that Shannon wasn't followed.

"Good afternoon, Mr. Murphy," Shannon said, approaching the counter. "Would you please fill this order for me while I select some warmer clothes?"

Murphy grunted.

"And Mr. Murphy?"

He grunted again.

"Keep your thumb off the scales," Shannon said crisply.

The storekeeper grinned. "Whip told you."

"He didn't have to. I've known for years that you cheated me. Silent John accepted it as the price of doing business close to home. But I don't. If that means going into Canyon City for supplies, I will do so."

"No need to get your water hot, missy. I'm not about to go and get in Whip's bad graces."

"Or mine?"

"Or your'n," Murphy agreed. "Folks what is smart enough to come in out of the rain don't have no trouble with me."

"Good. My pack mule is outside. Please load the supplies for me when you're done."

"Cost you three dollars extra."

"One."

"Two."

"One and two bits."

"You drive a mean bargain, missy."

"Not really. You load Betsy and Clementine's supplies for free."

"They throw in a little, uh, extra for my trouble."

Murphy leered cheerfully.

"One dollar and two bits," Shannon said coolly. "Do we have a deal?"

Sighing, Murphy nodded.

Shannon handed over her supply list and went to the piles of clothing that were scattered about the mercantile's floor. By the time she had found two warm jackets, four warm shirts, two pairs of wool trousers, and everything else required to turn winter's icy winds, Murphy had sacked up and loaded her supplies on her pack mule.

"Add these to the total, please," Shannon said, dumping the clothing on the counter.

"Huh. Guess I'm gonna have to order some femi-nine frippery. Gets mighty wearisome for a man to see his gal tricked out like hisself."

Shannon's lips thinned, but she said not one word while Murphy totaled her bill. The amount made her eyes widen.

"May I see the bill, please?" she asked, holding out her hand.

"What fer?"

"To check your sums."

Murphy handed the bill over and watched nervously while Shannon checked his addition.

"You are thirty-one dollars and twelve cents over," she said after a few minutes.

Muttering, Murphy subtracted thirty-one

dollars from the total. Shannon handed over a fat poke of gold.

"I have Silent John's gold scales at the cabin," Shannon said. "I know precisely how much gold is in that poke. When I return home, I will weigh what is left."

Murphy shot Shannon a look that was part irritation and part admiration.

"Whip sure put steel in yer spine," Murphy said.

Shannon smiled thinly.

Murphy took the poke, opened it, and poured. A mixture of dust, nuggets, and flakes spilled onto one of the scale's small dishes.

"Well, I be go to hell," Murphy said, surprised. "Whip found some new strikes, eh?"

"What do you mean?"

"None of this gold come from Silent John's old claims."

Shannon looked startled. "I beg your pardon?"

"The color and shape is all wrong," Murphy said impatiently. "Silent John's claims don't give no coppery-colored flakes. No pale gold dust, neither. And as for these . . ."

Deftly Murphy sorted out some heavy, ragged nuggets of a rich golden hue. He pressed his thumbnail hard against one nugget. When he lifted his thumb again, a crease showed on the surface of the gold.

"These pretty gals be too jagged for river nuggets, but too blessed pure for anything else," Murphy said reverently. "Ain't seen their like since a fast-talking city boy tried to sell me a Colorado claim salted with pure Dakota bullion. That was reddish gold. But this here nugget puts me to mind of some I saw once on a poker table down to Las Cruces. The gold come from the Abajos. Spanish gold, pure as a baby's dreams."

A chill crawled beneath Shannon's skin as she remembered Reno and Whip talking about bars of pure Spanish gold.

No, she told herself quickly. *Whip wouldn't have done that to me*! *Murphy must be mistaken*.

The storekeeper glanced away from the gold and saw the shocked look on Shannon's face.

"Don't s'pose you be wanting to tell me where Whip found this here gold?"

Shannon swallowed and said firmly, "Silent John's claims."

Murphy laughed. "Don't blame you none for playin' close to the vest. If'n I had me any claims rich as these, I sure to God wouldn't tell no one neither."

"Whip told me the gold came from Silent John's claims," Shannon said, her voice toneless.

"Smart man, that Whip. What you don't know, you can't spill to strangers. But I seen all kinds of Echo Basin gold, missy, and you can take this direct to God's ear—not one speck of this here gold come from here."

Reno's words echoed in Shannon's mind, shaking her.

Way up in the Abajos, in a crumbling old mine . . . bars of pure gold so heavy Eve could hardly lift more than one at a time.

Shannon wanted to scream her denial that Whip could treat her so shabbily, but she didn't let herself make a single sound. She had too much to do to waste energy yelling at a yondering man who couldn't even hear her.

In icy silence, Shannon ticked off what had to be done. First she had to get Cherokee's supplies to her. Then she had to track down Clementine and Betsy. And after that, Shannon had to ride to the Black ranch and back home before the first heavy snows came, closing the passes for the winter.

For the first time, Shannon was grateful for the two racing mules she had reluctantly inherited from the Culpeppers. Both Cully and Pepper would get a hard workout in the next few days.

Just over a day later, riding one mule and leading the other, Shannon reined to a stop in front of Caleb and Willow's ranch house. Caleb rode in from the direction of the north pasture just as Willow stepped onto the porch.

"Shannon?" Willow asked, shading her eyes against the sun shining out from behind a thunderhead. "Is that really you?"

"It's me," Shannon said, dismounting.

"What a lovely surprise! Come in, I'll have tea on in a minute."

"No, thank you. Prettyface, if you snarl again, I'm going to feed you to the crows."

Prettyface stopped making savage noises and stood quietly by Shannon's side as Caleb rode up.

"Trouble?" he asked.

"Nothing that can't be cured," Shannon said, her voice clipped. "Would you remove the saddlebags for me?"

Caleb gave her a long look. Then he dismounted, went to the mules, and made an admiring sound.

"Nice pair of mules," he said. "Virginia bred, from the look of them."

"The Culpeppers favored Virginia mules," Shannon said, her voice remote.
"Good stamina," Caleb said.
"They'll need it," was Shannon's only reply.
Caleb started to ask a question, then gave a grunt of surprise as he lifted the saddlebags.
"Judas Priest," he muttered. "What's in these? Lead?"
"Whip's gold," Shannon said savagely, yanking free the cinch strap on Cully's saddle.
Willow and Caleb exchanged a swift look.
"It was my understanding," Caleb said carefully, "that Whip was working for wages rather than for a share of *your* gold."
"That was my understanding, too," Shannon said.
She yanked off the saddle with one hand and the blanket with the other. With a few quick motions she saddled the second mule.
"But I was wrong," Shannon said, mounting the mule. "Murphy told me the gold was wrong, too."
"You want to chase that by me again?" Caleb asked, puzzled.
Shannon turned and looked at Caleb, making no attempt to hide the cold fury she had felt ever since she realized how little Whip had truly thought of her.
"This gold never was dug in Echo Basin," Shannon said savagely. "Whip paid me off with his own Spanish gold and then lit out for the far side of the horizon. But he made a little miscalculation."
"Did he?" Caleb asked warily.
"Once I figured out what had happened, I suspected Whip had paid me too much, but I

didn't know the going rate, so I tracked down Clementine and Betsy and asked."

Caleb measured the flat rage in Shannon's eyes and decided not to ask who Clementine and Betsy were, and what they had to do with any of it.

"I was right," Shannon continued. "Whip paid far too much for what he got from me. So I brought his change. Every damned speck of it."

"Wait!" Willow called as Shannon picked up the reins. "You've had a long ride. At least come in and rest a while before you set out."

"Thank you, no," Shannon said. "The passes could close at any moment."

"But—" Willow began.

"In any case," Shannon continued with icy pride, "I respect you too much to bring your brother's whore into your home."

With that, Shannon spun the mule and kicked it into a long, ground-eating lope. The other mule and Prettyface followed at a rapid clip.

For a time neither Willow nor Caleb spoke. Then Willow let out a long, harsh breath.

"I wish I knew where my dear brother was," she said. "I would like to see him again."

"So would Shannon," Caleb said dryly. "Preferably skinned out and nailed to her cabin wall."

It was an icy dusk when Whip rode up to Willow and Caleb's home, his collar turned up against the wind. Snow flurries gleamed and swirled around him.

"Hello, stranger," Caleb said, stepping down off the porch. "We thought you were headed for San Francisco and the high seas. I didn't expect to see you for a year or two."

There was a question buried beneath Caleb's words, but Whip didn't know how to answer it. He was as puzzled as anyone else to find himself on this side of the sunrise.

"Neither did I," Whip said. "But here I am."

"And here you'll stay. The passes are closed every way but the south."

"I know. I came in that way. Damned cold on the desert now."

Whip dismounted and shook Caleb's hand.

"Where have you been for the past three months?" Caleb asked.

"Here and there," Whip said, shrugging. "I got as far west as that big canyon where the Rio Colorado lies like a silver medicine snake at the bottom of a deep gorge."

"Hell of a place, from what Wolfe tells me."

"It will do," Whip agreed. "I chased sunrise all the way around that canyon's edge until I found myself back where I started from. Wild, lonely country, every inch of it."

"Come on," Caleb said. "Willow should be finished putting Ethan to bed by now."

Whip hesitated.

"If you're thinking of riding off to the high country," Caleb said, "think again. The passes have been closed for months. They won't open again for months."

"I know. That's why . . ." Whip's voice died.

"That's why you came back? You know you can't get to her?"

Whip grimaced. "Yes."

"Just as well," Caleb said. "Last time we saw Shannon, she—"

"You saw her?" Whip interrupted instantly. "When?"

"Just before the passes closed."

"Did she finally get smart and stay with you?"

"Nope. She wouldn't even stay for a cup of coffee."

Whip frowned. "Was she looking for me, then?"

"After a fashion," Caleb said sardonically.

"What in hell does that mean?"

"I'll tell him," Willow said from the doorway. "Come on in, Whip. Shannon left a message for you."

"Is she—" Whip's voice dried up. He swallowed visibly. "Is she, uh, all right?"

" 'All right' as in 'not pregnant'?" Willow asked with false sweetness.

A red that had nothing to do with the cold wind appeared on Whip's cheekbones.

Caleb took the reins from Whip's hand and headed for the barn.

"Don't take too many chunks out of his hide," Caleb said to Willow over his shoulder.

"Why not?" Willow retorted.

"Shannon will want some to nail to her cabin wall."

"Don't worry." Willow's smile was all teeth and not one bit of comfort as she turned away. "Whip is a big boy. There will be plenty of hide to go around. Come inside, brother dear."

Whip looked at Caleb's retreating back and then at Willow's. With swift, hard strides he followed his sister. When they were inside, he shut the door and grabbed her arm.

"Tell me straight up, Willy," Whip said in a flat tone. "Is Shannon pregnant?"

"If she is, she didn't mention it to us."

Whip's breath came out with a harsh sound.

"I didn't think Shannon would come here unless she was pregnant," he admitted.

"Is that why you're not halfway to China? You were worried that Shannon might be carrying your child?"

"I don't know why I'm not halfway to China," Whip said, his eyes bleak, haunted. "I only know that I'm not."

Compassion softened the angry set of Willow's face. She could sense her beloved brother's unhappiness as though it were her own. With a sigh for Whip's untamed, restless soul, she touched his sleeve gently.

"Come to the kitchen," she said. "I'll pour you some coffee. I'll make up a batch of biscuits, too. You look like you could use a good meal."

"I'll settle for bread, if you have it. I've kind of lost my taste for biscuits. They remind me too much of . . ."

Whip's voice trailed away. With a weary curse he lifted his hat, ran his fingers through his pale hair, and tossed the hat onto the kitchen table. Automatically he pulled off the bullwhip, hung his jacket by the back door, resettled the bullwhip on his shoulder, and sat down.

With eyes that reflected too many memories, Whip watched his sister go about the homey rituals of stirring up the fire, pouring coffee, and slicing bread. If he looked through nearly-closed eyes, he could pretend that it was Shannon moving around the kitchen, fixing supper, bringing him warmth and food with her own hands.

But it wasn't Shannon, and Whip knew it all the way to the bottom of his painful, seething soul.

There was a rustling sound and a thump at the back door, as though someone had brought firewood and stacked it outside. Then the door opened and Caleb walked in with a pair of saddlebags thrown over his shoulder.

Whip didn't even look up from his coffee.

Caleb shut the door and glanced at his wife. Willow shook her head slightly. Caleb almost smiled. He had guessed that Willow would be too tenderhearted to tear much of a strip off Whip's thick hide.

Caleb, however, wasn't.

"You said Shannon left a message for me," Whip said. "What was it?"

Willow looked at Caleb.

"You forgot your change," Caleb said sardonically.

Two saddlebags thumped heavily onto the kitchen table.

Whip glanced at them without interest. Then his eyes narrowed and one hand shot out. Muscles corded in his arm as he lifted the joined saddlebags, testing their weight.

He hissed a word that made Willow flinch.

"That tears it," Whip snarled, letting go of the saddlebags. "Of all the stupid—"

"Did that gold come from Shannon's claims?" Caleb interrupted.

"What damned difference does it make?"

"To me, none," Caleb retorted. "It made a hell of a lot of difference to Shannon, though. The difference between being a widow and a whore."

Whip uncoiled out of the chair and slammed into Caleb, pinning him against the kitchen wall in a single wild rush.

"God damn you, she isn't a whore."

"Whip! Stop it!" Willow cried, grabbing one of her brother's arms.

Caleb stared into the quicksilver violence of Whip's eyes and smiled almost gently.

"Hell, I know that," Caleb said. "But if you'd feel better trying to beat the same words out of me, we can do a turn or two around the back yard."

Whip stared at Caleb's level, compassionate eyes, took a deep breath, and stepped back.

"Sorry," Whip said, looking at his hands as though he had never seen them before. "I've been on a hair trigger, lately."

"Then you better sit on your hands for a few minutes," Caleb suggested dryly. "I'd hate to have my brisket parted by that damned bullwhip of yours."

Slowly, Whip sat down.

"The long and the short of it," Caleb said, "is that Shannon came here riding one fine racing mule and leading another. She had a hellhound as big as a pony at her side."

"Prettyface," Whip said.

"If you say so," Caleb muttered. "Looked to me more like the north end of a southbound burro. Anyway, Shannon got off her mule and asked me to take the saddlebags. As soon as I did, she peeled the saddle off the first mule and put it on the other."

Whip frowned. "Sounds like she was in an almighty rush. Something must have been wrong. Really wrong."

"Same thought occurred to me," Caleb said. He hesitated. "Do you know some women by the name of Betsy and Clementine?"

Whip shot a look toward Willow, who was

fussing over some stew she was warming up for him.

"I don't exactly *know* them," Whip said in a voice that went no farther than Caleb's ears. "I've never even met them. They live around Holler Creek. They're, uh, saloon girls, if you take my meaning."

"Yeah, that's what I thought."

"How did you hear their names?" Whip asked.

"Shannon mentioned them."

"What!"

Caleb took a deep breath and hoped that Whip had a good grip on his temper. If the two of them got into a fight in the kitchen, there wouldn't be enough left of the room to make breakfast in.

"Seems that someone named Murphy told Shannon that her gold couldn't have come from Silent John's claims," Caleb said.

"Murphy! Damn his blood-sucking soul! I figured he would just take the gold and shut up."

"According to Shannon, you figured wrong on something else, too," Caleb said.

As Caleb spoke, he casually went behind Whip's chair.

"What was that?" Whip asked.

"You, uh, overpaid her," Caleb said.

"What the hell are you talking about?"

Caleb took a concealed breath, gathering himself for the fight he knew was coming.

"When Shannon learned the gold wasn't hers," Caleb said, "she went to Betsy and Clementine and asked them what the going rate for their favors was."

"What?"

Whip would have shot to his feet again, but

Caleb's big hands were bearing down on Whip's shoulders, holding him in his chair.

"Settle down and listen," Caleb said grimly. "Shannon took whatever amount the girls told her, figured out how much she had been overpaid by you, and came down off that mountain like a blue norther to give you your change."

When the meaning of the words penetrated, the fight went out of Whip.

Oh, God, honey girl. I never thought of you that way at all. You were as innocent as sunrise . . .

"She really said that?" Whip managed finally.

Caleb nodded.

"She thought that I'd paid her off like something I'd bought for the night?" Whip whispered.

Warily, Caleb nodded.

"I don't believe it," Whip said starkly.

Willow smacked the stew spoon against the kettle, knocking off clinging bits of meat.

"Believe it," Willow said succinctly. "Shannon wouldn't come inside the house, not even for a cup of tea."

"Why?"

"She said she respected me too much to bring my brother's whore into my home."

Whip made an anguished sound and slammed his fist on the table. His coffee cup leaped and turned on its side, sending a wave of searing liquid over him. He barely felt it. The pain that was tearing his soul apart left no room for anything else.

Abruptly Whip twisted aside and stood up, throwing off Caleb's restraining hands.

"I changed my mind about those biscuits, Willy," Whip said in a strained voice. "Make a batch of them big enough to take me over the mountain."

"But the pass is closed," Willow protested.

Whip turned to Caleb. "You still have those snowshoes in the barn?"

"Nope. They're outside by the back door. I'll go with you as far as my Montana horses can take us. After that, you're on your own."

"Thanks."

"But when you get there," Caleb said, "be damned careful."

"Why?"

"She was mad enough to set that hellhound on you."

Whip looked at the scars on his hands and smiled slightly. "Wouldn't be the first time we tangled."

He grabbed his jacket and hat and headed for the back door.

"What about supplies?" Caleb asked as Whip opened the door. "Will the two of you make it through the winter?"

"I made sure Shannon had enough to feed two people until the melt came."

"You were a little slow figuring out who the second person was, weren't you?" Willow asked dryly.

The back door slammed, cutting off the sound of Caleb's laughter.

"What if he can't get to the cabin?" Willow asked.

"He will. Getting back in Shannon's good graces will be the real trick. That was one purely pissed off woman who rode out of here."

"He'll have all winter."

"He'll need it," Caleb said.

"I doubt it. He has an unfair advantage."

"What's that?"

"She loves him," Willow said simply.

As dawn began to take stars and darkness from the sky, Whip resettled the straps of his backpack and set out across the meadow toward Shannon's cabin. Peaks lifted silently above the earthbound darkness, bathing their rugged faces in the first heady light of dawn.

The air was utterly still around him, as cold and sharp as freshly broken ice. His breath was a shimmering cloud around his face. Each step he took brought squeaks from the dry, frigid snow beneath his feet.

Whip didn't notice the sounds, for he felt as though he was moving through a waking dream.

I've been here before, in the winter, with sunrise all around.

But he never had . . . except in his dream of a cabin and a woman waiting for him.

By the time Whip crossed the meadow, dawn was stealing down the mountains and touching the evergreens with gentle tongues of fire. The dark square of the cabin suddenly showed slivers of yellow light between the shutters. As he came closer, the door opened.

Warmth and golden light flowed out to meet him. Shannon was standing in the center of it, waiting for Whip, knowing that only one man could make Prettyface dance with silent eagerness.

"If you're bringing that gold back," Shannon said icily, "you can just take it and—"

The words ended in a muffled sound as Whip pulled Shannon into his arms and kissed her with the soul-deep need that had haunted him every step of the way since he had left her. When he finally lifted his head, she was holding him as hard as he was holding her, and dawn was riding their shoulders like a golden cape.

"I'm staying," Whip said. "You can rage at me and pull strips from my hide for my damn foolishness, but I'm never leaving you again, ever, I—"

Her fingers touched Whip's mouth, stilling the tumbling words.

"Don't make promises it would kill you to keep," Shannon said shakily. "I don't want that. I never wanted that, once I understood about all those sunrises you've never seen."

Whip looked into the dawn reflected by Shannon's eyes and smiled oddly.

"That's what I'm trying to tell you," he said. "The sunrise I was chasing all over the world to find is the one that only love could give me. Nothing on earth calls to me the way you do. It just took me a while to get used to the idea."

Shannon went still, afraid to hope again.

"I wasn't searching for sunrises," Whip said softly. "I was searching for something I couldn't name, something unbearably beautiful, something unspeakably perfect that was waiting for me to discover it."

Whip bent and kissed Shannon with a gentleness that brought tears to her eyes.

"I found it in you," he said simply. "I love you, honey girl. You're the only sunrise I'll ever need."

Epilogue

Shannon and Whip spent winter in the small cabin, laughing and loving while wild storms blew over the land. When the passes opened once more, they went to Canyon City and brought a preacher back with them over the mountains.

They were married at Willow and Caleb's house, with Reno as best man, Eve's pure alto singing of love everlasting, Ethan scampering through the maze of adult legs, and baby Rebecca Black watching from Willow's arms with unblinking hazel eyes. Jessi and Wolfe brought the bride a shawl made of fine Irish lace and a mustang whose coat was the exact autumn shade of Shannon's hair.

Whip and Shannon settled in a hidden valley that was a half day's ride from the Black ranch, and not much farther from Reno and Eve's home. The men worked together to build a house, and the women worked to give the touches that made a house into a home.

At the end of summer, Whip and Shannon went to Avalanche Creek and coaxed Cherokee to come back down the mountain with them, bringing with her a rich knowledge of herbs and healing and life.

Every year the families gathered for roundups and holidays, sharing work and play equally. Each gathering was bigger and more lively, with babies being born and children growing at a reckless pace, and adults laughing as they remembered how it had all begun, and how unexpected life could be in its gifts.

Baby Rebecca soon had a playmate named Catherine Wolfe. Within a year, John Rafael Moran was born. Whip's son took his strength and yondering urge from his father, but it was his mother's sapphire eyes that looked out on the world with wary curiosity. The sisters and brothers who followed had different eyes, different faces, different dreams.

In the midst of all the changes brought by the years that passed over the land like cloud shadows, one thing remained unchanged and certain. Whether Whip was gone for an hour or a week, Shannon was waiting for him, reaching for him even as he gathered her into his arms, and there was a light in their eyes that only love could bring.